# MEG

Jason Medina

ISBN 978-1-957582-26-9 (paperback)
ISBN 978-1-957582-28-3 (hardcover)
ISBN 978-1-957582-27-6 (eBook)



This is a work of fiction. Names, characters, places, and incidents are either the product of the author's imagination or are used fictitiously, and any resemblance to any actual persons, living or dead, events, or locales is entirely coincidental.

Any photos used are the property of the author. Cover model: Lisa Flynn. Model for Margaret Elizabeth Garrett: Christina Marie Claudio. Anniversary Killer model: Daniel Calderon.
Other victims portrayed by: Stella Martinez, Lori Stella, Sylvia Medina, Nancy Hamill, and Lorraine Zadok.



Printed in the United States of America

# Introduction

Inspired by true events, this is a fictional story about a young woman, who is haunted by the spirit of another young woman, who was murdered over thirty years ago. It is an obscure cry for help with the possibility of solving a decades old missing person's case.

When the show "*Paranormal Witness*" first aired, I watched it. It was my kind of show. One episode from the second season was titled "*The Apartment.*" In the episode a woman named Jodi Foster, not the actress, discussed her ordeal, which began after she and her four-year-old daughter, Hannah, moved into an apartment in Chico, California. Strange unexplainable things would often occur, leading her to believe the apartment was haunted.

She started having vivid nightmares about people she had never seen before. One person in her nightmares stood out because Jodi kept dreaming about her. It was a pretty young woman with wavy, shoulder-length, brown hair, who looked like she could have been a model.

Eventually, Jodi realized the former tenant of her apartment, Marie Elizabeth Spannhake, was the one haunting her. Marie disappeared on January 31, 1976, at the age of 19. Jodi's daughter, Hannah, had actually seen her spirit in the apartment on several occasions. Hannah believed the beautiful spirit was her guardian angel, so she did not fear her. Her mother, on the other hand, was frightened and at her wit's end.

She learned Marie had once lived in the apartment with her boyfriend. The couple had plans to be married, but it would never come to pass. One day, while working together at a local flea market, they had a minor disagreement. Marie became upset and decided to walk home. She was never seen, again.

Years later, a sadistic man named Cameron Hooker was arrested for kidnapping a young woman and keeping her locked in a wooden box under his bed for the better part of seven years. He and his wife, Janice, tricked this poor woman into signing a contract and becoming their slave claiming a powerful secret organization called The Company would come for her and her family, if she failed to comply. Over the years, she was forced to cook for them and do their house work. In time, she became Cameron's sex slave, and nanny to his and Janice's two daughters. The case made news becoming infamous and spawning books, documentaries, and even a film aptly called, *"The Girl in the Box."*

Janice turned state's evidence against her husband testifying against him at the trial. She also confessed to an earlier crime she claimed they committed together, which it turned out involved the kidnapping and murder of a young woman named Marie Elizabeth Spannhake. She led detectives to where she claimed the body was buried. However, Marie's body could not be found. Janice changed her story several times adding to the confusion. Supposedly, she had trouble remembering the facts. In addition, developmental changes in the rural area throughout the years made it very difficult for her to recall the precise location.

As a result, her husband was not charged with any additional crimes involving Marie's case, although Cameron is currently serving 104 years in prison for his crimes against, Colleen Stan, who was the aforementioned girl in the box. Janice was granted immunity and acquitted of her crimes for her cooperation. She later divorced Cameron. Today, she is a free woman, who ironically found work as a social worker on the very same street, where Marie resided.

As for Marie, she is still classified as missing. It is doubtful her remains will be found anytime soon. It comes as no surprise her spirit cannot rest peacefully. Her body is still out there somewhere, and she's never had the justice she deserved.

After Jodi's haunted experiences regarding Marie, she has practically become an advocate for the missing woman. She's told the tragic tale through books and via television appearances. Her autobiographical book, *"Forgotten Burial,"* details her frightening experiences in the apartment, as well as her research over the following years on the subject of Marie's missing person's case.

During my 23 years working as a New York City police officer in Manhattan, I learned first-hand not every victim gets justice for the crimes committed against them. While it is a shame, sometimes there is nothing that can legally be done about it. The legal system is far from perfect and it is not always morally correct. We live in a society where the laws protect the perpetrators as much as it protects their victims.

As it happens, people go missing all the time, especially in a city populated by thousands of residents. Some run away, while others were never actually missing in the first place. Maybe they stayed out too late or overdosed on drugs. Perhaps, they ended up in jail or at a hospital under a John Doe or Jane Doe alias. Clearly, there are also those dreadful instances when a person is actually missing, as a result of a crime.

In those cases, it is rare for the person to be found alive, especially after they have been missing for so long. Often, unidentified bodies turn up, sooner or later, in wooded areas, garbage bins, ditches along the highway, washed up on shores, or buried in unmarked graves. Sometimes, it could take years for them to be found. Obviously, there are also instances where the missing person is never found, such as in Marie's case.

I decided to write this story as a way of paying homage to Marie Elizabeth Spannhake, as well as to Jodi Foster. If not for Jodi, I probably would have never learned about Marie's story. Throughout the time I have been working on this book, I think I have become somewhat obsessed with the original case.

It was my obsession, which led me to a similar case, featured in the film "*Karla,*" which is the true story of a woman, whose husband, Paul Bernardo, kidnapped, raped, and murdered young girls during the 1990s. He allegedly forced his wife to help him, and abused her regularly, making a victim of her, as well. Regardless of her abuse, she was an accessory to multiple murders, including her younger sister, Tammy. The couple was arrested and convicted for their brutal crimes. Despite certain similarities with the previously mentioned case, Karla was not acquitted, as was the case with Janice.

I used elements from both cases for my story combined with my own morbid imagination. I also drew from a few other sources, such as other true crimes and famous serial killers, including the Son of Sam. I can only hope the end result you are about to read will satisfy the reader in you, while also shocking the shit out of you!

Be warned, the prologue alone is a bit extreme when compared to my previous books, and it might be rough to get through for some. I warn you now, this story will contain graphic violence, vulgar language, and sexual content.

Every chapter is not filled with the stuff, but you will certainly come across it, especially during the prologue.

Unfortunately, not all endings can be happy, as was the real-life case of Marie Elizabeth Spannhake. Life is not a fairy tale. It is often harsh. I hope she can someday find peace in her eternal rest, since she could not find justice. After so many years, it may already be too late for her family to find the closure they needed, considering it has been nearly forty-five years since Marie's disappearance. I doubt many of her family members, who knew her, are still alive. It is a truly heartbreaking situation, which I try to mirror in my story.

I guess it is worth mentioning how I put in a great deal of time and effort to create a backstory for this book because I wanted it to be thorough and feel authentic. For example, at some point in my story, one of the characters will research numerous newspaper articles from decades earlier. To add credibility, I actually went through the trouble of typing up approximately thirty newspaper articles to serve as her research materials. While most of these articles will not even appear in this book, every single one of them can be found in a special limited companion photobook I've created entitled, "*MEG: The Crimes of The Anniversary Killer.*" However, this rare exclusive photobook cannot be purchased through the publisher, or from any other vendor. It will only be made available at my book signings, or directly through me via special order, and only while supplies last. Trust me, they will be worth owning. Samples can be seen on my website:

www.JasonMedinaTribalPublications.com.

# Dedication



This story is dedicated in memory of Marie Elizabeth Spannhake, an unfortunate person for whom justice was not properly served. May her beautiful soul find a way to finally rest in peace.

# Prologue

## The Prisoner

Yonkers, New York, August 31, 1988...

"Wake up, bitch!" The male voice shouting was followed by the sound of a Kodak instamatic camera clicking.

Margaret struggled to open her eyes. She was groggy and everything seemed blurry. It felt like she had been drugged. She was unsure where she was, and for the moment, could not recall what she was doing last. What she did know is she appeared to be tied to something and the realization scared the hell out of her. Her body leaned on the rough ropes holding her up. It was painful, as the tightness of the ropes burned into her flesh through her clothing. How long had she been in the same position? She tried to adjust herself and stand on her own two feet, easing off the pressure of the rope. Her body ached. She noticed she was barefoot. The ground was cold and hard.

She wondered where she was at. She blinked her eyes, while her eyesight gradually began to clear. It appeared to be a basement. The walls around her were brick. The floor was concrete and dusty. Bright sunlight came in from a window behind her, so she knew it was daytime. She hoped it was still Wednesday. She felt utterly bewildered. There were no other lights on in the large, cold, dungeon-like room. A brick support beam stood directly across from her. Is that what she was tied to? A beam? She looked upwards and to the sides around her. She noticed it was indeed another beam. There seemed to be a horse stall behind her over to her right. It was difficult to tell for sure from her angle.

*Where the hell was she?*

She began to panic. Hundreds of questions flooded her mind. How did she get to this place? How far was she from home? Was she still in Yonkers? More importantly, who was the man yelling at her to wake up?

She tried to speak instinctively, but there was something jammed into her mouth. She wondered how she did not notice before. It was a foul-tasting cloth of some kind, which seemed to be made of cotton. Another cloth was tied tightly around her head to keep it in place. The taste made her want to gag. Was it sweat? Was it her own sock? Gross! She wanted to scream, but how could she with her mouth gagged?

The man, who yelled at her, stood near the wall to her left, while hovering over an old wooden worktable with wheels on its legs. His back was to her. He was a twenty-five-year-old Caucasian man with medium-length, straight, brown hair. He wore an auto mechanic's blue button-down shirt, greasy blue jeans, and black work boots caked in mud. He was busy looking through a selection of assorted knives and tools on the table. They were spread out across a grease-stained grayish towel, which at one time used to be white. She spotted his black camera on the table, as well.

The mysterious man looked over his shoulder to make sure she was awake. He grinned at her and turned back toward the table. He wore prescription glasses over his brown eyes. His hair was almost as greasy as the towel. His chiseled face was mostly cleanshaven with light stubble on his chin. He switched on a portable radio, which also sat on the same table. Loud rock music began to play, filling the room and making use of its acoustics.

Finally, he turned around to face her and stepped closer stopping in front of her. He studied her, momentarily, saying nothing. She stared back nervously trying to avoid eye contact. His name appeared to be Hank, or at least, it was the name embroidered in white across the front right side breast pocket of his shirt. He wore a thick brown leather belt, which had a metal buckle in the shape of an "H" on it.

In the background, the radio was blasting "*Wild Side*" by the rock band, Mötley Crüe. It was too loud to speak over the music, most likely why he said nothing, for the moment. When Vince Neal sang the verse "*Take a ride on the wi-ild side...,*" it gave Hank a morbid idea.

His nineteen-year-old guest dreaded what he would possibly do to her. He took a step even closer to her. She instinctively leaned back against the brick support beam, not wanting him anywhere near her. He glared at her crude bonds and wished he had a hoist, so he could lift her up properly. It would be too much trouble to take the one from his garage and bring it down to the basement. It would require a whole new set up. He simply did not have the time to create something like that. Besides, he needed it up in the garage to work on car engines. He shrugged it off. It was no big deal. He got along fine without it all this time. Why worry about it now?

He reached for her face with his dirty hand and removed the gag from her mouth. She was disgusted when she realized it was indeed her sock. "You better not scream!" He warned over the noise of the music.

"Why are you doing this?" She demanded, as loudly as she could muster without yelling.

Either he did not hear her, or he chose to ignore her question. Instead, he grabbed some pliers from the table and turned back to face her. Her eyes gaped open, as he approached her with them in his right hand.

"No! Wait! What are you going to do with that?" She panicked.

He grinned and grabbed Margaret firmly by the jaw with his left hand, while reaching into her mouth with the pliers in his right hand. She closed her mouth tight, but one swift slap with the pliers caused her to cry out. He squeezed her mouth open and jammed the pliers inside chipping one of her teeth in the process. He began carelessly yanking out each tooth, one at a time. The blood mixed with saliva began pouring out from her mouth. She screamed and cried from the agonizing pain, but the music was too loud for anyone outside to hear her. Plus, the basement room under the garage was fairly soundproofed with its thick stone walls on the outside and brick layers on the inside.

The torture went on for nearly an hour, until all of her teeth sat in a metal tray on the work table. With each tooth pulled, there was a creaking grinding sound she would not soon forget. By the time Hank was done, his prisoner's white t-shirt was covered by splattered blood stains and drool. Unfortunately, for her the pain had only just begun.

Hank yanked down her blue track pants with ease, causing her to gasp, and then pulled them off her legs. He bundled them up and threw them into the horse stall behind her.

"You won't be needing these either, kiddo," he said in a mockingly kind voice, as he slid her black panties down. He did it ever so slowly savoring the moment. He practically drooled on himself when his face got close to her private area. She was a runner, so she had strong legs. She gave him a satisfying strike in his face with her knee, even though she knew it would only make things worse for her.

He shouted, "God damn it! You fucking bitch!" As punishment, he punched her in the abdomen repeatedly, using combinations with both fists to take the fight out of her. This lasted about thirty seconds. He then untied her and pushed her to the ground into the horse stall. She bent over in pain reeling from his punches. He knelt down on the floor beside her and forced her onto her back. He gave her a swift slap across the face with the back of his hand to make sure she complied. She did, but with great reluctance.

"I could beat the shit out of you or fuck the shit out of you," he said to her. "It doesn't matter to me. I will most likely do both anyway." It seemed she did not actually have a choice in the matter. He pulled back his fist, as if he were going to punch her in the face. She winced and turned her face to the left. He lowered his fist, smirked, and shoved her pants under her head to serve as a pillow. "Relax, babe," he instructed, "And enjoy the ride."

She closed her eyes tightly and tried to imagine she was somewhere else. Anywhere else, except where she was at the moment.

He moved his face close to her private area and closed his eyes, as he took a whiff of her womanly scent. "Oh, yeah. You smell *so-o-o* good. I like a sweaty pussy." He licked his lips and grinned from ear to ear. "I'm really going to enjoy this." He inserted his finger for the taste test. He pulled it out and sucked it clean.

Margaret whimpered quietly, fully aware of the next phase of horror about to take place. She forced herself to urinate hoping it would discourage him. She prided herself on her hygiene, so the warm wet feeling disgusted her.

He simply waited for her to finish and questioned her, "Did you really think that would discourage me?" He chuckled. "To be honest, it's a turn on for me. Have you ever tried a golden shower? I recommend it. By the way, thanks for the warm lubrication. It should make this much easier."

She could only cry.

"Get ready, baby. This is going to hurt you more than it hurts me," he snickered, as he unbuckled his belt and yanked down his jeans in almost one motion. He shoved himself inside her and she shrieked. He slapped her hard across the face, and then slapped her, again, and again, until her screaming died down into muffled sobs. Once she appeared to be subdued to his liking, he placed his hands around her neck and began choking her, as he pushed himself inside her.

Margaret couldn't breathe. Her eyes widened in desperation, as she gasped for air. In a frantic effort to survive, she grabbed his wrists and tried to pull his hands off of her, crying and kicking her feet as she struggled. However, he was heavy and much stronger than her. She could not budge his hands. Fortunately, he eased off and placed his hands on the ground next to her. He did not want her to die. Not yet. She coughed and tried to catch her breath, while spitting up blood. He continued to thrust away into her knowing she would be too weak to resist any further. He began breathing heavily when he neared orgasm. He pushed faster. Harder. She prayed for the ordeal to be over quickly, keeping her face turned to the side. She did not want to look at him. When he ejaculated inside of her, she vomited.

"Ah, come on! You fucking slob!" He stopped what he was doing and dismounted her.

She remained with her face to the side, so she did not see him getting dressed, or looking for something to clean the vomit, which was grossing him out far more than the urine. The combined stench made her want to vomit, again.

She was not a virgin, but she had always been careful with her boyfriend. They always used a condom. The thought of becoming pregnant from this sadistic bastard sickened her to no end.

Her mind was transported to another time and place, a couple of years earlier. She imagined herself at her high school prom. It was a wonderful evening. She dazzled everyone in her stunning white dress, which had gray stripes and black flower patterns. Her hair was pinned back, and the top was stiffened by nearly an entire can of hairspray.

Her date was Matteo Federico. It was their first date. It would not be their last. Before that night, they spent many times hanging out together with mutual friends in a group. It was obvious to all of their friends Matt had a huge crush on her. She liked him, too, so when he asked her to go with him to the prom, it was easy for her to say, "yes."

It was the beginning of a wonderful relationship. He became her boyfriend that night and she began to fall in love for the first time. Eventually, their make out sessions would end with heavy petting over the clothes, and then under the clothes, until the first time they had sex. It was in the backseat of his father's car, which he borrowed to take her on a date to Rye Playland. They barely got on any rides because they spent most of the time in the backseat of the car. Sure, it was not the most romantic experience, but they enjoyed the hell out of it.

Her memories were disturbed abruptly when Hank turned the hose on her and began spraying the vomit and urine with cold water pushing it into the corner behind her. He also sprayed her down before turning the hose off. The blast of icy water snapped her back into reality. She shivered, although she did not scream. Not this time.

A short time later, Margaret lay in the horse stall battered, beaten, and soaking wet with her damp track pants, which were still shoved under her head as a pillow. Her white bloody t-shirt had turned pink from the mixture of blood and water. Her bra and panties were missing. She would not be getting those back. She was still struggling to breathe normally. Her heart was practically beating out of her chest. It had grown darker outside. The sun was going down. She wondered if he was done with her, or if there would be more terror ahead.

Hank stood over her, looking down at her. "Damn, baby," he said. "You were so tight. I love it. I even tried to make it better for you by choking you a bit. I guess it didn't work out too well, huh?" He chuckled. She did not reply. He resumed, "Whatever. It's too bad you killed the mood by throwing up. Dumb move." He shook his head.

A feeling of dread came over her. She had a feeling he was going to do something drastic to punish her for vomiting. She found herself trying to cover her body with her hands, as if it made any difference.

He stared down at her lustfully and rubbed his groin. He liked how vulnerable she looked, while soaking wet. He was extremely tempted to go one more round with her, but he was exhausted and covered in her blood, urine, and his semen. What he really wanted was to take a shower. Later. He laughed to himself when he considered how she did not enjoy the experience as much as he did. It amused him.

Finally, he stated, "Okay, you may as well get dressed now. The fun part is over."


Hank turned on the work lamp, which was attached to the worktable. There was still music playing in the background. Apparently, he had a few ninety-minute cassette tapes ready to go. He made sure to keep the music going to drown out her screams. Another song by Mötley Crüe had come on. He began bopping to it and playing an air guitar to their song, *"Looks That Kill."*

Blood oozed from Margaret's mouth, which was aching badly. As much as she wanted to get dressed, she felt too weak to move. After having been tortured, beaten, strangled, and raped she wanted to die. The amount of shame and disgust she felt was overwhelming. She was a broken mess. She knew her life would never be the same.

Somehow, she found the strength to get dressed. She pulled on her wet track pants, gathered her socks and sneakers, which were on the floor nearby. She put them on, although the process took much longer than it should have. She could not stop shaking and it made it nearly impossible for her to tie her sneaker laces.

Once she was dressed, she sat in the cleanest corner of the stall with her back against the wall. The ground was wet, which made it quite uncomfortable. She still shook uncontrollably due to shock. She stared down at the remnants of her scattered vomit on the floor and it nauseated her. She tried to remove herself from reality and imagined a tiny ant crawling between the cracks on the floor. She wanted to be the ant, no longer wanting to be herself. It would make it easier to crawl through a crack and disappear into a hole. She wanted to disappear from the world.

Hank stood tall before her and asked, rhetorically, "What should I do with you next?"

She looked up at his smug face and decided she did not want to die. Instead, she pled for her life. "Please, mister," she begged, while choking on her blood and trying desperately to hold back her tears. She did not want to give him the satisfaction of seeing her cry anymore. She wanted to be strong. She needed to be strong, especially if she was going to survive this experience. "I promise," she uttered, and then coughed before spitting coppery blood out of her mouth. It was so painful to speak. Her voice and word pronunciation sounded different without her teeth. She now had a lisp and she hated it. She tried not to think about it. "I won't tell anyone. Just let me go."

Hank casually walked over to her and cocked his head slightly to the right, as if he were actually considering her request. He asked curiously, "Hey, do you like the Crüe?" He gestured toward the radio over his right shoulder with his right thumb, ignoring her request. "Personally, I think they kick ass. I saw them live at the Garden not too long ago during their *Theatre of Pain* tour. Man, what a great show. I believe it was in August of '85. Best day of my life." For the briefest moment, he seemed to be lost in his memories.

Margaret stared at him helplessly and sobbed. She bowed her head in defeat and began to feel nothing but despair. She wanted to be strong, but did not know how. What was the point? She knew she was going to die. This man is demented. There is no way he was going to let her go, not after what he did to her.

He raised his right hand up to his chin and rubbed it with his forefinger and thumb, as if deep in thought. After a moment, he sighed with impatience and asked, "What are you willing to do for me, if I let you go?" He had a sly smirk on his face when he posed the question.

Margaret could not believe her ears. Was he serious? She met his eyes with her own revealing a glimmer of hope. Would he actually be willing to let her go?

She blurted out hopelessly, "I'll do anything you want me to do... just don't kill me! Please, I want to live!" At this point, she just wanted to stay alive, no matter what the cost. What else could he possibly do to her that would be worse than what has already been done? The horrors he put her through over the last few hours will be burned into her memory for the rest of her natural life. It was probably a fate worse than death, to have to live with these memories.

Still, the thought of never seeing her family and friends, again, weighed heavily on her. Would they ever know what happened to her, if he killed her, instead? What would he do with her body? The thoughts going through her mind made her tremble with fear.

He considered what she said. At last, he flashed her a devilish grin and responded, "Anything?"

Margaret cried out reluctantly in answer to his question, "Yes!" She desperately longed to be free from this monster.

Hank smiled and nodded his head. He then returned to his worktable and grabbed a knife from the towel. After examining the sharpness of the blade's edge, he approached her and crouched down in front of her, so he could look her in the eyes. As he did, he held the knife in a menacing manner. His smile broadened when he noticed a renewed level of fear eminating from her. He pressed the knife to her blood-soaked t-shirt and moved the blade slowly along the space between her breasts.

She trembled with fear and forced a lump of saliva down her throat.

He stood up and unzipped his pants. "Open your mouth," he ordered. "Try not to bite. Oh, that's right. You can't. Can you?" He scoffed. He then stated with seriousness, "Do a good job and I'll let you go." He sounded sincere.

He then shoved his semen-covered member toward her bloody mouth. "Suck it clean!" As if it were even possible with blood in her mouth.

Margaret did what she had to do to survive. It was painful on her raw gums. She wept the entire time, despite trying unsuccessfully to hold it back. He had only removed her teeth about an hour or two earlier. Her gums barely had enough time to recover, and this was not helping. She felt her nausea building up, too. It felt like she was going to vomit, again. There was too much blood and saliva in her mouth. She had to fight it. She kept telling herself it will all be over soon. She just had to be strong and stick it out a little longer.

She closed her eyes tightly and tried to pretend she was with Matt, hoping to ease the disgust. No, not here in this moment. It was not helping to think of him. It would only ruin their time together in the future, when he returned to her from the military. She would end up thinking about this animal, instead. Maybe someone else, such as a famous actor or singer. It did not help. Try as she might, she could not fool herself. She tried to convince herself Hank was not such a bad looking guy. He was only ugly on the inside. It did not make the humiliation any easier, and it did not stop the gag reflex, which he began to notice.

"Don't you fucking dare throw up on me!" He shouted in warning. "In fact, enough of that! You're making a fucking mess and getting blood all over me, for Christ's sake! Stop the slobbering!" He pushed her head away. "Stop!" By this point, he was already turned off and no longer in the mood for any sexual activities. "I can't believe you killed my boner."

It was fine by her. She backed away from him and stared down at the ground in shame. She spit out saliva and blood from her mouth, and then cried. She could not help herself. It only annoyed him more. Once his pants were zipped up, he bent down to her eye level, once more.

"Hey!" He grabbed her chin firmly and pointed at her with his other hand. "Don't you give me any more of that crying bullshit! It won't work on me! What are you? Some kind of fucking tease? You said you'd do anything! Well, I'm holding you to it, or should I just kill you, right now?"

She shook her head anxiously and replied, "No! Please, okay, okay! I'll do what you want." Once again, she was regretting the words, as soon as they came out of her mouth. Out of desperation, she tried a different approach. She lied to him. "My family has money!" She added, "They'll pay you!"

"*Pay me?* That would imply you're going to tell them I have you. Are you really that stupid? If that's the case, I guess I'll have to kill them. Is that what you want? Well??? *Is it?!*" He became upset.

"No!" She exhaled and repeated softly, "No." She then added almost in a whisper, "Please, I just wanna go home. I won't tell anyone anything about you. I swear. My little brother is waiting for me."

"Is that so? Sure, you want to go home. It's perfectly understandable. That's what I thought," he replied in a kind voice with a smug grin on his face. In the next moment, he changed his attitude and snarled, "Let me tell you something, you high and mighty little *whore*. You can keep your damn money. I don't need it. Do you think I'm some poor lowlife piece of shit with no money? Do I look like some *Spic* or *Nigger* to you? I think not." He shook his head. "In case you haven't noticed, I have my own business. This isn't about money, baby." He glared at her. "It's about something you can never understand."

She stared at him not knowing what else to say. She was afraid of angering him any further. She just wanted to go home and did not want to keep pushing the issue.

"Get up," he instructed. "I'll take you upstairs to the bathroom, so you can get cleaned up. That's a promise. You have my word," he told her, trying to sound sincere. He left the radio playing in the background.

She stood up hesitantly. Her legs felt so weak, her knees almost buckled. She was surprised. She could not believe he was actually going to keep his word.


He escorted her through a set of wooden double doors, and then to the left up a darkened staircase, which went up and around to his garage. She noticed it was a business. There was a car with its hood up. He led her into a small bathroom, allowing her to enter alone. However, he did not let her close the door. He jammed his foot into the doorway to make sure she did not try.

"No. I think not. The door stays open," he instructed. "Hurry up and clean yourself off. There's mouthwash, too, so use it. Your breath is atrocious. It smells like dirty cock." He laughed maniacally to himself. He loved when he made himself laugh.

She obeyed, rinsing her mouth out several times with the mouthwash, as if she could not get the taste out, no matter how hard she tried. The cold mint flavor stung her raw gums, but she did not care. Between the foul traces of blood, vomit, and semen it was too much to endure. She had already swallowed so much blood. When she was done, she passed her wet hands over her face and hair using the soap to cleanse herself. She also used a small towel hanging on a rack beside her to scrub her breasts and her privates as best she could with soap and water. Nothing she could do would ever cleanse her body enough, but it would have to do. She felt like she would never be clean, again.

A short time later, she stood there in silence dripping wet. Not having a towel to dry herself with did not matter to her, since she had already been wet when she entered the bathroom.

Hank stepped into the small bathroom and stood closely behind her. Much too close for her liking. She tensed up, as he pressed his crotch against her behind and sniffed her hair. She cringed and swallowed nervously. The taste of blood was still strong in her mouth.

"Mm. Much better," he said softly, as he stared at her reflection in the bathroom mirror with his dark piercing eyes. "Now, you smell sweet, again, like a pretty little flower." She wanted to gag. He licked his lips hungrily and demanded, "Tell me your name, '*Amanda*,' and don't lie because I'll know it and I seriously doubt it's Amanda."

The name "Amanda" was written across her bloodstained t-shirt in white letters over a photo back drop of a pretty redheaded model in some kind of public restroom. It was recently purchased from a thrift store at Getty Square. The name was actually the title of a story from a book called "*No Hope for the Hopeless at Kings Park*," which had been written by a local author, although Margaret only bought the shirt because she loved the photo. She had never read the book.

She answered hesitantly, "M-Margaret," while boldly looking back at his reflection. "Are you going to let me go, now? You said you would."

"Don't worry," he replied in a creepy sweet voice. "You will be leaving here very soon, just like I promised. In fact, I need you out of here before morning. I can't have you messing with my business."

She practically became excited and declared, "Oh, thank you! I promise I won't tell anyone!"

He grinned sadistically and replied, "I know you won't, babe." He then placed his left hand on her forehead and began to caress her head awkwardly, before holding her head still, as he reached over with his right hand to slit her throat using the knife, which he had been holding. He stared at her reflection looking her in the eyes the whole time.

"Our time together has come to an end," he said coldly, as he did the deed. "Sorry, M-Margaret."

Her eyes opened wide when she realized what he was doing. It was too late for her to react. She tried to scream but gurgled, instead. The blood spilled down her neck onto her wet t-shirt. Her big brown doe eyes rolled up into her head, as her lifeforce slowly slipped away. She slid out of his grip and fell limply to the floor. Margaret was dead.

Hank stood over her for what seemed to him like several minutes, before he said, "They think they got me all figured out. Well, you and I, we're going to change the game. Things will be different from now on. They're never going to find you, not where I'm putting you. You can bank on it, baby. I'm changing the game." He grinned to himself feeling proud.

He then took a step back and watched the blood, as it oozed from Margaret's neck creating a crimson puddle on the tile floor of the bathroom. He sighed wearily. "Now, look what you've done. You are such a messy girl. First, the urine, then the vomit, and now more blood. Jesus Christ. Who do you think has to clean this mess? *Me*, that's who! I don't have a maid. I'll tell you this," he pointed down at her corpse. "It's a good thing my employees went home early today." His eyes moved slowly over her body, which was now surrounded by a large pool of blood. "Look at you… framed by blood like a piece of art. You sexy little bitch. You really know how to get to me."

He removed her clothing, again, and then pulled down his pants revealing a rock-hard erection. He used the same wet towel she cleaned herself with to clean himself, first. He then bent down on his knees, ignoring the blood. He climbed onto her corpse and began to have intercourse with her, once more.

He figured there was still time to kill before nightfall. He usually liked to take twelve hours from the time of the abduction to the time he disposed of the body. It meant he had until about 3:30 A.M., give or take a few minutes. It was when he would dump the body. He already knew the perfect place, where no one would ever suspect. This time, he was better prepared, thanks to the newspapers. They thought they had him figured out, but he was going to fool them all.

# End of prologue.

# MEG

Inspired by True Events

# Chapter 1

## Our Secret Adventure

Chico, California, the present…

Megan Forester has never been so scared in all her life. She swallowed hard, as she stared down the business end of a 12-gauge double barrel rifle pointed directly at her face. She did not want to die, especially not like this. Her life began to flash before her eyes. Her childhood in New York was not great, but it was better than the few years she spent in California with Herman.

It was nice in the beginning, until he started drinking heavily. It was around the time she got pregnant. Herman was stressed about having an extra mouth to feed. He even had the audacity to say it might not have been his child. He had his doubts. Megan came extremely close to leaving him, back then. She wished she had.

How was she to know he was not in the good graces of his boss, which left him on edge? Herman rarely spoke about work because it caused him too much stress. Once he lost his job, things only got worse between Megan and him. They argued all of the time. Everything seemed to be her fault, according to him. Neighbors complained about the constant yelling. It was a miracle they were not evicted, especially considering how far behind they were with their rent. Luckily, the landlord was a good man and took pity on them because of their newborn baby.

Little Josh was the best thing ever to come out of her relationship with Herman. Josh was a blessing. For a while, things actually got better because of him. They did not argue as much. Those days did not last long, though.

Herman was able to get a new job, which paid better, but the drinking never stopped. Every weekend, he would get drunk. Whenever he was drunk every little thing seemed to annoy him. He would blame Megan for the baby crying and soon he began to take his anger out on her. The beatings did not come often, but when they did, it was brutal.

Megan thought about leaving Herman, but where would she go? She did not have much money. She never really knew her father, since he divorced her mother when she was a little girl. He remarried and moved away. Her mother passed away about a year after Josh was born. Her grandparents died a few years earlier. The only person she could go to was probably her childhood best friend, Hannah Kasanka, except she lived in New York.

The only time Megan ever threatened to leave Herman, she ended up with a broken arm. That was a year ago. The reason she did not report him to the police was because he apologized and promised to change his ways. He swore things would be different and begged her to forgive him. Like a fool, she did.

Now, she had a black eye and a rifle pointed at her face. The only relief she had was Josh was asleep in his room. He would not have to see his mother get murdered by his father.

"I should blow yer fuckin' head off, Megan." Herman took a breath and lowered the rifle. "The only reason I won't is because it'll make a mess, and then I'll need to spend a fortune on babysitting fees. Someone's gotta watch the little shit, while I'm at work."

"That little *shit* is your son, you fucking asshole," she spat back with contempt, and then she cringed thinking he would strike her, again. She did not need a second black eye. The one from yesterday was good enough, along with the slap she received earlier.

As it turned out, he did not seem interested in beating on her anymore. Not this time.

"Sometimes, I wonder 'bout that. He gots too much of you in him," he muttered drunkenly. "He's gonna be a momma's boy. I can tell. Yep." He nodded dumbly to himself. "He pra-ca-tilly is now. He's always halfway up yer ass." He burped and blew it in her general direction. "That's for you, honey." He wagged his forefinger at her, smirked, and stumbled clumsily toward the bathroom. "I gotta take a shit. Make yourself useful and make me some coffee.

*Bitch*," he added with emphasis. He then went to the bathroom and closed the door behind him, taking the rifle with him.

This was the last straw. Megan was both furious and in fear for her safety. She was not going to wait for him to kill her in a drunken stupor. She hated the fact he even owned a hunting rifle. He only went hunting once and he did not come home with anything. She went into the bedroom and opened her drawers from the dresser. She threw a bundle of clothes on the bed. Next, she reached into the closet, grabbed her suitcase, and pulled some clothing from the hangers. Everything was jammed into the suitcase. She grabbed her purse and went into Josh's room. Quietly, she woke him.

"Josh. Wake up, baby. We need to go. Come on. Get up."

"Where are we going, mommy?" Her four-year-old son asked, while yawning.

"It's a secret. Think of this as a game. We need to be extremely quiet. No more talking. Okay? Here, let me get you dressed." She helped him with his pants and socks, before pulling a shirt over his head. She grabbed his sneakers and quickly fastened them to his feet. She collected some of his clothing from his dresser and stuffed them into his knapsack pushing its seams to the limit. She placed his arms through the straps, so he could carry it on his back. Next, she grabbed Josh by the hand and began to lead him out of his room, but he dragged his feet and hesitated.

She turned to him and whispered, "Baby, we need to go. *Now.*"

"I want my Mando," he whined, referring to his fifteen-inch "*Star Wars Mandalorian*" talking action figure. It was his favorite toy. He got it for his fourth birthday, which was not too long ago. He absolutely adored it and usually took it everywhere with him.

"Okay, fine. Bring Mando, but hurry up and remember, be quiet," she instructed in a whisper.

He nodded eagerly and grabbed his Mandalorian action figure from his nightstand. He resisted the temptation to press the button on his chest, which caused the toy to say one of its eight phrases, or the two buttons on the arms, which played laser and flamethrower sound effects.

Megan held Josh's hand and walked him to the front door of their ground floor apartment on Parmac Road, while carrying the heavy suitcase in her other hand. Her purse was hanging over her shoulder by its strap. She quietly grabbed the car keys and they slipped through the door to the hallway closing it gently. She did not bother to lock it.

"What about Papa?" Josh asked, perplexed by this new secret game they were playing. "Isn't he coming? He always drives." He scratched his head, messing up his short brown hair.

"No, not today, baby," she explained, while hurrying across the lobby toward the main entrance of the building. It was raining, as they stepped out into the night.

The rain was coming down fairly hard. It was the first day in February, so the air was cold out, which made it feel twice as bad.

"Come on," Megan rushed her son. "We need to hurry. It's raining and it's cold. The last thing we need is for one of us to get sick on top of everything else." She dragged Josh to the parking lot of their housing complex and placed him into the backseat of the suburban vehicle, along with her suitcase. He had a confused look on his face. He could tell something was wrong. She hurried into the driver's seat, and then started the engine.

"What's wrong, Mommy? Are you in trouble?"

"What?" His question caught her off guard. "No, baby. Everything is fine. We just need to go somewhere. That's all. It will be our secret adventure." The word "adventure" was enough to make him smile.

Seconds later, the red Ford Explorer pulled out of the parking lot and sped toward the nearest intersection at Rio Lindo Avenue. From there, they headed to the Golden State Highway. She had no plan of where to go, after that, but she knew they had to leave Chico and get far away from Herman before he realized they were gone.

Once on the highway, Megan opted to go north. She drove for several minutes. There was not a lot of traffic on the road. It was nearly midnight by the time they reached Red Bluff, which was a town about thirty miles north of Chico. She had never been there before. It seemed far enough away for tonight. Next, she needed to find a hotel. It was terrible driving weather, especially with her young son in the car. Not to mention with the way her anxiety was acting up, it was only a matter of time before she got into an accident. It was a chance she did not wish to take.

She drove through the main road of town, until she saw a large number 6 on a tall sign hovering over a shop to her left. She recognized it as a Motel 6 sign. It was located off of Antelope Boulevard, shortly before Interstate 5. It probably would not be the best accommodations, but it would have to do.

Megan pulled into the parking lot and parked in front of the office. She got out and grabbed Josh from the backseat. There was no way she was going to leave him in the car alone.

"Let's go, Josh! Hurry and get inside!"

It seemed to be raining harder in Red Bluff than in Chico. They ran into the main office and shook the cold water from their bodies, once they were inside. It was a game they played whenever coming in out of the rain. Josh giggled and she smiled at him with adoration.

She grabbed him by the hand and approached the counter. A woman sat behind the desk chewing gum and reading a newspaper. She did not bother to look up.

Megan cleared her throat to get her attention. "Ahem!"

The woman rolled her eyes and looked up lazily. "Yes?" She asked, sounding annoyed.

"I'd like a room for the night with a full-size bed."

The woman noticed Megan's black eye and her attitude changed. She peeked over the counter to get a look at Josh, who was shorter than the desk. He blinked innocently, as he looked up at her. She smiled at him sympathetically and seemed to soften up. She looked back at Megan and nodded.

"One room coming up. Do you have any preference for what floor you're on?"

"Ground floor would be great," Megan replied. Ever since Josh was born, she always preferred to be on the ground floor, whenever possible. She was afraid of him falling down the steps and getting hurt.

"Not a problem. I'll need to see a credit card and your driver's license, although you can pay tomorrow when you check out." Once the woman received the documents she asked for, she jotted down some information. When she was done, she gave everything back to Megan, along with a hotel keycard for a room on the ground floor. "You're all set. Is there… anything else I can do for you?"

"No, that will be all. Thank you," Megan responded shortly. She put her documents back into her wallet and stuffed it deep into her purse. She hated using the credit card to rent a room, but she did not have much of a choice. She was short on cash. Of course, she knew it meant they would have to be gone by the morning. It was too risky staying a second night.

Unless… yes, she knew what she had to do. It would buy her the time she needed.

As soon as they were settled in their room, she picked up her cellphone and dialed 9-1-1. She explained the situation to the operator and was told police would be responding to her location to file a report. She hated doing it, but this time, it had to be done. Herman had gone too far by using the rifle. He needed to know he was not going to get away with that kind of abusive behavior. Not anymore.

A Red Bluff police cruiser arrived within minutes. Two police officers exited the vehicle and walked straight to the hotel room door. They knocked loudly and announced themselves.

"Police," one of the officers stated in a commanding voice.

Josh had been lying peacefully in the bed tucked neatly under the covers. When he heard the police officer outside, his eyes opened wide, and he ducked his head under the covers.

Megan noticed and couldn't help but chuckle. "It's okay, Josh. They're the good guys. They're not here for you. As long as you are a good boy, you never have to worry about the police." She opened the door and invited them inside from the rain, so she could close the door. She did not want anyone else to know her business.

Over the next few minutes, she described what took place at her residence, as one police officer prepared an incident report. They asked her questions, which she answered truthfully. She also briefly went over the extensive domestic violence history, explaining how Herman had first become abusive when he started drinking heavily around the time when she became pregnant. She also mentioned the other times he hurt her, making sure to include the time he broke her arm. The police only really wanted to know about what happened tonight, so she focused on that, especially on the fact Herman pointed a loaded rifle at her face. Together with the assault from the previous day, it was enough for an arrest to be made.

The police officers contacted the Chico Police Department because the crimes occurred in their jurisdiction. An arrest was made, several minutes later. Of course, additional charges of resisting arrest, menacing, and the assault on one of the arresting officers had to be tacked on because Herman did not go without a fight. He was lucky they did not shoot him considering he still had his hunting rifle in his hand. The officers realized he was drunk and were able to gain the upper hand using proper tactics.

When Megan learned of Herman's arrest, she was relieved.


The next morning Megan and Josh checked out of the motel, grabbed a quick breakfast from the McDonald's across the street, and returned home. They would not be staying long. Megan began packing anything important into bags and boxes. She had to be picky. There was no time to take all of their belongings. She wanted to be gone before Herman had a chance to return. She loaded up the Ford Explorer as best she could. She had no intention of being in the apartment longer than she needed to be.

With nowhere left to turn, she called her childhood friend, Hannah, in New York. After she explained the situation, Hannah immediately invited her to come stay with her for as long as necessary.

Within a day, Megan and Josh were on the road heading across the country toward the East Coast. She wished she had money to make it a fun and memorable trip for Josh. However, she did not want to push her luck. It was a long expensive drive and she kept thinking the Ford Explorer would breakdown in the middle of nowhere in the dead of night. The thought kept her on edge for the entire drive across Interstate 80, which took her from California to New Jersey. She was also worried she might end up on Interstate 90 by mistake because it intersected and traveled along Interstate 80 for a great distance. The road trip took a total of seven days with her average driving speed going about ten hours a day and making overnight stopovers. Not to mention food stops and bathroom breaks.

The scariest part of the trip for her was driving across the Great Salt Lake Desert. It seemed to go on forever, which gave her anxiety. To counter her anxiety she played a game with Josh. They tried to count the different state license plates of the vehicles they passed, along the way. They also had to navigate around the Great Lakes. At least, that portion of the trip made for a nice view, which also kept Josh entertained. He loved seeing large bodies of water because it reminded him of the beaches in California. Megan was not too crazy about it.

They finally arrived in Yonkers, New York, on the night of February 10. By this time, any cash Megan had saved up was gone, mainly spent on food and gas. Her credit card was maxed out also from gas, as well as hotel stopovers. Not to mention, she had no money left in the bank. She was flat broke and dead tired.

She parked her vehicle on Van Cortlandt Park Avenue and gave Hannah a call. "Hey, I'm here, at last. I mean we're here. Josh is asleep. I just parked the car. I can't believe I found a spot in front of your building. Can you come down and help me with some of this stuff? Thanks." She hung up and waited for her friend to come outside.

Hannah took a moment to come out because she had to get dressed and put on her coat. It was cold outside. Fortunately, there was no snow on the ground. When she stepped outside, she shuddered and hurried to her friend, who was unloading items from the Ford Explorer's rear compartment. By this time, Josh was awake, but he was tired and cranky, so he remained seated in the front.

Hannah called out when she saw Megan, "Hey, you! Give me a hug!"

Megan's face lit up when she heard Hannah's voice. The old friends ran into each other's arms and embraced. They were more like sisters than friends. It had always been that way since school.

Hannah exclaimed, "Oh, my God! I've missed you so much! I'm so happy to see you, Meg! Wow! Look at you! You're so pretty! I totally love your long brown hair! It looks great!"

"Oh, please. I must look like crap. I just finished driving cross-country. I'm so beat. Besides, between your curly blonde hair and those gorgeous green eyes, you are so much prettier."

"Yeah, whatever! Hey, let me help you with your stuff, so you can come up and get warm. I ordered a pizza pie for us," Hannah said with a smile. "I know how much you miss New York pizza."

"Oh, Hannah. If you were a man, I'd marry you right now. I'm so stoked for pizza…" Her mind trailed off dreamily, as she imagined herself eating a slice. Maybe two slices, and then one more for good measure.

Hannah apologized, "I'm so sorry I ordered it too soon. It's already cold, but I put it into the oven before I came down."

"Cold?" Megan asked sounding disappointed. "When did you order it?"

"At around the time you called me to tell me you were in New Jersey."

"Oh, boy. Hannah, that was like an hour and a half ago!"

"Well, I'm sorry! Pies take like twenty minutes to make and another ten to fifteen to deliver It usually takes less than an hour to get here from Interstate 80. I thought I timed it perfectly," Hannah stated. "How was I supposed to know you would take so long?" Her green eyes seemed to sparkle with the street lights reflecting in them.

Megan placed her hands at her hips and stated, "Do you have any idea how much traffic there was crossing the GW Bridge? And stupid me went into the express lanes thinking it would be faster. I figured it would have probably taken me twenty minutes tops. Nope! Definitely not express. Plus, as if that wasn't bad enough, I had to switch from the 9-5 to the 8-7, where more traffic was waiting for me!"

Hannah stared at her and replied dryly, "You've become so *Californicated. The 9-5? The 8-7?* Around these parts, we call it I-95 and I-87." She shook her head disapprovingly.

Megan glared at her.

For a brief moment, there was an awkward silence between the two, and then they both erupted with laughter. They hugged, once more, before getting Josh out of the car. He was shy around Hannah. The last time she saw him, he was only a baby. He did not remember her, having only seen her in photos.

She said, "Hi, Josh! I'm your auntie Hannah!"

Megan explained, "Sorry, he's a bit shy. Give him time and he'll warm up to you."

"He's so cute!" Hannah smiled at him and said, "It's okay, Josh. You're going to love me soon enough. I bought you some cool toys. They're upstairs in my apartment."

His face lit up with anticipation.

Megan responded, "You don't have to spoil him."

"Nonsense. Stay out of this, Meg. This is between me and this handsome little guy." She tickled his chest and he giggled. "You see? You're already under my spell." She pointed at him. She then turned to Megan and suggested, "Let's get you guys upstairs. I'm freezing my butt out here."

Together, they carried as much as they could up to Hannah's third floor apartment. Of course, the elevator was out of service, which meant walking everything up the stairs. It was exhausting.

The ultimate reward was when they eventually got a chance to sit down and eat their reheated pizza. Josh had never eaten pizza before. He became an instant fan.

Once he was put to bed at around ten, Megan and Hannah stayed up late talking and catching up. They had so much to talk about. It had been years since they last saw each other. It was agreed Megan would find a job right away, so she could save up enough money to get her own place. Hannah said she would help her to find a job, but in the meantime, she could stay as long as she needed to stay. It would not be a problem. Megan was grateful, but she did not wish to impose longer than necessary. She wanted to get herself set up before Josh started pre-school in September.

The first thing she did during the week was to sell the Ford Explorer. She hated to lose her vehicle, but she needed the money. The title was in the glove compartment, and it was registered to her because Herman had credit issues at the time when they bought it. The insurance was also under her name. She was able to net $8,000 cash, which was enough to temporarily get her back on her feet. It appeared things were starting to look up.

# Chapter 2

## Moving Day

It was a sunny day on the first of May when Megan and Josh finally moved into their new home. It was a second-floor apartment in a white three-story building on Walnut Street called the Hill View. Megan wanted to get a place on the ground floor, but it was taking too long to find one. Besides, she could not resist the low asking price for this particular apartment, which came fully furnished. That alone would save her a ton of money.

The previous owner was an elderly woman, who died three months earlier. According to the kind, middle-aged, African American landlady, Leslie, the woman's son lived out of state. He came for the funeral, and then collected his mother's personal belongings, but he had no interest in taking the furniture.

The remaining apartments were being rented out to decent tenants, who generally keep to themselves. Leslie lived in an apartment on the ground floor. The building is conveniently located a few blocks south from Yonkers Avenue, which is a busy thoroughfare, where one could easily catch a bus or taxi. There is even a church across the street and a park on the next block, where Megan could take Josh to play.

Hannah's friend, Sam, helped them move with his Chevy Blazer suburban. Megan and Josh did not have many possessions, so there was not much to move. Hannah gave them a few other items to help out, such as an old futon, a box of spare dishes and utensils, and a used flatscreen television set, which had been taking up space in her closet. She also gave Megan a framed photo of them during their school years to make the apartment feel more like home.

"Hannah, thank you so much for everything you've done. I especially love the photo. You are truly a gift from God," Megan said to her, as they stood in the living room. They hugged and smiled at one another.

Once they were done bringing everything up to the apartment, Sam left, since he had to be at work. As for Hannah, she would be staying a little longer to help her best friend with cleaning and unpacking.

Once they were alone, Hannah stated, "I'm so proud of you, Meg. You've managed to save up so much money in such a short amount of time." She was also proud of how Megan finally took charge of her life and got away from her abusive husband. It was long overdue, in her opinion, and certainly a huge step in the right direction. Hannah knew it could not have been easy for Megan and Josh to leave their home in California to make the long cross-country trek. "This place may not be the Hilton, but it should make a nice home for you both," she told Megan. "And I have to tell you, I really love the old-fashioned furniture! It's so cool!" She looked around the living room with admiration at the vintage furniture. Some of it looked like it was over forty years old, based on the style, yet it had been well cared for by the previous owner. "I'm getting a Brady Bunch vibe." She guessed, "Maybe vintage '70s?"

Megan shrugged, "Maybe. I don't know. It's okay. I suppose. I try not to get too attached to furniture. At least, if I ever need more money, I could probably sell some of this stuff to an antique store," she joked. "It's got to have some value. I wonder if Leslie would mind."

"Ah, probably not. You could always give some of this stuff to me," Hannah replied. "I won't mind."

They laughed. While they talked, Josh wandered off into his new room, which was only down the hall. The walls were a light blue color. It reminded him of the sky. He examined the white dresser near the bed. The bed had a white headboard to match. The white furniture made him think of clouds. It made him happy being in the room.

He walked to the dresser and reached up, as he tried to sit his Mandalorian action figure on the surface, but it was slightly too high for him. Just then, he felt someone lift him up a little, so he could reach. It was as if he floated. Before he could react, he was surprised when the Mandalorian spoke because he did not touch the button on his chest. It said in its usual masculine voice, "This is the way."

"Hey!" Josh looked behind him and did not see anyone in the room with him. He looked back at his action figure and asked, "How did you do that, Mando?" He stared at his action figure waiting for a response. Naturally, there was none. Still, Josh waited. Nothing else out of the ordinary took place.

"Josh?" Suddenly, his mother called him, so he hurried to the living room to join her.

"Coming, Mommy!"

"Were you checking out your new room?"

"Uh huh," he nodded. "I put Mando on the big table with the drawers."

Megan smiled at him. "Oh, did you? That's good. It's called a dresser." She put her arm around him and began walking with him through the apartment. She was overly excited to finally have her own apartment. This was going to be a great new start for them. Before unpacking she wanted to walk through each room with Josh, so they could get a feel for the place. As she walked into his room, she noticed there was a chill in the air. The word "haunted" briefly came to mind, but she immediately dismissed the idea as silly. It was only her being paranoid in unfamiliar surroundings.

Josh explained with excitement, "You see? He's up there!" He eagerly pointed at his action figure.

"I see. It's very nice," Megan replied, sounding impressed. "Did you reach it all by yourself?"

He shook his head. "No, Mando helped."

"Wow! Mando is *hella* cool," she said not really taking Josh too seriously. He did not elaborate, so she thought nothing of it. She turned to him and suggested, "Hey, come on. Let's see Mommy's new room!"

They went across the hall hand in hand into her new bedroom. All of the furniture matched as if part of a set. There was a full-size bed with a large Chestnut headboard, two chestnut nightstands, a dresser with a large heavy mirror, and an armoire. The lamps were both beige with yellow lampshades.

Josh looked up at her and said, "Your room is very brown."

She nodded in agreement with a frown on her face. "Yes, it is." Even the rug and drapes were brown. She shrugged and added, "Well, I guess I can spice it up later with a little color."

Meanwhile, Hannah was nearby in the bathroom scrubbing the sink clean, while humming a tune. She felt a chill down her spine and stopped suddenly. The blonde hairs on her arm were standing on end. She looked up fast and could have sworn she saw someone in the mirror behind her. She turned around instantly, but there was no one there. She checked behind the shower curtains. There was no one else in the bathroom with her.

"I must be going crazy," she said to herself. She hoped it was probably nothing. Maybe her eyes were playing tricks on her. She sighed and continued cleaning. She decided to keep her strange experience to herself. There was no reason to scare Megan by telling her she thought she saw someone, who was not there. Besides, she knew Megan would freak out if she thought the apartment was haunted. It was no secret she had anxiety issues. She had been that way since they were in elementary school together.

Megan and Josh entered the bathroom and Megan noticed how clean the sink looked.

"Wow. Thanks, Hannah! The sink looks so white now. Do you do floors and windows?"

Hannah chuckled, "Yeah, I also take cash payments or PayPal."

Megan laughed and told Josh to play in his new room, while she got to work on cleaning the kitchen. She was excited to unpack the box of dishes and utensils. She called out to Hannah from the kitchen, "Oh, God! I hope this place doesn't have a roach or rodent problem! That's all I need! I don't wanna have to bail on another home!"

Hannah called back from the bathroom, "Well, let's make sure to clean everything good! We can get some glue traps from the store and put them around to see if you catch anything!"

"Gross! If I do, will you come to remove the traps?"

Hannah responded, while still in the bathroom, "I will if you pay me! It's all about the money, honey!"

Megan raised her eyebrows and mumbled under her breath, "I guess I'd better set aside a Hannah fund." She accidentally dropped the can of Pledge she was using to clean the wooden dining table, so she bent down to pick it up. It had rolled under the table. While bending over she noticed three letters etched into the wood beneath the table. It read, "MEG," which was weird because it was her name. "Oh, cool," she mumbled to herself.

The cleaning went on for another hour, and then they unpacked the rest of the items. It did not take too long. The dishes and utensils were placed into newly cleaned cabinets and drawers. Megan neatly folded their clothing and put everything into the drawers of the dressers, or into the armoire of her bedroom.

Meanwhile, Hannah helped to set up the television in the living room. Of course, there were hardly any channels to watch without a cable subscription.

Sometime later, the women plopped down on the sofa and stared at the television, which was showing static. The volume was low, although it could still be heard.

Megan chuckled and commented, "This reminds me of '*Poltergeist.*' *They're here!*"

Hannah thought about her experience in the bathroom, but she faked a laugh for Megan's sake. "Yeah," she said. "Classic ghost movie." She immediately shut the television off. "No point in keeping this thing on."

Megan replied sarcastically, "Yeah, stop wasting my electricity." Hannah smirked at her, as Megan stated, "I guess I will have to order one of the local cable subscriptions. Do you guys have DirecTV in Yonkers?"

Hannah scoffed, "Of course, we do! I'm sure we have whatever you had in California. This is New York, after all. We can arrange to get it set up. I'll help if you want, and then we can talk about dinner."

"Oh, yes! I am starving!" Megan agreed, while enthusiastically rubbing her hands together. "Oh, now that you mention dinner, I found something odd under the kitchen table. Would you believe someone scratched in my name? It looks like it's been there for years."

Hannah was shocked, "Someone scratched Megan under the table?"

"Well, it only said 'MEG' in all caps," Megan clarified.

"Wow! How odd. What a crazy coincidence, huh?" Hannah commented.

Megan replied, "I don't know. I really don't believe in coincidences. I think everything happens for a reason. I think it's fate. Maybe it's a sign I was meant to live here." Once she thought about it that way, she suddenly began to feel right at home. A welcoming sensation came over her. She had a feeling she was really going to like living in this apartment. The thought brought a smile to her face.

Josh sat on his bed looking around his room with wide wandering eyes. It was much bigger than his old room in California. Even his new bed was larger. He suddenly felt so small. The room was fully furnished. There was a bed, a dresser, nightstand, an old white storage chest, and a shelf on the wall. Still, he missed his old toys. He had so many when he was in California. Now, he only had a few. Hannah had bought him some new toys, while they were staying at her place. They were okay. At least, he had his good old Mandalorian. It was his favorite because it felt familiar.

He looked at Mando, seated atop the dresser, and wondered if he would speak on his own a second time.

"Hello," said the voice of a young woman, who sounded like she was sitting right next to him on the bed.

Josh leapt from the bed and turned to see who had spoken, but the bed was empty. He blinked his eyes in disbelief. For a moment, he stood there ready to run out of the room. Instead, he mustered up the courage to bend down and peek under his bed. He was relieved to find no one there. He decided it was a good time to check on his mother and auntie Hannah.

Josh entered the living room and sat down on the sofa between his mother and Hannah. It felt safer that way.

Megan put her arm around him. "Hello, baby. What's wrong?" She became concerned. "You look like you've seen a ghost. Did something scare you? Is everything all right?"

Hannah became alert at the mention of a ghost. She looked toward the hallway, and then down at Josh. She was eager to hear what he had to say.

"I'm not scared," he lied. "Just cold." There was a sudden chill in the air, so he was not lying entirely. He almost felt if he admitted to being afraid, he would somehow get into trouble. He certainly did not want that to happen. "I'm not a baby anymore. I'm a big boy," he added trying to sound brave.

"Yes, you are. Hey, you know what? You're the man of the house, now," his mother said to him.

Hannah agreed, "That's right, Josh. It's your job to keep Mommy safe. If something bad happens to her, you find her phone and you call me, or you call 9-1-1. Okay?"

He stared at her bewildered, as he nodded with uncertainty. He wondered what could possibly happen.

Megan looked at her and explained, "He has no idea how to do that. We never let him play with the phone."

Hannah responded, "Well, your situation has changed. He needs to learn these important things, Meg. Your life may depend on his knowledge, one day. Start teaching him early."

"I guess you have a point," Megan realized.

Josh sat silently between them, as they continued talking. He gazed at the blank television screen and saw their reflections seated on the sofa, only there were four people on the television. There were three on the sofa and another standing behind them. It was a pretty teenage girl with wavy, shoulder-length, brown hair. Cautiously, he looked up to see if he could tell who was standing behind the sofa. He saw no one, which confused him. When he looked back at the television screen she was still there! She smiled and waved at him. He reluctantly waved back, awkwardly smiling as he did so.

At that point, Megan saw what he was doing and asked, "Who are you waving at, Josh?"

He looked up at her and answered, "The pretty girl in the TV."

Hannah grinned, "Surely, he must mean me."

Megan glanced at the television screen and saw their three reflections. She tried to see if she could notice maybe a reflection of a painting or something, but there was nothing to make her think he actually saw anyone else, other than them. She brushed it off as him being silly and began thinking about dinner, again. She was hungry.

They ordered Chinese food, a short time later. They were thankful it did not take too long to arrive. They sat at the kitchen table and enjoyed their first meal in the new apartment. There was enough food left over for tomorrow's dinner, which pleased Megan. It meant she would not have to cook for another day.

After dinner, Hannah decided it was time for her to head home. She felt slightly uncomfortable being in the apartment. "I should get going. It's getting late and I have to work tomorrow."

"Oh, no. Already?" Megan was disappointed. She was enjoying the company. She was also a little nervous about being alone with Josh in their new apartment. Alone in Yonkers. Alone in New York. This would be the first time ever she was actually on her own. She felt her anxiety kicking in, so she tried not to think about it.

Hannah promised to return in a few days. She wanted to give Megan time to get settled. "I'll be back later this week to see how you're doing. Call me, if you need anything. Okay?"

"Okay. Thank you so much for everything. I owe you big time."

"No, you don't. I know if I am ever in need, I can count on you to be there for me."

"Absolutely," Megan nodded enthusiastically. "Take care, Hannah."

They hugged. Hannah bent down to give Josh a kiss on the cheek. "Bye, Josh. Remember. You take good care of Mommy. Okay?"

"Okey dokey," he nodded.

"You are too cute," she kissed him on his little nose, and then stood up and walked to the door. She unlocked it and turned to say goodbye, once more. "Goodnight, Meg! I love you!"

"I love you, too. Goodnight. Get home safe. Text me when you get there."

"I will," and then she left. Megan locked the door behind her.

At last, Megan and Josh were alone in the apartment. This would be their new home from now on. Megan looked down at Josh to see him looking up at her innocently. He blinked at her and she smiled at him.

She said, "You really are too cute, *but* I think it's almost someone's bedtime. What do you think?"

He asked, "You?" He then giggled.

"No, silly. Not *me*. You!" She tickled him mercilessly and he crumpled into a ball on the floor. She bent down over him and continued the torture.

"Okay! Okay," he laughed, flashing his little teeth at her.

She snatched him up and carried him to his bedroom. He giggled some more, as she carried him. They dropped down on his bed with a light bounce. He escaped from her arms, kicked off his slippers, and quickly crawled under the covers pulling them up to his neck. She slid closer and tucked him in, before kissing him goodnight. She turned off the light, as she was leaving the room.

From behind her, he shouted, "No! Leave the light on, Mommy! *Please!*"

His sudden reaction startled her causing her to jump slightly. She turned to him and asked, "Josh, are you trying to give your mother a heart attack?" He shook his head apologetically, and she stated, "You can't sleep with the light on, baby. Remember, you are a *big* boy, not a baby." He pouted when she reminded him, so she suggested, "I'll tell you what. I can turn on your new superhero lamp, so the *Avengers* can watch over you, while you sleep. Okay?"

"Yes!" He nodded eagerly and watched her, as she walked to the nightstand beside his bed to turn on the lamp. She made sure to buy him a Marvel superheroes lamp for his bedroom, before they moved in. She wanted him to have something new in the room belonging only to him, since she knew the room would be fully furnished with someone else's old furniture. At least, the old furniture was in good condition. The previous owner kept it well-maintained and looking like new. As for the lamp, it had several different Marvel superheroes from the *Avengers* gathered together in heroic poses at the base with several colorful comic strips printed around the lampshade. Megan thought it was kind of cool and, naturally, Josh loved it.

"Goodnight, baby," she kissed him, again.

"Goodnight, Mommy," he replied, shortly before closing his eyes.

She disappeared across the hall into her bedroom and quietly closed her door leaving it slightly ajar. She wanted to be able to hear Josh, in case he called for her in the middle of the night.

Meanwhile, Josh had opened his eyes, again. He stared anxiously at his doorway looking toward the hallway. He kept expecting to see someone appear there. Maybe the girl from the television. He wondered if she was the one who spoke into his ear when he was sitting on the bed earlier. He turned to his left, and then to his right to make certain he was alone in the bed. He was relieved when he did not see anyone. His eyes wandered onto his Mandalorian action figure on top of the dresser, which was across from the foot of his bed next to the bedroom door. The toy did not move or speak.

Finally, Josh stated, "Goodnight, Mando," and then he turned onto his right side and closed his eyes. In a matter of minutes, he had fallen asleep.

Across the hall, Megan had undressed and slipped into her sleepwear. She had turned on one of the two lamps on either side of her bed. The ceiling lights were off. She climbed into bed, but was not really tired, yet. The bed felt firm. She liked it that way. She had a feeling she was going to sleep well. Later.

Since she was not quite ready for bed, she decided to look through her new cellphone. She bought a new one right away, after arriving in Yonkers, and made sure to change the number. She did not want Herman to have the means to track her. She also deleted her social media pages on the week she arrived. It was time to start fresh. She checked her emails, since it was the only thing she could do. It was mostly spam. There was nothing from him, which was odd.

She wondered if he was still in prison. What would happen, once he was free? Would she try to find her? He might want to find Josh. There was little reason for Herman to think Megan and Josh would go all the way across the country to New York. He probably thought she was still in California laying low. Hopefully, it could buy her a few months' time, before he realized where she might have gone. Besides, he did not know where Hannah lived, which was good. All he knew was she was somewhere in New York state and it is a very large state.

Thinking about Herman was causing her anxiety level to increase. She immediately placed her phone down on the nightstand and turned off the lamp. She tried to relax her breathing by taking long, slow, steady breaths. She found herself staring at the window for a long while, until she eventually closed her eyes and finally drifted off to sleep.

That's when the dreaming began.

In her dream, Megan could see a pretty young woman, or was she a teenager? She looked to be in her late teens. The girl had shoulder-length, wavy, brown hair, big brown eyes, adorable chubby cheeks, full lips, and a toned body. She was in her black lacy underwear. She was getting dressed. The room was familiar. It looked exactly like Josh's room. The walls were sky blue and the furniture had been painted white. It was indeed his room, but it looked different for some particular reason. Everything seemed brand new. The atmosphere felt different, too.

The pretty girl pulled on a pair of blue track pants, and then slipped into her white sneakers. She already had on a pair of white socks. She looked through the top dresser drawer and pulled out a white t-shirt, which had a picture of a beautiful redhead girl on it. There was a name across the t-shirt over the image, but it was hard to read. The lettering was white. She pulled the shirt over her head and looked at herself in the large mirror of the dresser. She hummed something inaudible, yet familiar, as she tied her hair behind her head into a ponytail and set it in place with a white scrunchie. It sounded like a 1980s tune, although Megan could not quite place it.

Subsequently, the teenager walked out the door into the hallway, and then took the steps two at a time going down to the lobby. She was undeniably young and athletic. She stepped outside and was greeted by a bright sunny day. The brightness made her squint her eyes temporarily. It was quite warm out.

After a few moments of stretching her legs on the front steps, she jogged northbound toward Yonkers Avenue. She did not appear to be in a hurry. In fact, she paced herself fairly well. It was obvious, this was not the first time she had done this. She was a runner. Her breathing was steady.

Megan watched the teenage girl fade away into the distance, while still standing in front of the building, until she could no longer see her. The dream seemed so real. It was as if she were actually outside in front of the building. She could even feel the warmth of the sun on her face. She looked up at the sky. The clouds were extraordinarily puffy. It was as if she could touch them, if she stretched out her arm far enough.

Her gaze turned back to the ground level. She thought about the girl and wondered who she might be. Already, her beautiful face had been forgotten. Megan wondered why she dreamt about her. Was she a real person? Maybe it was someone from her past? Maybe even someone from the future, like a daughter or granddaughter. The possibilities left her intrigued. Who was she?

The next morning, Megan did not think about the dream for too long. It did not seem like a big deal, at the time. After all, it was only a dream. She went on with her day and followed her normal morning routine. What she did not realize is the dream was only the start of a long nightmare.

# Chapter 3

## Lizzie

The next day Megan realized she did not have any food in her refrigerator, aside from the leftover Chinese food from the night before. It meant they would be going out for breakfast. Once her and Josh were ready, they headed out to see what was nearby, where they could stop for breakfast and maybe pick up a few groceries. She never thought to take a look at the neighborhood shops when she had access to Hannah's car.

As they went by Leslie's apartment on the first floor, they noticed she was about to go out herself. She had her salt and pepper hair neatly pinned back and was wearing a light amount of make-up. She had on a pretty, blue, summer dress and matching low-heeled shoes. When she saw Megan and Josh, she smiled at them.

"Good morning, Megan," Leslie said. "Hello, Josh." She looked down at him cheerfully.

"Hi," he responded in a low monotone voice, while gripping his mother's hand tightly and hiding behind her leg.

"Hello, Leslie," Megan replied in a friendly manner. She looked down at Josh feeling slightly embarrassed and explained, "It's okay, Josh. Leslie is our new friend. You don't have to be afraid of her." She turned back to Leslie. "I'm sorry. Sometimes, he's a bit shy."

"It's okay, sweetie. It's better for him to be leery of strangers. He'll be safer that way," Leslie advised.

Megan nodded in agreement, "True, although I'd like to hope everyone in this building is safe to be around."

Leslie grinned. "I believe so. I don't think you have anything to worry about here. Some of these folks have been living here for longer than a decade. They never give me any trouble. Not once. I'm happy to say, things here have been rather peaceful."

"Well, that's good to know." Since she felt relieved, it was time to move on to another important subject. She decided to ask Leslie about possible food spots in the neighborhood. "Hey, I don't suppose you can point me in the direction of someplace where we can pick up breakfast? I was so caught up with the move yesterday, I forgot to buy groceries. Stupid me."

"No worries, sweetie. There are a couple of delis and Spanish restaurants about a block or two down Elm Street, which is right at the corner." She pointed toward the nearest corner, and then turned around to face the opposite direction. "Personally, I prefer the deli over on Yonkers Avenue." She pointed the way. "Sadly, there really aren't many other choices nearby."

Megan considered her options and said, "Thank you. I guess we will check out the deli on Yonkers Avenue, and then maybe later on we'll sit in the park for a while. I want to enjoy my days off, while I can. I was lucky to get an extra day. My boss must really like me."

"What's not to like?"

"Aw, thanks, Leslie."

Leslie smiled at her and suggested, "You know? We can walk there together, if you don't mind. I also happen to be going that way."

Megan nodded, "Okay, cool. That'd be nice." They began walking together toward Yonkers Avenue. Megan held Josh by the hand and kept him close. The women talked, while they walked.

Leslie said, "If you happen to come across any remaining items from the former tenant, you can just toss it out, or keep it, or whatever. I've been storing a few of her things in the basement for far too long. I doubt her son will ever come for them. I didn't have the heart to throw anything away. The poor old woman, who lived there, was so sweet. Mrs. Garrett. By the way, if there's anything you need, I want you to know all you've got to do is ask."

"Okay, thank you, Leslie. Now that you mention it, I plan on doing some extensive archaeological work in the apartment later today," Megan joked. "Don't worry. I won't damage anything. I basically want to do a thorough cleaning job, making sure to get every nook and cranny, while searching for hidden or lost items." She added, "It's a hobby of mine. I just have one question, and please, be honest. Has there ever been a bug or rodent problem in the building?"

"Honey, you're in New York. There's a bug and rodent problem everywhere." Megan raised her eyebrows and made a disgusted face, as Leslie continued, "That being said, I recently had an exterminator fumigate the entire building, so it should be clean. Why? Oh, Lord! Have you seen something?" She sounded concerned.

Megan immediately shook her head, "Oh, no! Sorry, I only wanted to make sure. It's all good."

"Thank heavens! You had me going for a second," Leslie said feeling relieved. When they reached Yonkers Avenue, Leslie turned to Megan and said, "I'd best be on my way. I have an appointment at the bank. The deli is right across the street," she pointed. "You be careful crossing. These people drive like they're in the Indy 500."

Megan chuckled, "Will do. Thank you so much, Leslie. Bye." She waved.

"Bye, bye, dears," Leslie waved at them both, before turning away and walking downhill toward Getty Square.

Megan was pleased to see there was a pizza shop on Yonkers Avenue, as well. She made sure to get the phone number and saved it to her cellphone for future reference. It was probably going to be dinner later. She could always save the leftover Chinese food for the next day. She was not fond of eating the same thing two days in a row.

After ordering two egg sandwiches from the deli and picking up a few necessities, Megan and Josh returned home to eat. They sat at the kitchen table. While they ate, Megan planned out her day. First, she would take Josh to the park for an hour or two. She wanted to make sure he enjoyed some time under the sun, so he could get a healthy dose of vitamin D. She had big plans for when they got back home. Leslie mentioned she could keep anything she found in the apartment. The idea excited her and inspired her to go treasure hunting, while she cleaned up. Perhaps, she might even find something good if she looked hard enough. She loved finding old things.

However, first, they went down to Cochran Park, as planned, after breakfast. The park was only a block away. It appeared safe enough. She sat on the grass and watched Josh, while he played with his Mandalorian action figure. He seemed content, which made her happy. She hoped he would not ask about his father anymore. He had done so during the first two or three weeks, after arriving in New York. She was grateful he finally stopped asking. He was still too young to understand why she had to leave Herman. Someday, she would explain it when Josh was older.

She also had other things on her mind. Soon, she would require a babysitter for him. She only had one more day off, before it was back to work. Fortunately, Leslie had already put her in contact with a decent teenage girl from the neighborhood, who was a trusted babysitter for some families on the block. It was a tremendous stroke of good luck. Her name was Misty.

In the meantime, Josh was having a blast at the park. He ran back and forth, while laughing and talking to his Mandalorian action figure. Megan wondered if she looked as silly when she was a little girl. It seemed like such a long time ago. She was only thirty years old, although she felt so much older, thanks to the seven long years she spent with Herman.


It was around two in the afternoon when they got back to the apartment. Megan would have let Josh play in the park longer, but she was starting to fall asleep on the grass. The ants were crawling over her. She had to make sure to get them all off before going home. She did not want to be the cause of an ant problem in the building.

Josh ran straight to his room when they returned to the apartment.

Megan called after him, "Josh, wash your hands! You've been playing outside!"

"Okay, Mommy!" He then made a b-line for the bathroom. She loved how he normally did as he was told without complaining or whining like some other children. He was such a good boy.

Megan went into her bedroom, took off her sneakers, and put on her flip flops. She also changed her clothing, tossing her dirty clothes into a plastic bag, and wrapping it tight. She wanted to make sure there were no more ants before mixing them with the rest of the dirty laundry in the hamper. She put on a pair of comfortable shorts and a loose t-shirt.

It was time to begin her treasure hunt. She had been looking forward to it all day. It excited her to imagine what she may find hidden away in her new apartment. She started her search in her bedroom checking beneath her mattress and under the bed. She immediately realized the rug in her bedroom could use a good vacuuming. Of course, she did not own a vacuum cleaner. Perhaps, she could borrow one from Leslie.

Once she was done checking there, she pulled out the drawers from her dresser and both nightstands, one at a time. She managed to find a quarter from 1988 within one of the nightstands, but that was it. It was disappointing, but something was better than nothing.

Next, she dug deep into her armoire. It was mostly empty, aside from a variety of plastic and wire hangers, as well as an empty shoe box on the top shelf. She used the opportunity to organize some of her clothing on the hangers. She liked to keep the dresses together and separate from business wear. It took up a lot more time than she thought, which pretty much put an end to her search for the day. Tomorrow was another day, she told herself.

By the early evening, she went into the kitchen and sat down at the table, so she could order a small pizza pie for dinner. She was eager to test out the local pizzeria. Before she could dial the phone number she had saved into her contacts list, her cellphone rang. It was Hannah. They spoke for nearly an hour and half about nothing in particular. Hannah mainly wanted to see how her friend was holding up. They also made plans for Hannah to stay over sometime soon.

While using the phone, Megan casually paced back and forth in the kitchen. She was completely unaware the seat she had been sitting on mere moments ago was gradually pushed in under the table on its own.

When Megan finished talking with Hannah, it was time to order the pizza. She was starving, so she knew Josh was probably hungry, too.

The pizza arrived a half hour later. As they sat together at the kitchen table to eat, Megan made conversation with her son. "So, baby, how do you like your new room?"

"It's great! It reminds me of the sky. Lizzie said she painted it that way on purpose. She loves the sky, too."

Megan was baffled by his response. Right away, she inquired, "Who?"

"Lizzie!" He exclaimed, while pulling a chunk of cheese from his slice of pizza, and then jamming it into his little mouth with his petite fingers.

"Josh, who is Lizzie?" She asked with concern.

He replied with his mouthful of cheese, "She's my new friend."

"Oh, really? Don't talk with your mouth full, honey. Chew, first." Once he did as he was told, she resumed with the interrogation. "So, how did you meet Lizzie?"

He explained in a matter-of-fact way, "She lives here with us."

"Really? Well, why haven't I met her?" Megan asked.

He shrugged innocently and responded with a shrug, "I don't know."

At first, Megan was uncertain what to think. Eventually, she simply told herself it was nothing to worry about. Many children without siblings make up imaginary friends as a way of coping with loneliness, or loss. She had a feeling something like this might happen due to the fact he is dealing with his father's unexpected absence. She thought it was funny how he created an imaginary friend, who is female, considering most little boys would much rather play with another boy. She assumed it was no big deal and disregarded it, before grabbing a second slice of pizza.

"Oh, man," she said, as she bit into it. "This is the bomb! God, I love pizza!"

"Me, too, Mommy," Josh agreed with a nod of his little head. His face was full of tomato sauce.

After dinner, she gave him a much-needed bath, before letting him play in his room. She deposited the quarter she found earlier into his piggy bank. There were not many other coins in it, since it was still fairly new. Once it filled up, her plan was to open up a savings account for him. Hopefully, by the time he was old enough, there would be a few hundred dollars waiting for him.

With the evening drawing to a close, she knew it was time to take a shower herself. After laying on the grass and digging through the darkened interior of her armoire, behind the drawers from her dresser and two nightstands, and under her bed, she felt quite filthy. She turned on the shower, got undressed, and stepped into the tub allowing the water to wash over her unkempt hair. It felt extremely refreshing. She tried to hurry, so Josh would not be without supervision for too long.

After she finished, she stepped out and wrapped a towel around her body. As she briefly glanced at the mirror, which had become fogged up by the steam, she could have sworn she saw someone behind her. It looked like a woman, but it was hard to tell. She gasped and immediately spun her body around to confront whoever it was, but there was no one there. She turned back to face the mirror. This time, she only saw a blurry reflection of herself. She wiped the mirror clean with her hand and brushed it off as her mind playing tricks on her. She then proceeded to brush her long, wet hair.

"You're losing it," she mumbled to herself, as she inhaled and exhaled a long puff of air. "Breathe."

Minutes later, she put on her pajamas and walked to Josh's room to put him to bed. It surprised her when she overheard him talking to someone. He seemed to be having a full conversation. He did not sound like he was playing a game. For a moment, Megan began to worry. Who could he possibly be talking to? She paused and listened from the hallway to hear what he was saying. She held her cellphone ready to call 9-1-1.

"My Mommy drove us here from Cafilorn… Cali-forn-ya. It was a really, really, really long drive. I was sleeping a lot." He giggled. "Hey, can you make Mando talk, again?"

Suddenly, the Mandalorian action figure spoke one of his eight phrases, "No droids."

Josh laughed hysterically.

Megan stepped into the room and was relieved to find him alone. "Who are you talking to, Josh? Mando?"

He shook his head, "Nope. I'm talking to Lizzie! Can't you see her? She's right here!" He pointed to his left on the bed.

Megan looked where he was pointing. Aside from a slight depression on the bed, she saw no one. She figured she may as well go along with it. "Hello, Lizzie," she said in a polite tone. "Okay, time for bed, Josh."

"Aw! Is it okay if Lizzie tells me a bedtime story?"

"Yeah, sure," Megan humored him. "Make it a short story, and then it's straight to bed, young man."

"Okay, Mommy. Thank you!"

She sighed, as she turned on his lamp and turned off the light to his room. She then walked across the hall into her bedroom, leaving the door slightly ajar. She never noticed a book float off the bookshelf on its own.


Later during the night, Megan had a frightening dream. It began with her jogging along a long trail, which went winding through the woods. She was unsure where she was, but she knew where she was going. It was a warm sunny day. Her hair was tied back into a ponytail. She felt it bouncing gently against her back with each step.

There were other people on the trail, but she could not see their faces because they moved by like blurs, as she went past them. They were all going the other direction. Some were also jogging. Others were walking dogs. They were not the main focus of the dream, so she did not pay attention to them. Eventually, she found herself alone on the trail.

She felt her body getting tired. Her legs became heavier with each step. Sweat dripped down her face. Still, she pushed herself harder, wanting to go further than usual. Apparently, this was something she did often, according to this dream. She liked to jog because she wanted to stay in shape. This was how she maintained her toned body. This was how she was going to get rid of the baby fat, which bothered her so much. For some reason, she was younger than she is now. She was a teenager.

Was this from a repressed memory? Megan did not recall ever jogging. It was not really her thing. She barely even exercised, although perhaps it would have been a good idea to start. She did observe her belly getting a little extra padding on it. A couple of days of exercise couldn't hurt.

Suddenly, there was a chill in the air, which was odd because it was hot moments ago. She was still sweating from the heat. Yet, something made her hairs stand on end, as goose bumps rose over her bare arms. She noticed she was wearing a white short-sleeve t-shirt. Something did not feel right. There was danger in the air. It felt as if she were being watched by someone. Yes! She was being stalked. The creepy sensation sent shivers down her spine like icy daggers scraping against her neck and back.

Megan ran faster, but she was startled when she heard a loud cracking sound behind her. It sounded like a branch breaking. She glanced back for only a split second, and then tripped and fell to the ground, sliding forward into the dirt and scraping the palms of her hands. Before she could get up, someone had pounced on her back from out of nowhere. Whoever it was, grabbed her arm from behind and bent it hard behind her back. As she was about to scream, a damp white cloth was placed over her mouth and nose. It became very difficult to breathe. She panicked and struggled to break free, but she could not. He was far heavier and stronger than her. She began to feel weak and dizzy, and then everything became blurry.

After pointlessly resisting for several seconds, she passed out. Somehow, she was still completely aware of what was happening to her, probably because it was only a dream. Someone was holding her from under her arms and dragging her over the grass away from the trail and up a hill toward a nearby deadend street. It was a Caucasian male, although she could not see his face clearly because her eyes were closed. Yet, she still knew exactly what was taking place. She could see it, as if it were playing out in a movie. It almost felt like it was no longer her, but another teenage girl. She watched from a safe distance.

The man dragged her out of the woods and waited for the coast to be clear, before dragging her over to a small blue car parked on the deadend street. He gently placed her on the ground and opened the rear door of the hatchback. He lifted her up and placed her into the rear compartment, and then closed the hatch. He looked around to make sure no one was watching. She saw he was wearing glasses. When he thought it was safe, he disappeared from her view and went around to the driver's side. The car began moving, heading south to the intersection. She could only see out through the window of the rear door, but she did manage to see the street sign passing overhead for Arthur Street. It did not ring a bell. Had she ever been there?

The car turned right, going downhill, before making another right. It drove straight for a few minutes, before turning right, again, and going uphill. Next, it turned left onto a long cobblestone driveway. She could feel the grinding beneath the tires. Soon, the car pulled into a garage. That's where it came to a stop and the rear door was opened.

She felt herself being pulled out onto the cold concrete floor. The man with glasses dragged her across the floor through a doorway. He bent over and picked her up, placing her over his shoulders, so he could carry her down a dark wooden staircase. There was a landing halfway down. From there, they turned facing the opposite direction to go down the rest of the way into a large, darkened basement room. Once there, the man carried her through a set of wooden doors on the right and entered another dimly lit room.

The man placed her down on the ground and pulled off her sneakers. He tossed them back against a wall behind him. He then pulled off her sweat-covered socks. One was shoved into her mouth, while the other was wrapped securely around her head to cover her mouth and hold the first sock in place.

Megan did not like this experience one bit and was ready to wake up. She tried hard to wake herself, but she could not force herself out of this terrible nightmare. She began to feel anxiety, for all the good it did her. She still could not move. She remained unconscious, while the man wrapped a thick rope around her waist and stood her up against some sort of brick column. It was a support beam. There was another similar one across from her. The man tied her securely in place, and then walked over to a small nearby worktable, which had wheels and a lamp.

He fiddled around with things on the table. It sounded like metal tools clanking against one another. She felt her anxiety level increase to an all-time high. She wondered what was going to happen to her. *Why* was this happening to her?

The man returned with an outdated point-and-shoot camera in his hand. He began taking photos of her from different angles. He did not use a flash when he did so. He wanted to capture the image utilizing the natural light coming in from the small window behind her. He seemed to know photography well. Somehow, Megan was aware of that detail, despite the fact she was still unconscious. She also knew the man enjoyed developing his own photos. These would become part of his private collection. He had more like this hidden away in a small metal box. She did not see the box, but she knew it existed.

Suddenly, the man shouted, "Wake up, bitch!"

At that point, Megan woke up with a fright. All the lights in her bedroom were on. She practically sat up, as she glanced over at her clock radio to check the time. She was quite upset when she realized it was only 3:37 in the morning. Frustrated, she lay there for a while squinting her eyes at the brightness. She thought about her nightmare and wondered what could have possibly brought on such an awful experience. Was it some kind of premonition? She certainly hoped not. Suddenly, she realized every single light in her bedroom was on.

She got out of bed to turn off the main light when she realized the light in the hallway was also on. She began to feel paranoid. Was someone in the apartment? Was it the man from her nightmare? Her heart was pounding faster than before.

She prayed it was Josh, who turned on the lights out of fear. Perhaps he had a nightmare, too, she tried to convince herself. Maybe he was having trouble adjusting to their new home and felt afraid. That had to be it. Just in case, she cautiously tiptoed out of her room. She saw the lights in the kitchen and bathroom had also been turned on. It seemed too weird to be an intruder. What intruder would turn on every light in the apartment? It made no sense. It had to be Josh. She calmed herself and went into his room. His lamp and light were both on, as well, although he was sleeping peacefully.

"What the hell is going on?" She asked herself. She was perplexed. Was he really so scared he needed every light on to sleep?

She thought about waking him up to make sure he turned on the lights, but she decided an explanation could wait until morning. It was better to let him sleep. If he did have a nightmare, waking him up, would only mean he would have to fall asleep all over again. He might still be afraid. It was not something she needed to risk. Besides, he looked so peaceful. At least, someone was sleeping soundly.

She quietly turned off the lights from his room, the kitchen, bathroom, and hallway, before retiring back to her bedroom. Once her lights were off and she was back in bed, she tried to go back to sleep. It was not easy. The disturbing images from her nightmare kept coming back to her. She hoped it was only a nightmare and not a premonition of things to come. She never had premonitions before, so why start now? It felt so real, it left her feeling frightened. She prayed there would be no more dreams like the one she just had. She shivered thinking about it. It took several minutes, until she finally fell asleep, again.

# Chapter 4

## I Don't Believe Your Problem is Electrical

The next morning, while seated at the breakfast table with Josh, Megan decided it was a good time to ask him about the night before. She was very curious to learn why he felt the need to turn on every light and also why he did not mention it. Surely, it must have been due to a scary dream. If that was the case, why didn't he try sneaking into her bed with her last night? It's what she would have done as a child.

"Josh?" She got his attention. "Baby, did you turn on the lights last night?" Rather than accuse him, she wanted to give him a chance to admit it.

"No, Mommy," he answered, while eating his bowl of cereal. He barely looked up at her when he responded. He was too focused on his breakfast.

Still, she was not buying it. She pushed the issue and explained, "If you had a nightmare and felt scared enough you wanted the lights on, it's okay. I won't be upset. I just wanted to know if you did it. I found all of the lights on when I woke up in the middle of the night. I thought it was strange to see them on. You know? I had a nightmare, too." She paused and waited for a response. There was none, so she asked. "Is that what happened to you? Did you have a bad dream, baby? You could tell me if you did."

He thought about it and shook his head, "No, Mommy. I don't remember any bad dreams. Only a good dream. I had a dream about Lizzie."

Curious, she asked, "What was your dream about? Can you please tell me?"

"Lizzie took me to a really big park." He smiled fondly. "She played with me and showed me the secret garden with all the statues and the swimming pool. We fed the fish, too."

"Fish? Secret garden? What garden?"

"The big one in the park with the statues and the water," he told her, as if she should already know. The only park she could think of was Cochran Park, where she took him yesterday. There were no statues, no water, and it was absolutely not a big park. She wondered if he was remembering a place from California. It did not matter. She was more interested in how the lights turned on, than the imagination of his dream.

She asked, "So, you don't remember turning on every light in the apartment?"

"It wasn't me. I didn't do it. Honest. Maybe it was Lizzie. She said it was dark, where she was."

Megan had no idea what that was supposed to mean, not that it made any difference to her. She could care less about his imaginary friend. She was becoming frustrated. She knew he turned on the lights, so why wasn't he admitting to it? Unless, he had been walking in his sleep and could not remember? She hoped it was not the case. All of a sudden, it occurred to her. What if she were the one who had been walking in her sleep? Could she have turned on the lights during her crazy nightmare? She remembered things occurring in the nightmare, which she could not explain. She prayed she was not going crazy.

After all, she was the one with the history of physical and emotional abuse, thanks to Herman. Not to mention she suffers from agoraphobia, an anxiety disorder characterized by a specific fear of places and situations, which make her feel anxious occasionally leading to panic attacks. This especially happens whenever she finds herself surrounded by wide open spaces, large crowds of people, or when she feels trapped someplace.

It was something she had a hard time dealing with, while driving cross-country from California to New York. She was forced to fight through it for Josh's sake. It was not easy. Could it be the stress she repressed during the long trip was finally starting to catch up to her? It seemed like a possibility, even if it was months ago. Perhaps, being in this new unfamiliar environment set it off. She could not rule it out. Nothing else made sense to her.

The mere thought of it was starting to make her feel dizzy. Suddenly, she began to have trouble breathing. She stood up and moved to the living room sofa, where she laid herself down. She felt minor chest pains and a sense of impending doom. She knew it was one of her attacks. It was how they often started. She had to get through it. She did not want Josh to think something was wrong. She closed her eyes and tried to relax. She tried taking deep breaths, but she still could not breathe properly. It felt as if someone were on top of her chest with their hands wrapped tightly around her throat, choking her. She coughed and struggled to breathe. The grip around her neck tightened like a noose. She kicked her feet making a fuss.

Josh noticed and instantly became worried. He hurried over to the sofa and asked, "Mommy, what's wrong? Are you dying?"

Dying? What did he know of death, she wondered?

At last, the moment of tension had passed her by almost as suddenly as it had come. She took several deep breaths and finally answered weakly, "I just had something stuck in my throat, baby. That's all." She coughed. "There's nothing for you to worry about. I'm fine." She hoped. She was not so sure. This was her worst attack in a long time.

She remained utterly still for a long while, as the coolness from the sweat on her head subsided. The trembling of her hands ceased, as her breathing slowly returned to normal. She got lucky. At least, she did not faint as she thought she might. To be on the safe side, she kept her eyes closed in an effort to relax her mind. Soon, she found herself drifting off to sleep. She was exhausted, after only sleeping a total of five hours.

Believing his mother to be okay, Josh eventually went to his room to play. Meanwhile, Megan had another dream.

Somewhere in Yonkers, New York, stands a blue two-story house built across from a two-story mechanic's garage situated in the woods near the Old Croton Aqueduct Trail. At a quick glance, beyond the long cobblestone driveway leading in from a bend in the road on a hill, it seems like any other ordinary home in the suburbs with an attached business. At least, it was the general appearance from the outside.

On the inside, there is an entirely different scene.

Roaches of all shapes and sizes have virtually taken over the interior of the messy home, scurrying back and forth, while exploring the floors and walls in search of food. They don't have far to look. Rotten food and fly-infested pizza boxes have been left out on the kitchen counter and dining room table. Scattered pages from old newspapers are spread across the floor of the kitchen and living room, as if they were thrown across the floor in a fit of fury.

Aside from the many roaches and buzzing flies, no one else seems to be home. Each of the rooms on the first and second floors are void of human life. Apparently, the homeowner is keeping busy in the basement of his garage, where he has a new guest. It's another young woman.

Today, it is Megan. As she awakens, she finds herself in this dark cool basement tied to a brick support beam. There is another brick support beam directly across from her. She instantly realizes it is the same exact basement from her other dream. Her mouth is gagged, preventing her from talking or screaming for help. Her shoes are missing. The concrete floor is cold and hard.

Megan feels very afraid, as she should. She knows this will not end well for her. She will likely die a very painful death. Tears fall from her eyes and slide down her cheeks.

Unexpectedly, she sees another girl standing in the same room. She is tied to the beam opposite from her. The girl is familiar. Who is she? Her hair is covering her face. A moment later, she realizes the girl is the only one tied up, while she is free. It is as if they switched places. Megan carefully steps around the brick support column and sees the girl's sneakers on the floor near the wall not far from a small table or cart. It has wheels attached to its legs. There is an array of tools on top of the table spread across a greasy old towel lit by a lamp. There is also a vintage camera and a radio on the table, which look like they are from another time.

Suddenly, the radio turned on loudly, blasting rock music from a tape cassette.

Megan woke up with a start. She popped up from the sofa to find the television on with the volume maxed out. A Mötley Crüe music video was playing, which struck her as odd, since she did not have cable, yet. She grabbed the remote control from the coffee table and lowered the volume. Curious, she changed the channel. The other channels showed static. She changed it back to the video, but it was gone. She turned off the television and immediately called for Josh. "Josh! Come here, please!"

He hurried into the living room, holding his Mandalorian action figure in his hand and asked, "Yes, Mommy?"

"Did you think that was funny?" She was obviously upset.

He stared at her with a frightened and confused look on his face. He could tell by her tone, she was not pleased with him, but he could not understand why.

"Why did you turn the TV on so loud?" She demanded.

"I didn't turn it on," he replied innocently on the verge of tears. He seemed sincere and quite nervous.

She saw his face and was unsure how to react. He never lied to her in the past. What if he was telling her the truth? She did not want to yell at him without just cause. First, the lights went on in the middle of the night and now the television comes on at full blast. Maybe it was not him. She wondered if there could possibly be something wrong with the electrical outlets in the building.

She calmed herself and stated, "Be honest with me, Josh. Did you have anything to do with turning on the lights last night or the TV just now?"

He shook his head, "No, Mommy. I promise!"

At that moment, the Mandalorian said on his own, "I did what I had to." Both Megan and Josh looked at it, not sure what to think. For the first time, Megan felt creeped out by the toy.

She commented, "Why does it feel like everything electrical in this house is turning against me?"

Josh replied, "I don't know, Mommy."

"It was a rhetorical question, sweetie," she explained. He looked at her with confusion on his face. "Never mind, Josh. Come here." He did and she hugged him. "I'm sorry I shouted at you. You can go play in your room."

"Okay," he said, before walking back into his room with less excitement than when he entered.

Megan sat on the sofa contemplating. She was puzzled. She still did not know what to think. By the time she finally stood up, twenty minutes had gone by. She went into the bathroom to take a shower.

Sometime later, after she was dressed, she began messing around with the lights to see if they were working properly. She checked every appliance, too. There had to be a logical explanation. She figured it could not hurt to speak to Leslie about her electrical issues. Maybe it was something, which could be easily fixed.

She grabbed Josh and they went downstairs to Leslie's apartment. She knocked on the door and Leslie answered.

"Hello, Megan. How can I help you?"

"Hi, Leslie. Sorry to bother you. I was wondering. Did you experience any strange electrical issues last night or maybe this morning? Perhaps, there was some kind of electrical surge or something?"

"No, why do you ask? Is everything okay upstairs?" Leslie seemed concerned.

"I think so," Megan responded. "Actually, I'm not sure. Last night all the lights turned on by themselves and this morning the TV came on with the volume at full blast. It scared the hell out of me." She laughed at how silly she sounded. "I have no idea how everything turned on, but it did. There was even a brief moment when my TV picked up a music video channel, even though the cable isn't hooked up, yet."

"How odd," Leslie replied. "I can call the electrician to check out your apartment, if you'd like."

"Can you? That would be great. Thank you so much, Leslie. I'm so sorry to be a pain."

"Oh, it's no trouble at all. I have a regular guy who I use. He's very good at his job and he's so nice. He lives nearby, so he can probably be here in a few minutes, if he's not too busy. I'll give him a call."

Megan smiled. "Awesome. Thanks, again."

"It's okay. Let me call him now," she grabbed her phone. "By the way, his name is Elijah. Just so you know, he's a handsome young man and he's single," Leslie winked.

Megan blushed and chuckled. She shook her head and replied, "I'm not ready for anything like that, but thank you. Please, send him up whenever he arrives. I will be home all day today."

Leslie smiled back and made the call. Megan and Josh went back upstairs to wait for the electrician. It did not take long for him to arrive. Maybe twenty minutes? When Megan heard him knocking, she asked who was there.

"Who is it?"

"Electrician, ma'am. The name's Elijah. I live down the street. Leslie said you were having trouble," he answered from the other side of the door.

She opened the door and greeted him, "Please, come in." She stepped aside, so he could enter. "My name is Megan," she said with a smile. He was indeed handsome. She tried to focus on why he was there. "Um, thanks for coming. To be honest, I'm not quite sure what's going on. Last night when I went to bed, I turned off the lights, but I had a nightmare, which woke me up in the middle of the night. I was surprised to see every light was on. This morning I asked my son if he did it, but he swears it wasn't him. I believe him. He never lies to me. *Never.* This morning I took a nap on the sofa. Not long after, I was woken up by the television. The volume was all the way up. My son claims it wasn't him. He was in his room playing. I believed him, again."

Elijah began to sense a pattern, but he did not want to dismiss her claims without making sure. "Okay. I'll take a look around, but it sounds to me like you may want to keep a closer eye on your son. I mean… kids. Right?" He chuckled.

She was not too pleased by his comment, but she remained civil and said nothing.

He checked and tested every electrical outlet. He checked the television and kitchen appliances. He took a look at the light switches and light bulbs in every room. He even checked the main fuse boxes for the house. Everything was in good working order, as far as he could tell.

When he was done, he stood at her doorway and said, "Well, I checked everything out, ma'am. There doesn't seem to be any problems with the fuse boxes, circuit breakers, or outlets. Your lights all seem to work fine. I hate to say it, but I don't believe your problem is electrical." He had no clue how right he was about his observation.

She knew what he was insinuating and she did not want to accept it. She trusted Josh. If he said he did not do it, she believed him. It was more likely she was doing it herself, while in her sleep. However, she did not dare admit such a thing to a stranger.

"Thank you for coming over and taking the time to check everything," she said with a hint of ire in her tone. "I'm sorry I wasted your time."

He smiled at her, "It's not a waste of my time. If you ever have anymore problems, don't hesitate to call me yourself." He handed her a business card, which she took. He then turned to leave.

She closed the door and sighed. She did not want to think she was responsible for her troubles. It scared her to death. The last thing she wanted was for something to happen to Josh because she did something without even being aware of it. She prayed she was not a danger to her son.

She looked at the business card, sighed heavily, and placed it in the drawer of the kitchen counter.

Megan cooked mashed potatoes and fried chicken for dinner. She chose to save the leftover Chinese food for tomorrow because she would probably be too tired to cook, after going back to work. Tomorrow would be Josh's first day with his new babysitter, Misty. She wanted to make sure he was comfortable with her, so Megan invited her over for dinner. Misty would be arriving shortly. Megan also wanted to spend time getting to know her, before she entrusted her son with her.

It was not long before Misty was at the door. Megan greeted her, let her in, and eagerly invited her to have a seat at the kitchen table. "Please, have a seat. You're right on time," she said. "Dinner is almost ready."

"Oh, good. Thank you, Mrs. Forester," Misty replied, as she took a seat at the table.

"It's Ms. Forester, but please, call me Megan. I want you to feel comfortable with me. Let's be friends."

Misty smiled, "Oh, okay. That would be great. Thank you."

Misty was an average looking teenage girl with shoulder-length black wavy hair. She was slightly chubby, but not fat. She was dressed in plain black t-shirt with dark blue jeans, and she wore thin wireframe glasses. There was only a hint of make-up. She had a friendly smile and a kind attitude. So far, Megan liked what she saw.

Megan called for Josh to join them at the table. He was still playing in his room. "Josh, wash your hands and come to the table! Dinner is almost ready, and I'd like you to meet someone! We have company!"

"Okay, Mommy!" Josh called back, before going into the bathroom to wash his hands. A moment later, he appeared in the kitchen at the table with his Mandalorian action figure.

Megan spoke, "Josh, this is Misty. She will take care of you, while I'm at work."

Misty smiled warmly at him and said, "Hello, Josh. It's so nice to meet you. I like your doll."

He looked down bashfully and responded, "Hi. It's not a doll. It's an action figure."

Megan scoffed and looked at him, as she said, "Josh, put Mando down and have a seat. I told you not to bring your toys to the table. You know I don't like it. Now, stop being so shy. I hear Misty is a very nice person. Let's give her a chance. Okay?"

He nodded reluctantly, "Okay, Mommy," and then placed his action figure on one of the empty seats, despite what she told him about not bringing his toys to the table.

Megan rolled her eyes and sighed. "Have a seat. Dinner is almost ready." She looked at Misty, "I'm sorry. He carries that toy everywhere he goes. I know it's only a phase, so I'm just waiting for it to pass. Honestly I think he uses it as a coping mechanism. He's very shy around people he doesn't know. I promise he'll be better, once he gets to know you."

Misty responded, "It's fine. I'm used to it. He's not too different from most kids I take care of. Don't worry. Josh and I will become great friends in no time. I have a way with kids. They tend to like me because we like a lot of similar things."

Megan smiled, as she placed a serving plate of fried chicken at the center of the table, followed by a large bowl of mashed potatoes.

Misty looked up at her and asked, "Do you need any help?"

"No," she stopped Misty from getting up. "You stay right there and relax. Today, you are my guest. I don't want you to help. You will be helping me enough in the next coming weeks. Please, feel free to serve yourself with as much as you want."

"Thank you, Megan. This food smells delicious. I can't wait to dig in!"

"Me, too," said Megan, as she brought out mini corn on the cobs and warm biscuits from the oven. The food smelled delicious. She buttered them and placed them on the table, followed by a pitcher of iced tea. Misty had already begun serving herself. Megan sat down to eat. She served Josh, and then herself, before asking, "So, how long have you been babysitting for the families around here?"

Misty replied, "Ever since I was twelve. I just turned eighteen in April."

"Oh? Perfect. So, you have plenty of experience with kids."

"Yes, most definitely. I've taken care of newborns, toddlers, preschoolers, and preteens. The only ones I have not taken care of are other teenagers. I won't do it."

"Really? Why not?" Megan asked.

"I know they won't respect me due to the close age difference, so I'd rather not take a chance. It might turn me off to future jobs. Besides, teenagers don't really need babysitting and I'd much rather deal with children. They may not always listen, but they tend to respect me."

Megan nodded, "Makes sense."

At that moment, the Mandalorian action figure spoke on his own. He said, "I know the drill." The room was quiet, as everyone looked at the chair, where the action figure was seated. He was too short to be seen, so it looked like the voice came from an empty seat at the table. Misty suddenly looked terrified. Megan was embarrassed. The last thing she wanted was for Misty to be scared away before she even began her job.

It was actually Misty, who broke the silence by asking, "So, is it true you guys recently moved here from California?"

"Yes, back in February," Megan nodded with relief, happy to change the subject. "It was time for a fresh start. Besides, I used to live in New York as a child."

"Cool," Misty commented. "Where in California did you live?"

All of a sudden, memories of Herman sprung to mind, which made Megan feel uncomfortable. She realized California was not the subject she wished to discuss. "I don't mean to be rude, but I'd rather not talk about California," she said. "We had some bad experiences, which I'd rather forget."

"Oh, my God! I am so sorry," Misty apologized. "I didn't mean to pry. I was only making conversation." Misty felt terrible. Her eyes drifted to the empty seat, but she quickly looked away from it.

Megan felt bad and told her, "It's fine. There's no need to be sorry. Why don't you tell me about yourself? What are your plans for the future? Do you have a career in mind?" She hoped it was not babysitting.

Misty took a long swig from her iced tea and responded, "I would like to become a famous singer, but I know it's not going to happen since my singing voice sucks. I'd settle for being a rich actress." She grinned.

Megan chuckled.

Misty added, "To be honest, I really don't have any future plans, at the moment. My father wants me to become a lawyer. My mother says I should become a doctor. I'm really not interested in any of those things. I really don't want to spend my life going to school. I start college this fall, but I have no major in mind. Not yet. I suppose I could study nursing."

"Nursing is good. What college will you be attending?"

"Herbert Lehman College in the Bronx."

"Oh, that's a good school for nursing," Megan replied. "It's the one near the reservoir, right?"

Misty nodded, "Yes. The Kingsbridge Armory is close by, too, if you're into history." Misty looked at Josh and asked, "Do you like history, Josh? What do you want to be when you grow up?"

He glanced at her, before looking back down at his plate and declared, "I wanna be a Mandalorian warrior." He faced the seat, where his action figure sat, as if he expected it to respond.

Megan rolled her eyes and smiled. "That's not a real thing, Josh."

Misty smiled at Josh and said, "Mandalorians are pretty cool. I really like their armor and all the cool gadgets. I like your Mandalorian, too. I love that show. It's one of the best series they've done, so far."

Josh looked up at her enthusiastically and asked, "You like Mandalorians?"

Misty nodded, "Heck yeah! I love Mandalorians! Anything 'Star Wars' is awesome, even Jar Jar! Although, my favorite character is BB-8."

Josh's eyes lit up and, all of a sudden, they were discussing all of the movies and animated series related to "Star Wars." Josh acted out his favorite scenes and Misty joined him. Megan suddenly began to feel way out of her league. However, she was extremely happy to see Misty and Josh had something in common. She had a feeling they would get along fine without her.

<h1 style="text-align:center">Chapter 5</h1>

❦

# Imaginary Friend

Megan went to bed and thought about her new acquaintance. She enjoyed having Misty over for dinner. She had a good feeling about her. Misty appeared to be a decent person with a good heart. Megan knew Josh would be in safe hands, which helped her to rest easily. She fell asleep instantly.

Unfortunately, for her, she was about to have another dreadful nightmare. Like the others before it, this one would be extremely vivid and maybe a little too visceral.

Once more, she found herself in the same creepy basement. The man with the glasses was there. Who was he? His face was still unclear to her, but she could see his devilish grin very plainly. It was as if the rest of his face was hidden by the shadows of the dimly lit dungeon-like room. One thing about him stood out, this time. She noticed he wore a distinctive metal belt buckle in the shape of the letter "H" on his wide brown leather belt. She looked at the rest of his clothing. He was wearing blue jeans and a blue button-down work shirt with black work boots. He appeared to be dressed like a mechanic or repairman. His clothing was covered with greasy stains. There was a name embroidered on his shirt's right side breast pocket. She focused on it and tried to read it. It began with the letter "H", which made sense considering his belt buckle. Hank! It said Hank. Was that his name?

Megan realized she was not tied to the brick support beam, but there was someone else tied to it. It was the same girl from the previous dreams. The teenage girl with the white t-shirt and blue track pants. Her shaggy brown hair covered her pretty face. She could barely recall how her face looked, although she remembered the big brown eyes. She could not forget those eyes.

Megan watched helplessly, as if watching a horror movie. She was there in the basement, but she could do nothing to help the poor girl. Hank grabbed a tool from the table and approached the girl. It looked like he was holding pliers. He grabbed her face and struck her with the pliers. Next, he began yanking out her teeth, one at a time, while she screamed and cried in agony. As he pulled each tooth, Megan could hear a loud cracking crunch, which chilled her to the bone. The torture went on for nearly an hour. By the time he was done, the girl's white t-shirt was drenched in blood.

Megan felt sick to her stomach. As much as she tried, she could not turn away from the sadistic scene. She was forced to watch every sickening moment, just as the girl was forced to endure it. It was horrible.

Meanwhile, Hank placed the teeth into a small metallic tray on the table. Was he planning to save them?

Megan felt an intense hatred toward him. She thought he was a cruel, demented, sick bastard. He was worse than Herman could ever be. She wished severe pain upon him. It was something she never would have done in the past. However, this man deserved to die a painful death for what he did to that poor young girl.

He kept grinning, as if he were having a good time at the girl's expense.

After a while, Megan felt like her teeth were beginning to ache. Just then, she noticed she was bleeding from her mouth. At that moment, she went into full panic mode, which woke her up. There was a slight taste of copper in her mouth. She leapt out of bed, ran into the bathroom, and flicked on the light to check if she was bleeding. She spit into the sink and was astonished to see blood. She opened her mouth and looked into the mirror. Her teeth were covered in blood. She turned on the faucet and rinsed out her mouth. There was *a lot* of blood. She became frightened and started hyperventilating. What was happening to her?

The next thing she knew, one of her teeth came loose and fell out into the sink. She freaked out and started touching each tooth, gently pushing on them with her fingers. Many of them felt loose. She cried, not sure what to do. She did not want to lose her teeth, especially not due to a freakish nightmare. It made absolutely no sense. How was it even possible?

Suddenly, she heard a female's voice behind her saying, "Did you see what he did to me?"

Megan screamed and, this time, she woke up for real, or at least she thought so. She was still in bed. It was dark in her bedroom. She turned over and the girl was lying in bed with her. Blood was gushing out from her mouth. Megan screamed and fell back off the bed onto the floor.

It was then when she actually woke up. She looked over at her clock radio and noticed it was 3:37 A.M. She got out of bed and hurried to the bathroom. She turned on the light and looked at her teeth. They were fine. She nudged a few with her forefinger to see if any were loose. They were all fine, although she did have a toothache.

"Holy fuck. I'm tripping out. That was too freaky," she uttered to herself. It seemed the nightmares were getting worse. This was the scariest one, so far. A dream within a dream within a dream. It seemed too realistic.

She returned to her bed and lay there for several minutes wondering about the strange nightmares. Why was she dreaming about the same girl and the creepy man in that damned basement? This was a new experience for her to dream consecutively. Ever since moving into the apartment, she has been dreaming about them in what appears to be a story playing out in her nightmares. Who are they? She did not remember ever seeing them before the dreams. How did she get them into her head?

Hank. She knew his name, but who was the girl? The poor girl. Why is it sometimes Megan sees things through her eyes? It was probably the strangest part about these nightmares. She sees and feels everything the girl experiences, but *why?* What's the reason for it all? And when will these nightmares end?

Megan knew she needed to go back to sleep. Otherwise, she would be dead tired at work the next day, but she really did not want to go to sleep. She was afraid of returning to that awful nightmare sequence. She did not want to be in that basement, ever again. Instead, she spent the rest of the night worrying about falling asleep by mistake.

She was relieved when her alarm went off in the morning. Of course, she was also exhausted, but off to work she went without too much of a fuss. She was grateful to have found a job at the Cross County Shopping Center. Retail was not really her thing, but she had the experience. The hours were not too bad either. She did not have to be there, until half past nine, which was better than starting at the crack of dawn. It allowed her to sleep later, although sleep was becoming something she wanted to avoid.

Misty arrived on time to take care of Josh. Megan was glad she took the time to meet her, first. At least, it was a comfort to know she and Josh would be okay together. He would not be shy around her. Josh had made a new friend in her… a real one.

Misty and Josh started off their first day together with a marathon of "*Star Wars*" films. She brought along her Firestick, which had plenty of movie options for them, and connected it to the television and her Wi-Fi. Misty knew watching movies would keep Josh occupied and happy for several hours. She also enjoyed watching the films, thanks to her father. He turned her into a fan at day one. She loved geeking out over sci-fi classics. It was how she spent a good deal of her childhood. It also helped to win the hearts of many children she took care of, over the years.

They sat together on the sofa with Josh's Mandalorian action figure seated between them. Josh was completely taken in by the first movie, which was a relief. Some children did not have the patience to sit through an entire movie without becoming restless. Not Josh. He loved every exciting second.

They began with the prequel trilogy. Misty's plan was to go through every movie in chronological order. It would keep them quite busy for a few days, if you took into account bathroom breaks, lunch times, and an occasional breakfast, in case Megan was running late for work. Misty had a feeling she may also have to pause frequently to answer questions. She did not mind. She enjoyed training a new padawan in the ways of the Force. At least, it was how she preferred to think of it.

About an hour or so into the movie, Misty noticed Josh became distracted. He kept looking to his left side away from her. She wondered what was so interesting on that side of the living room to cause him to keep looking away from the television. All she saw was the hallway leading to the bathroom and bedrooms.

A strange feeling came over her. It was a familiar sensation. One that made her feel uncomfortable. She paused the film and asked, "Why do you keep looking over there, Josh? Is there something over there you want? Do you need to use the bathroom?" She hoped it was something as simple as a needed bathroom break.

He turned and looked up at her with his innocent eyes. "I was looking at Lizzie," he answered.

The name gave her chills. "Lizzie? Who's Lizzie?" She expected him to say it was a pet of some kind, which she did not know about. Maybe Megan forgot to mention it. Perhaps, it was a cat? They tend to hide from strangers.

"Lizzie is my friend," he stated. "She lives here, too."

Misty became intrigued. She asked, "Really? Can I meet her?"

"Okay," he replied. He beckoned for something or someone to come closer. Misty still could not see anything, but she felt a presence. "Come here," he said. "My new friend wants to meet you."

She watched the floor waiting to see a cat or dog, but there was nothing. Instead, she felt a cold chill in the air, which made the little hairs on her arm stand on end. She genuinely sensed a strong presence she could not explain, or understand. Misty was clairsentient, which meant she could sense spiritual energies around her. It was an ability yet to be developed, mainly because she normally kept her distance whenever she felt these strange spiritual energies. It made her feel uncomfortable. Normally, when she felt this kind of energy, she did not like sticking around for too long.

While she did not say anything, she had felt something similar the night before when she came over for dinner. It happened when Josh's Mandalorian spoke on its own. It sent a shiver down her spine. It was why Misty immediately tried to strike up a conversation, hoping to distract herself and get her mind off of it. Walking out during dinner would not have made a good first impression and she needed the job. Besides, she knew she would not be staying long, after dinner. This time, it was different. She was alone with Josh and could not leave, if the urge came over her. She had to remain here with him, as well as with whatever presence was in the room. She did not like the idea one bit.

Josh looked at her and noticed she had zoned out. He nudged her arm and asked, "What's wrong, Misty? Can you see her? Do you see Lizzie? Isn't she pretty?"

His last question made her heart skip a beat. It confirmed there was indeed a presence, who could not be seen by everyone. Apparently, Josh saw someone, who was not imaginary. Misty knew children were more susceptible to the paranormal. They were innocent and did not understand fear enough to block such things out like she tried so hard to do.

"No," she responded with almost a whisper. "I don't see her, and I hate to sound mean, but I don't want to, Josh. Please, tell her to leave. Can you do me that favor?" There were practically tears in her eyes.

Josh sympathized and turned toward the hallway. He said, "I think she's afraid of you. Can you come back later?" He paused, waiting for a response, and then said, "Thank you. Bye, Lizzie." He waved seemingly at nothing.

All of a sudden, Misty felt the heaviness in the room lift. The presence was gone, for the time being. She knew it could easily return, if it felt inclined to do so. She could tell this presence was attached to the apartment and maybe to Josh. She felt it stronger than the night before and it scared her. Yet, Josh was not afraid. The presence did not feel evil, but it felt angry and sad. Either way, it was more than Misty could handle. She shuddered.

Once she regained her composure, she turned to Josh and asked, "Josh? Exactly, how did you meet Lizzie?" She was almost afraid to ask.

He replied casually, "She lives in my bedroom. She was here when we first moved in. She said we can share the room because I'm little and don't take up a lot of space."

"Does your mom know about Lizzie?" Misty inquired.

"Yes," he nodded much to her surprise.

"Has she seen her?"

Josh shook his head, "Uh, uh. Mommy can't see her either, like you."

Misty did not want to put fear into his head, especially if it was not there already. She figured it might be best for them to drop the subject and resume the movie. "Let's get back to the movie, okay?"

"Okay!" Josh enthused.

They spent the next few hours watching the first two movies of the prequel trilogy. Misty only paused when Josh needed to use the bathroom. She did not want to think about anything but the movies. She focused on the screen and tried to keep her mind clear.

She was ecstatic when Megan finally got home from work.


Megan had gotten a job at Macy's. She spent her day at work trying to keep busy. Anytime she had too much down time, she began to feel the lack of sleep catching up to her, and then she would become drowsy. When it was time for her lunch break, she cut it short to avoid sitting down for too long. On the up side, her department manager was very impressed by her enthusiasm to get back to work with a vengeance, after being off for three days. Somehow, Megan also managed to get a few people to sign up for the store credit card. Her work efforts did not go unnoticed. They earned her a lot of points with her boss. If only the manager knew the real reason why she was working so hard.

It was difficult for Megan to forget the horrific nightmare she had, or rather the series of nightmares she was having each night, since moving into her new apartment. She could not get the poor tortured girl out of her mind or that lowlife degenerate scum named Hank. She felt haunted by them and had a hard time focusing on work. Despite her unwanted distraction, she worked hard and did her job well.

By the time her shift was over, she was more than ready to return home, after being on her feet for most of the day. She rode the bus back across Yonkers Avenue. From there, she stopped at the deli to pick up some groceries, before walking up Walnut Street to her building. She walked the couple of blocks much like a zombie. Her mind was unfocused on what she was doing or where she was going. She merely followed where her feet took her.

Had someone tried to rob her, they would have had an easy time.

The crazy thing was she had plans to stay up all night. She hoped by avoiding sleep, she could also avoid the nightmares. Considering how badly she felt today, there was no telling what a mess she would be, after a night without any sleep at all. It was a gamble, but she was willing to try it. That was how desperate she felt to put an end to these unwanted dreams.

Megan entered her building, the Hill View, walked up the stairs, and opened her apartment door. She went straight to the kitchen table to put down the two bags full of groceries.

Both Misty and Josh greeted her with excitement from the nearby living room sofa.

"Mommy!" Josh ran to give her a hug. She lifted him up and gave him a great big hug.

Misty said, "Welcome back, Ms.… I mean Megan. It's so good to see you. How was work?"

Megan was taken aback. "Wow! You guys really missed me, huh? You keep this up, I might get used to the attention. My day was blah." She shrugged. "I kept busy, which seemed to impress my boss. Come to think of it, I guess it was a good day at work. What did you guys do?"

Josh answered before Misty could. "We watched '*Star Wars*' movies! Jedis are cool!"

"Oh, goody. Again?" Megan asked with feigned enthusiasm. "You really love those movies, huh?"

"Yep!" He nodded delightfully.

Misty smirked, "Sorry, I put him to watch them, again. I figured he liked them, so it would keep him happy and busy. It worked."

Megan scoffed, "Please, Misty. It's completely fine. I agree with you. I just never understood how a child could sit through the same movies every day and never get tired of them. I suppose it has been a while, since he's seen them, so it's not too bad."

Misty laughed, "I used to watch the same Disney movies all the time as a kid. Drove my mom crazy. She was relieved when I moved on to live-action films. There was less singing."

They both laughed.

Megan was unpacking the groceries, as they spoke. She asked, "Would you like to stay for dinner?"

"Thank you, but I actually need to get going. My mom is waiting for me. I will see you tomorrow, though," Misty replied, as she grabbed her stuff and quickly made her way to the door. "Bye, Josh!" She did not wait for his reply. She left the apartment and hurried down the stairs to the building's exit. She could not wait to get out of the apartment and put some distance between it and her. As soon as she did, it felt as if a weight had been lifted off her shoulders. She did not realize exactly how heavy the energy felt, until she left. She wondered if she would be able to deal with it each week. One thing was certain. It was going to take all the nerve she could muster to return the next morning. She hoped she would not feel any negative spiritual energy when she did, or she might have to rethink this job. At the same time, she did not want to leave Megan without a babysitter. It was wrong. Megan really needed her. Plus, Josh seemed like a good little boy. She liked him. It was his friend, Lizzie, who Misty was worried about.

"Teenagers," Megan sighed. She shrugged off Misty's hasty departure and took the Chinese food out of the refrigerator. It was finally time to heat up those leftovers. She separated the food into Tupperware containers and began to heat them up in the microwave oven.

When dinner was ready, she served two plates and called out, "Josh, dinner's ready! Wash your hands and come to the kitchen, so we can eat!"

He had gone to his room, while waiting for dinner to be ready. He was having a conversation with Lizzie. "Mommy's calling. It's time to eat. You can eat with us, if you want, Lizzie. Wash your hands, first!" He went into the bathroom to wash his hands, and then took a seat at the kitchen table.

Megan asked, "Did you enjoy your day with Misty?"

"Yes, Mommy. Well, she didn't like Lizzie. I think she's scared of her. I don't know why." His voice went up to a higher pitch, when he said the last part, which made him sound adorable.

Still, Megan wished he would stop talking about his imaginary friend, as if she were real. "I don't think she was afraid of Lizzie. She probably just doesn't understand what kind of friend Lizzie is. That's all."

"What kind of friend is Lizzie?" Josh questioned with curiosity.

"She's an imaginary friend," his mother explained. "Some people don't believe in imaginary friends. They don't understand why they exist."

Josh asked, "Imaginary means fake. Right?"

"Yes, baby. It means something created from your imagination. She's not real," she clarified.

"But Lizzie is real," he countered.

Megan sighed. "Let's stop talking about Lizzie and finish our food before it gets cold. Okay?"

Unexpectedly, Megan's plate flew off the table and smashed to the floor causing her to shriek. She was in shock, as her dinner lay spread across the floor.

Josh was not startled by what happened. It was almost like he saw it coming. He simply stated, "Lizzie said she's not fake. She's gonna show you she's real." He then continued eating, as if nothing happened.

At the same time, his Mandalorian action figure, which was still seated on the sofa stated, "I can bring you in warm, or I can bring you in cold. This is the way." It said two of its eight phrases back-to-back without anyone touching it, which was highly unusual. It did not help the situation, at all.

Megan turned and looked toward the sofa, before looking back at Josh. He did not seem to react. Instead, he kept eating as if it were completely normal for his toy to talk on its own. Megan stared at him momentarily, and then looked at her dinner scattered all over the kitchen floor. She was not sure how it happened, but she tried to convince herself she somehow did it by accident. Of course, what Josh said made it really hard to believe.

After cleaning up the mess from the floor, Megan sat down on the sofa to watch television. She hoped it would help to get her mind off of the craziness going on in the apartment. When she turned on the television, she remembered the cable person was not due, until next week. There was only static and a few hazy channels. She had nothing to watch. She was completely perplexed and wondered how Misty was able to put on "Star Wars" movies. She had no idea about Misty's Firestick, nor did she know what a Firestick was, for that matter.

She sighed heavily and turned off the television. "Great. So much for that idea. Now, what am I supposed to do?" She found herself faced with the realization it was going to be extremely difficult to stay awake all night with absolutely nothing to do. Soon, Josh would be in bed, and then she was going to be alone in her silent and somewhat spooky apartment.

The only option she had available was to surf the Internet using her cellphone. It was not much, but it would keep her entertained and busy. She did not have a social media page to check, since she deleted them all, which limited her options. She plugged the cellphone into the charger, since the battery was low in power, and proceeded to check the weather for the rest of the week. She also confirmed her appointment with the cable company. Next, she spent a little time going through entertainment newsfeeds, which in the end, she found to be boring and uninteresting. At some point, she felt her eyes getting heavier. It was the last thing she needed.

She went to the bathroom to splash cold water on her face. She looked at herself in the mirror and asked, "How in the world am I going to stay up all night? This is crazy."

Josh was still awake. She decided why not spend time with him, while he was available? She went into his room and sat next to him on his bed. He looked at her and she told him, "It's almost bedtime, little man."

He nodded, "I know, Mommy. Lizzie was only telling me about when she was a little girl. This used to be her room. She had stars on the ceiling and they glowed in the dark."

Megan really did not want to hear anymore about Lizzie. Holding back her frustration, she suggested, "Let's give Lizzie a rest for tonight. Okay? How about you and I talk for a bit?" She touched the tip of his nose lovingly with her forefinger.

"Okay, Mommy," he nodded in agreement, but it was obvious he was disappointed.

"Do you remember how Misty was able to get those movies to play on our TV?" She asked, hoping to learn what magic secret Misty used to get the television to work.

He shrugged innocently, "I don't know." Even he had no idea Misty used her Firestick device, which she connected to the television. All he knew was there were movies ready to go, once he sat down on the sofa. Megan pouted. "It was worth a shot. I guess I'll ask her tomorrow," she half said to herself. "Hey! Would you like me to read you a bedtime story?"

"Yes, please!" He responded with glee.

She looked through his little collection of Golden Books neatly placed on the small white book shelf against the wall. She randomly selected one from the bunch. "Ah, how about this one?" The book she grabbed happen to be one of his "*Star Wars*" Golden Books. She read the title. "*I Am a Sith*. Of course, it would happen to be a '*Star Wars*' book." Most of his Golden Books were and those were his favorite ones. She thought back on when she was a little girl and could actually read the classics about three little pigs, big bad wolves, wooden little boys, flying elephants, and children wandering through the woods. Not that those were much better, now that she thought about it. They seemed rather silly to her.

Josh climbed under his blanket and made himself comfortable, as he prepared for the story. Megan leaned closer to him and opened to the first page of the book. As soon as she began to read, the Mandalorian action figure interrupted her.

"They work for the Empire," it said from its perch atop the dresser behind her.

Megan turned around to face it. She was starting to think the Mandalorian was defective. It was not supposed to say anything without someone pressing the button on his chest. She turned back to face Josh and shot him a suspicious glance, causing him to giggle.

"It was Lizzie," he smirked. "She likes to press the buttons."

She became upset and scolded him, "Josh, I thought we agreed we were not going to talk about her."

"I'm sorry," he frowned. "But I saw her do it."

She sighed, "Forget it. Let's pretend it didn't happen." She began to read from the book. She went slowly to make it last, showing him each colorful illustration, before moving on to the next page. He listened intently, while she read about the Sith characters from the "*Star Wars*" saga mentioned in the book. By the time she got halfway through the book, she began to wish she had picked a different one. This book was all about the bad guys.

When she reached the end, she stated, "The end. Okay, time to go to bed, baby." She leaned in and gave him a kiss. "Goodnight," she said.

"Goodnight, Mommy." He closed his eyes.

She placed the book back on his shelf and turned on his lamp. She turned off the main light, as she left the room. She gave the Mandalorian action figure a hard look on her way out of the room. It was like she was daring it to talk, so she would have a reason to grab it and shove it into the closet. However, it remained silent.

She went into the living room and sat back on the sofa with her cellphone. Back to the Internet, she thought. She was extremely tired and had a hard time keeping her eyes open. She did not want to go to sleep, but she knew if she stayed up, she would be no good at work the next day. She was going to have to sleep, at some point. She could not risk losing her job.

After about an hour of debating with herself, she retired to her room, and got ready for bed. She fell asleep within seconds. The next nightmare would soon follow.

# Chapter 6

## Insomniac

Megan found herself lying on the cold, hard, concrete floor of a familiar dark basement. She was in the corner underneath a window. Bright rays of sunlight from the setting sun pierced the window and partially lit the room. There appeared to be a slight amount of hay scattered near her head. It looked like she was in a horse stall, but it did not smell like a horse was anywhere nearby. Instead, she smelled urine and her white t-shirt was covered in blood. She wondered if it was her blood. There was some kind of pillow shoved beneath her head. It was not very comfortable. Her pants were off. Were they under her head? She felt an intense feeling of anxiety come over her. She also felt cold and wet. Was it her urine? She was disgusted by her environment.

All of a sudden, she felt her lace panties being yanked off. Not by a person. All she saw was a dark shadow figure appear out of nowhere. It loomed over her menacingly. It looked like a demon with pointed white teeth and yellow eyes. She wanted to scream, but she lacked the strength and voice. It was utterly terrifying.

In the next moment, the shadow figure moved closer to her and turned into the same malignant man from her previous nightmare. Hank. Him, again. It turned out the yellow eyes were only his glasses, but his smile was almost as sinister as the demon. She feared what kind of torture this wicked monster had in store for her.

Megan wanted to get up and escape so badly, but she was paralyzed by fear and could not move, no matter how hard she tried. Hank pulled down his pants and got on top of her. She felt sick and swiftly turned her face away. It did not matter. She knew it would not deter him. He was going to have his way with her, one way or another.

He slapped her on the face hard repeatedly back and forth with his strong hand, until she became so weakened the fight had been taken out of her. Next, he entered her and there was nothing she could do about it. She was being raped. It was the worst most helpless feeling in the world.

As if it were not bad enough, he began to strangle her! She wondered why? She had already stopped fighting him. She could not breathe and struggled desperately to catch her breath. Her eyes began to roll up into her head. She thought, this is it. She is going to die.

Somehow, she managed to struggle so hard she was able to pull herself away from him, but the nightmare was not over. She stood in the center of the basement room between the two brick support beams, while the pretty young girl was now in her place lying on the floor. Hank was on top of her thrusting away with his bare ass to Megan.

She shouted, "Leave her alone, you fucking animal! Get away from her!"

It was a waste of breath. Either Hank could not hear her, or he chose not to listen. He continued to push himself in and out of the girl, while she lay there gasping for air and crying. She looked so helpless.

When he ejaculated into her, she vomited. Hank did not like that one bit. It was enough to make him stop. He shouted something and got up off of her. He then pulled up his pants and grabbed a hose from the other side of the basement. He sprayed her full blast with cold water drenching Megan in the process, since she was in the way.

Both women screamed simultaneously. When Megan screamed, she ended up waking from the nightmare. She was so thankful to be out of the basement and away from that horrid scene.

She sat up in a cold sweat almost as wet as she was in the nightmare. As she sat up, the blinds on her bedroom window shot up on their own. The loud noise startled her and nearly gave her a heart attack. The evening sky outside was exposed, along with bright street lights. Once she caught her breath, she looked to her nightstand to check the time on her clock radio. Once again, it was 3:37 in the morning.

Why did she always wake up at the same exact time? What did it mean? There had to be a reason behind it. It did not matter, at the moment. It was a puzzle for another time. Right now, she was fed up. She got out of bed and marched to the window. She yanked the blinds and closed them, again. She pulled them so hard, she nearly caused them to fall to the floor.

"No more! I've had it," she complained to herself. "I am sick and tired of these damned nightmares! I'm not going back to sleep! Not today! Not tonight! I don't care how tired I feel! No more of this fucking bullshit! I can't take it anymore! I can't!" She dropped to her knees and cried.

Minutes later, she stomped off to the bathroom to wash up. She took a long cold shower to wake herself. She knew she had to try and stay awake, as long as she could. She could not deal with the nightmares anymore. They were making her crazy. Her anxiety level was going through the roof. She certainly did not want to have a panic attack.

She spent the next couple of hours being angry. She was angry with herself for having the nightmares. She was angry at the apartment for causing them. She was angry because she had to go to work. She was angry because she could not sleep. She was angry with Herman for putting her in this predicament, in the first place. Had he been a better man, she would have still been living in California, but no! He had to be an asshole! Somehow, this was all his fault!

Megan made herself a cup of coffee and tried to calm herself. Misty would be arriving soon. She did not want her to see she was upset. She paced back and forth impatiently in the kitchen, until Misty was at the door. She was a little late, which did not help. Misty hesitated returning and had spent all night thinking about the negative energy she felt in the apartment the day before. She thought about Josh's invisible friend and knew what it meant. The apartment was haunted, although she never mentioned anything to Megan.

Megan went to work and kept busy, again. It was an uneventful day at Macy's and fortunately for Misty it was uneventful in the apartment, as well. She and Josh watched another two "*Star Wars*" movies. The entire time, Misty kept looking over her shoulders expecting something to happen. She felt the presence, but that was it. She was extremely grateful nothing out of the ordinary took place.

When Megan got home from work, she talked with Misty and asked about how she got the television to play the movies. Misty had to explain it came from her Firestick device, and then she had to explain what a Firestick was to Megan because she had no clue. She also told Megan how she could easily acquire one. It sounded too complicated, though. Megan decided to simply wait for the cable guy to connect the antenna. It was only a few more days. Soon enough, she would be able to watch television, again.

It meant a few more days without sleep or television to keep her busy. It was not going to be easy.

Two days had gone by and still Megan had not slept. She drank a lot of coffee, though. She felt like she was going out of her mind. It was a relief when Hannah finally returned for a visit, as promised.

Megan greeted her at the door with joy, "Hannah! I'm so glad to see you! Come in!"

"Hi, Meg! So, how are things going over here?" She sat down on the sofa and Megan sat beside her.

"Not good," was her response. "I've been having these crazy ass nightmares about a pervert, who abducts a teenage girl and takes her to a dark basement, where he tortures and rapes her." Hannah eyed her curiously, as she continued, "The crazy part is these nightmares have been happening in sequence like a movie playing out. Sometimes, I can see and feel everything the girl is going through. Other times, it's me who's going through it. I can't take it anymore. I've stopped sleeping."

"What? That's insane!" Hannah could not believe her ears. She was surprised by the odd nightmares, but more concerned her best friend had not been sleeping. "Girl, you need to get your sleep. It's not healthy to stay up for several days in a row. You have a son to think about, and a job, if you plan to keep it."

"I know," Megan admitted. "I don't know what else to do. I'm going stir crazy." She began to cry.

Hannah put her arms around her and gave her a heartfelt hug. "Well, I'm here now. We will think of something together. I promise."

"Thank you, Hannah. I can always count on you."

"And don't you forget it," Hannah reminded her. "Are you sure you're not feeling stressed over your break up? It was fairly recent and not the best experience."

Megan shook her head, "I'm way over that fool, although I do blame him for the anxiety I'm feeling because had it not been for him, I would not be here having these nightmares."

"Okay, fine. What can you tell me about these nightmares?"

Megan went on to tell her every detail of the frightening nightmares. She described the eerie basement and told her about Hank. The only thing she could not truly describe was the teenage girl, aside from her eyes. She was still a mystery. Megan recalled one thing, which stood out. In the first dream she had with her, it took place in the apartment. The girl was in Josh's room, before going out for a jog, but then it was Megan jogging, or was it? At first, Megan did not think anything of it, but maybe there was a reason behind it. Was the girl from her nightmares a real person? Did she once live in the same apartment? Perhaps, it was a premonition of things to come. She ran her theories by Hannah.

"I don't know about it being a premonition. It's only your paranoia getting the better of you. If you ask me, it sounds more like something that already happened a long time ago, maybe to a former tenant. It would make more sense, considering what's been happening around here." Hannah suggested, "Honestly, I think she's a ghost."

Megan scoffed, "No, absolutely not. It's nothing that crazy. I was just thinking… maybe somehow… oh, I don't know." She shrugged in frustration. "Maybe it's like you said. She used to live here, but that's all. There's nothing paranormal. For some reason, I am seeing what happened to her. It's the only thing I can think of, which makes any kind of sense, even if it makes no kind of sense. Do you know what I mean?"

Hannah nodded, "Yeah, I get it. It still counts as paranormal, Meg, which is fine because I think it's a ghost. I know you don't want to believe it, but there's something I didn't tell you about the day you moved in. I didn't want to say anything because I thought it would scare you and give you anxiety. I know how you get when it comes to these things."

"What??? You're scaring me, *and* you're giving me anxiety anyway!"

Hannah chuckled and said, "When I was cleaning the bathroom that day, I could have sworn I saw someone behind me in the mirror. When I turned to look, there was no one there. It creeped me out. I thought maybe I imagined it, but I swear on my grandmother's grave, it looked like a teenage girl."

Megan's eyes shot open. "Oh, my God!" She exclaimed. "Hannah! When I took a shower the other day, I thought I saw someone behind me in the mirror. I turned around and no one was there. I thought I was seeing things."

Hannah was convinced, "Do you see? It is a ghost! I told you!"

"No," Megan shook her head. She felt anxiety thinking about it. "Stop it. Don't even go there. I don't want to hear anything about freaking ghosts in my apartment. It's bad enough Josh has an imaginary friend."

"Wait. He what?" Hannah asked, sounding surprised. "Is this friend a female, by any chance?"

Megan hesitated, "Well, yeah. He calls her Lizzie."

Hannah smirked at her, "Meg, come on! It's gotta be her! I'm telling you it's a ghost!"

Megan thought about it, for a moment. She felt a chill down her spine, as the hairs on her arms stood on end. "No. It can't be a ghost," she shook her head. She did not want to believe it, although how could she keep denying it?

Just then, Josh entered the living room carrying his Mandalorian action figure.

Hannah smiled at him and said, "Hi, Josh! Get over here and give me a hug!" She bent down to his height.

"Hello," he said. As he approached her, his Mandalorian said, "I did what I had to."

Hannah grabbed Josh and squeezed him tightly, not paying attention to his toy. Megan, on the other hand, knew it was not a random phrase. It said what it said on purpose. She knew it was talking to her. She was sure of it. It was not the first time it happened. However, she thought twice about telling Hannah. Being afraid of a talking toy may appear borderline crazy. For now, it would remain her secret.

In time, Josh went back to his room to play, taking his Mandalorian with him. Megan was relieved.

She and Hannah continued their conversation in an attempt to formulate a theory, which sounded believable. Hannah was convinced it was a ghost, who was haunting the apartment. Megan did not want to believe it, which was understandable. She especially did not want to believe how her four-year-old son had been talking to and playing with the ghost of a teenage girl the past few days. It worried her and that was too much to bear.

Hannah stayed for dinner. She was actually planning to stay the night. Megan prepared some grilled chicken wraps for them. The three of them sat at the table, ate the wraps, and then relocated to the sofa. They talked with Josh about his imaginary friend. It was Hannah's idea. She wanted to probe for more information about Lizzie.

"Hey, Josh. I hear you have a friend named Lizzie," she asked in a casual manner.

"Yep," he nodded, just as casually.

Hannah smiled at him and said, "That's great. Is she a nice person?"

He nodded, again, and responded, "Yeah, she's the best."

"That's cool. How old is she? Do you know?"

"Nope," he shook his head. "I think she said she's really old."

Hannah frowned realizing there was no way someone who is "really old" could also be a teenager, even by a child's standards. For the time being, it put her theory to rest.

They moved on to playing a boardgame with Josh. He loved whenever they played boardgames with him. They played *Monopoly*. It was one of the only three boardgames they owned, along with *Life* and *Candy Land*. Josh enjoyed using the racing car token. It was his favorite. Megan used the shaggy dog because it was how she was feeling – shaggy and dogged. Hannah liked the new cat token, so she snatched it up.

Later that night, Hannah convinced Megan to go to sleep. "I will be lying right beside you," she said, hoping it would inspire a little confidence. It worked. They were like sisters, so sleeping in the same bed was not foreign to them. They had done it dozens of times, while growing up.

As they lay side by side, they stared up at the ceiling. This was usually the time when they used to discuss boys they liked. Things were different these days. Megan said, "I really appreciate you doing this for me. You're such a great friend, Hannah. You have no idea how scared I've been to sleep. I'm so tired. I hope this helps. I really do not want to continue that nightmare anymore."

"Well, I'm here with you, Meg," Hannah said with a smile. "I won't let anything happen to you. Think of me as your guardian angel. Maybe we can do like in the '*Dream Warriors*' movie."

"You mean '*Nightmare on Elm Street, part three*,'" Megan corrected her.

"Yeah, that one. It was called '*Dream Warriors*.' It had the cool song by Dokken, which I love. That's what we'll be. We'll fight Hank *Krueger* together." They both laughed. "Try and get some sleep. Think happy thoughts like in '*Peter Pan*.' Better movie?"

Megan scoffed, "Cuter movie. Not necessarily better."

Hannah began humming the theme song to *"Nightmare on Elm Street: Dream Warriors."*

Suddenly they both began singing in unison, *"We're the Dream Warriors! Don't wanna dream no more! We're the Dream Warriors and maybe tonight… maybe tonight you'll be gone!"* At that point, they burst into laughter. It felt like old times.

A short time later, Hannah said, "Goodnight, Meg."

"Goodnight, Hannah," Megan sighed. The thought of going to sleep left her feeling uneasy, despite their brief retreat into their childhood. She did not want to see what happened next in the nightmare sequence. It could not be good. She closed her eyes and tried to think of happy thoughts. She thought about Josh. He was what made her the happiest. He was her whole world. She remembered the day he was born, and when she held him in her arms for the first time. It was a magical moment for her. She tried to focus on that moment in time. It seemed so distant.

Soon, her mind drifted and she fell fast asleep.

Almost instantly, she was transported back to the same basement. She saw the teenage girl curled up on the floor in the corner of the horse stall. The girl was naked and wet. Once again, her face was hidden by her shaggy wet hair. She slowly rocked back and forth, as she began to sing something inaudible. Her voice was sweet and soft. She sounded so innocent. Megan moved closer, so she could hear her better. It sounded like she was singing a number over and over. Megan wondered why she would do such a thing. What was the number and what did it signify? She did not understand the girl because she was crying, as she sang, and kept sniffling.

Megan felt so bad for her. She wanted to help her more than anything. She reached out to touch the girl on her shoulder. "Hey, let me help you, sweetie."

The girl stopped singing, turned, and looked directly into her eyes. Her big brown eyes were hypnotizing. They stared at one another long enough for Megan to finally get a good look at her. She was so beautiful… and so sad. In that instant, Megan felt her pain. She felt her despair. It was so horrible that it made her cry.

The girl whispered to her, "I'm *real*. Please, find me. I was number five."

Megan did not understand. What did it mean? Before she could ask, she woke up to the sound of Josh's Mandalorian action figure saying, "I can bring you in warm, or I can bring you in cold."

Megan glared at the toy and wondered how it got on her bed. She looked over at Hannah, who was asleep and snoring lightly. Megan looked at the time and saw it was 3:37 A.M. She got out of bed, grabbed the toy, and went across the hall into Josh's room. He was asleep, too. She looked at the Mandalorian, again, and felt so tempted to throw him away. However, she knew it would break her son's heart. Reluctantly, she placed him back on the dresser, where he belonged, before going back to bed.

She lay there in bed, for a long time, staring up at the ceiling. She thought about the girl's face. Considering she saw it so clearly, this time, she would never forget it. She tried to remember what number she was singing, but had not been able to understand her, so remembering it was going to be impossible. She did recall the girl said something to her. *"I'm real. Please, find me,"* and *"I was number five."* Megan had no idea what she meant, but it was a new piece of the puzzle. Maybe she was a real person, after all.

Eventually, Megan fell asleep with a new goal in mind for when she woke up.

Megan woke up tired, but in a much better mood. This time, she was on a mission. She got up earlier than intended, after having reset her alarm when she woke up at the usual time in the middle of the night. She grabbed a spiral notebook from her drawer, sat down at the kitchen table, and began to write down every nightmare she had ever since moving into the apartment. It was what she would do from this day forward. She hoped doing so would help her to make more sense of this mystery. She made sure to include every single detail she could possibly remember. Luckily, she had discussed each dream with Hannah the day before, so they were fresh in her head. She even drew a quick sketch of what the basement looked like using a ruler to keep the lines as straight as possible. She wanted to be able to show it to Hannah. She also wrote down everything she knew about Hank and the beautiful teenage girl. Megan especially made a note of what she said to her. It had to be an important clue.

When the girl mentioned she was number five it really threw Megan for a loop. It kind of scared her. Did she suggest she was Hank's fifth victim? Had there been other girls in his basement? Megan wondered where it was located. Maybe it was nearby. Or was there a more morbid meaning having something to do with where the girl's body was hidden? No! She did not want to think the girl was dead. It would mean Hannah was right about her being a ghost, which was totally unacceptable. Maybe there was a simpler meaning, such as she lived in apartment number five. No, that couldn't be it. It had to be something more significant, but what?

She recalled a previous dream when Hank took photos of the girl, soon after tying her up. The photos were to become part of his private collection. Somehow, she knew he had more like them hidden in a small metal box. Within the box were likely photos of other victims. *Four* other victims. The thought made Megan's skin crawl.

Elsewhere in the apartment, Hannah had finally woken up and brushed her teeth. She soon joined Megan at the kitchen table. "You're up early," she commented. "Did you sleep at all?"

Megan nodded, "Yep. I slept, had a nightmare, woke up, and went back to sleep. You were a big help. Thanks for nothing. Freddy would have made minced meat out of me." She referred to Freddy Krueger from the "*Nightmare on Elm Street*" films, who tormented his victims in their nightmares using a glove with knives as claws.

Hannah apologized, "I'm so sorry, Meg. Your bed is *super* comfy. I don't know how you can't conceivably sleep a good night's rest there. I slept like a baby." She glimpsed at the notebook and asked, "Hey, what are you writing? Did you draw this?" She pointed to the sketch and tilted her head trying to see what was on the notebook.

"It's the basement I told you about. I wanted to show you how it looks." She rotated the notebook, so Hannah could see it better. "Picture this room with those brick columns at the center." She pointed. "The horse stall is there in the left corner. There are bondage ropes tied on either side of the opening. The room is very dark, mainly lit by the small window on the side over the horse stall. This is where Hank tortures us. I mean her." She paused for dramatic effect, before adding, "Hannah, I saw her face last night. She's young, like about seventeen or eighteen. She's very pretty, too, but that's not all. She said something to me. Actually, she whispered it. It was really creepy."

"No shit! Well, what did she say? Don't keep me in suspense!"

"She told me she was real and that she was number five."

Hannah's jaw gaped open. "Holy shit! It means there were other victims in his basement!"

"Shh! Keep it down with the shitting. Josh will hear you," Megan scolded her.

"Oops! Sorry, Meg. My bad."

"Let's not jump to conclusions. The information I have is still kind of sketchy. It could mean any number of things," Megan tried to reason with her. She did not want to think there were more victims, who went through similar experiences. Yet, she knew that had to be the case. It was simply too ghastly to contemplate.

Hannah demanded, "What else could it possibly mean?"

"I don't know," Megan shrugged. "I hate to say it, but you're probably right. I've been writing down every nightmare, since I woke up, despite how much I hate thinking about them. I want to remember every important detail. It's the only way I can ever get to the bottom of this mystery."

"Yes! Great idea!" Hannah agreed enthusiastically. "Oh, sorry." She lowered her voice. "I think you should also make a note of the weird things happening in the apartment. It could all be connected. I'm telling you I think that girl is haunting you."

"Please, stop saying that," Megan replied angrily. "You know I don't want to think this place is haunted. Why can't she be alive, and maybe we have some kind of psychic connection? Why is it she has to be dead in your scenario?"

Hannah conceded and replied mockingly, "Okay, fine. You guys are telepathically linked for some absurd reason. Sound better?"

"Yes, thank you."

Hannah rolled her eyes and shook her head. "Whatever. Do me a favor, Meg? Please, get to the bottom of this mystery fast because I really need to know how you can possibly have a psychic connection with a teenage girl you've never met."

"I will do my best," she grinned ignoring the sarcasm.

"And how do you plan to start?"

Megan answered, "I'll ask around. See what I can learn from the people in the building. Leslie might be able to tell me who used to live here before the old lady, who died. What was her name, again?" She tried to recall. "Oh, yeah! I think it was Mrs. Bennett, or Garrett? Something that ends in double 'T's."

Hannah's eyes opened wide. "Wait. Did you say old lady?" A thought occurred to her. "Josh said his friend was 'really old.' *Remember?* Didn't the old lady, who used to live here, die a few months ago?"

"Hannah, I told you to stop that. Stop trying to make this about ghosts." Megan was becoming flustered. She felt her anxiety level going up. She did not want her new home to be haunted. She felt like the more Hannah suggested it, the more likely it was going to be true. She became dizzy and had to close her eyes.

"Breathe slowly," Hannah told her. She tried to be more openminded and said, "I'm sorry about the ghost talk. Don't listen to me. I'm only messing around with you. This place isn't haunted." She did not believe that for one second, but she tried to sound sincere. "It's like you said, it's only a psychic connection." She thought it might be a good time to change the subject. "Hey, I'm starving. What do you have here for breakfast?" She opened the refrigerator and peeked inside. "Do you want me to make us some eggs? How about pancakes? Do you have pancake mix?"

Megan nodded and pointed to the cupboard, "Yes, it's in there. Pancakes would be great. Thanks."

"Awesome. Then I'll make us some pancakes. Should I wake Josh?"

"No," Megan shook her head. "I'll do it, if he hasn't already heard all your yelling," she teased.

Seconds later, Megan woke Josh up and they sat down to have breakfast together. Misty arrived, minutes later. Quick introductions were made. It was almost time for Megan to leave for work. Hannah also had somewhere to be, so she prepared to leave. She grabbed her car keys from the counter, and then gave Megan and Josh hugs.

"I'll visit, again, really soon. It was so nice to see you both," she said. "And very nice to finally meet you, Misty."

Misty commented with a smile, "Thanks. It was nice to meet you, too."

Megan told her, "I'll keep you posted on my new project."

"Cool. You better," Hannah replied, as she turned to leave. Suddenly, she realized she did not have her car keys anymore. "What the...? Hey, didn't I just have my car keys in my hand?"

Megan nodded, "Yeah. You were holding them when we hugged. Check your pockets."

"I don't have any pockets. Do you?"

Megan checked her pockets, even though she seriously doubted the keys would be in there. They were not. "No, I don't have them. Why would I?" She looked around at the floor. "Did you drop them?"

Misty checked the floor with them.

Hannah responded, "I think I would have heard them fall. Where the heck could they have disappeared to? She checked her overnight bag thoroughly, thinking she might have placed them inside without thinking. "Wait a minute." Suddenly, she saw the keys on the kitchen table. "What the heck is going on here? I was holding these a second ago!" She walked over and picked them up. "How did they end up on the table?"

Josh was giggling quietly, but they did not notice. They were too focused on the keys.

Misty gasped in surprise, "Whoa! I saw them in your hands! There's no way they could have ended up on the table!"

Josh finally spoke up and said, "It was Lizzie! She took them and put them there." He giggled.

Megan swallowed nervously, as Hannah's eyes shot over to her. Megan did not want to hear what she knew Hannah was thinking. She gave Hannah a stern look and Hannah knew to refrain and keep quiet about it. Megan did not want to hear anything about ghosts, especially not in front of Josh and Misty.

Hannah lied, ignoring Josh's statement, and said, "Silly me. I must be losing my mind. It had to be me. I probably put them there without thinking when I hugged you guys."

Josh shook his head adamantly, "Nope, it was Lizzie. I saw her."

Misty became afraid. She could feel the spiritual presence in the room with them. She had been trying hard to ignore it.

Megan interjected angrily, "Josh, enough with the Lizzie stuff! Hush and eat your breakfast!"

He pouted.

Misty looked around the room and felt nervous. She sensed the presence was growing angry. She had a feeling something was going to happen.

Hannah felt bad for Josh because she believed him. She looked back at her friend and said, "Hey, take it easy on him, Meg. He's just playing around. It's fine. No harm done. Anyway, I gotta go. Make sure to write *everything* down, regarding your new project. Okay?"

Megan knew what she meant. She nodded, "Yeah, of course."

Misty became curious what project they were talking about, although she knew it was none of her business. She pretended not to listen, but made a mental note of it.

Before leaving, Hannah suggested, "You know? I have time." She was still standing in the doorway. "If you want, I could drop you off at Cross County, so you don't have to take the bus to work."

Megan was ecstatic. "Really? That would be great. Thanks, Hannah. Let me grab my purse and we can leave." She grabbed her purse, said bye to Josh and Misty, and then she left with Hannah. On the way down the stairs, they could be heard discussing what they believed happened with the keys. a short while ago. Hannah was rather loud when she got excited. After they left the building, it was silent.

Once again, Misty and Josh were alone in the apartment... with Lizzie. They sat at the kitchen table looking at each other. They were all out of "*Star Wars*" movies to watch. Over the past few days, they had gone through all three trilogies, "*Rogue One,*" and the Solo movie.

One of the empty seats between them slid out away from the table. Both of them watched, as it stopped, and then moved forward slightly. Josh smiled at Lizzie, who had just joined them. He then looked back at Misty, patiently waiting to see her reaction.

Misty swallowed nervously and wished she were somewhere else. Anywhere else, but there.

# Chapter 7

## Who's That Girl?

Josh had gone to his room to play, where he remained peacefully. He seemed content, so Misty did not disturb him. She sat down on the living room sofa prepared to read a book she brought with her. She pulled the seven-hundred-page novel out of her bag. It was a work of fiction called *"No Hope for the Hopeless at Kings Park."* It was long enough to keep her distracted for the duration of her stay.

Within minutes, she read through the introduction and first chapter of the first story. There were three stories in the book, which mainly took place at a psychiatric hospital on Long Island. Each tale was somehow tied together. The first was called *"Amanda."* It was a sentimental story about an adolescent girl, who was committed to the hospital, after attempting suicide.

As Misty began the second chapter, she felt a familiar sensation. Right away, she knew she was not alone. She closed her eyes and took a deep breath to calm herself. It's nothing, she told herself. Ignore it and it will go away. She kept reading. The feeling subsided, or rather it seemed to move to another room in the apartment. Josh's room.

Josh looked up toward his doorway and greeted his friend, Lizzie. "Hello, Lizzie."

Misty heard him say the words and her heart sank. She got up and went to check on him, placing the thick paperback down on the sofa. When she stepped closer to the doorway of his room, the sensation grew stronger. She pushed herself forward and stood in the doorway. Josh looked up at her curiously.

She asked, "Is everything okay, Josh? What are you doing?"

"I was talking to Lizzie. She's there," he pointed next to where Misty was standing.

Misty turned to look, but only saw the dresser and its large mirror. She moved further into the room, so she could look into the mirror. That's when she saw a teenage girl standing there for only a split second. Misty screamed, and then the girl vanished into thin air.

Josh was startled by her scream and became nervous. He did not know why she screamed so loudly. He stopped playing with his toys and sat on the floor frozen in fear.

Misty caught her breath and realized how loud she screamed. She turned to Josh and saw his expression. He was on the verge of crying. Immediately, she knew she had frightened him. She apologized, "I'm so sorry, Josh. I thought I saw a really, really big spider. My mistake. Hey, how would you like if we went to the park, for a while?"

"Okay," he nodded hesitantly. "What about the spider?" He seemed deeply concerned.

"Um, there is no spider. I was wrong," she explained. "Grab some toys, if you want, and I'll get some clothes for you to wear." Misty desperately needed to get out of the apartment. She had to escape the uncomfortable feeling of heaviness she was experiencing. It was suffocating her and giving her a headache.

Once they were ready, they headed out to Cochran Park on the next block over. Misty brought her book with her, just in case. She kept it in her denim duffle bag. At first, they walked around the inner perimeter of the park. Misty used the opportunity to talk to Josh and get to know him better, since they barely spoke, while watching movies. She asked him basic questions, such as what his favorite snack was and his favorite color. Brownies and blue were his answers. She also wanted to let him know where he was allowed to play and where he should not, for safety reasons. After the ground rules were established, she let him play on his own. She gave him a quest to keep him busy.

"See if you can find a rock shaped like an egg," she told him. He hurried off in search of a rock, while she found a nice shady spot to sit. She pulled out her book from her bag and resumed reading from where she left off. At last, she felt relaxed. Her mind was clear. There was no heavy sensation here. No spiritual energy. There was nothing but nature and fresh air.

She made sure to look up every few seconds at Josh. She did not want him to fall or get hurt. He seemed to be fine. He was walking around slowly with his head down, as he searched for an oval rock. Every once in a while, he bent down to check the ground.

Misty remembered walking along the beach with her father as a little girl doing the same thing. He would give her mini quests to occupy her time. She had a lot of fun with him. He took her on many adventures. Thinking about those days made her smile. It had been a long time, since she went anywhere with her father.

A look of excitement came over Josh's face, as he bent over to pick up a rock from the grass. He carefully cleaned it off with his fingers, before hurrying over to Misty. "Look! I found one!" He exclaimed.

"Wow! That's very good, Josh! Can I see it? Please!" He handed it to her. She examined it closely. It was incredibly smooth and a clean pearl white color. It actually did resemble a fossilized egg. She gave it a light tap with her long red fingernail. It was solid. She declared, "Hm. This one looks very special. I think it might even be a real petrified egg." He became excited. She suggested, "You should keep it. Maybe it will hatch someday." She handed it back to him.

"Do you really think so?" He held the rock carefully with both hands worried he may break it.

She smiled at his innocent naivety and said, "You never know. Strange things happen all the time."

He eagerly placed the rock into his pants pocket and wiped his hands.

She chuckled and put her arm around his shoulder. "Hey, are you hungry for some lunch?" He shrugged at her. She suggested, "Your mom said you like pizza. Would you like to go get some pizza with me?"

He responded with delight, "Pizza!" It had become an instant favorite of his, after moving to New York. He mainly enjoyed picking at the thick stringy cheese and eating it in clumps, although he was capable of eating a whole slice, aside from the crust. Most crusts were too toasty for his taste.

Within minutes, Misty and Josh were seated in the pizzeria on Yonkers Avenue eating their slices. Misty was in no hurry to go back to the apartment, so she ate slowly. She told Josh to take his time eating, as well, which he did.

After chewing and swallowing a hefty mouthful of cheese, he inquired out of the blue, "Why are you so scared of Lizzie?"

Misty had no idea how to respond to his inquiry. She was not expecting him to ask something like that. She did not wish to lie to him, but she also hated the idea of giving him a reason to fear this so-called friend of his. Instead, she strategically deflected the question. "Why would you ask that?"

"You look scared every time she's around. She thinks you're scared of her," he answered with a giggle, teasing her. To him, it was amusing how an adult could be scared of his friend, who he found to be very kind. Lizzie was always nice to him. He hoped she and Misty could also become friends. "I'm not scared of her. She's nice to me," he added.

"Good. I'm glad she's nice to you," she replied.

"And I'm not scared of her," he reminded her.

"Yes, that is also good. If you were afraid of her, she would not be a good friend."

"She's my best friend," Josh informed her. "She reads to me and plays with me. Sometimes, she tells me stories about her life and her little brother. She even told me about the bad man who hurt her."

Misty became intrigued. "What bad man?"

"The bad man, who took her."

"Took her from where?"

Josh shrugged, "I don't know. From her family. He took her and he hurt her real bad."

She hesitated to ask the next question, but her curiosity got the better of her. "What did he do to her? Did she tell you how he hurt her?"

"He did really bad things." He whispered, "*Nasty* things. I'm not allowed to say."

Misty had a lump in her throat. She did not want to push the conversation any further. It was time to talk to Megan about this imaginary friend. She needed to know this was no ordinary imaginary friend.


Later, when Megan got home from work, Misty was waiting to speak with her. "Hi, how was your day at work?" She asked.

"Brutal. It was so busy at the store. Everyone was shopping today. My feet are aching. I'm exhausted." Megan placed a bag on the table and sat down. "I brought home some burgers and sodas. There's enough for all three of us. I hope you're hungry." She called out, "Josh! Mommy's home! Wash your hands and come to the table for dinner!"

He called back from his room, "Okay, Mommy! Be right there!"

Misty took a seat and said, "Thank you, Megan. That's very kind of you. We had pizza at around noon, so I'm ready for dinner." She reached over to take a burger and the soda Megan was offering her. As she unwrapped the burger, she asked, "Do you know about Josh's friend, Lizzie?"

Megan sighed, "Yes, was he being a bother about her? I'm so sorry. Children and their imaginary friends!" She shook her head, trying to sound convincing.

"Um, about that. I don't exactly think she is imaginary," Misty stated awkwardly.

Megan stared at her and her expression changed drastically. She asked, "What happened?"

"Oh, nothing happened. I mean, nothing happened to Josh. He had a good day. I took him to the park. We had fun." Megan looked relieved. "It's just… well, I can sense things. *Energies*." Megan raised an eyebrow, as Misty went on, "Somehow, I can feel spiritual energy. I guess that's the best way to explain it. Whenever he mentions her…" Her voice trailed off, as Josh approached the table and took his seat. She waited.

Megan handed him a burger and unwrapped it for him. She pushed a small soft drink cup toward him, as well. "Where's my kiss?" She asked, as she pushed her cheek out for him.

He went over and gave her a kiss on the cheek, before sitting down to eat his meal.

Misty leaned toward Megan and continued in a low voice, "I can sense when she's around… like right now. She's here. Ask him." She gestured toward Josh with her chin.

Megan looked around nervously and asked Josh, "Hey, baby. Where's your friend, Lizzie?"

He looked up from his burger and a smile appeared on his face. His eyes lit up with immediate recognition. "There," he pointed at the empty seat next to him. "Hi, Lizzie!" He waved at her and took a bite from his burger.

Megan and Misty both looked at the empty seat. It was not completely pushed in against the table, so someone could conceivably be seated there. The women glanced at each other with concern. Megan then turned back to her son and asked, "Baby, how old is Lizzie? Can you ask her? You mentioned she was really old. How old is really old?"

Josh did not bother asking. Instead, he replied plainly, "She can hear you, Mommy. She's not deaf. You can ask her yourself. She said she's older than all of us."

Megan felt a hint of relief to know it was not the teenage girl from her nightmares. That meant it had to be Mrs. Garrett, the old woman, who used to live in the apartment.

Misty had not mentioned she saw Lizzie's teenage reflection in the mirror earlier, otherwise it would have ruined Megan's theory. Misty was not about to bring it up at the table with Josh listening either. She was not under the same impression as Megan and had no reason to suspect Mrs. Garrett and Lizzie were one in the same. All she knew was Lizzie was the wayward spirit of a teenage girl, who was somehow trapped in the apartment. Of course, she was also unaware of Megan's nightmares.

Megan stared at the empty seat, while eating her burger. She wanted to ask Ms. Garrett dozens of questions, but she did not know where to start.

Josh broke her chain of thought by stating, "Lizzie said she really loves burgers, but she hasn't had one since 1988. That's when she died."

Megan's heart skipped a beat and she almost choked on her burger. She began coughing at an excessive rate. Misty got up and offered to help her, but Megan waved her off. "It's okay. I'm good." She coughed once or twice and took a drink from her diet soda. The wheels in her mind started turning. If Lizzie died in 1988, there was no way she could be Mrs. Garrett, who only died a few months ago. Lizzie had to be a previous tenant from long ago.

Misty kept staring at the empty seat. She felt like someone was looking right through her. She sensed the spirit in the seat, which was next to her. It did not feel evil, but its close proximity terrified her. This was much closer than she liked being when it came to these things. It was making her extremely uncomfortable and giving her a headache.

Suddenly, her drink was knocked over spilling her soda all over the table and onto her lap. "Argh! Just great!" She complained. "How did that happen?" As soon as she asked, she knew. She glared at the empty seat.

Megan grabbed some paper towels and wet them. "Here. Use these." She gave a few to Misty.

"Thanks. I'm so sorry. I swear it wasn't my fault. I wasn't even touching the cup."

"Yeah, I know," Megan responded with a frown.

Both women cleaned up the mess together. As they did, the empty seat between Misty and Josh fell backwards to the floor.

Megan became upset. "Real nice, Lizzie," she reprimanded. She was obviously irritated. "Thanks," she added sarcastically. She bent over to pick up the chair and pushed it in against the table.

Once the mess had been cleaned up, Misty announced, "I think it's time for me to go. I guess I'll see you in the morning."

"Yes, of course. Thank you, Misty. By the way, the cable guy is supposed to be stopping by tomorrow anytime between nine and noon."

"Sure, no problem."

"Thanks, again," Megan said. "Please, let me know when you get home, so I know you're safe."

"I will. Bye, Josh!" She waved and he waved back, as she walked out the door.

"Bye, Misty!" He called after her.

Megan sat back down in her seat feeling frustrated and embarrassed. If there was a ghost haunting her apartment, why was she doing it? What good came from it? Was there a point? It certainly was not making her life easier. She looked at Josh and watched him finish his burger and drink. She loved him so much. Maybe he could help.

"Your friend, Lizzie, is making me nuts," she confided in him.

She had a feeling he did not quite understand. His response to her was, "I like nuts, Mommy. Almonds are my favorite."

She smiled at his sweet innocence. Too cute. However, being cute was not going to solve her problems. She suggested, "Maybe it might be a good idea if Lizzie found somewhere else to live. Can she hear me?"

Josh replied, "Nope. She left, after she knocked down the chair." He came to his friend's defense and stated, "Mommy, Lizzie is not bad. She said she will always protect me. She wants to be my guardian angel. I don't want her to leave. Can't she be my angel? Huh, Mommy? Please!"

Megan sighed in defeat. How could she say 'no' to such an innocent request from a child? Still, she tried, "Josh, I really don't know if that's even possible."

"*It is!* Lizzie told me so. She can always protect me for the rest of my life, so no bad man can ever hurt me like what happened to her."

Almost immediately, Megan shot him a look. "Bad man? What are you talking about Josh?"

"Lizzie told me a mean bad man with glasses hurt her, a really long time ago. He took her away from her family and he hurt her. He did very bad things to her. Nasty things."

Megan could not believe her ears. All at once, her nightmares came flooding back to her. The man with the glasses, Hank. He took the pretty teenage girl, who used to live in this apartment, and then he tortured and raped her in his creepy basement. Was it Lizzie? She certainly was not an old lady, as originally suspected. She liked burgers. What old lady eats burgers? She was only older because she died in 1988. She lived here that long ago. Hannah was right. She was a ghost. It was beginning to add up. More pieces of the puzzle. Megan became excited and especially interested in Lizzie. She needed to know more.

"Josh, what does Lizzie look like?" She asked. "What kind of clothing does she wear? What color? Do you remember? Can you please tell me everything you can about her?"

He nodded, "Sure, Mommy. She's very pretty. She has long brown hair down to her shoulders like you and big brown eyes. She always wears a white t-shirt with a picture of a pretty girl named Amanda. Oh, and blue pants. I don't think she has any shoes or socks because I never see her feet."

Megan's anxiety level began to go way up. She became dizzy and her vision became blurry. It was indeed the same girl from her nightmares. There was no doubt. They were being haunted by a teenage girl, who had most likely been murdered by Hank. Megan still had not seen it in her nightmares, but she knew. Even Misty was experiencing crazy things in the apartment. Megan could not breathe. Everything turned to black and she fell over onto the floor.

It was complete darkness. Megan could not see anything. She also could not move. She was on her knees. The floor was cold and hard. It was difficult to breathe. For some reason, it only got harder, as time went on. At this point, she was panicking. She felt herself choking. Something big had been shoved into her mouth. It was followed by the sensation of warm liquid rushing down her throat, which tasted foul. She tried to cough it up, but she could not. She felt herself gag. As her eyesight gradually began to clear, she realized she was in that awful basement, again.

Hank was standing directly in front of her. His pants were down and he was shoving his filthy penis into her mouth. "Suck it clean!" He instructed, as he held her head firmly in place with both hands.

She gagged and tried to throw up. Just then, cold water was poured over her head. The cold wetness woke her up. She soon realized Josh had tossed a cup of cold water on her head. She felt sick. She leapt to her feet and ran to the bathroom to vomit. She could still taste Hank in her mouth. It was repulsive!

"Mommy! Are you okay?" He chased after her, worried it was his fault she felt sick. "I'm sorry, Mommy! I was only trying to wake you up!"

She kept heaving into the toilet, unable to really speak, yet. "Stay back, Josh." She spit into the toilet. "It's not your fault. Mommy's sick," she warned. She did some dry heaving and a lot more spitting before flushing the toilet. She moved to the sink and rinsed her mouth out. She used mouthwash, gargled, and then brushed her teeth and tongue.

It was official. This was, by far, the absolute worst nightmare, by a long shot. The thought of his penis in her mouth made her gag, again. "Oh, God," she uttered, thinking she was going to vomit, again. She did not. "That was so bad," she stated.

"Mommy, what happened?" Josh stood at the doorway of the bathroom. He was worried about his mother. For all he knew, she was dying. He asked, "Are you going to die?"

She shook her head and replied, "Not today, baby. Mommy just had a panic attack. It's been a long time, since I've had one this bad. How long was I on the floor? Was it a long time?"

He nodded, "Uh huh. Hannah told me to throw cold water on your face, so I did."

"Hannah? When did you talk to Hannah?" She was bewildered.

"I called her. She showed me how to do it. Please, don't be mad at me." He still looked worried.

"Baby, come here." He did and she held him close. "I'm not mad at you. You did good. You saved me. You're *my* guardian angel and I love you so much!" She hugged him and was grateful for his quick thinking.

She realized she had better call Hannah back. "Where's my phone, baby?"

"On the kitchen table." He pointed toward the kitchen.

She hurried to the kitchen and dialed Hannah's number. She quickly explained what happened. She had a hard time convincing Hannah she did not need her to come over and tend to her. She was fine and had plans to go straight to bed. After a while, Hannah finally decided to turn back and go home. Apparently, she was already on her way over. She insisted on coming over the next day to check on her. Megan did not mind. She happily agreed and told her she had a lot to tell her regarding her new secret project. At the mention of the project, Hannah became very interested and almost wanted to keep coming over anyway.

"No, Hannah. Go back home. Get some sleep. I'm going straight to bed. I promise. Trust me. I'm good. We can talk tomorrow. You can even stay over, again, if you want. Hopefully, I'll have cable, by then, and I don't have to work the next day, so it will be perfect. We can work on the project together."

At last, she was able to satisfy Hannah. They said goodbye and hung up.

Josh was standing at his mother's side, gazing up at her. He asked, "Mommy, since you're sick, does it mean you won't have to go to work tomorrow?"

Megan thought about it and it sounded like a fantastic idea. "We'll see how Mommy feels in the morning. Hey, do you want to sleep with Mommy tonight?"

"Yes! Yay! Thank you, Mommy!" It was a special privilege whenever he got to sleep with his mother. He liked it better than sleeping alone, although he knew he had to get used to it. After all, he was not a baby anymore.

They hugged and a short time later, they were both ready for bed. They climbed into the bed. Josh brought his Mandalorian action figure with him. He did not want to leave it in the room alone. Of course, his mother did not want to sleep with that thing.

"Josh, Mando cannot sleep on the bed," she told him immediately.

"Aw, okay. Can I put him on the nightstand?"

She knew how much he loved his toy. She did not want to disappoint him. She reluctantly allowed it. "Fine. You can put him on the nightstand over on your side of the bed. We can leave the lamp next to you on, if you need to, but Mommy is turning off her lamp. Okay?"

"Okay, Mommy. Goodnight."

"Goodnight, Josh."

"Don't forget to say goodnight to Mando," he reminded her.

She sighed, "Goodnight, Mando."

"I know the drill," the toy replied.

Megan sat up immediately with a scared look on her face, but then she noticed Josh had pressed the button on the toy's chest. He giggled at her comical reaction. She threatened him playfully with her fist, and then began tickling him mercilessly.

"Okay! I'm sorry, Mommy!" He pleaded, while laughing hysterically.

She stopped her torture and stated, "Go to bed, Josh." He giggled a little more, before finally stopping. She warned him, "I'm going to kick your butt, if you don't stop laughing."

"Sorry, Mommy." He giggled a little more, but held it in.

She smirked and closed her eyes. She really did not want to go to sleep, but her body needed the rest. She knew it. She was fighting a losing battle. She hoped by having Josh in the bed with her Lizzie would leave her alone, this one time. Maybe she would show her mercy for Josh's sake. No nightmares, she prayed. Please, give me one night of peace, Lizzie, she added to her silent prayer. That's all I ask. One peaceful night. She kept repeating it to herself in her head, until she dozed off.

# Chapter 8

**Revelation**

Megan did have a dream, but this dream was different than the nightmares. It was daytime. She found herself standing in front of her building, but something was off. The paint around the entrance was a different color. Everything looked different. She speculated it might have been in the past, if this was still part of the same nightmare sequence.

There was a teenage boy sitting on the front steps. He looked around fifteen or sixteen years old. He had short brown hair. He looked angry. No, not angry, deeply concerned. He was worried about something, or someone.

The boy kept looking at his watch, and then checking down the street, every once in a while. He seemed to be waiting for someone, who was late. Megan realized he was waiting for her. Lizzie.

Megan knew Lizzie would not be coming home. She had a feeling she would never return to the Hill View, at least not as a living being.

She got the impression the boy was Lizzie's younger brother. He had the same big brown eyes and thick eyebrows. If he only knew where Lizzie was, he would explode with furious anger. He would attack Hank and possibly try to kill him with his bare hands. Who would blame him?

The sad truth is he would most likely never learn what truly happened to his older sister.

Megan wanted to tell him so desperately. She tried. "Someone has her," she said with concern. There was no reaction. She spoke louder. "An evil man named Hank took her!" Still, the boy could not hear her. She even shouted, but he did not acknowledge her presence. It's like she was the ghost when it came to these nightmares.

She wanted to take him to the basement, but she had no idea where it was located. Come to think of it, she was not sure she wanted to know the actual location. The place scared her to death. She associated it with terrible things and never wanted to see it, again, let alone go there on purpose.

It made no difference. It was too late. The boy faded away and the dream changed. It was nighttime. Megan felt herself being pulled somewhere else. She could not fight the sensation. She lifted upwards and dropped back down into the basement.

No! Not here! She hated this place.

She managed to wake herself up, before anything could happen. She looked at the time. It was 3:37 A.M. Of course, it was. She faced the nightstand, where the Mandalorian action figure sat expecting it to say something. When it did not, she laid her head back down on her pillow and tried to go back to sleep.

Instead, she found herself deep in thought. She wondered how much further these nightmares would go to tell the sordid tale of what allegedly happened to Lizzie. What if the nightmares never ended? The thought made her panic. Sometimes, they were too much for her to bear. The last thing she wanted was to have these nightmares for the rest of her life. It was too disturbing to contemplate.

Just then, an idea occurred to her. What if she moved somewhere else? Would things eventually go back to normal? It was a wonderful notion. Unfortunately, she did not have the money to move, again. For the moment, she was stuck in this apartment. There was no way to know for sure if moving would end the nightmares anyway.

She hoped the situation in her home would not become so out of control to the point where her agoraphobia might cause her too much stress, or affected her son in a negative way. She already had one panic attack. Poor Josh must have been so worried. He's too young for this kind of drama, even if he did handle the situation appropriately. It's not something she wanted to put him through, a second time. It was already making her crazy. As a single mother, she had too much to lose. She could not risk ending up in a hospital for a mental evaluation. Not with her history of panic attacks and paranoia. She definitely did not wish to risk losing Josh to child services, if she completely lost her mind, as a result of these nightmares. She needed to toughen up and be strong for Josh's sake, no matter how hard it was going to be.

The sound of raindrops began hitting her bedroom window creating a soothing ambience. She loved being home on rainy nights. Normally, she found it relaxing. She thought about the night when she left Herman. It had been raining. It was cold wintry rain. There was absolutely nothing relaxing about that night. Taking Josh away from his father was a big decision. Megan wondered if it was the right one for her to make. Should she have stayed?

No. Had she stayed, she might not be alive today. He could have easily killed her, and then she would be the one haunting an apartment. He was drunk and he pointed a loaded rifle at her face. It was reckless and stupid. She hated him for it. He did not deserve to have Josh in his life anymore, but did Josh deserve to not have a father?

Where was he now? Was he still in jail? It was unlikely. He had to be out by now. Was he looking for them? Did he even care where they were? There were so many questions going through her mind. She was too frightened to learn the answers. Sometimes, ignorance is bliss, she thought.

All of a sudden, Megan began feeling claustrophobic. Her breathing became tight. She quietly climbed out of bed and tiptoed across the rug to the window. She opened it and took a deep breath. The smell of the rain helped to ease her mind. She closed her eyes and tried to steady her breathing, taking slow deep breaths. She inhaled through her nose, and then exhaled from her mouth. This technique usually helped her to relax.

This was Herman's fault. Every time she thought about him, it stressed her out. She had to get him out of her mind.

After a few moments, she opened her eyes and looked up at the nighttime sky. It was gray and cloudy. The rain began falling harder. Droplets splashed onto the windowsill wetting her hands and legs. She wore shorts and a t-shirt. It was her usual bedtime attire during the summer. The rain felt nice on her body. Far better than the freezing raindrops she felt on the night she left Herman. Him, again.

Tears began to fall from her eyes. She felt regret because of what she was denying her son. There was also sadness for the loss of her relationship. Her life did not turn out how she wanted it to be. She always hoped for a happy marriage, but Herman never even proposed. In time, it became apparent, he had no interest in ever marrying her. Had she known it from the start, she would never have had a child with him. However, then she would not have Josh and that would have been a huge loss.

Josh was her entire world. He meant everything to her. Everything she did was for him. She wanted to give him a better life than what he would have had living with an abusive alcoholic father. Josh did not need to grow up with that kind of stigma. This was better and she knew it. They did not need Herman in their lives.

Remembering that fact helped Megan to feel better. She wiped away her tears, returned to bed, and got under the blanket. The combination of the open window and ceiling fan, which spun steadily overhead, made the room feel cool and comfortable.

She looked over at Josh, as he slept peacefully. There were no nightmares for him. Only serenity. Watching him sleep made her smile. He was all that mattered to her. His happiness made it possible for her to go on each day. She was grateful to him.

It was funny how he was completely content living with a spirit, who he considered to be his guardian angel. Meanwhile, Megan was being tormented each night with crazy nightmares brought on by the very same spirit. She had to laugh at the irony.

Eventually, she was able to fall asleep, again. She did not have any other dreams or nightmares, which she could recall during the rest of the night. As it turned out, the sound of the rain helped her to sleep more peacefully.

The next morning, Megan called out sick from work. It was still raining. She called Misty and told her to stay home since she would not be needed today. As for Hannah, she would not be coming over, until she got off work later in the early evening. It gave Megan a good part of the day to spend alone with Josh. And Lizzie. Well, until the person from DirecTV arrived.

Megan and Josh sat at the table quietly eating their breakfast. Megan kept staring suspiciously at the two empty seats, wondering if Lizzie was in the room with them. Both seats had been deliberately pushed in against the table to discourage anyone, or anything, from sitting on them. Megan watched Josh for any hints of acknowledgment, indicating someone else was there with them. He seemed focused on eating his fried eggs and buttered toast, which was good. She liked when he ate his food without her having to push him to finish it. He generally had a healthy appetite for a kid his age.

The phone rang. She looked at the caller ID. It was an unknown number. Megan hated answering calls from unknown numbers. She hesitated. What if it was Herman? Maybe he managed to track her down and learn her new number. The thought sent a shiver down her spine.

However, then she realized how ridiculous it would be. How could he possibly know her new number?

She answered the call and panicked when she heard a male voice on the other line, until she realized it was only the guy from the cable service. He called to tell her he was on his way and would be arriving shortly.

"Okay. Thank you," she replied feeling silly, except now she felt paranoid. She began to worry the cable guy might be a pervert. It was not the same as when the electrician, Elijah, came over. Leslie knew him and recommended him. He could be trusted to a certain extent. Not this guy. What if he turned out to be Hank?

Megan became nervous. He was on his way, which meant he could knock on the door at any minute. Someone should be aware a complete stranger was coming over, just in case. Well, Misty knew. If only Megan had let her come over, before cancelling her so hastily. At least, she could have kept her company, until the cable person conducted his business and left. It was too late. Misty might have already made other plans. Megan's heart began to race. To be on the safe side, she sent Leslie a text message to let her know a man from DirecTV was on his way over. She was downstairs, so she could come up quickly. Megan asked if she was busy and did not mind keeping her company, until he left. She also apologized for any inconvenience, but insisted it was important.

It seemed like she waited forever before Leslie finally responded. She said she would be right up.

Several minutes later, there was a knock at the apartment door. Megan walked over to open it, but hesitated. It could be Leslie, but it could also be *him*. Thoughts of paranoia went through her mind. What if he already killed Leslie, and now he was coming for her?

"Who is it?" She asked with a hint of fear in her voice.

"Relax, sweetie. It's only me, Leslie. I'm sorry I took so long."

Megan breathed a sigh of relief and opened the door. She let the landlady into her apartment and greeted her, as if she saved her life. "Thank you so much for coming, Leslie! I greatly appreciate it."

Leslie responded with a smile, "It's not a problem, dear. I completely understand."

Moments later, someone was at the door. Megan approached it and, once more, asked, "Who is it?"

A male voice replied, "I'm from DirecTV. You called for cable installation?"

"Just a sec," she said, as she opened the door with caution. She felt a tremendous amount of relief when he looked nothing like Hank. "Come in," she told him and he thanked her politely.

As it turned out he was very professional and speedy at his job. He was done setting everything up, in no time at all. He handed Megan her new remote control, once the service was activated. Before she realized it, he was gone. He mentioned something about another appointment nearby, so he hurried off. She freaked out for nothing.

More importantly, she and Josh now had channels to watch!

Before Leslie left, Megan decided it was a good time to ask her some questions regarding former tenants. She began by asking, "Leslie, how long have you lived in this building?"

"Oh, since I was a little girl. My father was the landlord before me."

While it was not a specific answer, it answered the question sufficiently. Leslie appeared to be in her fifties or early sixties. It was not a stretch to think she would remember many former tenants by name.

"Do you remember a teenage girl named Lizzie?" Megan hoped to see a spark of recognition when she said the name, but there was none. It was quite the opposite. Leslie looked perplexed.

"No, I can't say I do. Lizzie?" She thought about it momentarily searching her memories for the name, in relation to a teenager. No one came to mind. "No. I'm sorry. It doesn't ring a bell. Why do you ask?"

Megan looked disappointed, as she said, "I was just curious. The name came to me... in a dream." She lied not wanting to admit how she really knew the name. She did not want to mention Josh's "special" friend, nor was she ready to share her theory about her apartment being haunted by a former tenant. At least, not yet. She remembered something else she could ask about. On the day she moved in she saw her name etched under the table. She had forgotten about it. "What about my name?" She asked. "Did anyone named Megan ever live here?"

"No, not that I can recall," Leslie answered. "Another dream?"

"No. I found '*MEG*' etched on the bottom of my kitchen table, while I was cleaning up a while back. I thought it was a happy coincidence, but I'm curious about it. Do you know where the table came from?"

Leslie walked over to the table. There was a white table cloth on it. She lifted it from the corner and examined the rough wooden surface beneath it. There was no doubt the table was old. She bent down and tried to see the etching underneath the table. It was clear as day. The large upper-case letters had been scraped in place with something sharp presumably long ago.

"This table belonged to Mrs. Garrett. I'm not sure where she got it from, but I think she had it for a long time," Leslie finally commented. "Maybe she had a young niece named Megan. I really can't say for sure. Maybe it was her son, Chris. He was a handsome boy. He probably had his sights on a girl named Megan, at one time or another."

"I suppose," replied Megan, disappointed. None of her responses were the answers she was hoping to hear. "Thank you, Leslie. I guess I'll do some cleaning up. My friend, Hannah, is stopping by later."

"Okay, I'm going back downstairs. I need to get back to watching my shows. My DVR is running out of space. I'm down to thirty percent! I need to catch up!" She chuckled, as she left and closed the door behind her.

Megan locked it and went into Josh's room to check on him. He seemed too quiet. She stopped at his doorway and saw he was playing with his LEGOs on the floor. He managed to build an elaborate building with balconies and evenly placed windows. The colors matched up nicely, too. It was far beyond his normal crude constructions. She was impressed.

"Wow! What an awesome building, Josh!"

"Thanks, Mommy. Lizzie is helping me." He said it so casually it took a second for her to register it. When it did, it caused the hairs on her arms to stand on end. It implied Lizzie was there in that exact moment. Megan's smile quickly faded away. She was not quite sure how to feel about Lizzie anymore, but the thought of a ghost still scared her.

Megan left the room and went into the bathroom. She closed her eyes and splashed cold water onto her face. She took slow and steady deep breaths, while keeping her eyes shut. She dried her face and hands with the towel and avoided looking into the mirror, at all times.

"Not today," she said.

Megan sat on the edge of her bed thinking back on her time with Herman and how it ended. It worried her to think he might be out of jail. She had a feeling he might be looking for her and Josh. It's something which had been on her mind a lot lately. There were only so many places he might think she could go in California. He knew she was born and raised in New York. She prayed he would not come looking for her. The only thing she had going for her is he had no idea where in New York she grew up. That small fact gave her a little bit of comfort. There was always the slight possibility he was glad they were gone.

Thinking about Herman was starting to depress her and stress her, again. She needed to do something else to get her mind off of him.

She still had a treasure hunt to continue. She could always get back to it. Besides, it was a good day to do some cleaning. She used a small stepladder, which she had purchased before moving in, to check the top shelf of the closet in the hallway. When she looked up there, she found an old newspaper from Sunday, October 30, 1988. It was covered in dust. It was a large stack of pages, although most of the pages had turned yellow from age. She wiped off the dust and brought it down, placing it on the floor.

"This is interesting. I'll look through it later for fun," she said to herself.

She used a brush and proceeded to clean the shelf slowly, not wanting to blow the dust into her face. She thought about what she could store on the upper shelf. It was hard to reach, so it would not be anything she needed anytime soon.

All of a sudden, she felt the stepladder give out from underneath her feet. Before she could react, she was on the floor. Fortunately, she landed on her behind, which padded her fall. She did not understand what happened. It felt as if the stepladder had been pulled away on purpose. She wondered if maybe it was precisely what happened.

Her hand was resting on the newspaper. She picked it up and checked the cover. It had a photo of George Bush facing Michael Dukakis. Bush had defeated him in the election that year and only days later became the next President of the United States. She carefully turned the pages, glancing at the articles and reading some of the comics.

She noticed Josh standing in the hallway watching her. She asked, "How long have you been watching me?"

He shrugged and asked, "Did you fall down? I heard a loud noise."

"Yeah," she nodded. "I fell on my butt. I'm okay, though. Were you checking up on me?" He nodded. "Come here," she beckoned him. He did and she gave him a great big hug. "Do you know how much I love you?" She asked.

"How much?"

She squeezed him, again. "This much!" He giggled and she laughed with him. "Thank you for checking on me. Hey, look what I found."

"What's that?"

"It's an old newspaper from 1988, *waaayyy* before you were born. Before I was born, too! Do you want to look at it with me?"

"Okay," he nodded with uncertainty.

She placed the newspaper on the floor and sat him on her lap. She held him close, as she leaned forward to turn the pages, starting from the beginning, again. She pointed out a few articles and made commentary for him. He looked on interested to see more. She liked how interested he always was in history and science.

When she reached page ten, there was an article about a missing teenage girl from Yonkers. Josh pointed at the photo of the girl and announced, "That's Lizzie! Look, Mommy! Lizzie is in the newspaper!"

Megan felt all the air leave her lungs, as she looked at the girl. She was extremely familiar. Megan knew those eyes. It was the same teenage girl from her nightmares. Lizzie was without a doubt the girl in the basement, except her name was not Lizzie. It was *Margaret Elizabeth Garrett.* Garrett! She was related to Mrs. Garrett. Lizzie was short for Elizabeth. Megan noticed her initials was "M.E.G.," the same initials etched beneath the table! It wasn't Megan!

At last, everything became clear. Megan read the article to herself.


## *Yonkers Teen, Still Missing*


*"On Wednesday, August 31, at approximately 3:30 P.M., Margaret Elizabeth Garrett, 19, of Yonkers went missing.*

*She had been jogging northbound along the Old Croton Aqueduct State Park Trail when she disappeared. She was supposed to meet with her younger brother, Chris, at their home on Walnut Street. She never came home.*

*Witnesses reported last seeing her approach Untermyer Park.*

*She was wearing blue track pants, a white t-shirt, and white sneakers. Her hair was tied back into a ponytail.*

*Police believe she could have been abducted. In recent years, whenever a young woman goes missing in Yonkers, it has resulted in a violent death, sometimes on the anniversary of another similar violent death. Margaret went missing on the 100<sup>th</sup> anniversary of what experts believe to be the first victim of Jack the Ripper, Mary Ann Nichols.*

*This 'Anniversary Killer' has presumably killed several other young women dating back to 1986. All of these women go missing in Yonkers and have been located throughout Westchester County.*

*Authorities are urging anyone with any information to contact the Yonkers Police Department as soon as possible."*

Megan read the article three times, until everything sunk in. It was everything from her nightmares turned into reality. Margaret lived here in the same apartment. She went jogging along a trail near Untermyer Park, leaving behind her younger brother, Chris. She was taken by someone dubbed, "The Anniversary Killer." Hank. Megan knew his name. Margaret was not the first victim. She said she was number five. These were things Megan learned and here they were in the article. She could not believe her eyes.

At last, she finally understood everything. Somehow, the spirit of this murdered girl was trying to show her what happened to her. She needed someone to know. Lizzie was not a bad person or a bad spirit. Yes, she was angry, sad, and frustrated. Who could blame her, after what she went through?

Megan even saw her brother, Chris, waiting for her to come back home. It broke her heart.

Josh looked at his mother and wondered why she had been so silent. He noticed her face was distraught with emotion, so he asked, "Mommy, why are you crying?"

"Give Mommy a moment, baby," she uttered. "I'm so sorry." She felt completely miserable. She had been such an insensitive bitch.

"Why are you sorry?" He stared up at her from her lap.

"Because I didn't understand, but now I do." She looked at him and asked, "Josh, did Lizzie ever tell you her full name?"

"Yeah, but I don't remember it. It was really long."

"Margaret Elizabeth Garrett," Megan stated almost in a trancelike state.

Josh became excited. "Yes! That's it! How did you know, Mommy? Did she tell you? Can you see her?" He looked back toward his bedroom doorway. Megan knew she had been in there with them.

She replied, "No. This article is about her. It says what happened to her long ago. She disappeared one day, after she went jogging."

"She didn't disappear, Mommy," he shook his head. "It was the bad man. He took her. The man with the glasses." Hank.

Megan became immediately concerned. She asked, "Have you seen him?" It never occurred to her how Josh might also be experiencing nightmares.

"No, Mommy," he shook his head, again. She felt relieved. "Lizzie told me about him. Don't worry. She said she will keep me safe, so he never comes for me." He seemed confident in what he was saying.

Megan was not so sure. She asked, "Does she know where he is right now? Is he still alive?" The thought of him still being out there somewhere was deeply disturbing.

Josh shrugged. "I don't know." He looked to his bedroom doorway, again, and then turned back to his mother, and said, "I think she said he's singing." He did not seem certain. His mother was baffled, but then he corrected himself. "Oh, he's at a place called Sing Sing. Lizzie said it's a prison."

Megan turned toward his room and, for the first time, was hoping to see Lizzie. She did not. She stated, "I'm sorry I didn't listen to you. I promise from now on I will."

Josh was confused. "You weren't listening to me, Mommy?"

"Yes, I heard you, baby. I was talking to Lizzie… to Margaret."

"Oh," he responded a little puzzled by her statement. He was still unaware of her nightmares, so he did not know the connection his mother shared with his friend. He had no idea how deep it went.

"Josh? The other day you mentioned dreaming about Lizzie. Do you dream about her a lot?" She wanted to know how much he had seen of her life through his dreams. She prayed it was not nearly as much as she had seen.

"Yes," he nodded.

Next, she asked, "What do you dream about?"

"Sometimes, we're in the park. The one with the pretty secret garden. It has walls around it, and statues. I like it there. So does Lizzie. It's her favorite place."

"What kind of statues? Do you remember?"

"Really tall ones. They look like lions with wings. There's lions spitting water into the swimming pool, too. All the buildings are white. Oh, and there are fish in the water. Sometimes, we feed the fish. I like doing that."

It certainly sounded like someplace from a dream to her. She had no idea of any place like that. Lions with wings? Lions spitting water into a pool. It sounded magical. She was relieved. As long as he was not dreaming of Hank.

For a long time, the two of them sat on the floor silently with the newspaper open to the article. Megan realized her secret project had only just begun. She had barely scratched the surface of this growing mystery. There was still so much more she did not know. It was going to take some serious research, but at least, she had somewhere to begin. She finally had names and an exact date.

She still was unclear what Margaret wanted from her, but this was a start. She had a sinking feeling more information would be revealed in her next nightmare. She knew it was something she would have to endure, if she wanted to learn the rest of the story. She would learn to overcome her fear and deal with it, if she was going to help Margaret. She wanted so much to help her. She knew it was the reason behind the nightmares. The poor girl desperately needed her help. This time, Megan would come through.

One thing was certain, she could not wait to tell Hannah about what she learned today. She felt newly inspired to search every dark corner of the apartment for more clues. Who knew what else was hidden away? Maybe there were more old newspapers.

# Chapter 9

## Paranormal Witness

Before Megan could turn her apartment upside down searching for lost treasures of the Garrett family, Hannah texted her to let her know she was on her way. She was able to get out of work early. She felt generous and offered to pick up some Spanish food on the way. Megan gladly accepted. It was something she had not eaten since living in Chico with Herman.

Herman was without question not who she wanted to think about.

When Megan mentioned Spanish food to Josh, it must have triggered memories of California for him, as well, because he brought up the subject of his father, for the first time, in weeks, much to her regret. It was the last thing she wanted to discuss.

"Mommy, will we ever see Daddy, again?" He tilted his head in an angle, as he stared up at her, waiting for an answer.

She took a deep breath before tackling his question. She knew the subject would come up eventually. It did not make it any easier to talk about. She was lucky to have avoided it for the past few months. She tried her best to answer his question without making her intense hatred for Herman too obvious.

"Well, I don't really know, Josh. He's very far away, all the way on the other side of the country. To be honest, we probably won't see him for a very long time." She hoped her response would somehow satisfy him. She hesitated before asking, "Do you miss him?" She swallowed nervously. She already knew the answer to her question. Of course, he missed his father.

"A little bit," he nodded. Not as bad as she thought. He asked, "He was mean, right?"

She looked down, as she responded, not wanting to make eye contact for fear she would reveal too much, "Yes, he was very mean, baby. He was not always a good person. Not to me and not to you." She looked at him and added, "*But* he is still your father. Someday, you will see him, again."

"Okay, Mommy," he commented with a sad look on his face.

She felt so bad for him. She needed to do something with him to cheer him up. "Would you like to sit and watch TV with me, until Auntie Hannah comes over? She'll be here soon."

"Yes," he nodded.

"Come on." She put her arm around him, as they approached the sofa together.

They sat down and Megan turned on the television. She flipped through the channels, until she found a movie appropriate for Josh. It was one of the "*Jurassic Park*" movies. He loved dinosaurs, so he was thrilled when he saw them on the television.

While they watched the movie, Megan pondered if Margaret's spirit was nearby. Was she watching them? She could always ask Josh. If only she had Misty's gift, so she could know herself. Megan speculated on her rare gift to be able to detect the presence of spiritual energy. While it could be a gift, it could also be a terrifying curse. Not all spirits are good, so actually knowing when one was nearby could either be good or really bad.

However, Megan did not believe Margaret was a bad spirit. Not anymore. After all, she treated Josh well. That had to count for something. She was a victim. She was only trying to make her story known. It's what Megan believed. She accepted it and was ready to learn the rest of the dark tale when it became necessary. It was her duty.

There were no signs indicating Margaret was in the room with them, although she was there. Margaret's spirit stood in the corner watching them. She longed for the life she lost so long ago. She watched these people living in her home. So much time had gone by, since her passing, although to her time was inconsequential. Her life from over thirty years ago did not feel like so long ago to her. She could easily be in that moment, again, in an instant. It was her ongoing nightmare. It never seemed to end. She felt the pain today, as much as she did back then.

The only time she could ever escape it was whenever she retreated back here to the apartment. It was her safe place. Her home. At least, it used to be. Now, it belonged to someone else.

She prayed Megan would be the one to finally help her. No one else ever listened to her before. Not her brother and not her mother. She tried to tell them so many times. She tried getting through to them any way she could. It made no difference. Her brother always ignored the signs, while her mother was in denial about her death. The poor woman would not give up hope, until the day she died.

Over the long years, Margaret was doomed to suffer alone, until Megan and Josh moved into her home. She knew things would be different with them. They noticed her. Josh acknowledged her presence, right away, and he accepted her. It took Megan a while, but she finally understood. She was no longer afraid, which meant she might actually help her. Margaret hoped so.

She cried alone in her corner, not wanting Josh to see her this way. She always tried to be happy when she was around him. He was such a sweet young soul. She truly cared for him. He reminded her so much of her little brother, Chris, when he was the same age. Oh, how she missed him. She continued to cry.

Margaret hated this miserable existence, but it seemed she was trapped indefinitely. Her only hope was for someone to find her body. Megan was that hope. First, she had to see it, which meant more nightmares for her. It was the only way to show her. She hated reliving those moments. She wanted to forget everything that happened to her, but she could not. It would be burned into her memory forever. She always knew it, since that day *he* took her.

She watched the television, which was much larger than any she ever owned. It looked like a mini theater to her. She envied Josh. He was going to have a good life. He would never know the pain she knew. So long as he lived under the same roof as her, she would see to it he was always safe. Her reach outside the apartment was limited at best. She would do the best she could to watch over him, as promised.

If her body was found, she could be free to go wherever she wanted to go. Then, she could truly watch over him for his entire life. For that reason alone, she felt it was crucial for Megan to help her. Of course, more than anything, Margaret longed to be free of the nightmares. She had to live them. She could not wake from them like Megan.

Margaret closed her eyes tight. The tears kept coming. She hid the only way she knew how by fading away into nothing.

About a half hour later, Hannah arrived. She was soaking wet. It was still raining outside. Megan helped her with her bags and put the food on the table. She began setting up plates and utensils for them to use, while Hannah put her duffle bag and purse on the sofa beside Josh. She gave him a big hug when she saw him, and then he continued watching the movie.

Hannah sighed and stated, "It is really coming down outside. Look at me. I'm drenched."

Megan glanced at her, while setting the table and said, "Well, you're the one, who insisted on coming over today. Don't blame me."

"Someone has to keep an eye on you, before you have another panic attack in front of your son."

Megan smirked, "That was a rare instance. I'll tell you why it happened a bit later when we have time to chat. Let's eat. This smells delicious and I'm starving. Wash your hands, Josh. It's time for dinner."

Josh went into the bathroom to wash his hands, while Hannah took a seat at the table.

She asked, "What do you have to drink around here? Got any wine?"

"Red?"

"You know it," Hannah grinned. She whispered, "So, what happened?"

Josh came out of the bathroom and approached the table. He sat down before Megan could say anything. She responded, "Later. Trust me. It will be worth the wait."

They dined on their Spanish cuisine enjoying every tasty morsel. There was white rice and red beans with beef stew for everyone. Josh drank soda from a cup with a straw, while the ladies sipped red wine in wine glasses. They were able to enjoy a peaceful meal together.

Later, Josh went to his room to play. It was story time. Megan told Hannah everything. She updated her on the nightmares, and then she brought out the newspaper. She opened it to page ten and pointed to the black and white photo of Margaret Elizabeth Garrett.

"It's her, Hannah. This is Lizzie. Her name was Margaret."

"Oh, my God! Meg, where did you get this newspaper?" She read the date, "1988???"

"It was up in the hall closet. When Josh saw the photo, he became excited and pointed at her, claiming it was Lizzie. Hannah, this is the girl I've been dreaming about. This Anniversary Killer they mention has to be Hank. She told me she was number five. He was abducting and killing women since 1986. The article mentioned she had a younger brother named Chris. It has to be the teenage boy I saw in the last dream. It all makes sense. You were right. Josh and I are both being haunted by a teenage girl, who used to live here."

Hannah was in shock, even though she already suspected it. To see the photo in the newspaper made everything seem much more believable. Finally, she commented, "I just had a thought. What if that poor girl doesn't even know she's dead?"

Megan shook her head, "I don't think so. I think she knows. Remember she told Josh she's really old. It must mean she is aware of the passage of time. It's been more than thirty years. Her mother is gone, if she was her mother. Yes, it has to be because Chris was Margaret's brother and Leslie told me Mrs. Garrett had a son named Chris." Megan thought about it momentarily and then suggested, "I wonder if Leslie could tell us more. I asked her about any former tenant named Lizzie. She did not remember. Maybe she never knew Margaret's middle name was Elizabeth."

"It would be worth a shot," Hannah admitted. "Let's get her up here."

"Hopefully, she's not busy." Megan pulled out her phone and gave Leslie a call.


Several minutes later, Leslie was in Megan's apartment seated at the kitchen table with them. Megan showed her the newspaper article and pointed out the photo of Margaret. She asked, "Do you remember this girl? She lived here. Didn't she?"

Leslie cocked her head and examined the photo. She pulled the newspaper closer. A look of recognition immediately appeared on her face. "Oh, my Lord! Where in God's name did you get this newspaper? Did you find it here?" She stared in amazement at Megan.

"Yes," Megan answered. "It was in the hall closet. So, you *do* know her?"

Leslie nodded eagerly, "Yes! Yes, I do know her, or rather, I did. She was Mrs. Garrett's daughter, Maggie." She pointed at the photo, still surprised to be looking at the old newspaper and a face she had not seen in decades. She continued, "She disappeared when I was a teenager. We weren't really friends, but I knew her. She was an acquaintance. I remember her being so nice. Everyone liked her. She was a sweetheart."

She paused, before reaching into the rest of her memories, which were much darker. "No one knew what happened to her. It wasn't until weeks later. The rumors started about her being one of the victims of some awful serial killer." She paused, again. A look of sorrow was on her face. A moment later, she added, "They got him." Both Megan and Hannah shot each other a quick look, before turning their attention back on Leslie. "Yeah," she nodded with some satisfaction. "He got arrested about a year later, but he was never charged with Maggie's murder. No one could ever prove he took her. I don't know. Maybe he didn't." She shrugged. "One thing was for sure. He took those other girls. He did terrible things to them, and then he murdered them. I think there were about five victims. I still say they should have given him the death penalty for the things he did to those poor girls." She closed her eyes and shook her head, as if trying to shake away bad memories.

Megan and Hannah sat there silently taking in everything Leslie told them. It all added up to what they already knew, while adding some more background information to the mystery. Two pieces of information stood out the most to Megan. Margaret never got justice for what she knew happened to her. Of course, no one was going to take the word of her nightmares as the truth. The other thing was the fact Hank got arrested and was doing time at Sing Sing.

She asked to get confirmation, "Is Hank still in prison?"

Leslie immediately stared at her in confusion. "How did you know his name was Hank? It's not mentioned in this article."

Megan was stumped. She slipped up and did not know what to say. She looked to Hannah for help. Hannah nodded at her, giving her a signal to tell her the truth.

"Okay," she nodded back at Hannah. She turned back to Leslie and began, "I have to tell you something you might not believe, but I swear on my son, it is all true."

Megan told Leslie everything, starting with the crazy nightmares, Josh's supposed "imaginary" friend, Lizzie, and finally she spoke of the strange occurrences taking place in the apartment. Afterwards, she mentioned how she finally started to connect everything together, once she found the old newspaper. Leslie was astonished. She could not believe her ears, but the things Megan told her, especially the nightmares, were too incredible to dismiss. Megan knew details she should not have known. She was able to describe Margaret's younger brother and how Margaret wore her hair whenever she went jogging. She even knew what was on Margaret's t-shirt on the day she disappeared, which was never mentioned in any of the newspaper articles. However, Leslie recalled the t-shirt because it was from a book she read called "*No Hope for the Hopeless at Kings Park.*"

By the time Megan was finished, she brought out the journal she had been keeping to show it to Leslie, along with the sketch of the basement. Looking at it gave Leslie chills. She had been there before, many years ago.

"I've been here," she confessed, while holding the sketch. "After it was abandoned. I went here with some friends during the early 2000s. Dear God. This is exactly how I remember it."

"Where is it?" Hannah asked. Megan shot her a look.

"Oh, I don't really remember. It was so long ago. I never went back." She shook her head. "People used to say it was haunted. It was too eerie being there. And you saw this place in your dreams?"

"In my nightmares," Megan corrected her. "This is where everything happened."

Hannah asked, "Do you think you could find the place, if we drove around tomorrow?"

Leslie looked disgusted. "Why on Earth would you want to go there?"

Megan admitted, "I think I need to see it for myself... to know it's real. Believe me, I don't want to go there, but I feel like I need to... for Margaret."

Leslie nodded, "I understand. I can try to take you there, if you'd like or, maybe at least, point you in the right direction. I don't really remember the exact location, but I know it was near the trail."

"Which trail?" Hannah asked.

Leslie responded, "The Old Croton Aqueduct Trail. That's where a few of the girls went missing, including Maggie." She looked sad when she thought about her. Old feelings from long ago were coming back. There was guilt because she never became friends with Margaret, even though they were neighbors. She also felt fear because she thought she would be abducted, too. She spent a good part of her young adult life being paranoid.

It was agreed. In the morning, Hannah would drive them near the trail, until something looked familiar to Leslie. She was hesitant about going back, but she knew how important it was to Megan. Hannah assured her, she only had to point the way. She could always wait in the car. Leslie liked the idea. Megan called Misty and asked her if she could watch Josh the next day.

Misty had other plans, but she was able to reschedule them. While she was not too wild about the idea of being back in the apartment on what should have been her day off, she reluctantly consented. She did not want to disappoint Megan, who sounded desperately in need of her services.

Later in the evening, Hannah prepared to sleep in Megan's room with her. She looked forward to sleeping on her comfortable bed. She claimed she would be a better sleep buddy than the last time she stayed over. Megan was half convinced she would not have a nightmare because of her newfound understanding of what happened to Margaret. She and Hannah spent several minutes planning their morning excursion, before falling asleep. Hannah wanted to be sure this was something Megan was ready to do.

She asked, "Meg, are you sure about this? Maybe we can find another way." She had no problem going, but she was concerned for Megan's well-being.

"I have to do this for her," Megan replied bravely.

Hannah accepted her reasoning. "Okay, then we'll do it together," she replied. Satisfied, she turned around and eased into a cozy slumber.

Not long after they fell asleep at around 1 A.M., Megan had another nightmare. Surprisingly, this one did not take place in the basement. She was standing in a small bathroom in a house. A white sink was in front of her. It was dirty and stained with yellow rings. She looked up into the mirror on the wall and did not see her face. It was Margaret's reflection, who stared back at her.

She proceeded to wash her face and hair at the sink using a worn bar of soap. She rinsed out her mouth with mouthwash. She was spitting out blood. Next, she washed her body using a towel, which she soaked in soap and water. She scrubbed herself clean with the towel. Yet somehow, she did not feel clean enough.

While it felt as if it were her doing these actions, she knew it was actually Margaret, who was in the bathroom cleaning herself.

When she was done, she looked up into the mirror and her heart began pounding in her chest when she saw Hank standing behind her. She wanted to close her eyes and make it all go away. She tried. It did not work. She dared not turn around. Seeing him face to face would only confirm he was standing there. She hoped she was only seeing things in the mirror, which were not truly there. Of course, she was wrong.

Hank leaned in close to her and sniffed her damp hair. They locked eyes in the mirror. He was not wearing his glasses. An evil grin spread across his pale face. He placed his left hand onto her forehead and began caressing her hair slowly. Her instinct was to pull away, but he held her head in place. His eyes told her not to try that again. Words were not necessary. She knew better, so she remained in place.

Hank stepped closer pressing his crotch against her rear end. He was erect. He held her head firmly with one hand, and then rapidly moved his right hand up to her neck. He cut fast and hard. It was a blur of motion so fast she did not realize what he was doing, until it was too late. She realized there was a sharp knife in his hand and he used it to slit her throat open.

She panicked when she saw the blood rushing out from the deep gash in her neck. All at once, she felt pain, fear, anger, and shock. She became lightheaded and blacked out. Her wet body slid down to the cold tiled floor of the bathroom, as the life slipped out of her.

Megan was horrified. He killed her! The evil bastard killed Margaret!

Hank stood over her limp body and looked down on her hungrily, while the blood spread across the floor like a blossoming red rose. He bent down to undress her, and then pulled down his jeans. Torturing her, raping her, and killing her was not enough. He had to humiliate her even further by having sex with her corpse.

The next thing he did was even worse. The demented monster began sucking on her breasts. He dug his teeth into her flesh and bit off one of her nipples. He then got back to his feet. He took the nipple out of his mouth and placed it on the sink.

Megan felt so disgusted she almost did not notice Margaret's spirit standing there in the bathroom looking down on the scene. She was crying. Suddenly, she screamed out in anger and slammed her fist into the mirror shattering it into dozens of pieces sending broken shards into Hank's face.

The loud crash of the smashed mirror woke Megan from her nightmare. "It's not real," she breathed out the words, except she knew it was real and it happened a long time ago. She sat up in her bed, just in time to see the blinds on her window get pulled all the way up on their own. She turned toward her nightstand to see the time. It was 3:37 A.M. She turned on the lamp and got out of bed.

Hannah woke up from the sudden movements. She was groggy, as she squinted her eyes at the light from the lamp and inquired, "Another nightmare?"

"Yes," Megan answered angrily, while walking to the window. She was not angry with Margaret or Hannah. Hank was the object of her fury. What he did was unforgivable. Megan examined the blinds and saw how the cord had been neatly wrapped around both ends. She was baffled. "How the hell did she do this so fast?"

"Huh? What are you talking about?" Hannah asked, still half asleep. She sat up.

Megan did not answer. Instead, she took a deep breath and broke down crying. Hannah climbed out of bed and hurried to her side. Megan collapsed into her arms sobbing hysterically. Hannah held her best friend close and tried to comfort her. She was at loss for words. While she was curious about the nightmare, she knew now was not the time to ask about it. It would have to wait. Her friend needed her.


The next day, they had breakfast in silence. Hannah did not ask about the nightmare. She knew Megan would tell her when she was ready. Besides, she knew not with Josh around. Misty arrived, soon after they were done eating. Megan took out her journal and began diligently writing down the latest nightmare. When she was done, she hid the journal in her bedroom. Afterwards, she and Hannah went downstairs and knocked on Leslie's door. When she came out, she was ready to go.

The three of them got into Hannah's car and drove toward Yonkers Avenue. Leslie sat in the front passenger seat to better guide them. Megan made herself comfortable in the seat behind Hannah. It was then when she told them about the latest nightmare.

"I know how he killed her. She showed me last night. This time, I was standing in a small bathroom. I was her. She washed herself, and then he appeared behind her. He pressed up against her and slit her throat open with a knife. That's how it happened. He killed her, and then the sick *motherfucker* had sex with her corpse on the bathroom floor in a pool of her blood." Both Hannah and Leslie listened in horror, while Megan disclosed the rest. "He bit off one of her nipples and saved it as a damned souvenir. How did the police not find it when they arrested him???"

Leslie commented, "Dear Lord! That's horrible! Honey, keep in mind, we are going purely by your nightmares. As real as they may seem, it doesn't mean that was exactly how things played out. We are assuming it is the case for the sake of learning the truth of what happened to Maggie. Sadly, her body was never found."

Megan turned to her and asked, "Really? Jesus Christ. No wonder she's been haunting me. She wants justice. She wants to be found. Maybe she's leading up to the moment. Maybe she can guide me there."

Hannah added, "Yeah, but first she wants to show you every sordid detail from that nightmarish day, up until the precise moment. Be sure to write everything down in your journal, no matter how inconsequential it may seem, at the time. Don't leave anything out."

"I know. I've been doing my best to remember every detail."

Leslie tried to guide Hannah which way to go, leading her to North Broadway. They took that road going northbound. She instructed, "If we go this way, we can stay close to the trail. You can't drive on it, so we need to follow it closely. I know I turned down one of these streets, but I forgot which one. It was so long ago and everything looks different. I don't have a car and normally don't come around this neighborhood. It brings back too many bad memories. This area is all unfamiliar to me."

Hannah responded, "It's okay. Pay attention and try to think about anything that stands out."

As the car approached Untermyer Park, Megan perked up and locked onto the entrance road. Next, she saw the long stone wall of the garden extending about a block long. "What is that place on the left?" She pointed.

Hannah replied, "Untermyer Park. Should I go in there?"

"Yes! Wait. No. I mean, I don't know. Maybe. What do you think, Leslie?"

Leslie shook her head, "No, not there. I would have remembered if it was in there. That's where he grabbed his first victim. Not Maggie. However, this park does have a wonderful garden, if you ever have the time to visit."

Megan leaned forward and repeated, "Garden? Are there tall white statues and water with fish?"

"Yes," Leslie replied, while looking back at her. "Have you been here?"

"Turn around, Hannah! I need to go there!" Megan demanded.

Hannah did not question her friend. She found a place to make a U-turn and went back toward the park's entrance road.

They entered Untermyer Park and found a parking in the lot. At that point, Hannah spoke, "Okay, we're here. What's up? Why do you need to come here? You never mentioned this place before."

"I need to see the garden. Josh said Lizzie takes him to a special secret garden in his dreams. It was her favorite place. He said there are tall statues of lions with wings and…"

Leslie interrupted, "Oh, yes. The griffin statues near the old theater stage."

Megan asked, "What? So, it's true. This place is real. Josh described it to me, except he's never been here for real. Only in his dreams. I *need* to see it."

Hannah stated, "Okay, okay. Calm down. Let's go check it out."

They exited the car and walked along a path to the walled garden. They had to pass through a gate to reach it. As soon as they entered, Megan soaked in the beauty. There was a long moat filled with water, leading to two sets of tall columns. The columns supported two griffin statues high above, which seemed like guardians overlooking the beautiful Persian garden. Colorful flowers and bushes lined the moat on either side.

"This place is amazing," she commented.

She looked to her left and saw a large white pavilion made up of a series of columns in a circular fashion. There was scaffolding around it, indicating it was being repaired. To her right was the wall she saw from the road. There was a bench under a small pergola awning. She wondered, where was the swimming pool Josh spoke about.

She turned to Leslie and asked, "Is there a swimming pool in here?"

Hannah looked at her like she was crazy.

Leslie explained, "There has not been a swimming pool here since the 1970s, as far as I can recall." She pointed past the pavilion. "It was just past that area."

They walked toward the pavilion. There were steps leading down to another section of the garden. They went down the steps and around to the other side of the pavilion. There was a large empty pit, which once served as the pool she referred to. The tiled floor in the pit was severely damaged and corroded. You could tell there were once fancy pictures of sea creatures, which were currently broken up into small pieces. Megan noticed small pipes sticking out of the wall behind the lower part of the pavilion, which curved in an arc.

She asked, "What were those pipes for?"

Leslie answered, "Oh, yes. I believe those were beautiful fountains shaped like lion heads. Water used to pour from their mouths into the pool. You know, it really wasn't intended to be a swimming pool, but a lot of kids used to swim in here anyway. I know I did. It was free." She smiled, as she reminisced.

Megan stated, Josh saw the lion head fountains in his dream. He said they were spitting out water. He described this garden to me, as if he'd been here, but in the past. She brought him here more than once in his dreams." She scoffed, "She shows him the dreams and gives me the nightmares."

Hannah replied, "Better that way, than the other way around. Don't you think?"

"Yeah, definitely," Megan agreed. "Hm. Maybe I should bring him here, someday. I mean, when this is all over."

Hannah nodded, "Yeah, *we* should do that. I'll drive you."

"Thanks."

"So?" Hannah asked, "Are we ready to move on? We have other places to go, in case you forgot, unless you're stalling because you changed your mind and don't want to go."

"No, that's not it," Megan responded. "I'm ready. Let's get out of here."


Within minutes, they left the park and were back on North Broadway going north.

Leslie stated, "I think it was further up, after this hospital, on the left. St. John's Riverside."

Hannah glanced at the hospital, as she drove by it, and continued north toward the next intersection. Megan looked back at the park as they drove away from it. She remembered the newspaper article mentioned Margaret was last seen jogging in the direction of the park. There was also what Leslie mentioned about the first victim being abducted there. Who was she? It was another mystery, but one to be solved another time, after some research.

They stopped at a red light and that's when Leslie saw something, which struck a chord within her. She looked at Odell Avenue. It was a winding hill going down westward toward the Hudson River. Leslie sat up in her seat and tried to see beyond the crest of the hill.

"Down there. Make a left here," she pointed. "We need to go down this hill. It's that way."

Hannah asked, "Are you sure?"

"Positive! I remember this hill."

Megan turned her attention toward the hill on Odell Avenue. They descended the hill slowly. The hospital and a rear parking lot were on the left side, while on the right was a tall stone wall marking the edge of the Alder Manor estate. They continued driving down the winding road, which eventually led them to Warburton Avenue. Halfway down, there were houses on both sides of the street and a building on the corner at the end. Megan felt a sense of familiarity, which she could not explain. She knew they were close, but they were facing the wrong way.

"We passed it," she announced, out of the blue.

Hannah glanced at her in the rearview mirror and commented, "Huh?"

Then Leslie agreed, "Yes, she's right. I'm terribly sorry. I did not realize it. We did go past it. I was distracted by the park on the left. Can you go back up the hill? This time, go slower."

Hannah made a U-turn and drove back up the hill. She found a parking, after the first curve and pulled into the spot. She stared straight ahead at the next turn, which went right. On her left was an opening into a park of some kind. She wondered if it might have been the trail. She pointed and asked, "What's over there? Is it the trail?"

Leslie stretched her neck and tried to get a better look. "Yes, I believe so. I think we're in the right place. We should walk from here. The trail entrance is on both sides of the street, but that is the one we want. It's all coming back to me, little by little."

Hannah turned to Leslie and asked, "Are you sure you want to come with us? Megan and I can go check it out, while you wait here. I'll leave the car running."

Megan did not wait. She got out of the car and started walking to the trail entrance on her own. Hannah called after her, "Meg! Wait for me!" She turned to Leslie. "What's it gonna be? It's go time!"

Leslie hesitated, before swallowing and saying, "Then, I suppose we'd better get going."

Megan stood at the entrance of the Old Croton Aqueduct Trail. Perhaps, she was waiting for the others. Something stopped her from walking along the trail. In her mind's eye, she could see the trail from her second dream about Margaret. It was totally different. This was not the right place. Yet, she knew she was very close. About a minute later, Hannah and Leslie were behind her.

Hannah asked, "Are you okay, Meg?"

"Yeah, I'm good. Just a little confused. I had a flashback. This place is… different."

Leslie informed them, "The place where Margaret disappeared is further south. It was before Untermyer Park. It's not where we were going. The house and garage with the basement are this way."

She pointed to what appeared to be a closed road between the trail entrance and the tall stone wall, bordering the rear of the Lenoir Nature Preserve. A metallic bar blocked a long cobblestone driveway, which seemed to disappear into the woods. The path was unkempt, cluttered with overgrown trees and weeds.

Leslie led them around the roadblock and onto the cobblestone path. They had to duck under a fallen tree. The wilderness around the path had grown so out of control, it was hard to see anything beyond the woods. At last, they reached a clearing near the end of the driveway. It led to an abandoned structure one story in height.

Leslie froze in place, as she acclimated herself with her surroundings. Hannah and Megan waited for her to get her bearings. Leslie took a few cautious steps forward and looked around in amazement. Finally, she spoke, "Please, give me a moment. It's changed so much." She looked ahead to her right. "The house was over there. It's gone now. Demolished." She turned back to the lone structure. "That was a two-story garage. It was the family business. People used to bring their cars here to get them fixed. No one ever suspected he was a monster."

Megan asked sounding disappointed, "Was the basement in the house?"

Leslie turned to face them. "No," she shook her head. "It was behind the garage." She turned back to face the structure and pointed to the far left. There was an opening in what appeared to be a rear storage area. "It's in there. This is as far as I'm going. I can't go back in there."

Hannah put her hand on Leslie's shoulder and said, "It's okay. Thanks for taking us this far. We've got it from here." She looked at Megan, who was already walking to the dark opening. Hannah started after her.

When Megan reached the doorway, she paused. She looked into the dark room. It looked like the basement of a warehouse. As soon as Hannah was at her side, she stepped through the opening. It was large enough for a small car. Graffiti covered the concrete walls. There were two rusted metal support beams in the center of the room. A large doorway on the left side at the rear led to another back room. They approached it together. Small windows situated close to the ceiling on their left allowed for some light to enter only slightly illuminating the way. There was rubble and debris scattered around and piled up in the corners.

The next room was darker, but more basement-like and less like a garage. There was a large puddle of rain water built up at the center of the room. It took a moment for their eyes to adjust to the darkness. Once they could see, they proceeded forward around the puddle. The walls in this room were brick and also covered with graffiti and years of dust.

The next chamber beyond it was much darker. There were more bricks and more graffiti. Insulation dangled from the pipes going across the ceiling creating an eerie effect and casting shadows on the walls and floor. At the end of the room was a set of broken wooden double doors barely hanging from their hinges. Megan knew right away, that was it. It was the basement room.

She ignored everything else and went straight for those doors. The second she entered the last room her heart sank. At the mere sight of the brick columns and horse stall to her left, she began having difficulty with her breathing. She felt dizzy and weak in her knees when she saw there was still rope tied to the wooden horse stall support beams, which went up to the ceiling. She could not breathe. How many women hung from those ropes? Her eyes began to roll back into her head and everything faded away to darkness. She slipped away and dropped.

Hannah stepped forward in time to catch Megan before she hit the dark, cold, wet floor. She tried to shake her, while calling out to her, "Meg! Meg! Wake up! Hey!" She had to lean against the horse stall to keep from falling with her. She was able to free up one of her hands. She slapped Megan's face softly. "Meg! Snap out of it!"

Megan began to come to and her breathing began to steady. She opened her eyes and felt so weak. Her face was cold with sweat. The first thing she saw was the brick column across from the horse stall. It was the very same view she had in several of her nightmares. She began to panic, again.

"No! No! I don't want to be here!" She pulled away from Hannah and ran out of the basement. She did not stop, until she reached daylight. Leslie was waiting outside to catch her before she ran straight into the woods.

"Megan, honey! Relax. I have you." She held her. "It's going to be okay. Shh. Try to relax," she told her. Megan cried, as Leslie held her.

Hannah came rushing behind her out of the abandoned structure. She was relieved when she saw Leslie had grabbed onto Megan. She walked over to them and took a moment to catch her breath. Hannah and Leslie gave each other a look of concern for Megan, who was crying onto Leslie's shoulder. Leslie tried her best to comfort her. Hannah turned and stared back into the dark doorway. She wondered how many poor girls died in there without the option to run out like they just did. Were there other victims no one knew about?

She had a feeling there were.

# Chapter 10

## It Has to End

Megan, Hannah, and Leslie sat quietly in the car, which was still parked on Odell Avenue. They sat in their previous seating arrangement from earlier. Each was lost in her own thoughts, after leaving the abandoned structure, which once belonged to a notorious serial killer. Megan closed her eyes and leaned her head back against the backseat. She was still reeling from actually standing in the infamous basement she had dreamt about over the last ten days. Being in there was a lot harder than she thought it would be. Hannah watched her in the rearview mirror. She was concerned for her best friend's sanity, although she remained silent. She knew Megan was not yet ready to discuss their experience.

Leslie sat in the front passenger seat feeling a combination of sorrow, anger, regret, and relief. She was sad for being reminded of what happened to Margaret so many years earlier. She was angry because it happened to more than one woman. She regretted never getting to know Margaret as a friend. Lastly, she was relieved because she would never have to return to the basement ever again.

For several minutes, none of them said a word. Hannah adjusted the air conditioner, making it cooler. It was a humid day and they were sweating from their short hike to the basement and back. She wanted to turn on the radio, but it did not seem like a good time. Normally, music always soothed her, but this was not about her.

At last, she broke the silence. "That was something, huh? It looked exactly like your sketch, Meg. Totally unreal, but at the same time, all too real."

Leslie nodded in agreement.

Megan still said nothing.

Hannah made a suggestion, hoping it would help. "Are you guys hungry? I know where there's an Applebee's not far from here. My treat." She glanced back at Megan. "Besides, I could really use a drink."

Leslie looked at her and responded, "I think I could use one, too."

Hannah eyed Megan using the rearview mirror. They made eye contact and Megan nodded. It was enough. Hannah pulled out of the parking spot and drove up the hill back to North Broadway. The ride to Applebee's was quiet. It only took a few minutes to get there. Once they arrived, they walked inside, and waited to be seated.

Seconds later, they were seated and began scanning their menus for something to eat. Hannah was really the only one who had an appetite. She planned to order a meal. Megan was not very enthusiastic about eating. She simply stared at the menu's cover. Leslie decided on something light to go with her drink. The drink is what she really wanted. It was what she needed.

Hannah looked across the table at Megan and asked, "What's going through your mind, Meg? Talk to me. You're being too quiet for my taste. I need to know you're okay."

Megan took a deep breath and replied, while still staring down at the menu, "I just can't believe how similar it still looks, aside from it being abandoned, and covered with graffiti and debris. Even the ropes were still there!" She looked at Hannah and continued, "It seems so much more real to me, after having seen it in person. You know? Before, I could tell myself it was only a dream, but now?" She shook her head in disbelief. "Oh, my God. Now, I keep thinking about the horrible things he did to her, and who knows what else he did to those other girls? This is worse than any horror movie I've ever seen."

"I get it," Hannah replied. "It's a lot to take in. Keep in mind, you don't have to deal with this alone. You have me. I am always going to be here for you. *Always*. I can stay with you, as long as you need me to."

"Thank you," Megan said. "I appreciate it. I just need time to process this whole thing."

Leslie added, "The important thing is what happens next. I believe there is a reason why Maggie has been visiting you in your dreams. She needs something done and she probably thinks you can help her."

Megan agreed, "Yes, I know. I think I know what she wants from me, but I still need more information from her. I think she wants me to help find her body. It's horrible how she's still out there somewhere."

Leslie sighed heavily and nodded, "Yes, the poor dear girl. She did not deserve this fate." She shook her head sadly.

Hannah stated with feeling, "No girl deserves this fate."

Megan was filled with anger and needed it to be known. She raised her voice, "Hank deserves worse! That piece of shit is probably relaxing in some prison cell knowing he literally got away with murder, even if he did get charged with other murders. He got away with killing *her*, and that is unacceptable, especially with the things he did to her!" She took a breath and added, "Oh, how I wish I could see him dead. I want him to die a slow painful death."

Hannah looked around at the patrons sitting at nearby tables. They were watching. She became concerned and spoke in a near whisper, "Easy there, Meg. Lower your voice. We're in a public place. Let's change the subject. Okay?"

"Yeah, sure," Megan responded unconcerned about any listeners. She finally opened the menu and began checking the meals for something she could handle. She was not too hungry.

They ordered their food. It arrived, a short time later. Hannah was the only one who ordered a full lunch. Leslie ordered a salad, while Megan merely picked at the appetizers. All three drank alcoholic beverages, though. It's what they really wanted, a little something to help them cope with the rough day they were having.

Once they were done, they returned to the Hill View. Leslie said her farewells and went to her apartment, while Megan and Hannah went up to Megan's apartment. Misty was glad to see them. She was eager to leave. Apparently, a certain spirit was anxiously awaiting their return, as well, so her presence was quite strong in the apartment, which was more than Misty could handle.

After a quick goodbye, she went home.


Megan and Hannah sat on the sofa in front of the television. Josh sat on the floor beside them, while drawing pictures of the Mandalorian. Hannah held the remote control and was channel surfing hoping to find something they could watch to help get Megan's mind off of the day's events. She finally settled on a romantic comedy starring Ben Stiller and Drew Barrymore. Right away, she began laughing.

Megan took a while to ease her mind. Her mind was not focused on the movie, but rather on her nightmares. She kept playing them over in her head. For the first time, she actually wanted to go to sleep, so she could find out what happened next. In a way, she simply wanted to get it over with already and be done with the nightmares. She wanted it to end, so she could lock it away and never think about it, again.

However, she also genuinely wanted to help Margaret to find the peace she deserved. It was long overdue.

She looked around the room and wondered if her spirit was there with them. She glanced down at Josh, who was busy drawing and coloring. He did not appear to be distracted by the television, or Margaret's presence, which led Megan to believe Margaret was not around. At least, not at the moment. Megan began watching the movie mainly to pass the time, while keeping an eye on Josh for any hints he might be looking at his friend. Eventually, she found herself smiling at the humorous scenes in the movie. Laughter was always a good cure for misery.

By the time, the next movie came on, Megan was focused on the television. She and Hannah watched *"Forrest Gump"* for the umpteenth time. It was a movie they both loved, but never watched together, until now.

Eventually, it was time to make dinner. Josh had to be hungry, even if he was not acting like it. Megan got up and went into the kitchen to make something for them to eat. She started peeling potatoes, so she could make fries. She also prepared some chicken legs to fry. Hannah was not too hungry, since she ate a full lunch earlier. However, she did get up from the sofa to help with dinner.

Megan was starting to feel like herself, again. Hannah could tell by looking at her. She merely needed a little push to get her right, again. It was a good thing Hannah was there to provide that push.

"Hey, Meg? How are you enjoying the job at Macy's?" She asked as a distraction. "I don't know how you can deal with it. I hate retail work."

"It's not so bad. I'm used to it. My boss seems to like me, which helps."

"Likes you?" Hannah became intrigued.

"Not that kind of like. I'm a hard worker. It doesn't go unappreciated."

"Oh, okay. Well, that's good. I'm glad you were able to find a job that works for you. Hey, we need to set a day aside to go to the spa. There's a nice one in Scarsdale. We should hit it up sometime soon."

"The spa sounds great," Megan replied. "I could sure use a day of being spoiled."

"Hell yeah," Hannah agreed with a grin. "Don't we all?"

When dinner was ready, the three sat down at the table together. This time, Megan left the empty seat slightly pulled away from the table. Hannah did not notice. She was too busy enjoying her glass of red wine.

"Meg, I was thinking of staying over tonight. Is it okay?" She said before taking a sip from her glass.

"Sure! I would love that," Megan answered. "You're always welcome here."

"Cool." Hannah turned her attention on Josh. "Hey, Josh. Do you want to play a boardgame, after dinner?"

"Okay," he said with a smile. "Can we play the game of Life?"

"Sounds fun, when it's only a game," Hannah smirked. The comment went over Josh's head.

After dinner, Megan washed the dishes, while Hannah and Josh set up the game on the table. Over the next hour, they played and were able to forget about real life, for a while. It felt good. Josh won, which made him happy.

When the game was over, it was time to get back to real life. Hannah put Josh to bed, while Megan took a hot shower. She allowed the steam to fill the bathroom and fog up the mirror. The water poured over her head washing away the bad memories from earlier. It felt fantastic. Too bad it did not work. She cried and allowed the water to wash away her tears. That worked.

She eventually went into her room, where Hannah was already waiting for her. They sat on the bed and knew it was time to talk.

Hannah asked, "How are you feeling?"

"Better, I suppose. This has to end, sometime. Thanks for putting Josh to bed for me."

"Don't mention it. Are you going to update your journal?"

Megan shook her head. "I'll do it in the morning, just in case I have a nightmare tonight. I'd rather write everything at once. I want to try and go to sleep with a clear head, if possible. I was hoping the shower would help get me there. I was wrong. My mind is all over the place."

"And here I am not helping," Hannah sighed. "I'm sorry. Why don't we talk about the old days? I think it may help. There's nothing like reminiscing about good times, huh? Man, we had some great times together."

Megan grinned. "We sure did." At last, she began to feel better.

They sat in bed talking about their youth. They talked about their school days from elementary school to high school, and then they discussed old boyfriends. They also talked about school trips and their junior and senior proms. Talking about these fond memories brought back feelings of happiness. They even had a few laughs. It was very helpful therapy for Megan, and for Hannah, too.

About two hours later, they finally felt ready for bed. They were both tired, especially after the day they had. This time, Megan was more ready for sleep than she had been the past week. She knew what was coming would not be easy to deal with, but it was necessary. She knew she had to face it, sooner or later. Better to do it, while Hannah was with her. Hannah fell asleep, first. Several minutes went by before Megan followed.

The next nightmare began, soon after she fell asleep. Megan only played the role as a witness in this one. She did not experience anything first hand. The nightmare picked up pretty much from where the last one left off, up in the small bathroom above the basement, where Margaret was murdered. Hank was there and he was naked. Megan wanted to look away, but could not. She had to watch everything. She had no choice.

Hank placed Margaret's nude body into the clawfoot bathtub and turned on the water from the shower. He let the body soak, while he gathered up her sneakers and clothing, which he placed into a dark garbage bag he kept outside of the bathroom.

He grabbed the towel from the sink and soaked it in warm soapy water. He left the bathroom and returned with a metal bucket and a scrubbing brush. He was only wearing rubber gloves. He proceeded to scrub the floor clean using the towel and brush. It was not an easy job due to the large amount of blood, which had spilled. It took roughly a half hour. When he was done, he placed the brush, towel, and gloves into the garbage bag with the clothing.

He then stood in the shower and bathed over the body. The water had been running the entire time. When he was done, he turned off the shower. Blood was still oozing from Margaret's neck, but not as much.

He left the bathroom, again. This time, he returned fully clothed and holding a blowtorch from the garage. He lit it and used it to scorch her neck and breast in order to cauterize the wounds and stop the bleeding. He also burned Margaret's hands and feet to make sure her body could not be identified using her prints. He had already removed all of her teeth, so no one would be able to use dental records either.

The teeth were wrapped in a small cloth pouch and placed on the floor of the basement. Hank grabbed a metal mallet and began smashing them into dust, which he poured into the toilet and flushed away.

Hank picked up the nipple he had bitten off from Margaret's breast in the previous nightmare. It was still sitting on the edge of the sink. He washed it with soap and water, and then left the bathroom.

All of a sudden, he was in the kitchen of his house. The change of scenery confused Megan, at first. There was a black iron frying pan on the stove. Vegetable oil was sizzling in the pan. Hank placed the nipple on a wooden cutting board. He rolled it in butter, garlic powder, and oregano, before carefully placing it into the frying pan.

It sizzled instantly and began to curl slightly at the edges almost like a pepperoni. He stood there watching it cook, making sure to turn it over, so it would not burn.

When it was ready, he removed it and put it on a small plate. He poured a dash of salt and pepper over it, and then picked it up using a fork. He took a small bite and closed his eyes, savoring the flavor. It was crunchy. Megan wanted to vomit. She was sickened by his actions. He took another bite, and then finished it off.

"Mm," he said to himself. "It kind of tastes like fried pork rinds."

Megan had a feeling she would not be eating pork for a very long time.

While it was not known to Megan, this was not something Hank did regularly. It was actually his first time eating the flesh of one of his victims. It was something he always wanted to try, but never had the nerve. Much to his delight, he found it enjoyable. It was definitely something he wanted to try, again. Maybe with his next victim.

Perhaps, he could look into buying a large freezer for storing meat, and then he would not have to worry about disposing of the bodies. He could simply devour them at his own pace and burn their belongings as usual.

Eventually, Hank returned to the bathroom with a large white blanket. He began to wrap the body in it. There was still blood underneath her, which had not been washed away. It left a stain on the blanket. Hank shrugged it off. It did not matter anymore. Once the body was wrapped tightly, he carried it out to his car, which was parked nearby in the garage. The rear hatch was already open. He placed the body inside and slammed the hatch closed.

It was then when Megan noticed Margaret's spirit standing beside her. It was as if she appeared instantly. She was nude and pale. She had the burn wounds from Hank's torch. Tears rolled down her face. She turned to Megan and acknowledged her presence. They made eye contact. Megan felt so bad for her. She wanted to hold her and comfort her, but she wavered. She was too afraid of touching her cold dead skin.

Margaret opened her mouth to speak. Her sweet voice came out as a soft whisper, "Tell my brother what he did to me." It was almost like she did not want Hank to hear her. Megan nodded dutifully.

The nightmare ended and Megan woke up. She turned her head and glanced over at the clock on her nightstand. It was the usual time in the middle of the night. Hannah was asleep next to her. Megan stared at the ceiling as her eyes adjusted to the darkness. Tears began to roll down her cheeks.

It took nearly an hour before she could fall asleep, again.


The next day Megan told Hannah about the latest nightmare. Hannah was horrified when she heard about how Hank cannibalized Margaret's nipple. She could not believe her ears. It was not easy for Megan to talk about. She had a hard enough time seeing it occur in person. It grossed her out. Of course, Megan made certain Josh could not hear when they discussed it.

Later, while Hannah prepared breakfast for them, Megan took the time to write the nightmare down in her journal, along with her experience at the abandoned basement the day before. It struck her as odd how she did not dream about being there last night. She was very grateful, despite the new horrors she witnessed, instead. She never wanted to see that place, again.

After this latest nightmare, she had a feeling she had seen the last of Hank's residence and place of business. The next dream would probably be the one she was waiting on. It should be the one to reveal where Margaret's body was taken. The mystery can finally be solved and Margaret could be laid to rest, at last.

Megan thought about what Margaret said to her in the nightmare. She wanted her to make sure her brother, Chris, knew what happened to her. It was a huge request. Megan had no idea how to find him. Where did he live? She already knew Leslie did not know and she was the only person she could think to ask. She hoped once the authorities knew the location of Margaret's body, they could contact him, somehow. Surely, they would be able to find Margaret's next of kin. Convincing them to search for the body was going to be the true difficult task.

Megan reminded herself it was best not to think too far ahead. One step at a time. First, she needed to find out where to find Margaret's body. Hopefully, that information would be revealed to her soon. All in good time. Bedtime was still hours away.

The rest of the day was spent not thinking about morbid crimes, missing girls, and death. Megan and Hannah took Josh to the movie theater at Ridge Hill. It had been a long time since they last did so. The last time was back in March, a month after arriving from California. It was so nice to go out and do something fun, again. Josh had a great time.

Later, they ate dinner at McDonald's, which Josh loved. It was his choice to go there. They wanted him to enjoy the day. He had a thing for Chicken McNuggets with sweet and sour sauce. He also liked Happy Meals because they came with toys and cookies. As for Megan, she loved the warm, crispy, apple pies. Maybe a little too much. It was a rare treat she allowed herself to enjoy, once in blue moon. Today seemed like a good day for it. Hannah loved the fries and swore they were the best in the world.

They took their time eating and discussing the movie. It was the latest Marvel superheroes film, which were some of Josh's favorite movies of all time. They were usually action-packed and fun to watch. Of course, this one was no different. It was pretty good.

With their outing nearly over, it was time to go home. Hannah dropped them off, before heading to her home. She did not bring enough clothing to stay two nights and was eager to get home, so she could shower. She promised to visit, again, soon.

Megan and Josh walked into their apartment and wasted no time getting comfortable. They changed into their pajamas and prepared for bed. Megan read Josh a bedtime story from one of his Golden Books. He insisted on holding his Mandalorian action figure beside him, so he could also hear the story. When Megan was finished, she put Mando back on the dresser and turned off the light. Josh fell asleep quickly.

Megan sat on her bed with the lamp on and thought about what was soon to come. She had to prepare herself mentally for the upcoming nightmare. It had been a good day. She knew that was about to change, once she went to sleep.

She prayed this would be the last nightmare. What more could there be to tell, after Margaret showed her where her body was dumped? The big build up from the previous nightmares had to be leading to the secret location of her body. The only thing remaining was for Megan to fall asleep.

She went to the bathroom to take a hot shower, before going to bed. She hoped it would help relax her. Her anxiety level was high. She stood underneath the rushing water for several minutes. It felt great, but it was a little too hot, so she cut it short.

When she climbed out of the bathtub, she wrapped a towel around her body. The room was filled with steam and the mirror was fogged up. She stepped to the mirror, so she could wipe it clean. Suddenly, she heard a squeaking noise. It looked as if someone were writing on it from the other side. She stared in disbelief, as the words "HELP ME" appeared one letter at a time written backwards.

Her breathing became uneasy and she began to feel lightheaded. She closed her eyes, leaned on the sink for support, and tried to calm herself. She did not want to have a panic attack.

She stated in a stern voice, "That's what I'm trying to do, damn it." She opened her eyes and saw the message was gone. The mirror was still fogged up. She exhaled, feeling frustrated. "Quit messing with me," she complained.

A moment later, she left the bathroom and returned to her bedroom. She was wearing her pajamas. As she entered the room, she was unaware she was not alone. Margaret's spirit stood near the bed waiting for her impatiently. Megan turned off the lamp and climbed into bed. Margaret was lying beside her, as the light was turned off.

Megan was so hyped she no longer felt tired. Her anxiety was preventing her from falling asleep, right away. Try as she might, she had trouble sleeping. She tossed and turned all night long. Therefore, she did not dream.

Margaret expressed her frustration by waking her up with a bang, once she finally drifted off briefly. At 3:37 exactly, the lightbulbs on both lamps in the bedroom exploded. Megan awoke and let out a shriek, which even woke up Josh, who was in his room across the hall.

"Mommy!" He called out in fear, believing something happened to her.

She caught her breath and crawled out of bed. She turned on the light and noticed the shattered lightbulb shards around the nightstand. She called out, "I'm fine, baby! It was only an accident! Go back to bed!" She walked into his room to reassure him.

He was sitting up in his bed when he asked, "What happened, Mommy?"

"I don't know, baby. The lightbulb from my lamp popped for no reason at all." She knew who did it. She just had no idea why. "Go back to sleep. I'm so sorry the noise woke you up. It woke me up, too."

"It scared me," he admitted.

"Me, too." She went in and sat down on his bed. "Do you want me to read you another bedtime story?"

He nodded, "Yes, please."

She silently cursed Margaret for driving her crazy and waking Josh. After reading him another story, she returned to her bedroom and tried to ascertain the damage. She had not realized the lightbulbs from both lamps had exploded.

"Oh, great. Damn it, Maggie. It's your fault I couldn't sleep, in the first place. I have to work tomorrow. Why couldn't you pull the bedsheets off, instead, like they do in movies? You had to bust two lightbulbs? I don't even know if I have two spares. This has to end sooner or later."

She shook her head, as she went to the kitchen to check if she had extra lightbulbs. Luckily, she had exactly two spares, but that was it. There were no more stored away. She carefully replaced the lightbulbs and swept up the broken fragments. By the time she was back in bed, it was after four. Within seconds, the bedsheets were yanked off and thrown to the floor.

"Oh, you bitch! I thought we were becoming friends. That's not even cute."

She got out of bed and placed the blankets back in place. Afterwards, she got back under the covers and held them tight. Now, she was too angry to fall asleep, although she eventually did about thirty minutes later.

# Chapter 11

❦

# Dear Diary

After a long night and a hard day at work, Megan came home ready to relax. She was exhausted. Misty and Josh were seated on the sofa watching some LEGO Marvel superheroes animated shorts. Megan went straight into the kitchen to prepare a fast dinner. She asked Misty if she wanted to stay for dinner, but as usual Misty could not wait to leave. She quickly gathered her things. Megan did not blame her. She knew Margaret's spirit was probably around in full force today, after her mayhem the night before.

As Misty headed for the door, Megan asked, "Misty? Was it an uneventful day?"

Misty turned to face her and paused to think about it. She faltered, "Um, kind of. I suppose it wasn't too bad. I could definitely feel her presence. At times, it felt really strong, which made me nervous and gave me a headache. It's like she was right on top of me. I kept expecting something to happen, so I was on edge all day. I don't think she likes me. She knows her being around is enough to get to me and she was around all day, but nothing weird happened, if that's what you're asking."

"Oh, good. Thanks. Yeah, I was just curious." Megan was surprised. She half expected to hear about some kind of dreadful experience.

"Sure. No problem. See you tomorrow." Misty waved, before leaving.

"Get home safe."

Megan locked the door and returned to preparing dinner. She poured a box of mac and cheese into a pot of boiling milk and began stirring slowly.

When dinner was ready, she called Josh to the table. He already knew to wash his hands, first.

They sat down to eat and Megan asked about his day. She wondered if he had anything different to report, than what Misty said. "What did you and Misty do today? Did you do anything special?"

"We watched TV a lot," he said. "We were drawing, too. She draws really good. She drew Iron Man for me. I drew a picture of Lizzie."

"Really?" She became interested. "Can I see your drawing?"

"Okay." He left the dinner table to retrieve his drawing, which was on the coffee table in front of the sofa. He showed it to her. "Here it is, Mommy." He handed it to her. "And this is Iron Man." He showed the drawing Misty drew. It was pretty good, but she was more interested in what he drew.

"Wow, that's great. I really want to see your drawing, though." She examined it closely. In the drawing Lizzie, as he still called her, was wearing a white t-shirt and blue pants. Her hair was colored brown and her lips were pink. Her big brown eyes were evident. Also in the drawing was a small gray rectangular object on the floor. Curious, Megan asked, "What's this supposed to be?" She pointed at the object.

"It's the metal box," he answered, as if she was supposed to know.

Right away, she demanded, "What metal box?"

"The one with the pictures in it," he explained.

How did he know about the metal box? She asked, "Where did you get the idea to draw a metal box?"

"From Lizzie. She said the bad man hid it in his basement."

The word basement gave her an instant chill. Is that where the box was kept? She hoped her son did not know anything else about the basement. She continued the interrogation. "Have you seen this basement?"

"No," he shook his head. "Lizzie told me about it."

"Oh, okay." She was relieved. "So, she told you this metal box was there. Why?"

He shrugged, "I don't know." He began to feel like he was in some kind of trouble.

"Does she know exactly where to find it?"

He turned to his side and looked up. He then looked back at his mother and said, "She can show you when the time is right. That's what she just said. What did she mean, Mommy?"

"It means not yet. Thanks, baby, and thank you, Lizzie." She looked to where she thought she might be standing. "Josh, can you please find out what kind of pictures are in the box?"

"Pictures of her," he answered right away.

Megan could not believe what she was hearing. Was that box still in the basement?

"And of the other girls," he added.

Megan almost choked on her own spit. She coughed and asked, "What did you say?"

"There are pictures of other girls, too." He looked at Lizzie and asked, "What other girls? Oh." He turned to his mother and said, "The other girls like her." She had to mean the other victims!

Right away, Megan knew this box had to be found. Of course, it meant returning to the basement. It was the last place in the world she wanted to go. What did Lizzie, or Maggie, mean when she said when the time is right? Would it be part of the story played out in her nightmares? Megan wished she could speak to Margaret in private. She really did not want Josh to know too much about what happened to her. She had no idea what he knew. She was afraid to ask. As far as she was concerned, he already knew more than he should.

Her interrogation was over. "Sit down and eat your dinner, Josh. It's getting cold."

"Okay, Mommy." He obeyed without question.

Megan kept staring at the metal box in the drawing. It gave her a rough idea of the actual size. She wondered how long she would have to wait to see the real box.


After dinner, Josh grabbed his drawings and went to his room. Megan washed the dishes and sat down on the sofa to rest. She put her feet up and laid back. She was so tired. She hardly slept at all. She did not want to take a nap. It was best if she waited until bedtime, so she could sleep when she was supposed to, and dream while Josh was already asleep. She had a feeling it was going to be one of those nights.

In the meantime, she needed to kill time. She decided to get back to her treasure hunt. It had been a few days since she focused on it. Where could she look next? She thought about all the rooms in the apartment, and then it came to her. Josh's room! It belonged to Margaret! She wondered what kind of secrets could be hidden away in there.

A few moments later, she appeared at Josh's doorway with a mischievous look on her face.

He looked up at her with curiosity. "Hi, Mommy."

"Hello, baby. Don't mind me. I just want to check your closet and make sure it's up to code." It was the first thing, which came to mind. Even after she said it, she realized how stupid it sounded.

"I didn't know there was a code to open it. Lizzie never told me." He was puzzled by her ridiculous excuse. "Was I doing it wrong?"

"That's what I want to find out," she lied. She found herself chuckling at her silly excuse. She stepped into the room and walked to his closet. She opened the door and looked inside. His coat, jacket, and sweaters hung from hangers across a thick wooden bar. On the floor were his boots, sneakers, and backpack. She looked up at the top shelf. It was a little too high to see all the way to the back even on her toes.

Josh stated, "That's Lizzie's shelf. I don't use it."

"Is it now?"

"I can't reach it anyway," he reasoned.

Suddenly, the Mandalorian asked, "What's your highest bounty?" He was seated on the bed, but Josh had not touched him. He looked at Mando, smiled, and then looked at his mother, waiting for her reaction. He enjoyed how she reacted whenever Lizzie pressed the buttons on his Mandalorian.

"My highest…?" She thought about it for a second and got an idea. "Right. Gotcha." She left and returned swiftly with the stepladder. She climbed up and was able to get a better look at the shelf. It appeared to be empty, which was quite a disappointment. She stuck her head inside and looked around to make sure. She noticed something over the doorframe on the inside. It was a small pink hardcover book held in place by a bent nail.

"What are you doing, Mommy? Did you find something?"

"Yep. I found something alright." She struggled to loosen the nail, so she could turn it and get the book. It was jammed in tight. She did not want to break a fingernail, so she tried to be careful. At last, it came loose. "Got it!"

She stepped down from the stepladder to examine her find. It appeared to be some kind of diary. It was a smooth, pink, hardcover book about the size of a postcard, only thicker. Unfortunately, it was locked and there was no key.

Josh became fascinated and asked, "What's that, Mommy?"

"It looks like a diary," she answered. "Maybe it belongs to Maggie. I mean Lizzie. Is she here?"

"Yes," he nodded.

"Good. Can you ask her where she hid the key?"

"She lost it when the bad man took her," he responded seconds later.

Frustrated, Megan went into the kitchen and searched the drawer near the sink, where she kept some tools. Josh followed her. She found a screwdriver and used it to get the lock open. Inside was an old worn school photo of a young girl. It was Margaret. It was the same exact photo used in the newspaper article. Megan checked the back of the photo to see if there was anything written on it. Someone wrote "Class of '87."

"Can I see it, Mommy?"

She handed the photo to Josh and said, "Be careful with it. It's very old."

He held it delicately and admired it, as if it were a valuable baseball card.

Before reading anything inside the diary, she looked to Josh and asked, "Does she mind if I read it? Will she be upset, if I do?" The last thing she needed was to anger the spirit of the girl haunting her home.

Josh looked up at her and said, "She wants you to read it, but you gotta read it in private. She doesn't want me to read it because I'm a boy." He frowned. "It's not fair."

Megan smiled at him and said, "I'll tell you what. I will read this and you can keep the photo. Okay? I'll get a frame for you and we can put it on your nightstand next to your lamp."

Her suggestion seemed to please him greatly. "Really? Thank you, Mommy!" He hugged her, before skipping into his room with the photo in his hand.

Seemingly alone, she examined the diary by skimming through a few pages. There was a lot to read. Margaret watched her from nearby. Megan went to her bedroom and placed it on her nightstand. Margaret followed. As much as Megan wanted to read it, she decided it could wait until later, once she was ready for bed. She would make sure to go to bed earlier than usual, so she would have plenty of time to read a few pages.

She returned to Josh's room to retrieve the stepladder. She did not want him to climb it and fall. She was upset with herself for even leaving it there for so long. He could have gotten hurt. Luckily, he was well-behaved and fairly distracted by the photo. She noticed he was sitting on his bed staring at it. It looked like he had a little crush.

"She was very pretty," Megan commented.

Josh nodded in agreement. "She's my best friend in the whole wide world," he said with a big smile on his face. It was obvious he really loved his Lizzie. "I'm going to keep this picture forever."

Megan smiled warmly. She prayed Margaret would never cause him any harm, or there would be hell to pay. She did not want to disturb him any longer, so she removed the stepladder and put it back in the hall closet.

Later that evening, she put Josh to bed and tucked him in. He did not need a story read to him. He was tired and ready to sleep. Instead, she kissed him goodnight and turned on his lamp. The photo of Margaret was resting against the base of his superhero lamp. Megan turned off the light, as she left the room and went into her bedroom, after a brief stop in the bathroom.

Once in her room, she turned on her lamp, which happened to be on the nightstand where the diary sat waiting for her. She changed into her pajamas and got into bed. She eagerly picked up the diary and decided to look through it, again, before reading any of it. She slowly thumbed through the pages to see how long it might take to read. The pages were small, but there was a lot of writing. Many pages were filled from top to bottom. Everything was written in cursive, so she hoped she would not have a problem reading the handwriting. It was the same handwriting as the back of the photo. She saw the dates of the entries were all from the 1980s. The earliest was from 1983. She did the math in her head and figured Margaret had to be in Junior High School at around that time.

"Hmm. This should be interesting," she thought to herself. She knew there would be nothing in the diary, which could help solve the mystery of her body's location. The only knowledge she hoped to gain from reading the diary was insight into who Margaret was as a person. Taking that into consideration, she wondered why Margaret wanted her to read it. Unless there was something else to be learned from the entries. There was only one way to know for sure.

She began by reading the initials on the inside cover. It said, "MEG," in bold letters. Megan thought about the initials etched under the kitchen table and recalled how she originally thought it was short for her name. It made her chuckle. In addition to the dreams, it was another special connection she shared with Margaret.

She looked at the first page. Almost immediately she felt like she was overstepping her bounds. The idea of reading someone's private thoughts bothered her. She had to remind herself, Margaret wanted her to read it.

Out of curiosity, she quickly checked to see when the last entry was written. It was from 1987, the year before Margaret disappeared. No, the year before she was *abducted and murdered.*

Megan closed the diary and shut her eyes. Her heart was racing. She took slow, steady, deep breaths. This is what she wanted to avoid. She did not want to read something that was going to trigger a panic attack. "Stop being a big baby," she scolded herself. "It's only a diary."

She opened the diary to the first page and began reading. From the first few pages alone she was able to learn a few basic facts about the much younger incarnation of Margaret Elizabeth Garrett. She was born and raised in Yonkers. Her birthday was on February 13, 1969, which made her thirteen at the time she began writing in the diary. Her middle name came from her mother's first name.

Her mother, Elizabeth aka Mrs. Garrett, was better known by everyone affectionately as Beth. She worked on and off as a waitress at various establishments, which apparently included the Broadway Diner, the Parkhill Diner, and the Yonkers Raceway Diner. Beth would often stop working at these places due to her husband's constant jealousy. It seems at one time he embarrassed her by showing up at her job and starting an argument because he believed she was cheating on him.

According to Margaret's writings, she believed he felt guilty because he was the one cheating on her. She even saw him once with another woman in the car. For several weeks, she was furious with her father, although she never told him why. She also did not tell her mother.

Her father's name was Frank. He worked as a mortician, which was a little too morbid for Megan's taste. The funeral parlor, where he worked, is not named in the diary, although it was located somewhere in Yonkers. That narrows it down. Frank drove a red Cutlass Supreme, which he took pride in because it was an American car. He enjoyed taking his family on long drives upstate to the Finger Lakes during the late 1970s-early 1980s, or as Margaret referred to them… happier times.

Her brother, Chris, was three years younger than her, making him only sixteen at the time of her alleged disappearance. They shared the room during these early years, after moving into the apartment at the Hill View in the Summer of 1980. Margaret was eleven years old, making Chris eight.

Margaret loved her brother dearly and always seemed to mention him with fondness. It seems they got along well and rarely argued, which made it possible for them to share a room for several years.

Margaret began high school in the fall of 1983, the year she began her diary. She attended Saunders, located on Palmer Road beginning with the ninth grade. Based on her entries, she enjoyed being there and spoke warmly of her school experiences. She was a straight A student in the honor classes, who had lots of friends. It is safe to assume she was popular.

One of her friends, who is mentioned a lot was a girl named Alessia. They were best friends since elementary school and went to all of the same schools together. It reminded Megan of her and Hannah. It was the same for them. Apparently, Chris had a crush on Alessia.

Megan wondered what ever happened to this Alessia. She kept reading, hoping to learn more about her. There were no clues as to her last name or residence. Most likely they stayed friends until the end.

Margaret mentioned several times how her parents often argued. She even wrote about how when she was a little girl she used to hide under the kitchen table. It would explain how she ended up scratching her initials down there. Ultimately, her parents were divorced by October of 1986. Chris ended up leaving with their father, while Margaret remained with her mother. From then on, Josh's room belonged only to Margaret.

She hated being separated from her brother. They spoke on the telephone frequently and visited each other more than they visited with their parents. They were very close. Megan knew it must have hit her brother hard when she went missing. She could only imagine what he went through.

It's no wonder Margaret wanted her to find him. She wondered if that was the real favor Margaret needed. Maybe it was not so much about finding her body, but finding her brother, instead. Or maybe it was both.

Megan continued reading the diary, until well after midnight, before she realized she had to wake up early for work the next day. She felt compelled to know this sweet young girl, who has been haunting her life and dominating her dreams. However, she would have to resume another time. It was getting late.

She placed the diary on the nightstand and turned off the lamp. It did not take long for her to fall asleep.

She had another dream, but this time, it was of happier times inspired by reading the diary. In the dream, Margaret was much younger, but still just as beautiful. Her hair was longer. Perhaps, she was around fifteen years old. She had a baby face, so it was difficult to know for certain. Her brother and parents were with her. They were at a lake surrounded by a wooded area probably somewhere upstate.

They would usually spend warm summer days at such places. It was always a pleasant family experience. All the drama would be left behind in Yonkers. These days were for fun times only. No exceptions. They were free of the stresses from normal everyday life. It was wonderful.

Margaret wrote about many days like this in her diary throughout the summer months. Writing about them put her in a good mood because she would draw happy face emojis and hearts. Sometimes, she might mention a cute boy she saw, who she liked. Other times, her best friend, Alessia, was there with her. It was obvious those were the best times of their lives.

In the dream, Margaret was with Alessia and Chris. They went swimming and played in the water. Later, they ate small sandwiches cut into triangles, while playing frisbee on the grass. Afterwards, they went for a hike through the woods. Chris could not keep his eyes off of Alessia. She was very pretty, if she looked the way she did in the dream.

Megan had a feeling she did. It seemed Margaret only showed her real memories.

The dream sparked a memory from Megan's youth causing the dream to change. She recalled being at Taconic Lake with Hannah. Their parents were there, too. They were young teenagers, as well. The memory in the dream was not of any particular day, but a general memory of the times they shared there together. The lake was a special place of adventure for them. It always began with a swim in the lake, followed by a picnic at one of the wooden tables on the grass under the shade of a big tree. They also went hiking along the trails.

It was exactly like Margaret's experiences. *Exactly*. Another connection they shared.

While walking along the trail, the dream changed drastically. Megan and Hannah were now walking along the Old Croton Aqueduct Trail together going northbound toward Untermyer Park. They began jogging, before breaking into a full sprint. It was not like a race. Someone was chasing them and they were afraid, but they could not see who was chasing after them. None of them dared to look back. All of a sudden, Megan tripped over a fallen branch and fell to the ground. She scraped her hands on the ground in the process.

Before she could get up, someone had pounced on her. It was Hank! He placed his hand over her mouth and nose. There was a damp white cloth in his hand drenched in chloroform. Her vision became blurry, as she saw Hannah still running off ahead in the distance. She had not yet realized what happened to Megan.

Megan passed out. When she came to, she was in the basement tied to the brick support beam. Her mouth was gagged with her sock. Hank approached her with the pliers in his hand. The recognition of what was about to happen caused her to go into full panic mode. She struggled and cried, but could not break free. Her breathing became heavy and soon she fainted, again.

When she awoke, she found herself lying in her bed. Surprisingly, it was not 3:37 in the morning. Instead, it was nearly six. Her alarm was set for 7:30 A.M. She was no longer in the dreaming mood, although she still had time to sleep a little longer before getting up for work. She planned on it.

"Jesus Christ. I can't even have a nice dream without it turning to shit," she complained to herself.

Margaret Elizabeth Garrett.

# Chapter 12

## The Passenger

After Megan left for work, Misty was at the apartment taking care of Josh. He was playing in his room, so she decided to read a book. It was the same book she had been reading for the past week, "*No Hope for the Hopeless at Kings Park*." She was almost up to the last story, which was the longest of the three in the book. She laid on the sofa in the living room with her feet up. Her sneakers were slightly touching the sofa.

The air in the room became heavy. Misty sensed she was not alone. She tried to remain focused on her book and ignored the spiritual presence in the room with her. She hoped it would move on to Josh's room. He did not seem to mind having it around. Misty wanted nothing to do with it.

"Go away," she whispered without taking her eyes off of her book.

At that moment, her feet were pushed away from the sofa, which startled her and caused her to put the book down and sit up.

"What do you want? Leave me alone," she spoke low enough, so Josh could not hear her. "You're not welcome here. Leave this house. You're supposed to be dead, so be dead."

Enraged by her insensitive words, Margaret's spirit pushed Misty completely off the sofa onto the floor. She did not stop there. She grabbed Misty's book, which was still on the sofa and tossed it across the room. It fell onto the floor and opened to the first chapter of the first story. The title of that story was "*Amanda*." It was the same story, which inspired the t-shirt Margaret was wearing when she was abducted and murdered. In fact, it was the only shirt her spirit was doomed to wear indefinitely.

Misty was both appalled and frightened. She picked herself up and grabbed her book from the floor, unaware of the fact it had been opened to a specific page on purpose. She closed the book and placed it into her bag. She was staring at the sofa and breathing heavily.

Josh heard the ruckus and entered the living room. He noticed Misty looking disheveled and asked, "What's wrong? Did something bad happen?" He could see the angry spirit standing over the sofa. "What did you do to make Lizzie so mad?" He still called her by the name familiar to him.

Misty was offended when she replied, "She started it! I was laying on the sofa reading my book. I wasn't bothering anyone. She pushed my feet, and then she pushed *me* off the sofa! She even threw my book across the room. Ask her what her problem is. This was all her."

Josh looked to Margaret, who faded away. Confused, he said, "She's gone."

Misty could still feel her presence, but it was not as strong. It was the same as it felt before she was pushed – the normal sensation she felt whenever she was in the apartment. "She's still around somewhere," she stated.

Josh shrugged and replied, "I can't see her all the time. Sometimes, she's here. Sometimes, she's not. I don't know where she goes. You made her mad. She doesn't like you." He shook his head.

Misty thought about what she said to the spirit. She was only being honest. She did not admit to Josh what she said. As far as she was concerned, the spirit only did what she did because she did not like her. She wanted to leave so badly, but Megan would not be home for a few more hours. There was another option.

"Josh, what do you say we go out for a while?" She suggested.

"Okay. Where are we going?"

"Do you want to go to the park?"

"Yes! Can I bring Mando?"

"Of course," she responded.

They got ready and were heading outside in a matter of minutes. Misty needed to be somewhere else. She could not take being in the apartment. Not today. She was seriously considering giving up this job. She dreaded being alone in any room. It was not so bad, as long as she stayed near Josh.

Misty made sure to stay out of the apartment, until she knew Megan would be returning home from work. At that point, she and Josh went back to the building and sat outside on the front steps. She was in no hurry to go back upstairs to the apartment.

Soon, Megan approached on foot from Yonkers Avenue. Misty noticed her, right away, and felt a sensation of relief wash over her. When Josh saw her, he became excited.

"Mommy!" He ran to greet her.

"Hi, baby! What a nice surprise it is to see you out here waiting for me." She hugged her son and they walked back to the building hand in hand. "Hello, Misty. Were you guys out here long?"

"Hey. Actually, we just got back from the park. I noticed it was almost time for you to get home, so I figured we may as well wait out here for you. I thought you two would be happy to see each other." Misty decided not to tell Megan about what happened earlier. She was worried it would only upset her. As it turned out, she had no idea how interested Megan would have been to hear about it. "Well, I'd better get going," Misty said.

"Oh, you're leaving already?" Megan was not really too surprised.

"Yeah, my parents are waiting for me. Take care! Bye, Josh." Misty began walking off.

"Bye!" Josh waved. He was disappointed when she did not wave back, or look back.

Megan waited for Misty to be out of range, before looking down at Josh and asking, "Josh? Did anything strange happen today?"

He looked up at her and answered in a whisper, "She made Lizzie very mad."

"Really? How?"

He shrugged and replied, "I don't know. Mommy, I'm hungry. What's for dinner?"

Megan frowned wondering what could have happened. She had a feeling Misty would not last much longer. She was probably going to need a new sitter for Josh. It saddened her. She liked Misty. She turned back to her son and suggested, "Would you like a Manwich sandwich?"

"Okay!" Josh liked the idea. There did not seem to be anything he did not like when it came to food.

They went into the building and up to their apartment.

After dinner, Josh sat on the sofa with his Mandalorian watching the Cartoon Network. He appeared to be entertained, considering how much he was laughing. Megan sat nearby at the kitchen table with Margaret's diary. She continued reading from where she left off. It was hard to focus with the noise from the television and Josh's laughing. Eventually, she decided to save it for later. She returned the diary to her nightstand, for now.

Next, she gave Hannah a call and eagerly told her all about the diary and the supposed metal box hidden in the basement. They spoke for nearly two hours, before hanging up. Hannah was enthusiastic to see the diary in person.

Megan had almost forgotten. She brought home a small wooden frame for Margaret's photo. She pulled it out of her purse and went into Josh's room to find the photo. It was still leaning against the lamp on his nightstand. She tore off the clear plastic wrapping from around the frame and opened the rear, so she could place the photo within. Once it was in place, she stared at the photo.

A rush of emotions suddenly came over her. At first, she found herself smiling. She felt warm and happy, but soon she began crying and could not understand why. Thinking about Margaret made her emotional. What she did not realize was some of the emotions were coming directly from Margaret, who was in the room with her. The two shared a special bond. The same way Megan could see through her eyes in the dreams, she could feel her emotions.

Margaret was delighted to see her photo in a frame. It touched her in a profound way because Megan cared enough to buy a frame for the photo of her. It also made her sad because she hated how they could not interact normally. She wanted to hug Megan for agreeing to help her and for finally understanding what she had been trying to show her over the past two weeks. As for Megan, she was very pleased to have a photo of Margaret. She was also sad and angry because of how Margaret died. She hoped she would be able to help her find peace, after several decades. However, she was not sure how she was going to accomplish that goal.

One step at a time, she told herself.

She took the framed photo to the living room to show Josh. She knew he would also be pleased. "Look, Josh. I got a frame for her photo." She held it up for him to see.

"Ooh! Thank you, Mommy! You made Lizzie very happy." He hopped off the sofa and walked closer to get a better look at the frame.

His Mandalorian spoke from the sofa. "This is the way," it said. Both Josh and Megan looked at it. Margaret was sitting beside it on the sofa looking at them.

Josh replied, "You see, Lizzie? I told you Mommy liked you. Can you be her guardian angel, too, and make sure she doesn't get sick anymore like she did last time?"

Megan looked down at him lovingly. She was touched by his concern.

He smiled at his mother and proudly informed her, "Lizzie said she will be your guardian angel, too, from now on."

"Tell her I said thank you, Josh."

"She can hear you, Mommy. She said you're welcome." He hugged her.

She bent down and held him in her arms tight. She truly hoped Margaret would keep her word and always watch over him. Once more, she found herself feeling emotional and cried. "I love you, baby," she said to her son.

"I love you, too, Mommy. And I love Lizzie." He paused and asked, "Do you love Lizzie?"

Did she? She really could not answer the question honestly without hurting Josh's feelings. She was still trying to like Margaret, but incidents like the night before was making it extremely difficult to do so. Rather than get into it, she lied to her son. "Of course, I do. She's like part of the family."

Her words may have satisfied her son, but Margaret knew better. She knew exactly how Megan really felt. It did not upset her. She understood why Megan felt the way she did. She realized her antics could be terrifying at times. She did what she had to do to get Megan to understand what she wanted. She let her know it.

"I did what I had to," said the Mandalorian, once more.

Megan felt as if Margaret could somehow read her mind. She responded, "I know."

Josh looked up at her and grinned. "I'm glad you can talk to each other thanks to Mando."

His mother nodded hesitantly, "Yes, it is amazing how we can do that. I only wish there were an easier way. Maybe something less creepy." She made a funny face, which caused Josh to giggle. "Why don't you get ready for bed and I will read you a bedtime story?"

"Okay, Mommy." He hurried off leaving his Mandalorian on the sofa.

Megan walked over to the sofa and sat down next to it. She picked up the fifteen-inch action figure and stared at it. She was trying to figure out how

Margaret was using it to speak. There was a button on the chest to activate its eight phrases, as well as buttons on either shoulder for the weapon sound effects. She pressed the right shoulder button, which made a laser blast sound. She pressed the left one, next, and it lit up an orange glowing light effect for the flamethrower, while making it sound as if fire were shooting out.

She began, "Lizzie, um, Maggie? I'm not sure what you prefer to be called. Can I call you Maggie? Use the laser for 'yes' and the flamethrower for 'no.'"

The laser blast sounded off, surprising her. She did not expect her idea to actually work.

"Is it okay I'm reading your diary?"

She heard the laser blast sound, again, and still seemed surprised.

"Wow. We're talking." She grinned. "Is there a particular reason you need me to read the diary?"

Again, she heard the laser blast.

"Okay, then I will get back to it very soon. I have another unrelated question. Can you truly keep Josh safe for his entire life? Be honest. I'll understand, if you cannot. I won't be upset."

The laser blast button was pressed three times.

"I will take that as a hell yes," Megan grinned, again. "Thank you, Maggie. I promise, I will try my best to help you. Just please, no more scares. Not for me and not for Misty. Okay?"

There was silence. Megan waited, but nothing happened.

"That's not nice!"

Josh called out from his room, "I'm ready for my story! Can you bring me my Mando?"

"Okay! I'll be right there!" She stood up and took a deep breath. She looked at the Mandalorian and whispered, "I mean it. Stop the scaring. If you want me to help you, then you have to behave. Please."

She went into Josh's room, put the Mandalorian on the dresser, and grabbed a book from the shelf. She sat beside her son and proceeded to read him a bedtime story.

A short time later, Megan went into her bedroom and sat on the bed. She picked up the diary from the nightstand and opened to the page, where she left off earlier. By this time, she felt like she knew Maggie on a deep personal level. That fact only made it harder to think about what fate had in store for the doomed teenage girl. Megan became so angry knowing how this precious young girl's life would end so dramatically. It was a tragedy.

She had to temporarily stop reading, so she could clear her head before resuming. It was not easy to put aside what she already knew would happen and focus on these earlier years of innocence. She closed her eyes and took a few deep steady breaths. While it did help to relax her, the dark images were still there in the back of her mind, haunting her thoughts. She wished she could forget them.

Music! The thought came to her in a flash. It was not her thought, but it did not matter. It seemed like a good idea. Music would certainly serve as a great distraction. It's what she needed.

She got out of bed and retrieved her laptop from the top of her dresser. She brought it over to the bed and hit the power switch. Once it loaded up, she lowered the volume, and searched for mellow music to play in the background. For some reason, she was in the mood for a particular song from the mid-1980s. It was a song by Crowded House called *"Don't Dream it's Over."* It's what she needed to find, so she did.

As the song began, she felt like she could focus on the diary easier. She went through the rest of the 1986 entries quickly, and then began on the final year, 1987. It was the year before Maggie would meet her end. Don't think about it, she reminded herself. Keep reading. Maggie spent a lot of time writing about a boy named Matt. He became her first love. They shared many classes in school and he would often walk her home. The rest of the school year finished with parties and other good times with friends. Next, were the summer months, which were more family oriented.

In one entry from the middle of July something stood out. Maggie mentioned the Old Croton Aqueduct Trail for the first time. She said she went with her father and brother to get the car checked at a repair shop. The shop was near an entrance to the trail, past a cobblestone road. Maggie liked the feel of the wheels going over the cobblestone. While her father dealt with the mechanic, Maggie and her brother sat down on a leather sofa and waited. It was then when Maggie noticed another young mechanic, who kept staring at her. It made her feel uncomfortable enough to cause her to get up and wait outside with her brother.

The mention of the trail's close proximity made her think about a certain garage just off Odell Avenue, which also had a cobblestone road leading to it.

It sounded a lot like Maggie was talking about Hank's shop. Could it be they actually went there to do business a year before her disappearance? What were the odds? The possibility blew Megan's mind.

Nothing more is mentioned about it. Maggie moved on to discussing what she learned about the trail, which she found fascinating, as it did have a rich history. Even if she only mentioned the repair shop this one time, her notice of the creepy young mechanic was more significant than she could ever know. It had to be him. Megan felt it in her bones.

Maggie wished she had the Mandalorian in the room with her, so she could use it to communicate with Maggie. Still, she asked, "Is this what you wanted me to read? Give me a sign, so I know."

The laptop froze up causing the song to stop playing. Megan shut it down since she no longer needed the music. She was now completely focused. She continued reading, until she reached the end of the diary. Maggie's last entry was on New Year's Eve of the same year. She spent it here in the apartment with her mother. They were alone. Chris was with his father visiting family. The divorce left the family divided. Maggie wanted to be there with them, but it would have meant leaving her mother alone and she was not about to do that. It was a sad time for Maggie. She was feeling torn between her parents and her brother. There was also her boyfriend, Matt, who she wanted to be with, as well. Needless to say, the year ended, along with her mood to continue writing in a diary.

There were still some pages left, but they were blank. Based on the average length required for each day of entries, the pages would have only lasted until February of 1988. Perhaps, it was the reason she chose to stop. Megan considered the possibility of a second diary hidden around the apartment. It seemed unlikely.

Megan placed the diary in the top drawer of her nightstand. She got up and put the laptop back on the dresser. Within seconds, she was lying in bed and ready to sleep. It was several minutes after midnight.


Megan tossed and turned, until she found herself wrapped tightly in her blanket. It was hard to breathe. She tried to stretch her arms out, so she could free herself, but her movement was limited. She wondered how she managed to get herself so tightly wound and almost wanted to laugh at how silly she felt.

However, no matter how much she struggled, she could not break free from the blanket. After a while, she began to panic. It was not so funny anymore. It became more difficult for her to breathe.

"Help! Josh! I'm stuck in my blanket!" She shouted. He could not hear her. She screamed at the top of her lungs. Still nothing. Again, she screamed. She was freaking out. She pushed and pulled at the blanket, but it was wrapped too tightly. "What the hell is going on? Maggie? Are you doing this?"

Surprisingly, a realization came over her. She was Maggie.

In that moment, everything grew dark around her. She heard the car engine start. Soon, she felt the movement. They were turning out of the garage. Hank was driving her somewhere to dump the body. Where was he taking her? She felt the car going uphill. They were going north on Odell Avenue. She could tell when they reached North Broadway and turned left heading northbound. Next, they turned right and went downhill. She remembered they had to be near the Applebee's. The car went uphill, and then turned, as it went downhill, again. Finally, they were on a highway. There were no more pauses for traffic lights. Where was he going? The dark ride seemed to last forever.

Megan tried to remove herself from the blanket. She kept telling herself she is not Maggie. She can get out. She is not the one, who is trapped. She is not dead. Finally, she managed to find a small opening. She could see the dark nighttime sky over the vehicle through the rear hatch. Trees passed overhead. There was an overpass. Where are they now? How far had they gone? She had no clue. There was another overpass.

She heard what sounded like singing. It was Maggie. She kept singing the same monotone tune she sang in previous dreams, only now Megan could understand what she was saying. V-3-5-6. She repeated it over and over in a low voice to the tune of a familiar children's lullaby. What did it mean?

She asked Maggie, "What are you singing? What does it mean? Does it have something to do with where we're going?" She could have asked a million questions. None of them would have received a reply.

Maggie ignored her, as if she could not see her. She kept singing the tune, "V-3-5-6," repeatedly, while her eyes remained closed. It was too eerie, especially since Megan knew she was already dead, by this point.

At last, the car pulled off to the side and came to a stop. It was still dark outside, but it was a clear night. There were many stars overhead. The rear hatch was opened. Hank lifted the body and pulled it out of the car. He dropped it on the ground and grabbed a shovel from the car. He then closed the hatch.

Suddenly, Megan was standing outside of the vehicle on the side of the road. It was a highway or a parkway. She noticed there were a lot of trees along the side. She glanced briefly at the license plate of Hank's car. She could only read part of it. It ended with "677." She had no control of her vision, but tried to pay attention to the details she saw. She could only see what Hank was looking at through his eyes.

He held the shovel and looked around. He was nervous. There were no other cars in sight, aside from a single car driving past them on the opposite side of the highway. Hank hesitated, and then bent over. He lifted up the legs and dragged the body over the ground. It was still wrapped in the blanket. He hurried toward the stone overpass ahead. Megan noticed a pole of some sort to their left. There were numbers on it that read, "HU457." She tried to remember it. She looked ahead and could tell the stone overpass was part of a highway exit. There was a large sign over it. She only caught a glimpse of it, but she managed to see a number. She could not tell if it was a "3" or "5". It seemed to change, which mystified her.

They reached a patch of trees to the right of the overpass. Hank went into the trees to use them as cover. They would hide him from any passersby. Once through the trees, Megan noticed a body of water beyond the tall grass. It was still. She could not tell if it was a river or a lake. There were silhouettes of tall buildings on the other side of it. The water stretched about a mile across. The area near where Hank stood was swampy.

He dropped the body into a hole, which was about two feet deep, two feet wide, and six feet long. The hole had already been dug, most likely by him during an earlier visit to the site. He used the shovel and quickly began covering the body with a pile of dirt that must have originally come from the hole. It only took him several minutes to bury the body.

Again, he looked around nervously to make sure no one was watching. He stepped into the trees and paused. He turned to look across the water. He stared at the buildings and swallowed nervously. It was dark. Regardless, he hoped no one saw him. He tossed the shovel into the water and left.

Hank quickly returned to his car and got in. He started it up and drove off. Megan stood on the side of the road watching, as the car drove away.

She hurried back through the trees and searched for the mound of dirt. She could not find it. It was too dark to see. She could not remember which way to go. She panicked and had trouble breathing. It got even darker, until it was pitch black. She tripped and fell. She turned to get up, but she could not move. She was paralyzed.

"No, no, no…" She tried harder to move. She could not get up. She could not see anything and she could not breathe. "Help! Help me!" She fought and struggled to move, until she forced her eyes open. Was she in the grave?

She was in her bed. She turned to look at her clock. It was 3:37.

"Holy shit!" She tried to get out of bed, but was wrapped in her blanket. She tore it off and jumped out of the bed. She was free, at last. She breathed slowly, taking deep breaths.

She stood there momentarily, almost afraid to get back under the blanket. She thought about going to the bathroom to throw water on her face, except she knew if she did, then it would only be harder to fall asleep.

There was something she needed to do, before she forgot. She grabbed a small pad and a pen from inside her nightstand drawer. She immediately wrote down the numbers from the nightmare, while they were still fresh in her head. She started with the partial license plate from Hank's blue hatchback, which was "677." Next, was the pole along the highway. "H-U-4-5-7" was written there in white, going down in a line. She did not know what the digits signified, but knew they had to be important. There was also the highway sign. There was either a "3" or a "5" on it. Perhaps, it was the exit number for the road on the nearby overpass. Finally, there was the song Maggie sang, which she was finally able to understand. She kept singing, "V356," but why? It made no sense. Whatever the reason, Megan did not want to forget these numbers and letters. She knew they would all have some significance with learning the location of where Maggie is buried. She could always add the information to her journal, after a good night's sleep.

The thought made her laugh. How ironic. What was she thinking? She had not slept a good night's sleep, since moving into the apartment. What made her think she could have one now?

Then again, maybe the nightmares were finally at an end. She reached the climax of the story. The body was in the ground somewhere near a highway and a body of water, which could be anywhere in New York. For now, it would have to suffice. It was more than what she knew before. What else could Maggie have to show her? It seemed the rest would be up to Megan to figure things out. She was not looking forward to the challenge, although the thought of no longer having nightmares was a good start.

She wondered if she would be able to sleep well tomorrow night. She had a feeling she might. Of course, first, she had to get through the rest of this night.

There was still a matter of the small metal box hidden somewhere in the basement under the garage. Maggie said she would show her the location when the time was right. Exactly when was that supposed to be? Tomorrow??? Next week? Next month?

Megan took a deep breath. She knew this was far from over. After much consideration, she got back into bed. However, she pushed the blanket aside, before trying to go back to sleep.

# Chapter 13

<hr>

# Victims of The Anniversary Killer

The next evening after dinner Megan sat at the kitchen table reading the old newspaper article about Maggie's disappearance. Her journal and laptop were within reach. She pulled the laptop in front of her and typed a name into the search bar. She wanted to search the Internet and see what she could dig up regarding The Anniversary Killer. There were a few interesting results, which popped up during her search.

Surprisingly, there was a book by Stevie Shaw called "*The Anniversary Killer.*" She was thrilled and wondered if perhaps it could have been inspired by true events. After reading the description, she immediately realized it was an unrelated fictional story about another serial killer/rapist, who just happened to share the same name.

"Hm. It might be a good read anyway," she mumbled to herself. "It's been a while since I read a good book." She decided to make a mental note of the book's title, so she could order it later. Remembering it would not be too difficult.

The search continued. A few newspaper articles from the late 1980s showed up in the search, which were more rewarding than she expected. She printed them and resumed her search. She knew instantly she was on the right trail. One article in particular was quite helpful. It was dated August 20, 1989. The headline read, "*Anniversary Killer is Charged with the Murders of Four Women.*"

*"Two weeks ago, following the arrest of Yonkers mechanic Henry Paul Cameron, the pieces of a 3-year-old mystery finally began to fall into place. On*

*August 9, Doreen Stanley, 22, of Yonkers, nearly became the next victim of The Anniversary Killer. Instead, she managed to escape and lead police to his door. After an all-night stand-off, Cameron was arrested and charged with kidnapping, unlawful imprisonment, sexual abuse, and assault.*

*At last, additional charges have been filed against Cameron to include his vicious crimes against Erin Christine McAffy, Tamara Lyndsey, Linda Homolkan, and Dawn Ross. These additional charges include rape, sodomy, and murder. There has been enough evidence found to indicate Cameron has committed these crimes, after a thorough search of his home and business located on Odell Avenue last week, which revealed souvenirs from his victims. Police have also impounded his light blue 1981 2-door Dodge Colt hatchback as evidence used in the commission of at least two of the abductions.*

*His home and business, which was a mechanic's garage, are conveniently situated right next to the Old Croton Aqueduct Trailways State Park, where he allegedly did most of his hunting.*

*As of yet, police have not been able to link him to the disappearance of Margaret Elizabeth Garrett, who disappeared last year on August 31, when she went for a jog along the very same trail that runs beside Cameron's home. Several witnesses placed her on the trail at around 3:30 p.m. approaching Untermyer Park, which would be south from Cameron's home and business. He claims to have been home sick with a stomach virus that day, but no one can verify his alibi.*

*"Until a body can be found, she will remain a missing person," a police spokesman said. "That does not mean we'll stop looking for her. She'll turn up sooner or later. If she was indeed one of his victims, she won't be hard to find. We just haven't looked in the right place, yet."*

*Considering it's been nearly a year since her disappearance, chances of finding her alive are slim. Her family are still hoping she will emerge someplace with amnesia.*

*Cameron is set to stand trial for his crimes in the next coming weeks once psychiatrists deem him to be sane. The gruesome methods involved in some of his murders have left some questioning his sanity."*

Megan printed the article and placed it on the table with the rest of her research materials. She was going to need a folder to keep everything together. This new article alone proved to be a treasure trove of information, which could easily lead to more. She finally had Hank's full name, the names of his other victims, as well as a time span for her research. She would focus her attention on 1986-1989.

Her online search continued. She entered the names of each victim into the search bar to see what came up, including the name of the one who got away, Doreen Stanley. She found more articles and more information, including dates of disappearances. She printed whatever she could and saved everything on her laptop as a back-up.

She knew searching the Internet was not going to be enough. Not for what she needed. She would probably need to take a trip to the Yonkers Public Library, so she could search for more articles using the names of the victims and killer. She wanted every piece of information she could find on the case of The Anniversary Killer.

In time, her search yielded a photo of Henry Paul Cameron aka Hank aka The Anniversary Killer. It stopped her dead in her tracks. Seeing his face on her computer screen made her nauseous. In her nightmares his face had always been somewhat unclear and shadowy. This time, his face was clear as day. It sickened her.

Megan closed her eyes and took a deep breath. Her hands were trembling. She pulled them away from the keyboard and made two fists. She did not want to have an attack. She clenched her fists tightly, but then felt at ease. Although, she could not feel it, Maggie had placed her hand on Megan's shoulder to give her the strength she needed to go on. Megan opened her eyes, her hands returned to the keyboard, and she downloaded the photo of Hank. She also printed it.

Megan felt such hatred and disgust toward him. Those feelings were amplified by Maggie's equal hatred and disgust. She could never forgive him for what he did to her and to those other women. He robbed them of their dignity and filled their last moments with terror. He stole precious years from their lives. They were all young women like her, who might have had full lives ahead of them had it not been for his cruel intervention.

Later that night, Megan had another nightmare. She was lying in her bed surrounded by complete darkness. It was extremely silent. Maybe too silent. At first, she did not realize it was a nightmare, until she tried to move and could not. She was experiencing sleep paralysis. Right away, she began to panic. She struggled, but nothing happened. Her limbs felt stiff. It seemed she was paralyzed from the neck down. It also became difficult for her to breathe. It felt like she was having an attack. The air around her was stale and cold. Her body also felt cold.

It occurred to her she was experiencing what it probably felt like to be in Maggie's place, buried underground. Before she knew it, dirt began to fall in around her at a rapid rate. She cried out, "Oh, God! What's happening to me? Somebody please help me!" The dirt eventually covered her face to the point where she was forced to keep her eyes and mouth closed.

Of course, Maggie had not been buried alive. She was dead, so she never had to suffer in the way Megan was currently suffering. She had already endured more than enough. Megan wondered if it were possible Maggie's spirit experienced it and maybe it was why she was currently going through it. Normally, she experienced the same things Maggie went through during these nightmares. Then again, Maggie's body had been wrapped tightly in a blanket. This was different, unless you combine it with her previous nightmare.

The air quality worsened making it harder to breathe. Dirt continued to cover her face, so she tried turning her head sideways. She hated how the dirt felt on her face. Unfortunately, she still could not move, but she could scream. As soon as she did, dirt fell into her mouth causing her to swallow some. She began choking and tried her best to cough it back up. It tasted awful.

A moment later, the nightmare changed, much to her relief. She was no longer buried alive underground. She took a deep breath. The air smelled foul. She looked around and noticed she was standing at the swampy shore of the same dark body of water, where the body was buried. It was night like in the nightmare. She gazed across over the water, although she could barely see a thing. It was dark and foggy. She could only faintly make out the outlines of the buildings in the distance.

It made her think of California's June gloom, which was a foggy time of year, often confused with pollution. She thought the same when she first moved out west. Eventually, she learned it was not caused by pollution. It was merely the typical weather out there. By mid-day, the fogs usually cleared up.

She did not expect to reminisce about California. It felt odd.

She turned around to face the trees and noticed there was a large hole in the earth directly in front of her bare feet. It was the grave, except it was empty.

She glanced down at her body and saw she was naked. Her body was pale and filthy. Furthermore, it did not seem like her body, at all. It was different.

She turned back to face the water and stepped closer. She looked down to see her reflection and was not too surprised to see Maggie's sorrowful face staring back at her. It pained her to see Maggie looking so dreadful. For a long time, she simply stared at the reflection feeling sad. She wished she could take away the pain Maggie felt. After a while, she realized she was crying. She had not even noticed. It was becoming so natural.

Her legs started to feel weak in the knees, until it was too much effort to remain standing. She dropped to her knees. The ground was soft and cold. Her hand slowly reached for the water and touched her reflection, causing ripples that moved outward away from the shore into the fog. The reflection soon faded and disappeared leaving the darkened still water. It was quiet. There were no crickets or any indication of wildlife around her.

"What else do you want me to see?" She asked in a soft voice, which could hardly be heard.

A loud whisper answered back from behind her, "Come with me." It was Maggie's voice.

Megan looked back over her shoulder and saw the dead teenager standing naked over her own grave. She held out her ghostly hand for Megan to take. Megan was herself. Her strength had returned to her legs. She stood up and approached Maggie. She took her hand and, in an instant, they were transported to the basement of the garage.

Megan dreaded being there, but it was necessary for what Maggie wanted to show her.

Hank entered the room holding a small metal box about the size of a shoebox. He looked different. He was not dressed the same and his hair was slightly longer. He also had facial hair. It appeared to be a different night from when he murdered Maggie. He was carrying a new shovel with him, since the previous one was tossed into the water, after he buried her.

Maggie pointed to the metal box in his hand. "Look," she stated.

Hank placed the box down on the worktable and walked toward the far corner of the room, where he then began to dig a small hole about one foot deep. The women looked on in silence.

Once he was done, he opened the metal box and examined its contents one final time. There were nearly twenty photos of women in bondage inside.

Souvenirs of his victims. For some reason, he decided it was time to part with them. Perhaps, he was worried someone would find them. If so, Megan wondered, why not simply destroy them? Instead, he closed the box and locked it, placing the tiny metal key into his pants pocket. The box was carefully placed into the hole and buried. He made sure to flatten the surface well when he was done.

He then left the room and returned, a short time later, pushing a heavy-duty wheelbarrow. It was weighed down significantly by a large square-shaped boulder, making it very difficult for him to push. Somehow, Hank managed to move it into place. He dumped the boulder on top of the area, where the metal box was buried. Afterwards, he used a crowbar to push the boulder firmly against the wall.

It seemed like a lot of trouble to go through.

Suddenly, Maggie turned to Megan and said, "Find it." She reached up with her forefinger and poked Megan's forehead causing her to awaken in an instant. She opened her eyes and saw her ceiling overhead. She turned to look at her clock. As usual, it was 3:37 in the morning.

"Right on time," she uttered groggily, before turning over and going back to bed.

The next day, Megan asked Hannah to give her a ride to the library. Misty agreed to keep an eye on Josh, but asked if she could do it at her home, instead. Megan had no problem with her request. She trusted Misty and understood why she preferred not to be in the apartment. Misty had already informed her of the way she was treated by the former ghostly tenant. Megan hoped that would soon change, once she helped Maggie to resolve her issues.

At the library, Megan and Hannah split up to double their efforts. They examined old newspaper articles on microfiche. They searched for any mention of the victims, Margaret Elizabeth Garrett, Erin Christine McAffy, Tamara Lyndsey, Linda Homolkan, Dawn Ross, and Doreen Stanley. Of course, they also searched for Henry Paul Cameron, The Anniversary Killer.

When Megan focused on the date of Maggie's disappearance, August 4, 1988, she located a missing person's report, which she promptly printed. Apparently, it had also been issued with each copy of the August 20, 1989, Sunday Edition of the *Yonkers Herald Tribune*, which featured an article titled,

*"Margaret Elizabeth Garrett – Missing or Another Victim of The Anniversary Killer?"*

Hannah tried searching for anything she could find regarding the girl who lived, Doreen Stanley. She found an article about her from two days after the killer was apprehended. A photo of her was included. It seemed Doreen was able to escape by using Judo on Hank. Megan wished it was something she could have witnessed in a dream, when Hannah told her about it.

There were about two dozen articles to print out by the time they were done. Some concentrated on the other missing women, which was helpful. The two sleuths gathered everything together and sat at a table to review their findings. Hannah put the articles in chronological order to make it easier.

Megan suggested, "Let's take these home and combine them with the stuff I printed from my laptop last night. I'd prefer to read everything in order."

"Okay. Sounds good to me," Hannah agreed.

They left the library and picked up Josh on the way home. Megan turned on the television and found something for him to watch, so he would be occupied. Next, she and Hannah sat down at the kitchen table and combined both sets of printed newspaper articles. There was also the missing person's report and another report from the March 4, 1990, Sunday Edition of the *Yonkers Herald Tribune* called *"The Anniversary Killer's Victims,"* which actually had photos and significant dates for all six women in order.

They went over every bit of information they had and began reading.

Erin Christine McAffy, age 25, was the first reported victim to be taken on Tuesday, July 29, 1986, while leaving Untermyer Park. She had been abducted on the ten-year anniversary of the first Son of Sam shooting attack, which resulted in the death of Donna Lauria. Witnesses observed Hank grab Erin and pull her into his blue two-door hatchback, before speeding away south on North Broadway.

Sadly, her nude body was discovered in a ditch along the northbound side of the Bronx River Parkway in Yonkers two days later.

The next victim was Tamara Lyndsey, age 26, who was abducted on Thursday, January 15, 1987. She had been walking her dog along the Old Croton Aqueduct Trail in Yonkers, when she seemingly disappeared without a trace. Her dog was found unharmed and tied to a tree near a break in the trail at Arthur Street.

Megan recalled one of her earlier dreams, in which Maggie was abducted. After being dragged to the blue car and placed into the rear compartment, the car drove by Arthur Street on its way to Hank's garage. This could not be a coincidence. It proves the trail was Hank's hunting ground.

This second abduction took place on the forty-year anniversary of the infamous Black Dahlia murder in California. Like Elizabeth Short, Tamara's corpse was severed in half at the waist. Both halves of Tamara's nude body were discovered two weeks later in a ditch near the Saw Mill River Parkway going northbound, between the exits for Mt. Kisco and Bedford. Again, it was the northbound side of a parkway.

Victim number three was Linda Homolkan, age 25, who was abducted on Monday, November 16, 1987. She was supposed to be starting her new job at the Hudson River Museum on the same morning, but never made it into work. Her abandoned car was located later in the evening on Warburton Avenue south from Odell Avenue. It had a flat tire. There was no indication anyone tried to repair it.

Linda disappeared on the thirtieth anniversary of Ed Gein's final victim, Bernice Worden, who had been hung upside down and gutted. Ed Gein's crimes later became the inspiration for horror movies, such as "*Psycho*" and "*The Texas Chainsaw Massacre.*"

Linda's nude headless body was found a week later in a wooded area of Wave Hill Park in the Bronx. Her head was located the next day along the nearby railroad tracks. It was believed her body was also hung upside down because her blood had been drained.

The fourth victim was Dawn Ross, age 24, taken on Friday, January 15, 1988. She was the second victim to be abducted on that particular date. Dawn was abducted, while walking to her car on Odell Avenue, not far from Warburton Avenue, and conveniently very close to Hank's garage. She had been visiting a friend, who lived in the area. Her car was found parked exactly where she left it upon her arrival.

The crime took place on the tenth anniversary of one of Ted Bundy's more famous attacks of four women in a sorority house, in which two were brutally murdered. They were Lisa Levy and *Margaret Elizabeth* Bowman.

Margaret Elizabeth was also Maggie's name. Again, it felt like this was no coincidence. It made Maggie's eventual death so much more significant.

It begged the question, was he stalking his victims prior to abducting them? According to her diary, they first saw each other a year earlier.

Dawn's nude body was not found, until two weeks later, near the northbound side of the Taconic State Parkway before the Memorial Bridge, which crosses the Croton Reservoir. Again with the northbound side! Dawn had been strangled to death, which was Ted Bundy's modus operandi.

Margaret Elizabeth Garrett aka Maggie aka Lizzie allegedly went missing on Wednesday, August 31, 1988, which happened to be the one hundredth anniversary of Jack the Ripper's first official victim, in which he murdered Mary Ann Nichols. Margaret was only 19 years old, at the time, making her the youngest victim.

Finally, there was Doreen Stanley, age 22, who was Hank's final victim. She was abducted on Wednesday, August 9, 1989, while walking to the Elizabeth Seton School on North Broadway. Hank asked her for directions, and then used Chloroform to render her unconscious. He intended to stab her to death, but instead, she managed to use her Judo training to render him unconscious. She freed herself and fled to a neighbor's home, where she called the police. It led to an all-night stand-off, which resulted in Hank's arrest early the next morning.

This crime took place on the twenty-year anniversary of the Sharon Tate murder by the Manson family in California.

By early September of 1989, Hank was found fit to stand trial. He was convicted of five counts of kidnapping, five counts of unlawful imprisonment, four counts of rape and sodomy, several illegal weapons charges, menacing, and four counts of murder, as well as an assortment of various charges for assault and torture.

He was sentenced to life in prison on Tuesday, March 27, 1990. According to the latest newspaper article from March 28, 2000, he should still be serving time at the Sing Sing Correctional Facility in Ossining, New York. Megan noticed that particular article featured a photo of him with longer hair and no glasses. His smug look had been replaced with the look of a hardened criminal.

And what of the girl, who lived? Where was Doreen Stanley today? Was she still alive? Megan most certainly wanted to know, so she and Hannah did a search of her name. They came up with several possible matches on Facebook, which they checked using Hannah's profile, but it was difficult to tell if any were the right person based on the photos available.

Hannah asked, "Do you really think she might still be alive? I mean, I suppose it's possible."

"Next to Maggie, she was the next youngest victim. She can't be too old," Megan figured. "It was only about thirty-five to forty years ago. She should be somewhere in her sixties. Or seventies? Okay, maybe she could have passed away. Personally, I like to think a tough lady like her is still alive and kicking," she smirked.

"Yeah, she must have been a bad ass in her day." Hannah smiled in admiration. "Thanks to her, they caught that jerk. So, what now, Meg?"

"Now, we try to figure out where he put Maggie, and then we'll worry about the metal box." Megan was in no hurry to return to the basement. Besides, she had a feeling searching for the box was something better left to the proper authorities. It's like she reminded herself once before, one step at a time.

# MISSING

## HAVE YOU SEEN THIS WOMAN?

**Margaret Elizabeth Garrett aka "Maggie" aka "Liz" aka "Lizzie"**

**Race:** White
**Sex:** Female
**Age:** 19 years old
**DOB:** February 13, 1969
**Height:** 5'2"
**Weight:** 130 lbs.
**Eyes:** Brown
**Hair:** Long, wavy, and brown
**Identifying Markings:** No tattoos, no scars
**Last Seen:** Wednesday, August 31, 1988, 3:30 pm, Old Croton Aqueduct State Park Trailway, Yonkers.
**Circumstances of Disappearance:** Margaret was jogging north along the Old Croton Aqueduct Trail, which she often did several times a week. She was wearing a white t-shirt, blue track pants, and white sneakers. She never returned home and there was no evidence to indicate foul play. She was not dependent on anyone, nor was she under any stress, according to her brother. All of her clothing and possessions were still at her residence in her room, aside from what she had with her, at the time of her disappearance.
If located, please contact Yonkers Police Department at 914-555-0105.

# THE ANNIVERSARY KILLER'S VICTIMS...

1. Erin Christine McAffy, 25
Abducted July 29, 1986
Body Found July 31, 1986

2. Tamara Lyndsey, 26
Abducted Jan. 15, 1987
Body Found Jan. 28, 1987

3. Linda Homolkan, 25
Abducted Nov. 16, 1987
Body Found Nov. 28, 1987
Head Found Nov. 30, 1987

4. Dawn Ross, 24
Abducted Jan. 15, 1988
Body Found on Jan. 28, 1988

5. Margaret Elizabeth Garrett, 19
Disappeared Aug. 31, 1988
Still Missing

6. Doreen Stanley, 22
Abducted Aug. 9, 1989
Escaped Aug. 10, 1989

Doreen Stanley is presumably the only victim to survive her abduction, while Margaret Elizabeth Garrett's disappearance remains a mystery. There are still those who doubt her alleged status as a victim of The Anniversary Killer because her body has not been found. The question remains, is she still alive? No one knows for certain. One can only hope she is alive and well. It has been nearly two years since her disappearance.

3/4/1990

# The Anniversary Killer – 10 Years Later

It has been ten years since Henry Paul Cameron was sentenced to life in prison for multiple charges of kidnapping, assault, rape, sodomy, and murder of several women in Yonkers. However, since that time, he's become something of a model prisoner. It does not, by any means, change what he's done, nor does it ease the pain he has caused for so many families. To make matters worse, he still shows no remorse for his actions, even a decade later.

In a recent interview at the Sing Sing Correctional Facility in Ossining, N.Y., where he has spent the last decade, he explained coldly, "People die. It's part of life. When it's your time to go, you go. It's simple. There's nothing you can do about it, so why feel bad? Listen, I just helped those girls on their way. It's no big deal. You know? It was their time. They just didn't know it."

There is little doubt with an attitude like that, Cameron will continue to do time – for the rest of his life. Cameron is currently serving life in prison with no chance for parole.

When asked about Margaret Elizabeth Garrett's disappearance, he had this to say, "You know? I'm getting really tired of hearing people ask me about her. Is she one of my victims? I'm asking *you!* She's not the reason I'm here. Is it? They charged me for the murders of *four* girls. Four! Jesus. If I killed that girl, show me the proof! You show me proof, and then maybe I'll fess up to it. Not a moment sooner."

While it was not exactly a confession, it was also not exactly a denial. If there is any proof out there to show that Cameron abducted and murdered Garrett, we can only hope it comes to light, while he is still alive, so justice can finally be served.

Originally published March 28, 2000

# Chapter 14

## The Next Step

Megan and Hannah sat at the kitchen table going over the research materials they gathered. Newspaper articles were spread across the table in chronological order. Megan's journal was opened to one of the recent entries. Together they tried to make sense of the facts, as they knew them. They had the names of each victim, dates of abduction, and the dates the victims' bodies were found. They also had Hank's full name, photos of him, and of his house, which had been demolished some time ago. After comparing the crimes and Maggie's diary, they noted several obvious coincidences, which led them to believe the way Hank chose his victims may have been premeditated.

Megan was floored by the idea. "Dear God. Do you really think he could have planned each crime in advance down to the victim he chose? That is so demented."

"Totally!" Hannah replied. "There's no question in my mind. He saw Maggie a year earlier, according to what she wrote in her diary. Her name was nearly identical to Ted Bundy's victim. Who's to say the sick fucker didn't follow her around and spy on her for a year, so he could learn her jogging routine and wait for her?"

Megan scowled, "Take it easy with the language and lower your voice. I don't need Josh to hear what we're talking about. Use your whisper voice."

Luckily, Josh was playing in his room, so he was out of ear shot from their conversation and heard nothing.

"I'm sorry, Meg. I get so heated whenever I think about this jerk." She sighed in frustration and tried to focus. "Where could he have buried her?

Based on what you wrote in your journal, it sounds like he got on the Saw Mill River Parkway and headed south. It could be anywhere from there." She frowned. "If he took the Cross County Parkway to the end it could have led him up into Connecticut."

"Well, it was a highway near the water somewhere. I think it was a big lake," Megan guessed. "I know there were tall buildings across the water."

"A lake? Hmm. I can't imagine where it could be. Are you sure it was a lake?" Hannah asked.

"No," Megan shook her head. She had no clue. "It was somewhere unfamiliar to me."

"Then maybe it was Connecticut. *Or* maybe it was near the ocean. I suppose it could have been the Long Island Sound. Ugh! There are so many possibilities. For all we know that same area might have been undeveloped back then and looks completely different today."

"True. Hey, what about the numbers on the pole?" Megan asked. "It has to mean something. H-U-4-5-7."

"Beats me. If I had to guess, I'd say the 'H' stands for highway. The 'U' could be utility or urban. Maybe it was a significant number, which had nothing to do with the pole or highway. It was only on the pole in the dream, so you could see it."

"I guess." Megan was uncertain. She thought about the sign before the overpass. It also had a number on it. "What about the green highway sign in front of the overpass? I'm not sure if it had a '3' or a '5' on it, but I think it might have been the exit sign. Maybe it was the exit number."

"Yeah, probably," Hannah agreed. "It's too bad you can't remember the exact number, not that it matters since we have no idea which highway it was on." She exhaled in frustration. "What are we doing, Meg? I mean, what's the end game plan? Are you going to contact the police with the information you have?"

Megan nodded, but then shrugged. "I don't really know, yet. I think it's what I should do. It would be the best way for Hank to get what he deserves. There's nothing I can do to him, if he's in prison. It has to be them, right?"

"Well, yeah, but what are you going to tell them? Hello, my name is Megan and a ghost told me how to find her body. That's gonna go over well."

"What else can I do?" Megan was stumped.

"Maybe you can make an anonymous phone call to the police. Tell them you have some information regarding a missing person case from 1988, and then give them what you got. Be sure to hang up before it reaches thirty seconds, so they can't trace the call. You should probably use an outside line."

Megan scoffed and shook her head. "You watch too many movies," she said. "They're not going to trace the call. Besides, when is the last time you noticed a payphone anywhere in Yonkers? I've only been back in New York for a few months, but I can tell you I have not seen one, yet."

"I don't know. Maybe you're right." Hannah shrugged. "So, what's the plan, then? There has to be something we can do to help her without sounding like complete loons."

Megan frowned and asked, "Why can't we just be honest? I can call the police, explain what happened, give them the information I have, and the ball will be in their court."

Hannah was stunned. "Are you insane?" She exclaimed. "First of all, if you call them with the information you have, they're gonna want to know how you know what you know, which is a lot more than you should know. You know?" Megan glared back at her unamused. Hannah smirked and continued, "Second, how will you know the person you call will take you seriously and follow up on the information you give them? What if they think you're just another kook calling with nothing better to do and ignore your call? Maggie won't get the justice she deserves, and how will you even know by calling some random dope on the phone? Bad idea." She shook her head disapprovingly.

"And how would an anonymous call be any different?"

Hannah considered it. "Okay. You got me there. This is why we need to think of a good fool-proof plan, where we can involve the police, stick it to Hank, and give Maggie the justice she deserves."

"Don't forget about the metal box," Megan added.

"We can find it ourselves."

"No way!" Megan shook her head. "I won't go back there. Besides, if we find the box and hand it over to the police, why would they believe we got it from Hank's basement? As far as they know, we found it somewhere else and lied. Trust me. *They* need to find it. Not us."

"Good point, Meg," Hannah agreed. "That's pretty smart. We shouldn't risk contaminating the evidence. I suppose we can make the anonymous call about the metal box. What do you think?"

"Will you forget about the anonymous calls? I don't trust doing it that way. I need to know the information I provide will be put to good use. I need to be in touch with someone on the inside, like a detective. It's the only way this will work."

Hannah nodded, "Yeah, you're right, again. However, what if you tell them all about the whole ghost in the nightmares thing and they think you're batshit crazy and take you to the mental hospital in a straitjacket? Think about Josh."

"That's why I have you to back me up," Megan replied.

"Except I can't corroborate any of the dream information. That stuff is all you, Meg. All I can really do is say I thought I saw what might have been a woman in the bathroom on the day you moved in. You're the one with the crazy unexplained experiences. Josh is a kid. They won't take his word for it. Unless maybe Misty can help."

"I should give her a call and ask her to come over. It might be time to bring her in on this project."

"Yes! Good idea! What about Leslie? Maybe we can have her come up, too. We can all brainstorm on the best course of action. Ask a detective to come here to the apartment and we explain what we know, as a group."

Megan had doubts. "I don't think police detectives randomly come over upon request," she said. "Let me call Misty and see if *she* can come over." She dialed Misty's number and made her request. After some reluctance, Misty agreed. Next, Megan sent Leslie a text message and asked if she had time to come upstairs, for a while. She said she would be right up.


When Misty arrived, Megan invited her inside. Leslie was already there with them. Megan and Hannah spent a few minutes filling them in on what kind of research they had available and what they intended to accomplish. Megan did not leave anything out. She informed them of her nightmares, and then showed them the journal and diary. In return, Misty disclosed her experiences within the apartment during the times she would take care of Josh.

Once she was done she added, "For the record, she is here with us, right now. I can feel her."

Megan stated in a clear voice, "We are going to do what we can to help you find peace, Maggie. You have my word. Just please work with us, not against us."

Leslie suggested, "What about the phone number at the bottom of the missing person's report? Why not simply call the number and ask to speak to the detective in charge of the case? If they put you through to him or her, then and only then, should you give out the information you have."

Hannah agreed, "It's a great plan. I like it."

Misty nodded in agreement, "Yeah, let's do that."

It was settled. Megan picked up her cellphone and dialed the number on the bottom of the report. A male police officer answered the call stating his name and rank. He then asked how he could help her.

Megan felt nervous, as she began, "Hello. Um, my name is Megan Forester. I live in Yonkers. I'm calling in regard to a missing person case from 1988. Her name was Margaret Elizabeth Garrett. She was nineteen years old, at the time. I believe I have valuable information, which can help any detectives working on the case. Can you please transfer me to the detective bureau, or whoever I can talk to about this case? I can wait."

The police officer paused, before putting her on hold. When he returned to the line, he asked her a few basic questions, such as what kind of information she had and how she came across this information.

She held her ground and stated, "All I will say is I strongly believe I might be able to help find her. I'm sorry, but it's a lot of information and I'd rather not waste time telling everything to someone, who has nothing to do with the case, because I'm only gonna have to repeat it to someone else, after I tell you. No offense. So, can I please speak to the detective in charge?"

A moment later, he transferred her to the Detective Division. She spoke to a detective named Johnson, who answered the call with suspicion. "This is Detective Robert Johnson. Who may I ask is calling?"

"Hello, Detective Johnson. Thank you for taking my call. My name is Megan Forester. I live on Walnut Street in the very same apartment once occupied by Margaret Elizabeth Garrett, who was reported missing in August of 1988. This might sound very hard to believe, but I have come across information, which may help you to solve what actually happened to her, and it has to do with Henry Paul Cameron, The Anniversary Killer."

"Oh, really? This I have to hear," he sounded both skeptical and sarcastic. "By all means, what can you tell me that we have not already went over a few hundred times in the more than thirty years, since her disappearance? And this better be good. I don't like people wasting my time with conspiracy theories."

"This is not a conspiracy theory. I can prove Hank Cameron abducted Margaret, and I might have an idea of how to locate her body."

"Please, do tell," he replied. "I'm all ears."

"Hank's other victims were easy to find because they were left out in the open along the highways or other outdoor wooded areas. He didn't like the newspapers knowing his M.O., so he changed things, by the time he got to Maggie. He buried her."

He sighed impatiently and inquired, "And how can you prove this theory?"

"It's not a theory. I know that's what he did for a fact. I also have information on the area, where he buried her. A description and numbers that can help. I would like to give you this information."

"Let me guess," he stated with cynicism. "For a small reward?"

"No, of course not! I'm not looking for anything in return." She felt insulted by his insinuation. "I'm doing this for Maggie. I want to tell you everything I know. I just need to know you'll believe me and follow up on it."

"Okay, fine, but tell me this. How did you come across this information? Please, don't tell me you're another psychic or that you and old Hank are pen pals." Apparently, she was not the first to call with new information.

"*Pen pals???* Ugh! Gross! I hate that bastard, especially because of what he did to those women! And what he did to Maggie is unforgivable!"

"I am still waiting to learn *how* you came across this information," he reminded her.

"Um, right," she hesitated. She hoped he would not hang up, as soon as she admitted the truth. She warned him, "This is the part which is going to sound unbelievable. Please, don't hang up when I tell you."

"I can tell you now, ma'am. That does not inspire my confidence in what you are about to tell me. I behoove you to make it sound as believable as you can because I am not one bit amused. It just so happens I was looking over Margaret's case file before you called, so I am already thinking this is a prank. Convince me otherwise."

"Oh, my God! You were looking over her case?" She could not believe it. Neither could her friends when they overheard. "That settles it. This is fate! I am so glad I called."

"Can we please get on with this?" He urged her. "I'd like to skip to the part where I'm glad you called."

"Oh, sorry. Okay." She tried thinking of something she could start with, which was never mentioned in any of the newspapers, to gain his confidence. "I know Hank wore a belt buckle with the letter 'H' on it. Hank was written across the breast pocket of his blue mechanic's shirt." The detective became intrigued, as she went on, "He abducted a total of six women. He tortured, raped, and sodomized most of these women in the basement of his garage with the exception of Doreen Stanley, who escaped. Each woman was tied to a brick support beam next to a horse stall in the same basement. There was hay residue in the stall," she added. "The hay isn't there anymore, but it was there, back then. Hank used tools from a small wooden worktable to torture them. The worktable was more like a cart. It had wheels. He also took photos of each victim, which he placed into a small metal box the size of a shoebox. After he killed Maggie, he buried the box in one of the corners of the basement. He covered it with a large square-shaped boulder. If you find the box, you will find photos of Maggie and the other girls, which should tie the crimes together. Hank used his blue two-door hatchback to abduct each of these women. I know the license plate ends with '677.' After murdering Maggie, he wrapped her body in a white blanket and drove to an isolated highway near some kind of lake and buried her along the shore. There was a stone overpass nearby and the exit sign was either number 3 or number 5. I also know another number, which could help with learning the exact location, but I don't know what it means. The number is 'H-U-4-5-7.'" She paused. It was too quiet on the other line. "Are you writing this down or something?"

"I'm listening and taking notes. Let me ask you something, which amazingly you still have not mentioned. *How* do you know about this information? You mentioned a few details not available to the public, so you have my attention."

"Oh, good!" Megan was pleased. "I was hoping I said something only the police would know."

"Ms. Forester. How. Do. You. Know? It's a simple question."

She wavered, before spitting it out, "Maggie showed me." She bit her lip, after the words came out.

"Maggie showed… what? Maggie the dead girl???"

"Yes! Her spirit showed me everything that happened to her, beginning with when she went for a jog along the Old Croton Aqueduct Trail, and then Hank approaching her from behind near Arthur Street, as she was heading toward Untermyer Park. He used something to put her to sleep, dragged her to his car, and drove her to his garage. He tied her to the brick beam in the basement and yanked out all of her teeth using pliers. Afterwards, the monster raped her. She had blood all over her white '*Amanda*' t-shirt. He slit her throat in the bathroom, but that wasn't all. He had… *relations* with her body." It was difficult to think about it, again. She had to look and make sure Josh was not listening, "Next, he bit off and ate one of her nipples, after frying it in a pan on the stove." The other women cringed. "He wrapped the body, drove it to some deserted highway in the middle of the night, and buried her along the shore of a lake. There were tall buildings across the water. He threw the shovel into the water. There was a pole along the highway. On the pole I saw the numbers 'H-U-4-5-7,' as I said before, and the exit sign before the overpass either had a '3' or a '5' on it."

"Okay, that is quite the graphic story." He sounded to her like he wanted to hear more. "Can you please explain how the spirit of a teenage girl, who died over thirty years ago, was able to show you these things in such detail? Believe me, I'd really like to know."

"She showed me through my dreams," Megan confessed. "Ever since I moved into her old apartment in the Hill View, I've had these awful nightmares. I saw everything play out in order, over a period of two weeks. At first, I thought they were regular nightmares, so obviously, I didn't pay them any mind, but eventually I noticed it was an ongoing story with the same characters. I saw her, a girl I've never seen in my life, until the first dream. The same girl who has been haunting my home. My four-year-old son has also seen her numerous times. He knew her as Lizzie, which is short for her middle name, before I ever knew her name. How would he even know, unless it was true? I only know her name because I read it in an old newspaper from 1988, which I found hidden away on the top shelf of my hall closet. Her 1987 high school picture was in the paper. It's when we both realized we were dealing with a common entity. I also found her diary in my son's bedroom closet. One of her last entries from 1987 mentioned her father, Frank, going to get his car repaired at a garage near Odell Avenue. She said one of the young mechanics looked at her in a creepy way. It had to be Hank! I know his creepy look. I've seen him in my nightmares with his glasses and that creepy smile." She detested thinking about his smile. It gave her chills. Luckily, she recalled another fact she could add, which got her mind off of it. "Oh, and I always wake up at 3:37 A.M., after these nightmare. I believe it was when he buried the body."

"I see," he responded. "That would make it approximately twelve hours, after she disappeared."

"She did not disappear. She was taken," she corrected him.

"Right. Well, I guess we'll see. Huh? As I told you, I took some notes based on this conversation. I'll tell you what. Let me do some digging and see if everything you said checks out. I want to compare what you said to what I have in my files. There are a lot of details. I will certainly be in touch. You said you're living at Margaret's old address?"

"Yes," Megan confirmed. "In the exact same apartment."

"Okay. Good. It simplifies things. Can you give me a phone number, where I can reach you?"

She did and they hung up.


Hannah, Leslie, and Misty were at the edge of their seats at the kitchen table. They had been listening intently to one side of the conversation. They were extremely eager to know what was said on the other end of the phone by the detective.

Hannah blurted out, "Well?! What did he say?"

Megan repeated what the detective told her, while the others listened with great interest. She hoped he would believe her, after checking the facts. How could he not? When she was done filling them in, she paced back and forth, before saying, "I guess the only thing to do now is to wait."

Misty was still astonished by the whole story. "Wow. This is really an incredible story. I know it scared me to death being here with her, at first, but I feel privileged to be a part of something so special. To be able to help a spirit find peace in the afterlife is truly amazing. By the way, she's still here with us. I can tell. I wonder if she's just as anxious as the rest of us to learn what the detective will say when he calls you back."

Leslie also felt privileged to know Maggie was in the room with them. After feeling guilty for decades, she took the opportunity to say her piece. "Margaret, if you can hear me, I am so very sorry for what happened to you. For many years, there wasn't a day that went by when I didn't think of you. I honestly wish we had the chance to become friends before it was too late. I wish I knew what a great person you were before you were taken away. Everyone in this building tried to find you. We all helped your momma anyway we could." Her eyes filled with tears, as she spoke. "I hope you know that."

Hannah put her arm around her and said in a comforting tone, "I'm sure she knows."

Megan nodded, "She can hear everything we say and she understands, too. Trust me. We won't let her down, regardless of what Detective Johnson says. If we have to, we'll go find the damned metal box ourselves, as much as I hate the idea of going back to that horrible place. I'd do it for Maggie. I would." She was adamant about her decision. She promised Maggie justice and she intended to deliver.

Hannah turned to her and said, "You won't be alone either. I will be there at your side every step of the way. I have no problem going back there."

Leslie took a deep breath and uttered bravely, "Me, too. This time, I *will* go inside with you. I swear it." She looked at Megan, who nodded back. "That place puts a wicked fear in me that shakes my heart to the core, but I will go there with you."

Misty had only just learned of the basement. She was curious about it. "I wonder what I would feel, if I went there," she speculated aloud. She looked to Megan and Hannah, and asked, "Do you think it's haunted?"

"Hell yeah," responded Hannah in a flash. She remembered how scary it was to be there. It was cold, dark, damp, and lonely. It did not help seeing how badly being there affected Megan. She almost lost it that day. The thought of returning there with Megan made her worry. She knew without a doubt she had to look out for her best friend, no matter what.

One person who was not as eager to go to the basement was Misty. She swallowed nervously. It was not the kind of place she preferred to visit… ever. She hated the feeling she got whenever going to cemeteries and allegedly haunted locations. It's not something she did on purpose. Normally, she would find out a place was haunted, after the fact. It was always the same. It felt so overwhelming. The air itself felt unbelievably heavy. Usually, she ended up with a migraine. Not to mention, the intense feelings she got from the spirits around her. Therefore, she tended to avoid haunted places like the plague.

Her grandmother used to tell her, "Dying is like waking from a dream, or a nightmare. It's an ending and a beginning." It was something, which always remained with her. Her grandmother intended to take away her fear of death and the unknown. Instead, she only put more questions into Misty's mind, which she did not want answered. Death scared her, plain and simple. She hated being anywhere near it.

Needless to say, she made no such offer to join the others on their potential adventure. She hoped they would understand. No one mentioned it.

In fact, no one said anything for a while. It was very quiet. They were all lost in their thoughts.

Eventually, Leslie excused herself and went back downstairs to her apartment. Not long after, Misty decided it was also time for her to leave, so she said her goodbyes and was gone. Hannah remained, for the time being. She was in no hurry to leave. After locking the apartment door, she walked into the living room and sat beside Megan, who was on the sofa.

She placed her hand on Megan's shoulder and said, "I'm so proud of you, Meg. You did good today. You were right. Being honest was the best idea. It was brave, too. I hope the detective takes you seriously enough to investigate the information you gave him. If I were him, I would look into it."

"I hope you're right," Megan said, while staring down at the floor. "I guess we wait, for now."

# Chapter 15

## Reopening the Investigation

Detective Robert Johnson has been a member of the Yonkers Police Department for fifteen years. He spent his first ten years as a police officer on patrol. The last five were spent as a detective in the Detective Division at 104 South Broadway. A few years ago, he inherited a cold case from a recently retired colleague, Detective Jack Roe.

Good old Jack Roe. Everyone loved him. He was a stand-up guy with a great personality and a nice sense of humor. He was pretty tall, too. Jack spent fifty years on the job. His first twenty were as a police officer. He worked in every precinct in Yonkers. During that time, he made many friends and enemies along the way. When he was promoted to detective he considered retiring on his twenty-fifth year. It's not what happened.

In 1988, he picked up the now infamous case of The Anniversary Killer. Although Henry Paul Cameron was convicted and sentenced for his crimes, there remained the question of what happened to young Margaret Elizabeth Garrett. The official word and department reports indicated she was a missing person. Jack knew better.

Everything about her case screamed the same thing. She had to be another victim of The Anniversary Killer. The evidence all pointed to it. The only problem was there was no body. Without a body, there was no murder. No matter how hard the department searched for her, they never found her.

Naturally, her parents wanted closure, but did not want to believe she was gone. The supervisors wanted the case closed. They hated unsolved cases. It was bad politics. However, Jack kept pushing the issue saying he could link her disappearance to Cameron. He only needed more time. One more month. Another year. A decade. Thirty years later, there was still no evidence to tie her disappearance to Cameron. The trail had gone ice cold. Too much time had passed.

As it turned out, Jack was out of time. His health had gotten worse. His heart was giving him trouble. Before he knew it, he was forced to retire. He retired with a great pension, but he was unsatisfied because he left his most precious case unsolved. The man could have gone on world cruises all year round, if he wanted to do so. Instead, he was still obsessed with a cold case file he had no say so over anymore. It was sad.

For weeks, after Johnson inherited the case, Jack would often call and ask how the search was going. At first, Johnson tried his best to solve the case. After a while, he realized it would not be easy. Eventually, he would give Jack the usual answer. "I'm still working on it." Sometimes, he would do whatever he could to avoid Jack's calls, mainly out of guilt. In part, he was tired of being bothered about it. For the most part, he stopped putting in any real effort to solving the cold case. The truth was Johnson always thought it was a wasted effort. That girl was not going to be found alive, after all this time. There was no doubt in his mind, she was definitely dead. Whether or not Cameron killed her was irrelevant, at this point, although he probably did it. Regardless, Cameron was already going to rot in prison for life because of his other crimes. As for the girl's parents, they were both gone. It was too late to give them the closure they wanted. It became more about giving Jack the closure he needed, which seemed impossible.

That is until a week ago, when Jack's heart finally gave out. He passed away sitting in his chair in front of his computer. On the screen was a photo of Henry Paul Cameron. Even in retirement, Jack was still on the case. Meanwhile, the man he entrusted his case to had completely ignored it, until recently.

The day after the funeral, Johnson pulled the file and finally looked at it for the first time in months. An hour later, he got a call from some random woman, who wanted to give him information about the case, which could tie Cameron to the disappearance of Margaret Elizabeth Garrett. What were the chances this would happen, just as he decided to look at the old case file? It had to be one in a million. It was crazy. That's what it was.

It was no wonder he sat at his desk with his mind blown for several minutes, after speaking to Megan Forester for a half hour.

He had to admit, he thought she was full of it. However, the things she said made a lot of sense. Well, most of the things she said. How she got the information was another story entirely. It sounded more like something out of a movie. Ghosts in dreams showing the events of a crime. It was laughable, at best, but was it real? Was she telling the truth? She sure sounded like she believed it. She was very sincere.

Johnson decided he needed to take this as a sign from Jack. Somehow, he was pulling the strings from Heaven and making the planets and stars align, so his case could finally be solved with his heavenly touch. Johnson had to laugh at this farfetched theory. How was it any less insane than Megan believing Margaret's spirit was haunting her dreams to get her to solve her murder? It was almost the same damn thing!

Johnson went into the bathroom to throw cold water on his face. He stood in front of the mirror and stared at himself. He seemed like an average African American middle class working man based on his appearance. He was cleanshaven with an average build standing at six feet tall. He was far from average in his mind.

He served in the military for two years, prior to joining the police department. Most of that time was spent in the middle east. During that short time, he saw a lot of death. More than the average American should ever see.

The police department seemed the likeliest next step for him when he got back to the States. He enjoyed it, for the most part. He felt like he was making a difference in the community, and maybe he was. He earned several medals over the years and was quite proud of them. When he became a detective, he thought it was his time to sit back and relax. He would take on cases, solve them, and eventually retire.

Instead, here he was with the case of a lifetime. It was most likely the oldest cold case in Yonkers. If not, it was right up there with it. Somehow, he had to solve a case almost as old as him. It was crazy. This time, there could be no more dismissing it. No more excuses. Apparently, the spirits of the dead were at unrest and they wanted it solved. He could not ignore their demands. Could he?

"Okay, let's do this," he psyched himself up.

He returned to his desk and looked through the case file. Where to begin? He read the recent notes he took down, while talking with Megan. The numbers she gave him for the partial license plate matched up with Cameron's 1981 blue

Dodge Colt hatchback. How could she know? Why only part of it? Why not all of it? If she had seen a photo of it on the Internet, she probably would have seen the entire plate. Not a partial. If she was getting her information directly from Cameron, maybe he was only giving her part of the information. Maybe he forgot the rest. Then again, why would he be stupid enough to give her any information, if it could link him to Margaret's disappearance?

It made no sense. Plus, this woman insisted she hated his guts.

Could she really be acquiring this information through her dreams or nightmares? If so, it would be pretty damn incredible, but was it impossible? Johnson was a huge science fiction fan. He loved anything that had to do with "*Star Trek*" and "*Star Wars*," his two biggest loves. So much technology could be imagined from watching those movies and shows. For example, cellphone technology actually came about from the inspiration of the original 1960s "*Star Trek*" series communicators. Johnson always believed if it could be imagined, it could be achieved. Keeping that logic in mind, did this qualify? A ghost making contact through a dream. It was certainly food for thought.

There was one thing he could look into, which was fairly easy. Not to mention, it was probably the most important piece of information, too. She mentioned a certain small metal box containing photos of Cameron's victims, including Margaret. If it actually existed, it could be the key to convicting Cameron of Margaret's murder. Supposedly, this box is buried in his basement underneath a large square-shaped boulder. It would be easy enough to verify with a brief field trip to the location. Hopefully, the structure is still standing.

Johnson grabbed the keys to an unmarked car and stepped out of the office. It was time to go for a ride.


Detective Johnson parked his unmarked department vehicle on Odell Avenue, and then walked across to the closed deadend road, which led to the remains of the abandoned garage, where the basement was located. He walked around the barricade and headed back into the wooded area, which was once home to Henry Paul Cameron. When he reached the remaining structure he scanned for the opening to the basement section. It had been years since he was last there.

To the best of his recollection, the main house and upper levels of the garage had been demolished back in the 2010s. The people of the community signed a petition to tear it down. It had become unsafe and was attracting drug addicts, vandals, and gangs. The company that signed up to do the job went out of business, before the main section of the garage was razed. For some reason, no other company was ever hired to finish the job. Ironically, the one section, which should have been destroyed first, was the only portion still standing.

Johnson walked toward the left down the hill to the basement entrance. That part of the building was closer to the Old Croton Aqueduct Trail. The open doorway led into the first room of the basement, which stretched back below the garage. Scattered debris littered the far corner of the entrance room beyond a pair of thin metal support beams. It got darker when he stepped into the second room. A large puddle covered most of the floor in that room.

He began to think this was not a good place for a man wearing a gray suit and loafers.

Johnson turned on his flashlight by the time he reached the third basement room. In this room was a staircase to his right, leading up to the garage. However, the room he needed to check was straight ahead at the rear of the basement. He proceeded forward and stepped through the broken wooden double doors. They barely hung in place. He froze in place, while his eyes took in the scenery.

Ahead, were the two brick support beams. The one to the left was where the victims were tied, before being moved to the horse stall, directly to his left. Ropes were tied to either side of its doorway. Definitely not the same ropes, though. He wondered if it was how victim number three, Linda Holmolkan, was hung upside down to drain her blood? He stepped in past the horse stall. His gaze still drawn by its menacing facade. He thought about how Cameron must have tortured and brutalized his victims in there. He remembered the crime scene photos clearly showed hay.

Megan was correct. The hay was gone, except how would she know it was even there without having seen it?

Another puddle of water had built up in front of the horse stall. Johnson stepped around it and continued past the two brick support beams. The bricks on the beams and walls were covered in graffiti and pocked full of random holes. Bricks were missing or chipped. The floor was filthy with debris and trash.

The back of the room looked different from the crime scene photos. The room had been altered over the years, probably by trespassers. The old worktable, which would have been in the back of the cold chamber, had been taken in as evidence years ago. It was used during the trial. The last victim, Doreen Stanley, testified how she kicked it over and picked up one of the tools with her bare feet to cut herself free, after using Judo training to put Cameron to sleep with the strength of her legs around his neck.

Johnson noticed a large square-shaped boulder with another heavy rock set on top of it. Could it be the one Megan told him about? Would he really find a metal box beneath it? The possibility enticed him. He could not recall if the boulder was in the crime scene photos. Then again, the photos really did not focus on this side of the room. They mainly showed the areas where the victims were held captive, beaten, and sexually assaulted.

Unfortunately, there was no way the boulder was going to be moved by his hands alone. It looked way too heavy. He was going to need assistance. He was also going to need a search warrant, if he was going to use the metal box as evidence against Cameron. His work was cut out for him.

He made a call to one of his contacts at the courthouse and explained the situation, making sure to leave out the part about ghosts. Basically, he said he needed a search warrant to check on a lead based on new information given to him by an anonymous source. The location was abandoned, so it would not be an issue.

Once the warrant was secured, he called for the Yonkers Police Department's Emergency Service Unit to move the boulder for him. They had the tools necessary to get the job done. Photos were taken of the scene, before and after.

In less than an hour, the boulder had been removed. Johnson personally used a shovel to dig in the dirt where it lay. It did not take long before he hit something metal. He cleared away the dirt only to reveal a rusty old metallic safe box, which was indeed about the size of a shoebox. Prying it open was easy enough with his leatherman multi-tool.

When the box was opened, it revealed a stack of old photographs depicting women in bondage. Upon closer scrutiny, Johnson immediately recognized some to be the victims of The Anniversary Killer. He had memorized their case photos. At a glance, there were six women in total, which added up, if you included Margaret.

Johnson looked to his colleagues and stated, "We got that prick red handed." He held up the photos for them to see. In reality, he was talking to his old friend, Jack, but he would never admit it.

Later, back at his office at the Detective Division, Johnson examined the photos at his desk under a bright light, while using a magnifying glass. He checked each one closely looking for identifying features and consistency. Each photo had a white border around it and was worn from age, so it was clear these were not recent photos. They were vintage 1980s. There was no doubt the majority of photos had been taken in the basement. For each of the basement photos, the lighting was the same. Cameron only used natural light from the window behind his victims. In most shots, the faces are not easily identifiable. They were obscured using blindfolds or by their own hair. Despite the sick theme, Cameron seemed to have an artistic quality with his photography, even if it was demented.

It is likely he developed his own photos because these were not the type of photos one took to the local shop to get developed, although there was no evidence of a photo lab on his property. The photos were far too intimate. Not to mention quite incriminating. It was clear they were of his victims. There were multiple photos of each woman.

Erin Christine McAffy was the easiest to identify with her long dark hair. She was wearing the sleeveless dress she had on when she was abducted from Untermyer Park. Her face was the only one visible. She was his first victim, so it was highly possible Cameron still had not figured out how he would do things. Essentially, he was an amateur, at this point. Her arms were bound to the horse stall's doorway. She was alive and had not been beaten, yet. Therefore, the photos were likely taken soon after her capture. It was still daylight.

The poor woman had no idea what was in store for her.

Linda Holmolkan was the next one to be identified. In the photos, she was tied to the brick support beam. She wore the white button-down blouse she was last seen in, which she wore for what would have been her first day working at the Hudson River Museum. Alas, she would never make it there. Her blouse was opened revealing a dark colored bra. A common red handkerchief was used to cover her face. She also appeared to be alive. Who knew how long it would be before her head was severed from her body and her blood drained? Did he really hang her upside down?

Johnson was incensed when he thought about Cameron. The things he did to these women was horrible. The pain and terror they experienced was unimaginable. He shook his head and studied the next photo.

Tamara Lyndsey was wearing a black t-shirt, as described in her missing person's report. Like Linda, her eyes were covered by a dark blindfold. She was tied to the horse stall and alive when the photos of her were taken.

Johnson had to wonder where she was severed in half. Was it in the basement or somewhere else? A bathtub? There did not seem to be any indication of large amounts of blood on the floor, unless Cameron washed it away.

The photos of Dawn Ross showed her topless, although she was also wearing her bra. In one photo her bra appears to be stained with blood beneath her left nipple and she seems to be unconscious because her head was bowed. She had been tied to the brick support beam, like Linda, who was abducted several months before her.

At last, there was the *coup de gras*. There were photos of a woman, who could only be Margaret Elizabeth Garrett. She had been tied to the brick support beam, as well. While her frizzled wet hair covered her face, her white t-shirt was unmistakable. It said *"Amanda"* across it in white letters over the image of a woman. The t-shirt was based on a book written by a local author. The exact description of her t-shirt was never in the original missing person's report or in any of the newspaper articles, but it was in Jack Roe's follow-up report, after an interview with her mother. This was not public knowledge, yet Megan was aware of it. She described the t-shirt and said it was covered in blood. It is still clean in the photos, indicating they were taken before she was beaten, perhaps soon after her abduction.

Johnson could not believe his luck. This was the evidence he needed to prove Cameron took her. He had her in the basement on the day she went missing. He placed photos of her with photos of his victims and deliberately hid them. However, it still did not prove he murdered her. Where was the body? Johnson needed to locate her body.

Megan described a highway near a lake. She gave him a set of numbers, as well. He looked them over and figured the numbers were probably a highway marker. It was a typical set of numbers, which every highway in the country had. There were consecutive numbers every few feet. It made it easier to identify specific locations along the roadways. He knew this from his experience as a police officer.

H-U-4-5-7 did not sound familiar. A few seconds later, it occurred to him. The Hutchinson River Parkway. It was surrounded by water on both sides in the Bronx near Co-Op City, a region of high-rise buildings bordering the river. He could call the New York City Department of Transportation to find out exactly where that specific highway marker was located. Of course, the call would have to wait until normal business hours.

In the meantime, there were still a bunch of other photos to investigate. Originally, he thought they would be of Doreen Stanley, the woman who escaped death. When he looked closer, he realized it was someone else entirely. The remaining photos were all of this same woman. There were no photos of Doreen. In fact, the name "Leanne" had been handwritten by Cameron on some of the photos in very small print along the white borders. There were close to a dozen photos of this particular woman, but who the hell was she? As far as Johnson could tell, she was not one of Cameron's victims, or was she?

One thing, which stood out, was how the photos of Leanne were somewhat different than the rest. While most of her photos were taken in the basement of the garage, there were a few taken elsewhere. Like the others, she was also tied to the brick support beam and to the horse stall. However, the other photos looked like they were taken within the main house. It was hard to tell, if it was Cameron's home. In one of the photos she was chained to the shower in a bathroom. Another was of her lying on a striped blanket, perhaps on a bed. She was not tied up or bound in any way. There was also one which looked like she was standing in front of a light-colored wall. Again, her hands and legs seemed to be free. What was crazier was in another photo she actually looked like she was smiling, although she was chained in what might be the basement. The window behind her looked like the window behind the horse stall.

As was the case with his victims, Leanne was an attractive, young, Caucasian woman with a nice body. She had long, straight, blonde hair. No tattoos were visible. She might have been a Goth girl because she had long fingernails, which were painted black. It was not something commonly done by other women during those days. In every photo she wore black panties and a bra. Her eyes were covered in each photo using a blindfold or handkerchief.

Her different eye coverings are the only things hinting the photos could have been taken on different days. She appears to be wearing the same blindfolds used by the victims, which makes one wonder, were her photos taken before the murders? Was she another victim, or was something else going on?

Johnson was extremely baffled by this set of photos. Why had they been placed in the same locked box as the photos of his victims, and then buried under a boulder? There had to be a good reason for it. What was Cameron trying to hide?

"What the hell is going on here?" Johnson asked aloud. "Who are you, Leanne?" He stared at her photos going over each one several times.

He contemplated if perhaps Megan could shed some light on her identity. It was the only person he could think to ask, besides Cameron himself. He checked his watch. It was getting late. He did not realize the time. It was time to go home, although tomorrow he would most definitely be paying Megan a visit.

The next morning, when Johnson arrived at work, he started his day with breakfast and a medium coffee. He had a feeling it was going to be a long day. Once he was done eating, he made a call to the District Attorney's office to inform them of the newly acquired photographic evidence against Henry Paul Cameron. At long last, it was time to start building a case against him regarding the alleged murder of Margaret Elizabeth Garrett. It was long overdue. Of course, it took a lot of convincing and explaining, considering how many years had gone by. The D.A.'s office in White Plains, where the Westchester County courthouse was located, was interested in what he discovered, but they were without a doubt going to need a body, if they were going to get a conviction. Otherwise, it was a waste of the tax payers' money.

Johnson agreed. He only hoped the information he got from Megan would prove to be useful. Based on the fact she had told the truth about the photos, he felt inclined to give her the benefit of the doubt.

Next, he called the NYC DOT. He asked if they could identify the precise location of highway marker H-U-4-5-7. He was quite pleased with their speedy response. It turned out he was correct. The marker was located along the Hutchinson River Parkway going southbound, just before the exit for Orchard Beach and City Island, which was now Exit 3. It used to be Exit 5, but the numbers had been changed. It was a straight section of the parkway surrounded by water on both sides, which also happened to be directly across from the high-rise buildings of Co-Op City.

"Thank you," he said, before hanging up the phone. He could not help smiling to himself. He had a good feeling about this. Jack Roe would have been ecstatic. He decided he would take a ride along the parkway, sometime during the day, when traffic was not too heavy, so he could check it out.

He also planned on visiting Megan, so he could speak to her in person. He still had a lot of questions for her. He gave her a call to set up a time for their meeting. Unfortunately, she was at work and would not be done, until six in the evening. Talking to her in person would have to wait. He considered asking her about Leanne, but she seemed to be very busy. It was kind enough of her to take his call, while at work. He did not want to push it. It was best to save his questions for when he could look her in the eyes and see her reactions.

Of course, there was another way he could find out Leanne's identity. He could always arrange for a visit with Cameron at Sing Sing. It was worth a shot. Besides, now that he had those photos of the victims, he absolutely wanted to have a little chat with The Anniversary Killer. He had a feeling it was going to be an enlightening conversation, to say the least. He could not wait to see the look on Cameron's face.

Johnson made a few more calls over the next hour and arranged an appointment to see Cameron, later during the week. He was grateful he would not have to wait too long. Hopefully, by that time, he would have some concrete information and more incriminating questions for the convicted killer.

He checked the time. Rush hour was over. He decided it was a good time to take a ride along the Hutchinson River Parkway. Traffic should not be too bad and he was not going far.

A half hour later, when he arrived at the location, he pulled over on the shoulder prior to the exit for Orchard Beach and City Island. He observed the exit sign before the stone overpass was indeed Exit 3. He stepped out of the unmarked car and walked to the nearest utility pole. He saw the highway marker was H-U-4-5-7. It went down the pole one digit at a time. Satisfied, he looked across the river and could see the tall buildings.

There was no doubt in his mind, this was the right area Megan described. It had to be, but where was the body? He looked around at the trees and saw the tall grass beyond. It could be anywhere.

He stepped back and took a few photos of the location using his cellphone and got back into his car. Perhaps, he could show these photos to Megan later to see if anything was familiar to her. Maybe she could point out the exact location. So far, he was impressed by her input. She had been right about everything. Either she was telling the truth, or this was a very elaborate lie. What would she have to gain by lying, though?

Only time would tell.

Johnson returned to the Detective Division and went into his office. Over the next few hours, he kept himself busy making copies of the victims' bondage photos and faxing them down to the D.A.'s office. He held off on sending his notes from his bizarre conversation with Megan and anything to do with the possible location of the body, until he could meet with Megan and interview her. If what she said sounded legit, he would arrange for a team to check the site. This time, he would record their conversation and make sure she understood the penalties for lying to a sworn officer of the law during an official investigation. He needed to know whether or not she was going to give him the same answers or if she was going to change her story. If she were lying to his face, he'd know it.

At six o'clock he left his office and drove to the Hill View on Walnut Street.

# Chapter 16

## The Interview

Megan got home from work carrying a pizza pie. She called Josh to the table to eat and asked Misty if she could stay longer because she was expecting a police detective to come over. Hannah was also on her way. Megan hoped to speak with the detective without worrying about Josh, so she needed to make sure he was being looked after. Hannah would be talking with the detective, as well. Misty had no problem with taking care of Josh.

They sat down to eat the pizza, while they waited.

"Thanks for the pizza," Misty said. She grabbed a slice. "I don't mind staying longer. I know it's for a good cause. By the way, *she* didn't give me any problems today. Maybe she doesn't hate me as much anymore, since she knows we all want to help her." Suddenly, Misty turned to the empty seat beside her and a look of worry came over her face. "Maybe I spoke too soon. She's here."

Josh smiled cheerfully and said, "Hi, Lizzie!"

Megan turned to Misty and explained, "I don't think she hates you, Misty. She just has a lot of anger, which is perfectly understandable."

"Oh, I agree. Sometimes, I can feel her anger." Misty cringed. "Anyway, I can keep Josh busy in his room when your guest arrives. No worries. Um, can you try to keep her in this room with you guys?"

Megan scoffed, "No promises, but I think she will want to hear what we have to say. Thank you so much for your help. I really appreciate it." Megan bit her slice of pizza.

Josh looked up from his plate and asked, "Who's coming over, Mommy?"

Megan finished chewing and swallowed, before answering. "Well, Hannah should be here soon and we are also expecting a detective. He wants to talk about our special friend, Maggie."

Josh's eyes brightened. "A real-life detective? Is he gonna help her, too?"

She smirked and nodded, "Yes, I believe so. When he arrives, I want you to do me a favor and stay in your room with Misty. Okay? We will be talking about adult things, which you should not hear."

"Okay, Mommy. I will." He looked disappointed. He looked to the empty seat between him and Misty and exclaimed with excitement, "Oh, goody!"

Megan was curious and asked, "Did Maggie say something to you?"

Josh nodded, "Yes, Mommy."

"Well, what did she say?" Megan asked impatiently.

"She said you're gonna help the detective find her."

Megan looked to the empty seat. She sure hoped so.

Misty noticed Megan looked worried and asked, "Are you sure you're going to be okay to speak with him today? You don't look too good."

"Huh? Oh, um, don't mind me. I'm fine. I was just thinking about her. Plus, I didn't sleep too good last night. My mind was all over the place, kind of like now. I was thinking about this stuff all night. I thought I was going to worry myself to death. I tend to overwork myself with panic. I keep thinking I'm going to fail her, somehow. I really want to help her. You know?"

Misty nodded. She understood.

Megan added, "Well, at least, I didn't have any nightmares last night. I suppose that's a good thing. As if I wasn't stressed enough, work was pretty hectic. I was on my feet all day with barely a chance to rest. It felt like every moron in Yonkers decided to go shopping today, considering the amount of stupidity I had to deal with. It was unreal."

Josh giggled.

Misty smiled at him, before responding, "I'm sorry to hear that. It sucks how you can't even take this time to relax and take a nap with this detective coming over soon."

"Yeah. Tell me about it. He should be here any minute. Hopefully, I can finish enjoying this pizza, before he arrives." She checked the time on her cellphone and added, "I also hope Hannah gets here before he does."

Misty chuckled and took a bite from her slice. "Hmm. This is good pizza."

"I love pizza!" Josh grinned, while taking a sideways bite from the cheese he was pulling up with his fingers.

Megan noticed and admonished him, "Please, don't make a mess, Josh."

He swallowed his food and replied, "I won't."

Megan's phone chimed with a text message notification. After checking it, she felt relieved. "Oh, good. Hannah is downstairs. She's parking her car."

A moment later, Megan opened the door to greet her best friend. "Hi, Hannah! Come on in. Thanks for coming. I picked up a pizza pie. Grab a slice, before the detective gets here. They're still warm."

"Hey, Meg. Thanks. I don't mind if I do." She approached the table and said hello to Misty and Josh, "Hi, guys."

Before she could take a seat, Josh stopped her. "Wait! Lizzie is sitting there!"

Hannah hesitated, but then Megan suggested, "You can sit in my seat. I'm done." She pointed to the other seat.

"Uh, okay. I'll do that," Hannah replied. It felt strange having to leave a seat available for a ghost. Of course, it was better to be polite than to deal with the consequences later. She sat in Megan's seat and grabbed a slice of pizza.

Meanwhile, Megan went into the bathroom to rinse out her mouth with mouthwash. She did not want Detective Johnson to smell the garlic on her breath from the garlic powder. It would be too embarrassing. Their conversation was going to be awkward enough without adding bad breath into the mix.


Detective Johnson arrived at exactly 6:30 P.M. After greeting everyone and introducing himself, he took a seat at the kitchen table opposite Megan. Hannah sat in one of the seats between them. The other was left vacant for Maggie. Misty took Josh to his room and closed the door.

The detective began by placing a small, black, digital voice recorder on the table. "I hope you don't mind, but I will be recording this interview."

"Oh, okay," Megan nodded hesitantly.

He pressed record, and then informed them both they were not suspects in any crime. He explained how it was illegal for them to lie to an officer of the law during an official investigation. They both understood and assured him they would only be telling the truth. Megan added there was no reason for them to lie.

Before he could ask anything else, Hannah asked, "Shouldn't you read us our rights?"

Johnson explained, "No, I am conducting an interview, not an interrogation. From this point on, I must ask you both to refrain from blurting out anything irrelevant to the conversation. It is very possible this recording could be used as evidence against Henry Cameron. Is that clear, Ms. Kasanka?" He eyed Hannah with a raised eyebrow.

"Yes. Totally clear. So sorry!" Hannah felt like a fool. She zipped her lip.

Megan glared at her disapprovingly, before smiling politely at Detective Johnson, and then signaling for him to continue with the interview.

Satisfied, he proceeded. He stated his name, rank, and the date, as well as their location, before he started with any official questions. "Ms. Forester, how long have you resided at this address? Please, be sure to speak in a clear audible voice," he instructed.

"I only moved in two weeks ago," she answered casually.

"Can you tell me the exact date?" He asked, which she did. His next question was more to the point. "When did you first learn about the disappearance of Margaret Elizabeth Garrett? Please, be precise with your answer."

"Well, it was the day I found the newspaper from 1988 in my closet. Hold on. I can give you the exact date." She opened her journal and reviewed it, before stating the exact date and day of the week. Her research materials were stacked on the table in front of her for easy access. The pizza box had already been thrown away.

Johnson glanced at her journal and became curious, although he figured it was probably a daily planner. He moved on to the next question. He was careful to avoid asking anything about the paranormal. "When did you find out this was the former residence of Margaret Elizabeth Garrett? Remember, be precise."

She thought about it and answered, "It was fairly recent. Honestly, it was the same exact moment when I read the newspaper article about her." She repeated the date for the sake of being precise.

"Do you still have this newspaper article in your possession?"

"Yes, it's right here on the table." She pulled it out from under the rest of her research materials.

"Very good. I will need to make a copy of it, if you don't mind."

"Will you give it back?" She asked with a look of worry on her face.

"Of course, I will," he assured her with a nod of his head.

She nodded back, "Okay." She passed it over the table to him.

He looked at the article briefly and noticed it did not state Margaret's address, so he asked, "How is it you were able to ascertain that Margaret Garrett, the missing teenage girl mentioned in this newspaper article from 1988, resided here in this very apartment?"

This was when the conversation took a turn for the strange and unexplained. "Well, I had seen her here before reading the article. She was in my son's room getting dressed to go jogging. It used to be her room. While I knew her face, I did not know her name, yet." Megan tried to avoid mentioning she saw her in a dream, so she would not sound insane. "On the day I moved in, I found her initials etched under this table." She pointed to the table. "I was told by my landlady that the former resident was an elderly woman named Mrs. Garrett, Maggie's mother, Elizabeth. She lived here for many years. Once I saw the newspaper, I was able to identify the photo of her from the article, as the same girl I saw in my son's room. I noticed her name matched the initials etched under the table. Plus, my son said he knew her as the girl, who used to live here. He'd seen her many times before, except he knew her by her middle name, as Lizzie."

Johnson swallowed nervously. He really did not want to ask the next question, but he had no choice. "How were you and your son both able to see her, before finding this newspaper?"

This time, it was Megan, who swallowed nervously, when she replied, "I saw her every night in my dreams, starting on the day I moved in. My son actually saw her here in the apartment on more than one occasion, not in a dream, but in person. She shows herself to him often. She also speaks to him and reads him bedtime stories."

Hannah confessed, "I've also seen her, but only once. It was the day they moved in. I was here helping with the unpacking and cleaning. I saw her in the bathroom behind me when I looked into the mirror. And Misty is clairvoyant. She can sense her presence and her mood. So, believe it or not, there are actually multiple witnesses to the paranormal events, which have occurred in this apartment. We're telling the truth, as crazy as it may sound."

Johnson wished she had not used the words paranormal or crazy. This was not going to go over well with the District Attorney or in a courtroom. He could not think of what to say next. He figured he may as well go along with it, at this point. "I see," he tried to sound skeptical. "Ms. Forester, can you tell me in as much detail as you can recall, exactly what the alleged spirit of Margaret Garrett showed you."

At that exact moment, Maggie's spirit leaned over the recorder and stated, *"I am not alleged. I am real."* Of course, no one in the room could hear her speak. However, her voice was registered by the recorder. It became part of the official recording unbeknownst to them.

Megan proceeded to tell the tale as she saw it in her nightmares starting from the first one, in which Maggie was in her room preparing to leave. She told how she went jogging and was grabbed from behind by Hank Cameron. She described the basement how it used to look. She mentioned the heinous crimes committed against Maggie in morbid detail. She left nothing out because it was still fresh in her head, no matter how hard she originally tried to forget it. She explained how Hank slit her throat in the bathroom, had sex with the body, cooked and ate the nipple, and then cleaned the bathroom before wrapping the body in a white bedsheet.

Maggie's spirit relived each moment, as she heard it. The torment still very real in her mind. She cried out in pain as if once more she felt being struck in the face with the pliers, each tooth being yanked from her mouth, her face being slapped, the rape, and slitting of her throat. Although no one in the room could hear her, the cries were recorded on Johnson's recorder. Josh could also hear her in the next room. Misty had a hard time keeping him distracted.

Meanwhile, discussing it caused Megan to feel emotional bringing tears to her eyes. Yet, she kept going. She described how it felt riding in the trunk of the car, and then arriving at the burial site. She described the location in exact detail. Johnson listened carefully and could imagine it clearly, after having visited the area only hours earlier. Megan said how the body was dragged through the trees to a hole near the shore. She was then placed into the hole and buried. Megan knew that feeling, as well, so she described it. She then spoke of seeing Maggie's spirit outside of the grave and being transported back to the basement in time to witness Hank, when he buried the metal box filled with photos of his victims. She explained how Maggie also told her she was number five.

Johnson had the dates memorized. According to the dates each woman was abducted, Maggie's disappearance would make her the fifth victim, assuming what he was being told was the truth.

By the time Megan was done telling the story, Johnson had forgotten it came from a ghost. He was fully drawn in by the tale. He kept hoping Megan would say something to hint at the existence of another victim, mainly Leanne. However, Megan finished her haunting tale and never said one word about Leanne. Did it mean she was unaware of her existence?

Johnson asked, "Have you ever heard the name Leanne, in association with any aspect of this case?"

Megan looked confused at the mention of the name. She shook her head and answered, "No, sorry. I've never heard of any Leanne. Who is she?"

"I was hoping you could tell me," he admitted. "I'm still trying to find out." He decided it was time to see their reactions to a few revelations. "I went to the abandoned basement under the garage yesterday, after we spoke." Both women perked up waiting to hear what he would say next. "I saw the square-shaped boulder you told me about and I had it moved."

Megan could no longer hold back. She blurted out, "Did you find the metal box?"

"Yes," he nodded. "I did. It was still locked, but I managed to open it." Megan looked at him, as if he were about to propose marriage. "It was filled with photos of what appears to be the victims of The Anniversary Killer."

Hannah cried out, "Oh my God! The box is actually real?" She seemed genuinely surprised.

Megan ignored the comment and asked, "Did you find any photos of Maggie?"

He nodded, again, "Yes, I believe I did, based on what she is wearing. However, I cannot see her face. Come to think of it, most of their faces are obscured in some way. For all I know, they could be anyone. These days, it is not unheard of to digitally age a photo using an editing program. Maybe the photos were planted, after the fact. I really cannot say for sure." He watched carefully for their reactions to his insinuation.

Megan's heart broke. Her expression broke with it. Her eyes filled with tears as her biggest fear began to come true. He did not believe her. "No! Those photos were placed there by Hank! Maggie showed me! I saw him do it! Those are the actual victims! You have to believe me!"

Hannah tried to comfort Megan. "Shhh! Meg, keep it down. Josh will hear you."

Without warning, the recorder slid across the table on its own toward the unoccupied seat. Johnson was disappointed. He was hoping they would not resort to cheap parlor tricks to make their semi-convincing haunted tale seem believable. Annoyed, he grabbed the recorder and placed it back at the center of the table. When he did, he felt someone grip his wrist tightly. His eyes opened wide with fear, and then the recorder moved back in front of the empty seat by his own hand being forced by some cold unseen force. He let it go, instinctively.

Maggie's spirit spoke into the recorder, once again, and declared, *"Megan is telling the truth!"* Again, her voice was not heard by them, but it was recorded.

The three sat quietly staring at the recorder. Johnson was afraid to move it back to the center of the table, so he decided to leave it there.

"Can anyone tell me what just happened?" He asked. He tried and failed to hide his fear.

Hannah answered plainly, "It was her. Maggie. She usually sits there."

Megan nodded, "She's right. We tend to leave that seat available for her. She doesn't like when people sit in her seat. She also doesn't like when people deny her existence."

Johnson found their explanation difficult to believe. Still, someone or something grabbed his wrist extremely hard. There was no way he imagined it. It felt so cold. He asked, "So, she grabbed my wrist?"

Megan shrugged, "I really can't say. I can't see her, unless it's in my dreams. Only my son can see her and only he can hear what she says."

Johnson hesitated, but then asked, "Can we ask him to join us? Misty, too?"

Megan carefully considered his request. Before she would ever agree she needed to make sure of a few things, first. She requested the detective not mention the details of the crime to Josh. As far as he knew, a bad man took Maggie and hurt her. He knew she was dead, but he did not know how she came to be that way. It's the way Megan preferred it. She also requested Johnson ask no questions about Josh's father. He was an asshole and he was completely irrelevant to the investigation. End of story. Johnson agreed.

She walked to the room and soon returned with them. Misty was nervous about talking to the detective. She hoped he would not ask her too many questions. To be on the safe side, she stood away from the table near the sink, out of view. Megan took her seat and sat Josh on her lap to keep the other seat free. Misty did not dare sit there.

Johnson smiled warmly and addressed Josh, "Hello, Josh. I'm Detective Robert Johnson. We met earlier. Is it okay if I ask you a few questions about your special friend, Lizzie?"

Megan was glad he remembered to refer to her as Lizzie for Josh's sake.

Josh nodded nervously. As usual, he was being shy around strangers.

Johnson spoke in a friendly voice, "I am recording this conversation, so you will have to speak up. Don't just nod your head. Can you please say your answers out loud, from now on?"

"Okay," Josh responded in a low voice.

"Excellent. Thank you, Josh. Can you tell me who is in this room with us?"

"Yes. It's me, Mommy, Lizzie, Hannah, Misty, and you."

Johnson found it interesting how Lizzie was not the last name mentioned. It was as if the boy considered her to be as real as everyone else. He asked, "Where is Lizzie, right at this moment?"

He pointed to the empty seat and said, "She's right there."

"Can you ask her what she did a moment ago, while you were in your bedroom?"

He did not bother. Instead, he answered, "She grabbed your hand cause you tried to take away the tape recorder. She wanted to use it."

"Use it?" Johnson could not believe his ears. And how could Josh possibly know what happened, unless he was telling the truth? Was he psychic? Why would he refer to it as a tape recorder? Had he ever even seen one?

"Lizzie called it a tape recorder," Josh replied. "She wanted to tell you something. She said I'm not a sidekick." He looked at the empty seat and corrected himself. "Oh, I mean she's not psychic."

Johnson was in shock. How did Josh know what he was thinking? He decided to take a chance and asked, "Who is Leanne?"

Josh listened to Lizzie, and then responded, "Lizzie said you should ask Hank when you go see him soon." Josh seemed confused by his own answer. He asked Lizzie, "Who's Hank?" A second later he acknowledged, "Oh, he's the bad man."

Megan became concerned. She hated not being able to hear what Maggie was saying to him. She explained in a soft voice, "Josh. If you have any questions, ask me, not Lizzie. Okay? I'd rather be the one to tell you."

"Okay, Mommy," he said, while looking up at her.

Meanwhile, Johnson was stunned by Josh's casual reply. How in the world could he possibly know he was planning to see Cameron? This kid was incredible. Johnson certainly planned to ask Cameron about Leanne. There was no doubt about it. It seemed he might be the only one, who could reveal her identity.

Josh then stated, "Lizzie also knows who she is, but she said it's not her place to tell."

Again? Johnson asked unexpectedly, "Josh, can you read my mind?"

"No!" He giggled and they all laughed briefly, until Josh added, "But Lizzie can."

Johnson's smile faded. He requested, "Ask Lizzie where I went this afternoon."

Josh sighed and replied, "She can hear your questions. She's not deaf. You can ask her yourself. She said you went to the highway to find her."

"Incredible! Was I close?" Johnson asked sounding hopeful.

"Yes," Josh nodded. He looked up at his mother and added, "Mommy knows where to go. Right, Mommy?"

Johnson looked at Megan, who nodded awkwardly, "I think I can point it out, if you can take me to the same section on the highway. You know where it is, Detective?" She gazed across the table at him.

"Yes," he nodded. Somehow, he felt guilty for not mentioning it earlier. "I found it today… with your help. The numbers you gave me are what's known as a highway marker. Using highway marker numbers, I can find the exact location on any highway in the country. This particular highway is the Hutchinson River Parkway, right before Exit 3. It used to be Exit 5, until it was changed not long ago."

Megan's eyes opened with excitement. "That explains why I couldn't tell if it was a '3' or a '5'! So, you *were* there???" She was overjoyed. Soon, they would find Maggie!

"Yes, I was there, *but* I may need you to show me the exact location. Tell me, Ms. Forester, are you up for a ride?" He decided to hold off on showing her the photo he took and see if she would be willing to accompany him to the location, instead. If she were lying, chances were she would not want to go.

"What? Now???" She was taken aback by his request.

He replied, "Don't you want me to find her? I'm going to need your help, Ms. Forester. I'm starting to think she's counting on us all to play our part. It seems we each have a role to play in this mystery. I don't think any of us can solve it alone." He really hoped she was legit. He needed her to be, so he could solve this case.

She knew he was right. Suddenly, she felt afraid, as a flurry of questions went through her mind. The thought of going to that location in real life –

the place where Maggie was buried. What would they find? Would her body actually be there? Did she want to see it? Could she really handle something like that?

Megan began breathing fast. Her heart raced and she felt dizzy. She was experiencing a panic attack.

Hannah grabbed her hand and said, "Relax, Meg. Take slow steady breaths. Misty, can you please take Josh to his room."

Misty did as she was told. Josh left willingly, although he kept looking back at his mother. He was worried she would pass out, again. He became scared for her life. He did not understand what was wrong with her. Tears filled his eyes, as Misty led him into his room. Meanwhile, Megan tried to take deep breaths.

Johnson became deeply concerned, as well. "Is she okay?" He asked. "Ms. Forester? Do you need me to call an ambulance?" He reached for his portable radio and was about to speak into it, when Megan stopped him.

"No! Don't call an ambulance! I'm fine. I have panic attacks. I just need…" She took a deep breath before continuing, "…I need to rest."

"Okay, I understand. I'll give you time to think about it. Here. Take my card." He handed her a business card. "Whenever you're ready, give me a call. If you think of anything else to tell me, give me a call. Please, don't hesitate. I'd like you to think of me as a friend. We are on the same side, Ms. Forester."

She nodded in agreement and said, "Megan. Please, call me Megan."

He smiled at her. "Thank you, Megan. I think I will leave now, so you can get some rest. Please, think about what I said. I don't think I can do this without your help."

"Okay. Let me think about it," she replied.

"That's all I ask. Hey, I don't suppose I can borrow your research materials to make some copies? I promise I will bring everything back tomorrow."

Megan faltered, but she knew her research would be extremely helpful to him. It was what she needed to do if she wanted to help Maggie, so she agreed. "Fine. You can borrow everything." She reluctantly handed him the stack of printed newspaper articles, Maggie's diary, and her journal. "Please, be very careful with this stuff. I would very much like to have everything back, as soon as possible."

"Is tomorrow fast enough? I can bring it over by the time you get home from work."

Hannah suggested, "Or you can take it to her job tomorrow and give her a ride home, so she doesn't have to wait for the bus."

Megan leered at her, dismayed by her suggestion. "Hannah!" She turned back to him and said, "Pay her no mind. Bringing it here will be fine. Thank you very much."

He chuckled and replied, "You got it." He then turned to leave, but Megan got his attention, again.

"Detective, are you really going to see him? Hank?"

Johnson turned back to face her and nodded, "Yes. I have an appointment to see him, later this week. I have a few questions for him, as well."

"Can we go find her, after you see him?" Megan requested. "For some reason, I think she would prefer it that way."

Johnson considered it, for a moment, and then responded, "Sure. I think we can do that. I suppose it can't hurt to wait a few more days. Can it? However, once I see him, I want you to take me to her. No more excuses. Do we have a deal?"

"Deal," she agreed without question. Once more, he turned to leave. However, there was one more thing she wanted to say to him. "Detective? I'm so sorry. One more thing, before you go."

By now, he was opening the door and standing in the doorway. He turned and asked, trying to sound patient, "Yes?"

"Thank you for believing us."

He scoffed and admitted, "To be honest, I'm still quite not there, yet, Megan, but I'm trying really hard to keep an open mind. I need a little time to think things over is all. Let me get back to the office, so I can review this recording. Enjoy the rest of your evening, ladies."

"Thank you," Megan replied. "You, too."

Hannah called out, "Goodnight!" Once he left, she turned to Megan and said, "He's kind of cute. Reminds me of Denzel Washington. Don't you think?"

Megan rolled her eyes and punched her in the arm.

"Ouch!"

Megan scowled at her, as she demanded, "What the heck is wrong with you asking him to pick me up at work? Are you nuts?"

"Okay, okay! I'm sorry!"

They laughed.

# Chapter 17

## Reviewing the Evidence

Detective Johnson returned to his office on South Broadway. He placed the research documents and books he borrowed onto his desk and began to go through them. He started with Megan's journal. He had a feeling it was going to be the most interesting item of the bunch. Would it be believable, though? Probably not, he figured. He thumbed through the pages and saw there were a lot. It had to be approximately two weeks' worth of entries. He set it aside and picked up the small pink diary, which once belonged to a much younger Margaret Garrett. He did not expect it to reveal much in the way of clues or evidence, since it was written before she went missing. Still, it could provide some insight into her character. It couldn't hurt to have it as reference material. The rest of the papers were copies of newspaper articles and what appeared to be missing person's reports. Most were from the late 1980s. There were thirty loose pages in total, counting the page from the old newspaper.

Johnson decided to make copies in triplicate before taking the time to read anything. One set would go into Margaret Garrett's file. Another set was for the District Attorney, in case they ever found her body. The last set was for his records. He began by copying the newspaper articles, first. It did not take long. After he finished with those, he made copies of the pages from Megan's journal. He was eager to read those pages, but knew it could probably wait, until he got home later tonight. He was already on pre-approved overtime and did not want to push his luck. The diary was next to be copied. It was going to take a little longer. It spanned several years and the pages were small. The binding of the hardcover book made it an awkward fit onto the scanning screen of the copier.

He wanted to be done with all of Megan's items before he went home. Once he was finally done, he sat down at his desk and pressed 'play' on the recorder. He needed to make sure the recording was clear and audible, before making a record of it. While the interview played in the background, he separated and sorted the copies. The actual recording was thirty-five minutes long. After listening to it, he would end his shift. As it played, he wrote down a few notes in his pad every once in a while, mainly whenever something significant was said. He jotted down the times when necessary, so he could easily go back and replay certain parts.

Right after he asked Megan to describe exactly what the "alleged" spirit of Margaret Garrett showed her, he was greatly surprised to hear an unfamiliar female voice whispering closely into the recorder. It said, "*I am not alleged. I am real.*" Johnson looked up from what he was doing and immediately rewinded the recording. He played that part a second time and heard the whispered voice, again. "*I am not alleged. I am real.*"

The eerie whisper gave him chills. "Who the hell was that?" He asked aloud. He wondered if somehow Hannah was able to whisper into the recorder when he was not paying attention. It was the only thing, which made any sense to him. He refused to believe Margaret's spirit spoke into his recorder. It would have been impossible, not to mention ridiculous. He was not what is known as a firm believer of the paranormal.

He dismissed it, for now, and resumed listening to the interview. The thought of entertaining a silly notion, such as ghosts, was not on his agenda tonight. He went back to sorting the rest of his copies. He was almost done.

A few moments later, when Megan began to describe everything Margaret experienced, as witnessed through a series of cleverly told realistic nightmares, something very strange could be heard in the background. Johnson quickly stopped the recording and rewinded it, so he could hear the same portion of the interview, again. This time, he listened to it closely, as Megan spoke. He swore he could hear what sounded like a female crying in the background, but how was it possible? The recording left him bewildered.

"What the hell?" He tried to recall if he heard the crying during the interview. At the time, it was only him and the two women in the room. The boy was down the hall from them in his bedroom with the door closed. Nobody was crying. He was certain. Besides, had he heard anyone crying, it would have surely distracted him and he would have mentioned it to Megan and Hannah. He figured it had to be one of the neighbors being heard through thin walls.

He let out a long breath of frustration and pressed 'play,' again, but only after taking a few notes down in his pad. He wanted to document the strange sounds. However, what would come next was even more disturbing.

When Megan spoke about how Hank yanked out Margaret's teeth one by one with his pliers, Johnson almost had a heart attack. The sound of a woman screaming loudly could be heard quite clearly. It sounded like someone in the room was in agony. It was terrifying. The screaming continued, until Megan moved on to what happened next.

Again, Johnson stopped the recording. "What the fuck was that?" He exclaimed. He knew no one had been screaming. Immediately, he recalled the moment when it felt like something cold grabbed his wrist tightly. It was all too real. He began to wonder if it really could have been Margaret, who was screaming.

He was almost afraid to listen to the rest of the recording, although he played it anyway. Every single time Megan described a painful or horrible experience Margaret had allegedly gone through, Johnson could either hear a woman crying or screaming. It was unreal.

He was relieved when Megan's retelling of the nightmares was over. During the last few minutes of the interview, she had become upset. She ranted and shouted at him, insisting the photos in the metal box were real and she claimed how "Maggie" showed the box to her. She even argued she saw "Hank" bury the box herself. She pleaded for Johnson to believe her, at which point her friend, Hannah, tried to calm her down.

It was the exact same moment when the recorder slid across the table on its own toward the empty seat, where Josh said he later saw his friend, Lizzie. Margaret. When Johnson tried to move the recorder back to the center of the table, someone or something grabbed his wrist firmly and moved his hand with the recorder in it. As this moment played out on the recorder, it also played out in his head, once again. He was positive he did not imagine the icy sensation of someone gripping his wrist. A dreadful feeling came over him at the realization that maybe Margaret's spirit actually was there in the room with them the entire time. There was simply no reasonable way it could have been a trick.

What he heard next sealed the deal.

Right after he let go of the recorder, the very same female voice from earlier whispered quite clearly, *"Megan is telling the truth!"* The room fell silent, immediately after the words were said, although none of them heard the voice, at the time. Not long after was the moment when Johnson asked if anyone could tell him what just happened. However, he had no idea what truly happened, until this very moment. Hearing the unfamiliar whispered voice on the recording was too disturbing and way too real for him.

At last, he accepted the truth. It really was her! She was there with them in the same room! Megan and her son were not lying, which meant everything they said was probably true. It also meant the recording was nearly undeniable proof of another person in the room with them. It was a completely different voice from everyone else in the apartment. Johnson was sure of it.

A thought occurred to him. He could always have both women sign sworn affidavits indicating they were alone with him during that part of the interview. Maybe it would stand up in a court of law. After all, it was most likely the best evidence of Margaret's spirit he would most likely ever get. He knew instantly this recording had to be transferred to his work computer to make sure it was backed up somewhere, in case anything happened to it, or to the recorder. He uploaded it to his computer, as soon as it ended.

He gathered his copies together and placed them into a manila envelope. It was time to go home. Once he filed his overtime report, he left the office.


By the time, Johnson was on the road heading to his home in Yorktown Heights, rush hour was pretty much over. Traffic was fairly light.

When he got home, he loosened his tie and tossed his suit jacket over the back of the sofa seat in his living room. He plopped down on the seat and placed the research materials on the coffee table in front of him. He removed his shoes and slid his feet into a pair of slippers. After stretching his arms out and letting out an exaggeratingly loud yawn, he leaned back against the seat and closed his eyes briefly. He wanted to take a moment to relax, after a long crazy day. He was drained.

The eerie female voice from the recording was still on his mind. He could not get it out of his head. The clarity and intensity of it left him freaked out. It was a prominent part of the recording with the crying in the background, the unmistakable screaming, and the whispered full sentences. No one could deny it was genuine. At the same time, no one would believe it was a ghost, other than Megan and her friends.

Johnson never expected to reopen the case and be forced to rely on ghost stories, in order to solve it. It was a crazy day indeed, he thought. He pondered what Jack Roe would think. He probably would not care, as long as the case was ultimately solved.

"I'm trying my best with what I have, Jack," Johnson said to himself, while shaking his head.

Once he was ready, he opened his eyes, leaned forward, and grabbed his copies of the newspaper articles. He began reading starting from the first one, which was from July 30, 1986. The headline read, "*Woman Abducted in Broad Daylight.*" It referred to the first victim, Erin Christine McAffy. Cameron had abducted her from Untermyer Park, as she was leaving. Witnesses saw him pull her into his blue two-door hatchback and drive away going southbound on North Broadway. The license plate was covered. The second article was from the next day when her nude body was discovered by an off-duty police officer, along the shoulder of the Bronx River Parkway.

The next article was from January 16, 1987. It was about the unexplained disappearance of Tamara Lyndsey, who became the second victim. She was taken, while walking her dog, along the Old Croton Aqueduct Trail. For some reason, her dog was left behind unharmed. As for Tamara, she remained missing for two weeks, before her body was found severed in half. The poor woman. There were a few articles about her.

Another victim, Linda Holmolkan, was abducted and murdered later in the year, in November. She was beheaded and the blood was drained from her body. These crimes were unbelievably cruel and evil.

Johnson was disgusted, but he kept reading the articles about each victim, until he reached the first one about Margaret Elizabeth Garrett's disappearance. He placed her missing person's report right after it. He stared at the high school photo of her, which had been printed both with the article and on the report. She was so young and innocent, only nineteen years old, making her the youngest victim.

It made Johnson so angry to think about the horrific things Megan said happened to her. He wondered, was that how it really played out? Based on what Cameron did to his other victims, it was not hard to believe he would do the terrible things Megan described.

By then, the newspapers were onto Cameron's game. They were the ones who gave him the name that stuck. The Anniversary Killer. Everyone else ran with it. It was catchy and fitting. Johnson wondered if Cameron liked his new identity. Apparently, he did not like the fact they had him all figured out because he changed how he operated. Rather than dumping Margaret's body alongside a parkway, or in a park, she was supposedly buried. It proves he was smart. No one expected it. It made it impossible to locate her.

Until now. Hopefully.

Did Megan really know the exact location of Margaret's body? Even if she did, would there be a way to link the body to Cameron? Was he foolish enough to leave any DNA evidence? Not likely. Megan said he washed the body in the shower for several minutes, before wrapping it in a white blanket. A clean body was not going to have a lot of DNA evidence, other than her own, especially decades later. It would only be a skeleton, by now.

Johnson wracked his brain thinking about a way this could end with Cameron being charged with Margaret's murder. He had the photos to prove she was in Cameron's basement, after she was abducted. She was wearing the same clothing mentioned on the missing person's report. Still, it was not good enough. Her face is not clearly visible. The only victim, whose face can be seen in the photos is Erin, victim number one.

Come to think of it, maybe there was a place, where Johnson could find her DNA. Cameron's car. He wrapped Margaret's body in a blanket, placed it into the rear compartment of his car, and drove her to the burial site. However, when she was abducted, there was no blanket. Maybe there was a leftover hair or something from that time. Comparing Margaret's DNA from her remains, if the body is found, with any possible DNA evidence from the back of Cameron's car might yield some positive results.

Of course, she was not his last victim. Therefore, it is highly possible he could have cleaned out the car, at some point, after dumping her body. Another problem is when the car was impounded, the arresting officer checked it thoroughly and nothing was found, according to his *Impound/Recovered Vehicle Report*. Maybe he missed something.

It was a longshot, but what if the car was still being stored at a pound somewhere? Typically, when a vehicle is impounded by Yonkers police as evidence of a major crime, it is towed to the 4th Precinct garage, the location of the city's Auto Crimes Unit. Of course, there is no way the car is still in the garage, after all this time. There had to be a record of where the car went, after the Crime Scene Unit was done with it, and after Cameron's trial ended.

Then again, what if the car was not even an option anymore? Why in the world would it still be at any tow pound more than thirty years later? Johnson felt discouraged. He might be literally chasing after ghosts with this theory. A few phone calls in the morning could answer any questions regarding the car.

In the meantime, he got up and went into the kitchen to make himself something to eat. He was starving and dinner was long overdue. He looked through his cabinets and refrigerator, trying to decide what to eat. There were not a lot of options. He settled for a quick microwaved meal and ate at his kitchen table, before changing his clothing and getting ready for bed.

However, he would not be going to sleep, yet. It was time to read his copies of Megan's journal. He was very interested in reading what she wrote. Of course, once he started he noticed it was a lot of the same things he already heard during the interview, twice. Still, it was good to see she was consistent with her story.

He observed her sketch of the basement and speculated if she had ever been there, or if she drew it based solely on her nightmares. It had not occurred to him before that she might have gone there. He never thought to ask and she failed to mention it. He definitely planned to ask her when he returned her documents the next day. The possibility of her being there could only add more skepticism to whether or not the metal box was planted by someone else, other than Cameron.

This was not good, Johnson thought.

According to the original search of the location supplemental to Cameron's arrest, the entire basement had been searched thoroughly by a team of forensic experts. The ground in that particular room was dug up in an attempt to search for bodies and evidence because it was part concrete and part soil. It was not specified if the team checked beneath the boulder. According to the initial report, the search mainly focused on the central region of the room.

Johnson continued reading the journal. Something else stood out, which she also failed to mention during the interview. He wondered if this detail simply slipped her mind, or if by chance she deliberately did not mention it, for whatever reason. In the journal, she wrote about how Margaret was humming or singing a series of numbers in some of the nightmares. At first, she said it was difficult to understand, but she eventually heard it clearly.

Apparently, Megan wrote everything down when it came to the nightmares, as soon as she woke up. She did not want to forget anything. V356 were the numbers and letter, but what did they signify? Megan did not know and neither did Johnson. He knew it had nothing to do with the car's license plate number or Cameron's home address. He wondered if perhaps it was only a partial number. It was possible. Maybe it was a code of some kind?

Another mystery to investigate. He would start by asking Megan.

Before going to sleep, Johnson examined the copies of the diary pages. There were too many to start reading it now. It could wait, until tomorrow. He only hoped Margaret had neat handwriting like Megan. He checked. The diary was written in script, although it was legible. Satisfied, he put the pages aside, for the time being. He decided he could always ask Megan if she saw anything in the diary, which might have stood out to her, when she read it.

He turned off his light and got into bed. Sleep was beckoning him. Everything involving this case seemed so overwhelming and unbelievable. If he found the body, how was he going to state his case to the D.A. without sounding like a crazy person? Everything was counting on the supposed word of a ghost, as told through a third party based on her dreams.

Oh, yeah. Johnson had a feeling he was going to get psyched off the job, for sure. He still had not even ran this theory by his supervisor. That was going to be fun, too. Luckily, his supervisor was on vacation. It bought him some time to get results and maybe finally solve this case.

Sure, it was going to be easy. All he had to do was solve a cold case in less than a week, which has been unsolved for more than thirty years, with help from the victim's ghost. No problem. It was all in the timing.

It was so funny, he had to laugh.

To top it off, there was yet another mystery, which still needed to be solved. Who in the world was Leanne? Was she another one of Cameron's victims? Maybe she was the crime he really got away with because no one even reported her missing. Maybe her name was mentioned in Margaret's dairy. It would certainly be particularly helpful, although very unlikely.

Johnson analyzed the photos of her carefully. Leanne was smiling in one photo, which means she probably knew Cameron and felt comfortable around him. Hers were the only photos taken in places other than the basement. Some were taken at intimate locations, such as the bedroom and bathroom. It meant they were intimate with each other. Maybe his first bondage experience was with her.

If only there was a way to learn her last name. There was nothing about her mentioned in Megan's journal either, or in any of the newspaper articles. Perhaps, she was still alive out there somewhere with secrets of her own.

Johnson got out of bed and walked over to his computer in the living room. He sat down and turned it on. Once it was ready, he did a search of Henry Paul Cameron's full name together with Leanne's name to see what would turn up. There was nothing useful. Next, he searched Leanne's first name for obituaries in 1985, 1986, 1987, 1988, and 1989. There were sixty-four pages of results, which was a lot. Johnson only looked at the first few possible matches. None of them were of the Leanne he wanted to find.

"Oh, forget it. This is a waste of time," he complained, before shutting down his computer and going back to bed. Tomorrow was another day, he reminded himself. It was time to get some sleep.

# Chapter 18

## The Ghost Within

Megan woke up early the next morning feeling well rested, for once. She realized she had not been woken up in the middle of the night. It was the first time in days she slept through the night. While she did dream about Maggie, it was a different kind of dream from the usual nightmares she was having each night. This dream took place in the apartment.

She was sitting at the kitchen table with Hannah, Josh, and Maggie. Maggie was still a spirit, but they could see and hear her. She was not invisible. Instead, she was more like a living person. They were having a large meal together like a real family. No, it was a feast. It may have been a holiday. Thanksgiving or Christmas? Everything seemed so normal and everyone was happy.

While they ate, they talked about average everyday things. Trivial matters of the heart. They joked and laughed. It did not seem important enough to remember the specifics. The point is it was a normal family gathering, which was nice, for a change. And Maggie was part of their family.

This dream was clearly not scary. Actually, it was rather pleasant, although it did not last very long. When it was over, Megan wondered why she ever feared Maggie. She was not the monster. She was only an innocent victim, whose life was taken away too soon.

Hank was the monster. She had always known it. He was already rotting away in prison, where he belonged.

He was not the one, who haunted her apartment. He was not the one trapped with no way to move on. He was not the one trying to seek her help. No. That was sweet innocent Maggie, the beautiful teenage girl he tortured, raped, and murdered. She was the one who needed help because she was trapped in the apartment and could not move on. Why feel fear toward her?

Megan's perspective had definitely changed over the last few days. She wondered if it was part of the reason she did not have a nightmare. Of course, she was also trying her best to help Maggie to move on, which meant she knew what had to be done. She needed to go with Detective Johnson to find the body. It was like he said, there could be no more excuses. Maggie needed her to do this, so she could finally be put to rest.

In addition, Maggie wanted Megan to let her brother know what happened. She was not entirely sure how she was going to make that happen. She knew his name, Chris Garrett, but it was the only thing she knew about him. Maybe she could have Hannah search Facebook. She hoped he would not be too difficult to locate. She had a feeling Maggie would find some way to help her.

Megan got ready for work and served breakfast for her and Josh. Her mind was on other things, so she did not make conversation. However, Josh was not feeling so pensive.

"Mommy? How can you help Lizzie, if you can't even see her?"

She thought about how to answer his question without scaring him. The concept of finding a dead body did not make good breakfast conversation with a four-year-old child.

"I will have to go on a secret adventure with Detective Johnson." She knew he loved the idea of an adventure, especially considering how his expression changed to one of enthusiasm. To deter any further questions he might pose, she added, "I'm sorry I cannot say much about it. Just know, when we get to our destination, we will find her and set her free, so she can go to Heaven."

"Wow! You're going to help my guardian angel go to Heaven?"

She nodded, "Yes, I am."

"Awesome!" Suddenly, he became worried. He asked, "Does that mean she won't be my guardian angel anymore?"

"Aw, baby. Of course, she can still be your guardian angel. It will be even better, though. From Heaven she can watch over you wherever you go, unlike now, where she is stuck in this apartment." Except when she is showing off how she died and where she was buried, Megan thought.

"Oh, goody!" Josh cheered.

Megan smiled at him and began washing the dishes. Before Josh could go to his room, she asked, "Josh, can you do me a favor? Ask our special friend to be nice to Misty. Sometimes, I think she enjoys scaring Misty. It's not very nice."

"Okay, Mommy. I will ask her."

A short time later, Misty was at the door. Megan let her in and greeted her. A moment later, she was off to work.


For the first time, Misty did not feel as scared as usual to be around Lizzie, which is how she tended to refer to Maggie thanks to Josh. Now that she knew the whole story, she felt sorry for the wayward spirit. The things she went through before ultimately being murdered were absolutely awful. Misty wanted to help her in any way she could. She began by not showing fear when she felt her presence, which was not long after Megan left for work.

"Hello, Lizzie. I'm sorry I was so scared of you. I didn't understand. I've always been afraid of spirits. It was only instinct. I never thought about the fact you were a person like me. You have feelings, too. If I ever did anything to hurt your feelings or to make you angry, I am so sorry. I promise things will be different from now on."

She waited, as if there would be a vocal response to her apology. Naturally, there was nothing.

"I wish I could see you, too, the way Josh can. You can show yourself to me, if you'd like. I promise I will not be afraid. I was thinking maybe I could help you to somehow communicate with Megan. I can't hear your voice, but I can sense when you are happy or angry or sad. I know it's not much, but it's all I can do. I suppose you prefer Josh, since he can actually see and hear you. I don't blame you. He's so much cuter than me anyway."

She waited, again, and then asked, "Is there any other way I can help you?" She had seen many paranormal shows over the recent years, so she used one of the lines they often said. "Use my energy, if it will help you."

Just then, she felt a tingling sensation all over. It was something new. The spiritual presence felt much stronger than it ever had before. Misty felt an unseen pressure against her body. It was almost crowding her. Her body felt so heavy and time seemed to slow down. She felt dizzy and sat on the sofa.

Misty took a deep breath and closed her eyes.

Maggie opened her eyes and could feel herself breathing.

She looked down and saw Misty's body. It felt strange. She had forgotten how it felt to be alive. Her heart was beating fast. She reached up and felt it with her hand. She looked at her hand. She squeezed the fingers tightly into a fist. She stood up and walked around the room getting a feel for her legs and feet. She looked at everything through different eyes and touched whatever was in front of her. She could feel it all. She looked out of the window and felt the warmth on her face from the sun. She closed her eyes and smiled.

She turned around and opened the refrigerator. She examined the contents. She grabbed a chocolate chip cookie and pulled out the milk. She poured herself a glass and bit the cookie. Again, she closed her eyes and savored the flavor. She swallowed and drank from the glass. She only took a sip. She continued eating the cookie slowly taking small bites and drinking small sips of milk after each bite.

When she finished her snack, she danced around the kitchen table to a song in her head. She sat down in her favorite seat at the table. She tried to imagine seeing her mother and brother at the table with her like old times, but she had trouble picturing Chris. He was different. Older. She wanted to visit him, but he was too far away. She was still stuck in her own world. Her mother had moved on without her. So did her father long ago. They left her here alone.

She cried. It was nothing new. She always cries, these days. She wiped away her tears and tried something else. She spoke using an actual voice, which could be heard by anyone. "I am Margaret and I am real." The words sounded strange, since it was Misty's voice. It felt too weird even for her. "I am ready to rest. Thank you, Misty," she said.

In the next moment, Misty found herself seated at the kitchen table, which threw her for a loop. She looked around and noticed she was alone in the kitchen. She could not feel Lizzie. Every little thing, which had just occurred, came back to her as distant memories, as if they happened years ago.

"Whoa!" She exclaimed. "That was too weird. Not exactly what I had in mind, Lizzie." Misty remained in the seat for several minutes before she realized which seat she was sitting on. "Oh, snap! I'm so sorry." She began to stand, but felt a hand on her shoulder gently pushing her back down. She could not hear the words aloud, but swore she heard it in her head.

A sweet female voice saying, "It's okay."

Misty felt overwhelmed with emotions. She had no idea why, but she was crying.

"Oh, boy. I'm a hot mess today," she said to herself.

A short while later, Misty walked into Josh's room. She felt the presence growing stronger. Right away, she knew Lizzie was in there with him. Josh was sitting on his bed with a book opened in front of him and his Mandalorian at his side.

The Mandalorian spoke without him pushing the button. It said, "I did what I had to."

Josh looked at the Mandalorian, and then at Misty. He asked, "Are you okay? You look tired."

"Yeah, I'm a little tired, but I think I'm good." She did not react to the talking action figure. She knew, who it was saying the words. She was okay with it. It was on her. She did say, she wanted to help anyway she could and she gave Lizzie permission to use her energy. How could she complain?

Josh said, "Lizzie said thank you."

Misty smirked, "Tell her…" she paused and corrected herself. "I mean, you're very welcome, Lizzie. I'm glad I could help you. Hey, do you guys want to watch a movie with me?"

Josh looked at Lizzie, and then responded, "Which one? She wants to know."

"Whichever one she wants to see," was Misty's response. "Let her choose."

"She said she wants to watch '*The Lost Boys.*'" He made a funny face when he said it, as if he thought it was an odd choice.

Misty grinned and replied, "I believe that can be arranged. We can watch it on my Firestick. Have you ever seen this movie, Josh?" She led him to the living room TV.

"I think so." He asked, while following her, "Is it about Peter Pan?"

Misty scoffed, "Oh no. Definitely not, my young padawan. You are in for a real treat. I first saw this movie when I was little and I absolutely loved it. Even the music is great."

They sat on the sofa together. Misty turned on the television and set up the movie on her Firestick. When it started a huge smile came over her face. They began watching the film, which made it cool to be a vampire. One without glitter.

Detective Johnson spent the first part of his day at work trying diligently to track down Cameron's 1981 blue Dodge Colt hatchback. What he learned was quite discouraging. According to the police department reports he had available, it was stored at the 4th Precinct's garage for nearly a year, after the Crime Scene Unit went over it with a fine-tooth comb. At the end of the trial the vehicle was to be released to its owner, except he was in prison for life. There was no way it was going to remain in the precinct garage, once it was not needed as evidence. In the early part of May 1990, it was towed away by a private towing company, which does not even exist anymore, and then it was auctioned off to the highest bidder at a car sale.

Johnson knew the car could be anywhere, but it was probably demolished years ago. So, searching the car for possible evidence was no longer an option.

Fortunately, the Crime Scene Unit was able to collect evidence from the car. They had fingerprints from two of the victims. There were also various hair follicles. Not all of them matched the victims, so some were not used during the trial. The samples that were used and positively identified were destroyed, sometime after the trial ended.

At the moment, Johnson only cared about the samples, which were not used.

It seems there were no DNA tests conducted, at all, which he found to be odd. What he had forgotten was DNA testing for crime scene evidence had only begun in 1985. It was not yet widely used by 1988. Regardless, it did not excuse the later years when it was in use and became common.

He tried to figure out why Jack never ran DNA tests on the unknown hair follicles. Then again, maybe by then, he lacked anything with Margaret's DNA to use as a match. Of course, he could have tested her mother or brother for a possible match. What he did not know is Margaret's family refused to believe she was a victim of The Anniversary Killer. They never gave anyone permission to test for her DNA. They were in denial, which essentially built a wall in front of Jack Roe's investigation. His hands were tied and the case remained unsolved for decades.

Surely, finding a body would have changed their minds. It was too late for the parents, but the brother might still be out there somewhere. Johnson had his name and date of birth on file. He could always try to find him when the time came.

Once more, he had to remind himself, he was relying on the word of a woman, who was getting her information from a ghost in her dreams. Every time he said it to himself, he felt like he was wasting his time. However, since his first conversation with Megan, he had made the first progress with this case, since it was assigned to him years earlier. He could not easily dismiss that fact.

He got back on track and thought about the unknown hair follicles, which were taken into evidence. According to Jack's old records, there were two unknown long hair follicles. It could very well be Margaret's hair, or perhaps they belonged to Leanne. Johnson knew he had to locate those hairs as soon as possible, preferably by the time he went out to search the alleged burial site with Megan.

He had a feeling he knew exactly where those mystery hair follicles were being stored and it was not far. A few moments later, he visited the Yonkers Police Department Forensic Science Laboratory and Criminal Identification Unit, which was located in the same building as the Detective Division on South Broadway, where he worked. It was very convenient.

Over the next hour, he tried to track down the hair follicles, but was having trouble finding them because they were so damned old. The lab technician, Nick, who was also his friend, tried to do him the favor, but could not find them. Nick checked the logs, again, to make sure no one had checked them out and had not returned them, yet. The last person to check them out was Jack. Based on the log, they were returned long ago. Nick searched the computer to see if there was an update, which he might have missed. Nothing stood out. They were as good as lost.

"Sorry, Rob," Nick said with a shrug. "I can keep looking. Maybe they were misplaced or something. It's been a long time. I'll give you a call, if I find them. They should be together, wherever they are."

"Thanks, Nicky. I'll be in my office, if anything. Hey, if you find those hairs for me, I'll buy you lunch for a week," he promised his friend.

"Oh, nice," Nick grinned happily. "Thanks! *But* I get to choose where the lunch comes from. Okay?"

"Yeah, okay. Not a problem," Johnson agreed. "You got a deal, my friend. Now find me those hairs." He turned to leave.

"I'm working on it," Nick assured him, while still in front of the computer.

Johnson returned to his office and sat at his desk. He checked the time. It was still too early. He intended to pay Megan another visit, later today, so he could return her belongings. He also had a few questions for her. Plus, he wanted her to hear the recording to see what she made of the female voice. He could not wait to see her reaction.

In the meantime, he figured he could always take his lunch break. It was best to take advantage before Nick found the missing evidence. Otherwise, he was going to have to buy two lunches.

During the evening, when Megan arrived home from work, she began cooking spaghetti with ground beef. She also put some biscuits in the oven. She invited Misty to stay for dinner. Misty agreed. In truth, Megan wanted her around in case she and the detective needed to speak in private. She thought Misty could keep Josh occupied.

While she was cooking, she noticed Misty seemed in a better mood than usual. She was also not in a hurry to leave. She asked, "Did you have a good day?"

"Yes, I did," responded Misty. "Today, something weird happened. When I got here, I sort of had a talk with Lizzie, uh, Maggie. Anyway, I basically told her I was sorry for being afraid of her. I offered my help to her, in any way I could and gave her permission to use my energy." She paused, and then added, "Well, she did one better. She used my body."

Megan was astonished. Her mouth gaped open when she asked, "She did what???"

"You heard me right. She entered my body and took over for like an hour. It was pretty bizarre. One minute I was sitting on the sofa, and the next thing I know I am here at the table sitting in her seat. When I checked my watch an hour had gone by. She even let me stay in her seat when I tried to get up."

"Oh my goodness!" Megan could not believe it.

"Little by little," Misty continued. "I began to remember everything she did, while she was in control. The strange thing is those memories seemed like they happened long ago. I barely remember the details. I think she danced and ate a cookie." She laughed. "I remember something about her sitting at the table, but the memory is vague."

"I still can't believe she just swooped into your body and took over." Megan was amazed.

"Yeah, tell me about it. I was a bit shocked myself, but I realized I kind of gave her permission. I guess she misunderstood." She shrugged. "No harm done. It worked out in the end. She even thanked me. Not to mention she let me sit in her seat, although I don't plan to make a habit out of it. After everything was said and done, Josh and I sat down on the sofa and watched a movie with her. Crazy, huh?"

"Well, yeah! That is insane. I can't wait to tell Hannah about this. Wow! My mind is blown." Megan still could not wrap her mind around it. It was the kind of thing she thought Maggie would have only done to her. She probably would have allowed it, considering the connection they already shared. She almost felt jealous.

Moments later, Detective Johnson arrived. Megan opened the door for him and let him into her apartment. "Please, come in, Detective Johnson."

"Thank you, Megan." He handed her the stack of research materials. "I also want to thank you for letting me borrow these. I found everything to be incredibly interesting, especially your journal."

"You're welcome." She placed the stack of paperwork on the kitchen table. "Sorry, I'm in the middle of making dinner. Would you like to join us? We're having spaghetti with ground beef and biscuits."

"Oh, that sounds delicious, but I just ate, not too long ago, and I have to get back to the office. Still on the clock." He pointed to his Rolex watch.

"Nice watch," she commented.

"Thank you, again. I do have a few quick questions, if you don't mind."

"Shoot," she said without turning away from the pot on the stove. "Wait. Poor choice of words. Don't shoot. I mean, go ahead."

"I hear you," he chuckled. "Okay, first question. In your journal, you wrote about Margaret singing a tune. V356? You never mentioned it during our interview. What does it mean?"

"Wow. I am so sorry. I completely forgot about that," she said. "I really have no idea what it means. I barely understood what she was singing, until we were in the trunk of the car on our way to the highway. Whenever she sang it, she was always kind of zoned out. It was pretty creepy."

"It does sound kind of creepy," he admitted. "So, you don't know what it means?"

She shook her head. "No, sorry. Not yet anyway. I guess she will show me when the time comes. It's how she works. She shows me things when she's ready. Sometimes, I get a tease about something. It's why I write it all down."

"I see. Did she show you anything last night?"

"Actually, last night I had a normal dream, although she was in it. It was not a memory like the nightmares. It was more like a fantasy." She told him her dream, while mixing the spaghetti with the sauce.

"Interesting. Hey, I got another question for you. I saw the sketch you drew of the basement. Tell me, have you ever been there? I mean physically, not just in a dream."

"Yes, I went once with Hannah and Leslie, my landlady. I totally started tripping, as soon as we stepped through those wooden doors. I had to bail fast. I thought I could go there, but I barely stayed a minute before having a full-blown panic attack."

"You have panic attacks?" He asked.

"All the time. I had one yesterday. Remember?"

"Yeah, that's right. You didn't want me to call you an ambulance. I didn't realize it was a panic attack. I thought you were really sick. I was worried about you."

"I was really sick. Sort of. Okay, maybe not that sick. I take meds for it," she explained. "I hate it. I'm trying to ween myself off of them slowly. I've been practicing a breathing technique to relax myself."

He asked, "Is it working?"

"Sometimes. It depends on how stressed I am, at the moment."

He realized there is no way she could have taken the time to plant the metal box and cover it with a boulder, if what she said is true. Not to mention, her, Hannah, and Leslie would not have been able to move the huge boulder by hand. It was extremely heavy. The Emergency Service officers had to use heavy duty equipment to move it.

Satisfied, he moved on to the next question. "Did you find anything significant when you read Margaret's diary? I've only had time to peruse through it."

"Absolutely!" She nearly shouted at him. "There was an entry toward the end from 1987. She went with her father and brother to get their car repaired. Guess which shop they went to?"

"Cameron's Autobody Repair?"

"Yeah, and she saw him there. She said there was a young mechanic, who kept looking at her in a creepy way. Trust me. The man is creepy. If he looks at you, it feels creepy. His smile is creepy. He's basically an all-around creep."

"Okay. Thanks. I guess I will check it out tonight. Oh, by the way, I wanted you to hear something before I leave, but I know you need to finish cooking. I will skip to the good parts. I memorized the times. She was intrigued. He pulled out the recorder and skipped to the first part when the unknown whisper was heard.

Megan became excited. "Oh, my God! That was her! I know her voice! I'd recognize it anywhere!" She tried to speak more calmly. "I've heard it enough times in my nightmares. It's definitely Maggie."

"There's more," he teased. He skipped ahead to the part when Megan was talking about Hank pulling teeth with pliers. The screams were intense.

"Jesus Christ! It's how she sounded in my nightmare. I'll never forget her screams for as long as I live. I don't want to hear this part. Please, stop it."

She looked distressed. Johnson noticed she was taking deep breaths. He did not want her to have another panic attack, so he skipped the parts where the spirit was crying and went to the last whisper. Megan was surprised.

"She was backing me up," she smiled proudly. A tear came to her eye. "Wow! This is the bomb! I'm totally stoked, right now!" She wiped away the tear, and then paused before asking, "Hey, is there any way I can please have a copy of this recording? I know the girls would love to hear it. Josh, too. Well, some of it. Or is it against the rules because it's official evidence or something?"

He thought about it, before answering, "Well, technically, I originally made this recording for my own records, but I do plan on making it part of the official investigation. It's too good not to include it. I'm really not supposed to give you a copy, but I think I can make an exception under these unusual circumstances. However, first, I want to make sure this recording gets heard by the D.A." She nodded, as he went on, "Until it does, you need to keep it under wraps. Do NOT post it on the Internet." She shook her head obediently. "If you do, it could jeopardize the entire investigation. I can't emphasize it enough. Do you understand?"

"Yes," she nodded eagerly. "Don't worry about me. I don't use social media anymore."

"Good because if I send you a copy, you cannot share it with anyone. I mean anyone. If you want Hannah and whoever to hear it, they need to listen to it here on your computer. Do not forward it to them."

"Not ever? So, it's like top secret?" She asked with a smirk on her face.

"Yes, exactly. Once this is all over, you can share it on TV for all I care, but until then, treat it like it came from Area 51. You get me?"

"So post it on social media and send it to the *National Enquirer*?"

He looked flustered. "What? No, you can't." He shook his head adamantly. "Okay, you know what? Forget Area 51. DO NOT POST IT. Are we clear?"

She chuckled, "I was only yanking your chain. Don't get so butthurt."

"Excuse me?" He seemed both confused and offended, although he was *cracking* a smile.

"Oh, sorry. California slang. It basically means to stop being so sensitive," she explained. "I lived in California for a few years. It kind of stays with you. I only moved back to New York in February, after I left Josh's dad."

He nodded. "Ah, yes. He who shall not be named. Right?" He was unsure if she would get the "*Harry Potter*" reference.

She smiled at him bashfully, and then said, "Yeah, something like that, although he is more of an asshole than Voldemort and less magical."

Johnson laughed both at her vulgarity and the comparison she made.

She turned back to the stove to check on her meal, before asking, "Hey, are you sure you can't stay for dinner? There's a lot and it's almost done." She opened the oven to check on the biscuits. "Yep. Just a few more minutes." She turned to face him gazing up at him warmly. He was much taller than her. Suddenly, she realized Hannah was right. He did look a little bit like Denzel Washington.

Johnson smiled back at her. He was tempted. "I'm not gonna lie. It smells really good and it looks tasty, but I honestly need to get my behind back to work. Maybe we can all have a celebration dinner together when this thing is over."

"That would be very nice," she said.

"Great. I'd better go now. Thank you, Megan, for everything. I will see you soon. Right?" He eyed her admonishingly.

She nodded, "Yes, definitely. Um, so, when are you going to see that sick son of a bitch?"

He laughed and replied, "In two days, and I expect to see you on the day after for our little rendezvous. Does that day work for you?"

"Yes, it's a date," she answered plainly. She quickly changed her tone and became flustered. "I mean, yes! I will be ready, this time. Uh, you know what

I meant." She felt embarrassed. Did she really say date??? Stupid. Stupid. She wanted to put her head in the oven.

He laughed, again. She was on a roll tonight. He was enjoying himself and wished he had more time to stay longer. She was pleasant company and dinner was looking tempting. Of course, that would be unprofessional. He had to behave, at least, until the trial was over.

She felt like a silly schoolgirl. She regained her composure and explained more seriously, "I know it's what she wants me to do, so I will do it. She's waited long enough."

He responded, "Yes, I would imagine she has." He thought about the three-decade-old cold case and was glad he might actually be able to solve it. He kept his fingers crossed. "Well, I'd best be on my way. I'll be in touch. Enjoy your dinner," he said, as he opened the door to leave.

"Thank you. Goodnight, detective." She smiled at him warmly.

"Goodnight." He waved at her and left.

After he was gone, she smiled. She then called Josh and Misty to dinner. She could not wait to tell them all about the recording and how Maggie's voice was on it.

---

# Chapter 19

# Inside The Anniversary Killer

Two days had gone by and Detective Johnson was still waiting to hear back from his buddy, Nick, regarding the two unknown hair follicles. He was starting to worry they may never be located. It was all he needed, for them to be gone. It figured the least important evidence from the original trial was currently the most important evidence he might need to close this case and link Margaret's death to The Anniversary Killer case. And what a big surprise it was to learn they just happened to be misplaced.

"Life enjoys kicking me in the balls," Johnson thought to himself.

He left the office feeling frustrated and got into his unmarked department vehicle. He took a drive upstate, traveling along Route 9, as he headed to Ossining. He had an appointment to keep.

It was sometime early in the afternoon when he arrived at the Sing Sing Correctional Facility. After showing his credentials and the appropriate paperwork, he checked in. He handed over his firearm for safekeeping, and then was escorted to a private visiting room. The small square-shaped room had two large windows. The only furniture was a long table, which was bolted to the floor, and two seats.

The corrections officer, who escorted him to the room, was a sergeant. He was a short stocky Hispanic male in his late forties. It looked like he had just gotten back from a very sunny vacation, based on his overly tanned skin and pleasantly relaxed demeanor.

"Wait in here," he said to Johnson, who nodded. "I'll arrange to have him brought in for you." He spoke into his portable handheld radio, as he turned to leave. "Alonzo, can you bring Henry Cameron out to the visiting room? You'll find him waiting in his cell, V-356. He's expecting a visitor. The detective from Yonkers is here to see him."

"10-4, Sarge," a male voice answered casually.

The officer turned back to face Johnson and stated, "He'll be right out. You can have a seat, if you want. Make yourself comfortable, but not too comfortable. Keep in mind, no matter how nice these guys may seem, most of them are assholes, who will try to test you." He then left, leaving Johnson alone in the small square-shaped room.

"Thanks, I'll keep that in mind," Johnson said half-heartedly, as he took a seat. He barely paid any mind to the sergeant's warning. He was too distracted. When he heard him mention Cameron's cell number, his eyes gaped open. V-356! It was exactly what Megan said Margaret was singing in her nightmares. Somehow, Margaret knew exactly where her killer was spending his days."

Johnson snickered to himself. Yet, one more amazing thing about this case. The mysterious occurrences and coincidences kept on coming. Megan was going to be quite surprised when he told her what the numbers meant. There was no way she could have possibly known his cell number without Margaret's help. He was gradually learning to believe in everything she said. She had not been wrong, yet.

He looked at his watch and waited patiently. He wondered how Cameron would look, after thirty plus years of being incarcerated.

A moment later, the door opened. A much older scruffy looking Henry Paul Cameron shuffled lazily into the room with shackles on his ankles and handcuffs on his wrists. He was tall and lanky. His gray hair was long, down to his shoulders, and it was starting to thin out. He had gray stubble on his chiseled face from not shaving for days. He wore his wireframe glasses, a plain white t-shirt, and dark slacks with black shoes. It was not quite the same vision Johnson imagined. He had only ever seen the photos on file or from the newspaper articles. The sixty-something-year-old Hank Cameron was escorted by Officer Alonzo, who remained near the door, after closing it behind him.

Cameron leered at Johnson and slowly made his way to the seat opposite from him at the long table. He sat down and placed his hands on the table. The handcuffs on his wrists made a loud clanking sound when they hit the table.

Officer Alonzo cleared his throat loudly, as a not-so subtle warning.

Cameron grinned mischievously. Megan was right. He did have a creepy smile, even now.

Johnson nodded at him politely and stated in a loud clear voice, "Good afternoon, Mr. Cameron. My name is Detective Robert Johnson. I'm with the Detective Division in Yonkers." He did not specify which unit. "Thank you for seeing me. I appreciate your time."

"Yeah, yeah. Whatever," Cameron replied with uninterest. His voice was harsh and nasally. "Time is all I have. Everyone wants to see a famous serial killer in person. What's your reason?" He was rude and obnoxious

"I merely want to talk," Johnson answered smoothly. "Maybe ask you a few questions."

"I bet you do," Cameron sneered. He chuckled briefly.

Johnson placed his digital recorder on the table and turned it on. "Mr. Cameron, do you mind if I record our conversation?" He wished he had a camcorder, instead, to capture facial reactions.

"Like I got a choice in what you do?" Cameron scowled. "You writing a book or something?"

"Or something," Johnson replied casually with a half-smile. As a formality, he read Cameron his rights, first, before beginning. "So, are they treating you well in here?"

Cameron sucked his teeth. The Miranda Warnings left him leery. "What do you care?"

"Fair enough. I'll cut to the chase, but before I do, I'm kind of curious about something. Why anniversaries, if you don't mind me asking?"

"Why not?" Cameron shrugged. "I like history. Always have. Watched a lot of documentaries, back in the day, especially about famous serial killers. Read a lot of books on the subject, too. Maybe something we have in common, huh? A special interest in serial killers?"

"Yeah, maybe," Johnson agreed with a nod. "Did they inspire you to do what you did? I can't help noticing you seemed to pay homage to them."

"No," he answered quickly and shook his head, but then he thought about it. "Well, maybe a little. You see, I had all these dates on a calendar. Murder dates," he explained. "It was a special calendar, which I made when I turned twenty. It was private. I burned it, so you guys never found it. Typically, I would see how the weather was going to be and if it wasn't too bad, I'd pick a day. The murder on the calendar would dictate how things would have to be done."

"*Have* to be done?" Johnson inquired. "So, it was like a game?"

"Yeah! I mean, what's the point in picking a special date when a murder occurred, if I wasn't going to do something similar? Right?"

"Okay, but you didn't like to copy it exactly. Did you? You liked to make it your own."

Cameron grinned, "Doesn't every artist?"

"So, you consider yourself an artist?"

"I *am* an artist!" Cameron declared angrily. "I can draw, paint, sculpt, build, destroy! Whatever!" He sucked his teeth and spoke more calmly. "I don't need your opinion. I know what I am. My brother used to call me an artist all the time. He knew I was good, too."

"Your brother, huh?" Johnson became intrigued. While he had a few questions he wanted to ask, he never thought to ask about Cameron's family. It might be helpful to learn what he had to say. Johnson hoped by letting Cameron ramble on, he might slip up and say something significant. Maybe about Leanne. "Can we talk about your brother for a moment?"

"Sure," Cameron agreed. "What do you want to know? I love talking about my brother. I worshipped Paul. Man, I miss him like crazy."

"What did he think about the things the newspapers said about you?"

"He never knew. He died a long ass time ago, back in the '70s. I was fifteen. Just a kid."

"My condolences," Johnson said with sincerity. "Was it natural causes? 'Nam?"

"He served in 'Nam, but that's not where he died," Cameron shook his head. "The war was over by then. Paul was killed in Yonkers, but it's not what the official reports say. They're filled with bullshit lies about an overdose. My brother kicked his drug habit a year before. He was clean. I would have known if he wasn't. Someone planted the drugs in his apartment and made it look like an O.D. Personally, I think it was crooked cops."

"Why would you think that?"

"Because he knew it was coming. He warned me. He said someone was probably going to kill him. Let me tell you, he knew a lot of bad people. They had a few Yonkers cops in their pocket, too."

"How can you be sure? What proof do you have to back up your claim?"

"Proof? Please! Like cops give a shit about proof when it makes them look bad! Remember back in the '70s with those Son of Sam shootings David Berkowitz got blamed for doing?" He asked.

"Yeah. Of course," Johnson nodded.

"Well, I hope you know he didn't do those shootings alone. There were a bunch of others doing it with him and sometimes without him. They called themselves the 22 Disciples of Hell. My brother, Paul, was one of them. Berkowitz was just their patsy. He was the fall guy. Took the blame for all the crimes, since he was the only one to actually murder any of the victims. The responsibility kind of fell onto him. You know? He was okay with it, though. He wanted the fame. Old Dave was a glory hound. Needed some recognition." He grinned.

"And how do you know all of this? Have you been watching one of those recent documentaries?"

"Shit no! I don't watch a lot of TV no more. Nothing but reality bullshit. Dave told me. He's here. You know? Besides, I knew this way back then. It's like I told you, my brother was part of the crew. Sometimes, he used to take me with him to Untermyer Park. That's where they liked to meet in one of those old pump houses along the trail."

"The Old Croton Aqueduct Trail?" Johnson felt like they were getting somewhere, once he mentioned the trail.

"Yeah, man. I loved that trail." He reminisced for a second, and then continued, "I guess he was training me to follow in his footsteps. But after everything went down and Dave Berkowitz was arrested, the leader of the crew started putting out hits and killing everyone off. Getting rid of loose ends, including Paul."

"Who was the leader? Do you know his name?"

"Shit, even if I did, I ain't gonna tell you! I don't need his disciples coming after me. To be honest, I'm only telling you what's already common knowledge. It doesn't really matter anymore. Most of those 22 Disciples of Hell are probably in Hell. They were being killed off left and right. These were professional jobs, mind you. They usually looked like accidents or suicides, like with Paul."

Mentioning his brother refocused him on his death. "Man, I know he didn't kill himself with no overdose. I'm the one, who found his body. I had a key to his place on Warburton. Someone made it seem like he had an overdose. He was too smart for that shit. That's why he quit using. He just wasn't smarter than them. I'm pretty sure the cops got to him because they showed up way too fast when I called, almost like they were waiting for the call."

"I see. It must have been hard to see him like that. I'm really sorry." Johnson wanted to see how he reacted to sympathy, since he did not seem to mind raping and murdering young women. There was no reaction.

The conspiracy theories and talk of crooked cops was becoming a little too overwhelming for Johnson. It was time to change the subject and move on to his questions. "What you're saying about these disciples is very interesting, but to be honest I don't want to go down this rabbit hole with you. I'd rather get back to your case, if you don't mind. Refresh my memory. How many victims was it, again?" He was hoping Cameron would accidentally reveal a number other than five, which was the amount he was convicted on.

Cameron was too smart, though. He took a moment to think about it and shrugged, "I can't remember. It was a long time ago. You gotta have a list somewhere. Check it."

"You're right. I'll check it later. So, who was the first victim? Do you remember?"

Cameron took a deep breath and asked in a pleasant voice, "What's new in Yonkers? Been a while since I was there. Is crime down? Let me guess. You guys have nothing better to do. I mean, there's gotta be a good reason you're chasing down ghosts. Am I right?" Suddenly, his demeanor changed. "This shit happened decades ago. It's in the past. Who cares? Get over it." Johnson noticed he showed no signs of remorse.

Johnson realized he must have hit a nerve. Maybe Erin McAffy was not the first victim, after all. Could it have been Leanne? He decided to push a little harder and asked, "Tell me what you know about Margaret Elizabeth Garrett." He purposely did not pose it as a question because Cameron would have given a simple 'yes' or 'no' answer. Instead, his request required a more elaborate response.

"She's dead… or missing. How should I know?" He shrugged. "That girl's been gone for decades. Right?"

"I find it interesting how you said 'dead' before 'missing.'"

"Oh, whatever, man!" Cameron became agitated. "She's not one of my victims. There's no proof connecting me to her. You got nothing."

"Maybe. Maybe not. I'm a patient man."

"Is that what this visit is about?" Cameron asked, sounding surprised and irritated. "Man, you really are chasing after ghosts. Huh?"

"Who's Leanne?" Johnson paid close attention to Cameron's face when he asked the question. He wanted to watch for any specific reactions.

Cameron swallowed hard and his face froze. There was a slight hint of emotion on his face. Eventually, he looked away and responded, "How should I know?"

"So, you've never known anyone named Leanne?"

"Nope," he shook his head, but would not make eye contact.

Johnson asked, again, "Are you sure? Pretty Goth girl with long blonde hair? Ring any bells?"

Cameron's facial expression changed. He looked worried. He swallowed, again, and then shook his head. "No, man. I don't know no Leanne. Why? She say something about me?" He faked a laugh.

Johnson asked, "Is that possible? Can she say anything about you? When is the last time you saw her?"

"A long time ago," Cameron answered with a distant look in his eyes.

"So, you do know her?"

"Wait. What?" Cameron realized he got caught in a lie. "Are you trying to confuse me, man?"

Johnson pulled out an envelope from his jacket pocket and placed it on the table. He opened it and pulled out several copies of photos, which he spread out across the table in front of Cameron. It was the photos of the women in bondage from the metal box. His victims. "Still feeling confused,... *man?*"

Cameron swallowed hard, once more, as he looked upon the photos laid out on the table in front of him. He became obviously nervous and began fidgeting with his fingers. He began shaking his legs nervously under the table.

Johnson smirked and urged him, "Go ahead. Pick them up. Take a closer look at your art." He gambled on the chance they were genuine and not planted by the girls. Cameron's reaction would reveal the truth. "I imagine these must be very familiar to you, since they came from the basement of your garage. Did you forget the Crime Scene Unit did a thorough search of it back in 1989?" He did not specify the photos were found, as a result of that particular search, but he wanted Cameron to think it, so he would not deny them."

"I didn't know they found these," he admitted. "Why weren't they used during the trial?" He was baffled.

"Come on, Cam. They already had so much other evidence against you. You took trophies and kept them in your house. Plus, you messed up with the last girl. I heard she kicked your ass." He teased.

"What? That's bullshit, man! She distracted me and got lucky is all."

"Oh, okay. My bad. Sorry. Can you just do me a favor and humor me? Which one of these girls is which? It's kind of hard to tell without their official photos in front of me."

Cameron examined the photos one by one. They were in order of how they were murdered. When he noticed the ones of Margaret, he pushed them away. "How am I supposed to remember?" He lied.

"Fine. Never mind. Tell me, who is this girl, Leanne?" He pointed at her photos. "She's a beauty. I see you wrote her name in the corners of some. You didn't do that for the others." Cameron stared at her. Johnson stated, "I notice you don't like bullshit, so why don't you stop bullshitting me and be honest? Was she another victim?"

"No!" He shouted, but then immediately calmed himself and said, "Sorry. She was no one. I didn't kill her."

"Oh, she *was* someone," Johnson nodded positively. "Who was she? A girlfriend?"

Cameron looked down at the table shamefully.

"You liked her, huh? She was special. It's okay." He spoke as if talking to a child. "You can tell me about her. I promise I won't judge you." Mainly since it was not his job to judge, only to investigate and arrest.

"We dated," he confessed. "It was all her. She put the bondage shit in my head. I didn't know about that stuff before she came along. She liked it."

"I got that impression from her smile in one of the photos. What happened to her?"

"She left me. Broke my heart. I don't like talking about it. Okay?" Cameron looked away.

Johnson nodded, "Okay. Fine. Tell me her last name and I will not mention her, again."

"Flynn… I think," Cameron quickly added. He shook his head, unable to believe he blurted out her last name. He became upset. "Are we done here?" He looked like he was done talking. He was eager to get back to his cell.

"Not just yet. Give me a few more minutes. Please. I only want to know what you think about Margaret Garrett and her proximity to the Hutchinson River Parkway."

"Oh, fuck this!" Cameron stood up from his seat and shouted, "We're done here! I'm through talking to you, nigger!" He pointed accusingly at Johnson, who was quite surprised by his guilty reaction. "Take me back to my cell, Alonzo. I'm not talking to this prick anymore."

As the corrections officer escorted him out and back to his cell, Johnson waved and said, "I think I'll be in touch, Cam! See you soon, pal!"

He turned off the recorder and gathered the photos back into the envelope. He placed them into his pocket and left. His level of suspicion was at around six when he arrived. Now, it was at nine. He had enough suspicion to continue with this investigation based on everything Megan said and his talk with Cameron. He had a sinking feeling they were going to find Margaret's body exactly where she said it would be.


Henry Cameron was furious by the time he returned to his cell. The officer had removed the handcuffs and shackles, before locking him inside. At last, he was alone. He punched the wall hurting his hand in the process.

"Fuck!" The hot pain shot through his fingers, through his fist, and to his wrist. He hoped nothing was broken. He sat down on his cot and slammed his other hand down beside him. He cursed himself for foolishly agreeing to speak to Johnson and he cursed Johnson for getting under his skin. "Stupid motherfucker and his Goddamn questions!"

He took a deep breath and leaned back against the wall. The photos of Leanne came to mind. He had not thought about her in years. He closed his eyes tight and took a trip down memory lane.

Leanne Flynn.

It was the summer of 1985, when she walked into the garage. His father, Henry Senior, was still alive and running the family business. He wanted his boy, young Hank, to earn his keep. He told his son to take care of the customer and winked saying she was a cutie.

Hank was kind of shy back then, but he dealt with customers before. Why should this one be any different? He did not realize she would be the single most interesting and significant customer he would ever deal with in his life.

He walked over to her and noticed she was very pretty. Her long, straight, crimson red hair hung loosely behind her back. She had black lipstick on her perfect lips, an excessive amount of eyeliner that accentuated her lovely bright blue eyes, and a small tattoo of a black star on the inside of her right wrist. She wore a black Mötley Crüe "*Shout at the Devil*" t-shirt, tight black Levi jeans with a chain for a belt, and combat boots. She was perfect.

She smiled at him when she saw him approaching, which made him feel bashful. She found it cute.

He asked, "What seems to be the problem, miss?"

"Hi, it's my stupid Volkswagen Beetle. It's right outside." She had a nice voice. She walked out of the garage to her car, which was parked out front. He followed, as she explained, "Sometimes, the starter doesn't work and it keeps shutting off on me. I live out in Jersey, so I know it's gonna break down when I'm on the bridge. That's how my stupid luck works." She smirked in a cute way and shrugged innocently.

"Okay. Pop it open and I'll take a look at the engine," he said with a smile. She opened the rear compartment and he looked inside. He checked the battery to see if it was connected properly. Nothing was loose. After briefly examining everything, he said, "It might be the alternator. What year is it?"

"It's a 1972."

"Yeah, the *Consumer Reports* did not have good things to say about that year's model. A lot of issues with the starter, battery, and alternator. Bring it inside."

"How long do you think it'll take to fix?"

"An hour, two? Are you in a hurry?"

"To get back to Jersey?" She shook her head. "I hate waiting around is all."

"Understandable. By the way, I love the shirt."

"Yeah, man! I *love* the Crüe," she said proudly. "You a fan?"

"Shit yeah," he replied. "I wanna see them at the Garden in August. I just haven't gotten around to buying a ticket. I guess I kind of hate the idea of going alone."

"Shit! I'll go with you!"

"Yeah?" He asked with a look of hope on his face.

"Absolutely. You get me a ticket for the show and I promise it will be the best night of your life," she said flirtatiously.

He smiled at her and she smiled back. It was the moment their relationship was born. After that first day, they dated every single week. Sometimes, Hank would drive to New Jersey to see her. Other times, she would come to New York. In August, they saw Mötley Crüe at Madison Square Garden, as planned, on their two-month anniversary. It was the best night of his life.

Sex with Leanne was always a great adventure. She was super kinky. She liked role playing and got him into it. Her favorite was the rape scenario, where he pretended to break into her place and rape her. She would resist only just enough to make it feel real. It made him so hard, whenever she resisted. He liked the sex more, when it felt forbidden. Not that it mattered, she was an amazing lover. She made him feel alive.

Eventually, she wanted him to start tying her to the bed using her clothing. It was the beginning of the bondage stage for them. She loved that feeling of being helpless, while he took her. Bondage became their guilty pleasure. They bought chains and blindfolds to make it more fun. She liked it more than he did, although he enjoyed it, too.

By this time, she had dyed her hair blonde. She changed her hair color almost every month. It was black during the month of the concert.

After Hank's father died in September, he changed. He lost a part of himself. He began to feel so alone in their big house. The business had become his full responsibility. It left less time for him to travel to New Jersey to see Leanne and she could not always come to him. They saw less of each other over the next few weeks.

Whenever they were together, she wanted to make it memorable. She upped the ante and got the idea he should take photos of her in her underwear, while she was chained up on the bed or in the bathroom. She knew how much he loved photography and wanted to cultivate that side of him. She even urged him to take photos of her in the basement of the garage, since it had such a unique look with that old horse stall. She hoped her sexy poses would motivate him to take more daring photos, specifically of them having sex. However, he always insisted on no nude shots and nothing showing intercourse. He did not want to think of her as a slut, which she could appreciate.

The rape scenarios continued, until one day in late October when things went horribly wrong. She resisted and like always he forced her, except this time, when she said she could not breathe, she was not faking it. He accidentally strangled her too hard and broke her windpipe. She died seconds later.

At first, he thought she was joking. "Quit fooling around, Lee." Lee was his nickname for her. When she did not respond, he became worried. He checked to see if she was breathing. She was not. Her heart was no longer beating either. He panicked and tried to shake her into consciousness.

"Lee? Lee! Wake up!"

It was too late. She was gone.

Her unexpected death broke his heart. However, it scared him even more. What was he going to do? What would he tell the paramedics – he strangled her by accident? Surely, they would call the police and he would end up going to jail.

No. Unacceptable. There was no way he wanted to go to jail for murder.

He tried to figure out what to do. She was dead in his home. He had to do something. He had to get rid of her body, at least. It occurred to him, aside from his father, no one knew they were dating. His father was gone. They kept their relationship private, mainly due to its unique nature. She never talked about her family because they banished her long ago. She had a bit of a drug problem, but was trying to get over it. He could not risk being seen with her body at her residence, so he could not take her back there. Not to mention she lived on the second floor of an apartment building.

He had an idea. He cleaned her up and carried her downstairs. He did not think to dress her. He simply brought her outside and placed her naked body into the trunk of his car. He drove her back to New Jersey. Once over the bridge, he started out on Route 4 and kept going west, until he found himself in a largely wooded region near the Point View Reservoir. It was somewhere they visited together once before during one of their normal dates.

He drove his car along a dirt path going far out of view. He then took her body out of the trunk and carried her to an isolated area in the woods. He gently placed her nude body lying face down onto a log, where he would leave her. He positioned her face down out of respect, so her privates would not be exposed. Years later, that area would become known as the High Mountain Park Preserve, but it would not be established until 1993. For now, it was in the middle of nowhere, which was good enough for him.

Hank drove back home and burned her clothing in a garbage can behind the garage. He placed the photos he took of her in bondage into a shoebox and shoved it deep into his closet. He wanted to hide them. It would be months before he had the courage to look upon them, again.

For nearly a week, he had no idea, if her body had been discovered. There was nothing in the news. He was paying attention. Waiting for it. Finally, while watching the news, there was mention of an unidentified Caucasian woman found nude in a wooded area about two miles northeast from the reservoir. He knew it had to be her. He waited for more, but that was it. He never heard anything else about it. She remained unidentified, as far as he knew. Just another Jane Doe gone and forgotten by everyone, but him.

He felt bad. He really did like her.

He never did learn she was eventually identified and her family was notified. They did not make a big deal of it, since she was the black sheep of the family. They wanted her buried in private. No publicity. There was no murder mystery, as far as they were concerned. She hung out with bad crowds and met the wrong person, which resulted in her demise. It was bound to happen, sooner or later. They never knew she was happy for a few months. They could care less.

The police had nothing to go on. To them, she was another cold case, which would never be solved.

Hank felt guilty for a very long time. He missed her terribly. In his own strange way, he loved her. They had only dated for four months, but it was the longest romantic relationship he ever had. Had she not died, he would have stayed with her, until she got tired of him. He never got tired of her. He might have even married her. She kept his life exciting. It was an excitement he also came to miss.

In time, he longed for a similar kind of sexual excitement. The raping. The bondage. He wanted to do it, again, with someone else, but how does one find a person, who wants to do things like that? In those days, there was no such thing as dating apps or websites. He certainly was not going to put an ad in the classified section of the newspaper. He would be too embarrassed to do such a thing.

Instead, he entertained the idea of kidnapping a woman and forcing her into bondage, and maybe even slavery. He was mainly unsure what to do with her, after he was done having his way. He lacked the resources to keep her in captivity for too long, and he certainly could not let her go back home. He would easily end up being arrested, which was not an option. For a while, it remained a secret fantasy.

Of course, he did manage to get away with murder once, even if it was by chance. He thought maybe he could do it, again. It was a very tempting idea. He wondered how he would go about doing such a thing without getting caught. He imagined different scenarios, where he would kidnap women. He tried to think of how things could go wrong, and then thought of ways to make sure they did not. He began scouting his neighborhood for ideal abduction points. The Old Croton Aqueduct Trail, which passed right behind his garage, was an ideal location. It was close to home, which made it convenient. There was also plenty of parks in the area. He could grab someone and force them into his car at knifepoint. The basement behind the garage was a great place to store them, until he had his way with them. No one, but him, ever went down there. His employees were not allowed to go to the basement.

Yes, it could work, he told himself. He could do all those things he loved, again. The bondage, the photos, and the rape scenarios. Only, this time, they would not be scenarios. They would be real rapes, which made it more enticing to him.

By the Spring of 1986, he began walking the trail and learning its ins and outs. He memorized choke points and made mental notes of ideal locations near the trail, where he could park his car. He even did practice scenarios dragging a heavy duffle bag to his car. He tried to make sure no one spotted him. He learned where to hide and to step lightly.

He also drove around to scout the larger parks in Yonkers. Untermyer Park was a favorite of his because it reminded him of his youthful years with his brother. As it turned out, it was where he would eventually find victim number one during the summertime of that year. He also began watching women to see who might potentially make good victim choices.

Over the next couple of years, he learned to perfect his crimes. It took time to get it right. He learned to be more careful and efficient with each kill. Good old "M-Margaret" was his perfect crime. He never forgot her or how good she felt around his dick. He changed his style with her, so they would never find her body.

Hank sat in his cell nursing his hand. It was still aching, after punching the wall.

He wondered how Detective Johnson knew about Margaret's location. Hank thought he did everything right. Yet somehow, that busybody detective had his suspicions. He was definitely on the right track, but how the hell did he get there? Hank could not figure it out, for the life of him. He knew Johnson had not found the body, yet. Otherwise, his little visit would have gone much differently. Surely, he would have informed him of additional charges, and then Hank would have been rearrested. There would be another trial just for her.

No, Johnson did not find her, but somehow, he was getting close. Too damn close for comfort.

After thinking about it, Hank realized he really had nothing to worry about. What was the worst they could do to him? Add more years to his life sentence? Really?

It was a joke. He smiled his creepy grin from ear to ear. They could not hurt him with more time. Why should more years matter to him? It was ridiculous to be stressed over it. It was laughable. In fact, it was so funny, it made him laugh out loud. Soon, his laughter grew louder and more maniacal. He started to feel like the Joker from the Batman comics he once loved as a child, which only made him laugh more.

Another inmate down the hall became annoyed and shouted, "Shut the fuck up already, you fucking lunatic, before I break your ass in half!"

Hank laughed even louder at the thought of his ass being broken in half, until his chest ached and his voice became hoarse. He laid back in his cot and felt good for the first time in ages. He felt invincible.

"Bring it, bitches," he grinned.

# Chapter 20

<hr>

# The Crime Scene

Detective Johnson stopped by Megan's building, after a long day at work. He was eager to tell her about his productive visit with Henry Cameron. He hoped it would be okay for him to visit unannounced. Before getting out of his car, he decided to play it safe and call her cellphone.

She answered, "Hello? What can I do for you, detective?"

"Hello, Megan. I was wondering if it would be okay if I… uh, give you a call." He saw the time on the clock in his car. It was almost nine o'clock. He thought a simple phone call would be more proper, instead.

"Sure, what's up?" She asked.

"I thought you might want to know how my little chat with our boy went today. It was quite an eye-opening experience. If it's too late, I could always tell you tomorrow when I see you."

"Oh, no, it's fine. I can talk," she replied. "What did that douche bag have to say?"

He chuckled at her vulgarity. She reminded him of some cops he knew. "Well, the first thing I learned did not even come from him. It was one of the C.O.'s, who said it. You are going to love this. V-356. I know what it means."

Megan became excited and inquired, "The numbers she sang???"

"It's his cell number."

"Holy shit! I can't believe it!" Megan was astonished. The mystery of those numbers had her baffled for days. She never expected them to be connected to the present. She thought for sure their significance was tied to the past. She asked, "How did she even know?"

"I wish I knew, but you're the one in connection with her. Maybe you can ask her yourself," he answered. "I'm not so sure she likes me."

Megan felt more hopeful. "I don't know. She knows you want to help her. If you do, I think she will like you. Trust me. Just never doubt her. Not believing in her upsets her. She is very real and she knows what actually happened. It took me a while before I accepted it, but I don't doubt it for a minute anymore."

He took a breath and responded, "I'm starting to realize it, especially after listening to the recording. I don't know how she's doing it from beyond the grave, but I do believe she is helping us to solve her own murder. I never would have believed it except I heard her voice with my own ears."

"I know. It's so crazy," she acknowledged. "It's also amazing."

"Yeah, it is," he agreed. "Oh, yeah. I asked Cameron about Leanne."

"You did? What did he say? Please, tell me he knew her."

"Yes, he did, although he tried to deny it, at first. Eventually, he told me her name is Leanne Flynn. I couldn't find much on her, except a minor misdemeanor arrest when she was eighteen in Manhattan. Shoplifting. The address she gave doesn't exist. She must have lied. I'm guessing no one bothered to verify it. Back then, the NYPD were not using computers like today. Reports were typed on type writers, filed in cabinets, and buried in boxes."

Megan scoffed, "How archaic. Gotta love technology."

Johnson chuckled, "Yeah." He then continued, "Anyway, Cameron unquestionably had feelings for her. He claimed she broke it off with him and he hasn't seen her since. I feel like there's more to their story, but I can't find anything. I don't know. Maybe it's nothing. I figure maybe now that you know a little something about her, you can somehow get Margaret to give you more information. It can't hurt."

"I'm not sure it works like that, but I'll see what I can do," Megan responded.

"Fair enough. I learned a few other things about Cameron's past, but nothing remotely related to Margaret's disappearance. I showed him the photos. I gave him the impression they were recovered by the Crime Scene Unit back in '89 to see if he'd show his hand. He did. I have no doubt he took the photos. I got him to look through them, but when he saw the photos of her, he pushed them away and became upset. I decided to push his buttons a little further. When I asked him about the connection between Margaret and the Hutchinson

River Parkway, he lost his mind. He blew up and cursed me out. He even called me the 'N' word!" He laughed. "We had been getting along so well, up to that point."

"Wow! So, you called him out on his bullshit and he got pissed? That's classic!"

He replied, "Yes, indeed. He gave himself away, again. There is no doubt in my mind, we will find her there tomorrow. Will you be ready, when the time comes?" She was silent. He asked, "Are you still there?"

"Yeah, I am. I'm just worried how I'm going to react when I see her," she confessed.

"I know it's not going to be easy for you. I understand. I'll be there with you every step of the way. You'll be fine, Megan," he assured her. "We need to do this… for her."

"I know," she practically mumbled. She swallowed nervously and confided, "I'm scared."

"I get it, but you need to be brave. I'm counting on you. I can't find her without your help. She's counting on us. We can't let her down. She's waited too long for justice. She needs to be at peace." He hoped his words would give her the courage she needed to face her fears. He thought it might help, if he changed the subject. "Let's not talk about it, right now. Hey! Do you want to hear something crazy?" He did not wait for her to answer. "Cameron is friends with David Berkowitz. The Son of Sam! Supposedly, his older brother and Berk were in the same cult back in the '70s."

"Really?" She inquired. "Sounds kind of sketchy to me. I guess it's possible. Small world."

"Yeah!"

He told her everything Cameron said about his brother and conspiracy theories. It helped to get her mind off of the daunting task, which awaited them on the next evening. It would have to be after she got off work. Simply thinking about it was going to cause her stress all day.

An hour had gone by when they finally decided to hang up.

"Okay, I'd better let you go," he said. "I can't believe we've been gossiping for an hour." He shook his head. "I feel like one of my aunts." They laughed. "You get some rest. Okay? I'll pick you up from work at around six. I'll send you a text to let you know where I'll be parked."

"Okay. Thanks for the update. Have a good night, Detective," she said with a smile.

"You, too. Goodnight." He hung up and drove home.


That night, Megan prepared for bed, after updating her journal with the additional information Johnson gave to her. It was all good stuff, she thought. She considered the possibility of writing a book about the experience someday, if they were successful in helping Maggie to find peace, but then she remembered she was still hiding from Josh's father, Herman, and decided, "Oh, hell no!"

She went into her bedroom and put away her journal in the top drawer of her nightstand. Before getting into bed, she went to the kitchen to make herself a hot cup of herbal tea. She felt anxious about the next day. It was going to make it difficult for her to fall asleep, so she hoped the tea would ease her mind.

Maggie's spirit placed a comforting hand on her shoulder.

While Megan sat at the table sipping her tea, her mind drifted to Maggie. One more day and the big mystery will be solved. It was hard to believe. A few weeks ago, the last thing on her mind was solving a decades old murder mystery. She was more concerned about Herman finding and murdering her.

He probably forgot all about her by now. She wondered if he ever truly loved her. A tear came to her eye. Thinking about him was depressing. She reminded herself he was an asshole.

Maggie tried to refocus her mind on the task at hand by placing an image of Hank in her mind. She made her think about what he did to her.

Out of the blue, Megan thought to herself, Hank was a bigger asshole. She looked forward to helping Detective Johnson stick it to him for Maggie's sake. She wished he could get the death penalty, instead. It was no less than that miserable bastard deserved. What did it really matter to him, having a few more years added to his life sentence, as if it made any difference? Megan felt intense hatred for him. He needed to suffer. Badly. The only way it would happen was by the state giving him the death penalty. She found herself wishing for it. She prayed for it.

A wicked grin spread across Maggie's face, although Megan could not see it.

Of course, while New York remains one of the twenty-seven states where capital punishment is legal, issuing the death penalty has become unconstitutional. The last execution in New York was in 1963, so it was unlikely Hank would end up on Death Row. It was a fact Maggie could not comprehend.

It made Megan angry to think he would essentially be getting away with her murder, even if he was charged with it. She clenched her fists and wanted to pound something. However, it was not her style, so she relaxed her hands.

"Jesus Christ. What the hell is wrong with me? I feel so angry. I'm tripping out. I need to get my behind to sleep."

She went to bed and tried very hard to get some sleep. Somehow, instead of feeling more relaxed, she was more agitated than before. She turned onto her side and shut her eyes. As it turned out, she fell asleep fairly fast.

The dream she had was definitely not something, which occurred a long time ago. It was purely fictional. It did not feel as vivid or unbearable as the nightmares were either. She actually enjoyed this one.

In the dream, she was at the prison watching, while Hank was being strapped into the electric chair. He cried and begged for them to let him go. He kept saying he was sorry for what he did, but nobody wanted to hear his bullshit.

When it was time, they let Maggie throw the switch. She was ecstatic. She grinned when she yanked it down. It was one of those vintage old-fashioned levers from those 1950s horror movies. Almost instantly, one thousand volts of electricity shot into Hank's body, causing him to tremble violently in his seat. Plumes of steam rose from his burning limbs. Megan clapped, and then Maggie hit him with another two thousand volts, for good measure. He fried like a greased chicken on a grill. Megan watched in awe, as his skin turned a charred blackened color. It kind of smelled like bacon.

After it was over, Maggie was awarded with a special medal of honor. Everyone cheered for her. It really was a strange dream. It was also kind of morbid.

This time, Megan did not awaken in the middle of the night. Instead, she slept straight through, until her alarm woke her to go to work. Once she was up, showered, and dressed, she happily jotted down the dream into her journal. As far as she thought, the dream came from her own mind, and not from Maggie. She was wrong. Regardless, she did not care. She wanted to add it, as part of the overall experience. Deep down, she wanted it to be true.

Misty arrived to take care of Josh and Megan left for work. She informed Misty, in advance, she would be delayed in coming home. Misty was okay with staying longer. It was for a good cause, as she put it.

Today was the big day, although Megan still did not feel ready. She wondered would she ever feel ready to see a dead body? Probably not.

As for Detective Johnson, he spent the entire first part of his day preparing for the big reveal. He had a team of diggers on standby. He made a call to the D.A. in White Plains and provided updates regarding the case. His supervisor was brought into the loop, after having returned from vacation. It took a long time for Johnson to convince him he was not going on some wild goose chase. He played the recording, showed the photos of the victims in bondage, and went over everything that happened when he was speaking to Cameron. It helped.

Unfortunately, he was still waiting on those hair follicles to be found. He hoped Nick would come through.

In the meantime, it came down to finding a body. If it turned out there was no body, Johnson was going to be in deep shit for wasting valuable time and manpower. He had faith, though. He would not let Margaret down and he knew she was not going to let him down. He felt it in his gut. The only thing left was to pick up Megan from work and head over to the alleged burial site.

He checked his watch. At last, it was time to go.


Detective Johnson arrived at the Cross County Shopping Center only five minutes later than planned. He sent Megan a text message to let her know he was at the agreed upon pick-up location near the bus stop behind Macy's. It took her a minute before she responded saying she would be right out. While he waited, he made a few calls to his team letting them know to be ready.

Fifteen minutes later, he spotted Megan. She looked worn out. She walked over to the unmarked police vehicle and climbed into the front passenger seat without a word. She slowly buckled her seatbelt and did not make eye contact with him. Instead, she rested her head back against the seat and exhaled.

"I'm sorry I'm late. It was a hectic day," she finally said. She sounded defeated.

"Not a problem," he replied. He studied her demeanor and could tell she was very anxious. Her hands seemed to tremble. Beads of sweat glistened on her forehead. He reached over and gently touched her arm in a comforting way. She looked at him and he said, "It's okay to be scared. I understand. If things become too tough, you can always look away. I mainly need you to show me the spot. I don't expect you to stand there and watch the whole thing play out. It's going to be a bit much."

"Thank you," she replied.

He nodded, and then he asked, "Have you ever seen a dead person in real life?"

She nodded back, "Yes, my grandmother."

"Okay. Well, I'm not going to lie and tell you this will be similar. It's not. It's going to be extremely different. In fact, it's going to be a lot more like watching a horror movie, except you're in it. Kind of like your nightmares. You may even feel the urge to throw up and it's fine."

She leered at him and said with a shake of her head, "You're not really helping me. My stomach is in knots. If you keep this up, I'm probably going to throw up here."

"Please, don't throw up," he begged in such a pitiful small voice, while shaking his head.

She could not help, but laugh. He laughed, as well.

A moment later, he shifted the car into gear and began driving. They followed the flow of traffic, leaving the shopping center, and took the Cross County Parkway to the Hutchinson River Parkway going south. Megan looked out of her window and tried to keep herself distracted by the view. It was not helping either.

Johnson spoke into his portable radio to someone and informed them he was heading south on the parkway. He said he would contact them, once they arrived at the rendezvous site. Megan felt herself becoming more nervous by the minute. This was actually happening. She was in a police vehicle with a detective on her way to find Maggie's dead body. Her heart began beating faster and her breathing became uneasy. She felt dizzy.

Unlike the last time, Johnson was now aware of her health condition. When he noticed she did not look well, he stated, "Take long deep breaths, Megan."

"Yeah, I know," she nodded impatiently. "I'm trying."

"Try harder. You got this, Meg. Don't let it get the better of you. You're strong. You can do this…" His voice seemed to trail off, as he rambled on.

She closed her eyes tight, blocking him out, and tried to focus on something else. Josh. She thought about her sweet little boy. Josh was home waiting for her. She simply needed to do this one thing for Maggie, and then she could go home to him. She pictured his happy little face. She thought about his cute innocent voice. It made her smile. She loved him so much.

He was going to be incredibly happy, when he learned how his brave Mommy helped the hero detective to finally find Maggie, so she could be at peace. Josh was going to be very proud of her.

So, why was she so scared? She was doing something good.

Maggie's face popped into her mind. She was only a teenager. Such a pretty young girl. Stop being such a damn baby, she told herself. Help this poor girl find peace. Thinking about Maggie made her cry.

She felt the car slowing down and pulling off the road to the right. When she opened her eyes, she wanted to close them, again. She knew exactly where they were. They were there in the same place, where Hank parked that night in her nightmare. She looked straight ahead in front of the car and saw the gray utility pole with the highway marker numbers H-U-4-5-7 going down its smooth metallic surface, one digit at a time. Beyond the pole, just before the stone overpass, was the green highway sign indicating it was Exit 3. The large exit sign was for Orchard Beach and City Island with an arrow pointing right, toward the exit. To the right of the overpass was a bunch of trees. It was a lot more than she remembered. Some had grown tall. She had to remember when she first saw them it was how they looked over thirty years ago. Obviously, they would be different.

Aside from that slight discrepancy, everything else was pretty much as it was in her nightmare, except there was still daylight. In her nightmare, it was dark since it was around 3:37 A.M. She checked the time on her cellphone. It was 6:55 P.M. The days were much longer during the summer months. It was May, which was close enough. Darkness would not arrive for another hour.

She realized Johnson had already exited the vehicle. He stood in front of it and was looking directly at her. She knew he was waiting for her to be ready. He did not rush her. Instead, he was being very patient, which she appreciated. However, she knew they were wasting precious daylight. It would seem more real to her if they waited around, until dark. Therefore, she needed to do this immediately.

She forced herself out of the car. Her legs felt weak, for a moment, but she regained her strength and held her head up high. She took a deep breath, walked over to Johnson, and stated in a firm voice, "I'm ready. Let's get this done."

He held out his hand and she took it.


Johnson patiently led Megan by the hand toward the tree line near the overpass, where he then let her take the lead. She swallowed nervously and walked into the trees. He followed silently. When they emerged on the other side, they reached a small clearing near the river surrounded by tall grass. She took a moment to gaze across the river at the tall buildings of Co-Op City. At last, she could see them clearly.

She turned and pointed down at the ground. "There. That's where he put her."

"Are you sure?"

"Yes." She was never more certain of anything in her life.

He spoke into his radio and called for his team to meet him along the shore beyond the tree line to the right of the overpass. Pretty soon, an NYPD Harbor boat approached along the river coming from the south. It did not come near the shore. Instead, it waited for further orders. Not long after, Megan heard sirens in the distance, as the rest of the team made their way through rush hour traffic to reach the shoulder, where Johnson parked.

Within minutes, an entire police team from the Yonkers Detective Division, Crime Scene Unit, Westchester County Police, and NYPD showed up. Megan was impressed by the combined effort being put into finding Maggie's body, even if it was several decades overdue.

Johnson greeted his colleagues. There were so many. Some wore uniforms. Others had on suits. A few guys wore blue jackets with "Crime Scene Unit" written on the rear in white letters. They were carrying shovels and evidence collection kits. Johnson moved off to the side to speak to an NYPD lieutenant named Sanders, leaving Megan alone amongst the uniformed officers.

A Caucasian female police officer with the name Foster on her name plate approached her and asked if she wanted to be driven to the precinct, where she could wait. "I can take you, if you're ready to go, ma'am. You shouldn't have to see this next part."

Suddenly, Megan realized she did not want to leave. She had to stay and see this through. She cried out, "No, not yet! I can't go!" She pleaded to remain at the crime scene. "Please, I need to be here!"

"Okay, okay," the officer nodded and walked away.

Large spot lights were set up and pointed in an angle, as not to blind anyone. A fellow detective was taking photos with a professional camera. A few officers surrounded the area with yellow crime scene tape. One approached her and said she could not be within the taped area, but Johnson intervened.

"She's good. She can stay. She's with me." He walked over to her and asked, "Are you okay being here? I can have someone take you home, whenever you're ready. You did your part. Let us do ours."

"Thank you, but I really think I need to be here. I don't think my part is over, yet." She shook her head.

He nodded and placed his hand on her shoulder. "Fine. Just... please, don't get in the way. Let them do their job." She nodded and several officers began digging. They watched. He then turned back to her and asked, "Tell me, again, what are we going to find down there? Be specific."

She thought for a second and responded, "Um, okay. It's a nude female body. She's wrapped tightly in a white blanket... stained with her blood."

"You heard her, boys," he said to the diggers. "Let's see if she's right. I'm willing to bet my paycheck on it." That was how certain he felt and how much he trusted in her.

"Big words, Johnson," one of the others commented.

"Don't ruin my confidence, Hale. I've got a good feeling about this," he retorted.

He never bothered to explain to everyone how he initially suspected there was a body in this spot. They did not need to know those particular details of the investigation. As far as they needed to know, they were digging based on the word of a possible witness, Megan, and that was sufficient. It was best not to get into the specifics, since he needed the cooperation of the NYPD to be within their city and in their jurisdiction. There was no need to mention nightmares or ghosts. Instead, they were merely informed it was a cold case from many years ago. He did not want them to be too surprised when they found the skeletal remains. Anyone who wondered, probably figured Megan witnessed it, as a child. No one asked.

"We got something," one of the diggers announced. He stood upright and pointed his flashlight down on the ground at something white sticking out of the dirt.

Megan felt weak in the knees. Her legs began to buckle, until she felt Johnson's strong arm around her. He held her up and she leaned on him for support and comfort.

The officers kept digging, only more carefully to avoid damaging or disturbing the cloth object in the ground. They uncovered more portions of what appeared to be a white blanket wrapped around something. The detective with the camera took more photos using the flash.

It was getting darker.

Megan heard an officer whisper to his partner, "Oh, shit. It looks like she was right. Damn."

Once the dirt was cleared away, additional photos were taken of the scene. They dared not lift the wrapped body and risk damaging it. Someone from the Crime Scene Unit stepped into the hole and carefully cut open the blanket to reveal a mummified female corpse.

"We have a body," he called out. "Nude female."

Megan turned her head to look away and dug her face into Johnson's chest. She cried. He held her, for a short while, before gently pulling away. He said to her, "I need to see her." She nodded and stepped back, while he moved closer to the hole. He looked at the body and felt a lump form in his throat. He had seen many corpses, since becoming a police officer, and then a detective. For some reason, this one hit home in a different way than the others. It was almost like he knew this girl personally. He spent so much time on the case, but ignored it for too long. Only this week, did he truly investigate her murder. He never expected results to come so fast.

"Let's see what she has to tell us," he said.

One of the forensic scientists named Merrifield examined her in the hole, still half wrapped in the blanket using a flashlight and an ultraviolet light. He studied her jaw, which had no teeth. It verified what Megan said about the pliers. He could tell where her throat was slit and burned. He pointed it out. She still had a lot of hair attached to her head. It was as if being wrapped so tightly in the blanket managed to preserve the body. Next, he examined the blanket and could see the dried blood. He identified all his findings aloud for everyone to hear. Each confirming what Megan described from her nightmares.

She felt sick. If there was any doubt whatsoever in her mind, it was gone. Everything she witnessed in those nightmares was real. This was the ultimate proof. Did this mean the nightmares were finally at an end? She hoped so for the sake of her sanity.

Johnson grabbed her to snap her out of her stupor. She was staring at the body with her mouth gaped open. He got her to refocus her attention. "Megan, listen, I need your help one more time. You mentioned Cameron tossing a shovel into the water. Do you know where he threw it? How far out was it from here?"

She faced the water and pointed to a spot nearby. It was only a few feet away from the shore. "There."

He contacted the Harbor police via radio, who sent out two divers on a rubber raft. They came closer to the shore with underwater lights and began searching. One diver named Smith climbed into the water with a metal detector. It was not very deep in that area, but it was muddy and soft. The diver reached into the water and grabbed a dark metal object covered in barnacles. When his hand emerged he was holding an old shovel.

A smile appeared on Johnson's face. He looked at Megan, who looked like she was still in shock. He asked, "How are you feeling?" He wondered if she was as excited as him.

She was still watching the divers, who were approaching the shore, as she answered, "Honestly, I feel like a weight has been lifted off my shoulders. The tension I've been feeling the past few days is gone." She turned to him. "We did it. We found her." Her eyes were filled with tears of joy. She threw her arms around him and hugged him.

"Yeah, we did, huh?" He patted her on the back. He almost didn't believe it himself. He looked up and thought, I hope you're seeing this, Jack. This was for you, old friend.

# Chapter 21

## No More Nightmares

Megan walked into her apartment after a long crazy day. It was nearly nine o'clock in the evening. Misty was in Josh's room getting him ready for bed. They both came out to the living room to greet her.

Josh called out, "Mommy! You're home from your adventure!"

He ran over to hug her. She crouched down and held him in her arms for longer than he expected. She and Misty made eye contact. Megan nodded slightly at her and Misty knew, right away. They found her. Misty's hands shot up to cup her mouth in shock. She could not believe the nightmares were true. It horrified her.

Megan slightly pulled away from Josh to look him in the eyes. He was a site for her sore eyes, which were filled with tears. She still held him in her arms, while looking at his precious face.

"What's wrong, Mommy?" He asked concerned for his mother.

"Nothing's wrong, baby. Not anymore."

"Then why are you crying? Did you help Lizzie?"

"Yes," she answered. "We found her, Josh. She's not lost anymore." She shook her head, barely believing her own words. "Is she here? Can you see her?" She glanced around the room, as if she would see her.

"No," he shook his head. "Is she gone forever?" He sounded disappointed and sad.

She shrugged, "Honestly, I have no idea. I guess we'll find out sooner or later." She looked at Misty and asked, "When was the last time you felt her presence, Misty?"

"Sometime this afternoon. I think it was around noon," she answered. "She's been laying low all night. I thought maybe she was with you."

Megan considered it. She had no way of knowing. "I don't know if she was there. Maybe after she was found, I guess. I wish I knew. It would've made me feel better knowing what she was thinking and what she felt. I suppose I'm just used to knowing how she feels. It wasn't easy for me to be there, but I felt like I needed to be there… for her."

"Yeah," Misty nodded. "I totally understand. So, what happens next?"

Megan stood up and carried Josh in her arms, while she explained, "The police crime scene scientists have tests they need to do. They have to collect whatever evidence they can find. See if anything matches up. It's going to be a long process. I have no idea how long it will take, but I have a feeling things are going to be very different around here."

Josh whined, "I don't want Lizzie to go."

She faced her son and responded, "Baby, she was only here because she was stuck. She didn't want to be here. It made her sad. Now she can be free. Don't you want her to be free and happy?"

"Yeah," he nodded with reluctance.

"Well, this is how we make that happen," his mother clarified for him. "By finding her and setting her free. We have to let her go, so she can go to Heaven, where she belongs. She can still watch over you from there."

"Promise?" He asked.

"I promise, baby. She can still be your guardian angel. We'll get a chance to say goodbye to her someday in the near future at the cemetery, and then we will visit her there whenever we miss her. Okay?"

"She's gonna be at the cemetery *and* in Heaven?" He asked confused by her unintentional contradiction.

She thought about it and replied, "Her body will be at rest at the cemetery. Her soul will go to Heaven, so she can become a real angel. It's what she wanted, right?"

"Yes," he recalled.

She gave him a kiss and said, "I think it's time for bed." She really did not want to answer any more questions. "Maybe you'll see her in your dreams, if you fall asleep fast enough." She encouraged him.

She took him to his room and Misty followed. Once he was in bed with his lamp on, the women went into the living room and sat on the sofa. Megan was exhausted. Misty was eager to know the details, but was afraid to ask.

After a minute of silence, she inquired, "Are you okay?"

Megan was unsure. She answered, "She was exactly where I saw in my nightmare. Wrapped in a blanket like a mummy. It was awful. I felt so sad. I know this is what she wanted. So, why do I feel terrible?"

"Seeing her body couldn't have been easy," Misty replied trying to understand.

"Absolutely not," Megan shook her head. "It was depressing. She was a teenager, close to your age. This never should have happened to her. I feel so bad for her." She wiped the tears from her cheeks. "I still haven't stopped crying, since I saw her in that hole. I keep seeing the same image in my head."

"I'm sorry. Do you want me to make you some hot tea?" Misty asked.

"No, but thank you. You should probably get going. It's getting late and I've already sucked up your entire day by keeping you here. Besides, I think I just need to be alone. Maybe I'll soak in the tub or something."

"Okay. I'll see you tomorrow then."

"Thank you, Misty."

"Sure. No problem, Megan. Get some rest." She gathered her things. "Goodnight," she said, while walking toward the door to leave.

"Goodnight. Text me when you get home," Megan said.

"I will. I know the drill. Bye." She closed the door behind her.

There was one more thing Megan had to do before she could try to relax. She dialed Hannah's number and told her everything she missed, starting with the weird dream she had about Hank's electrocution. They spoke for almost an hour. Hannah had a lot of questions, but she could tell Megan was not in the mood to talk anymore. She reluctantly hung up, but promised to visit the next day.

Moments later, Megan filled the bathtub with warm water and bubbles, while she got undressed. She then slid into the tub and leaned back with her eyes closed. She wanted to erase the images of the crime scene from her mind, although seeing Maggie's mummified corpse in that dirty bloodstained blanket was impossible to forget. The image was stained into her mind in the same way Maggie's dried blood stained the blanket. It was something she would keep with her forever, whether she wanted it or not. She was never going to be the same.

She sighed heavily. She was grateful to Detective Johnson for allowing her to remain within the crime scene area. It was something she had to do, so she could have closure. She hoped Maggie could finally have the justice she deserved and stop haunting her.

It felt great to be home. The silence was welcome. She took long deep breaths. Her body began to feel relaxed. The day's tension was washing away, little by little. Soon, she would be in bed. She wondered what she would dream tonight. Would she dream? Would it be another nightmare?

"No more nightmares," she whispered. "Please, Maggie. No more." She was able to enjoy her bubble bath without incident.


That night, she had another vivid dream. She was lying in bed. Maggie was lying beside her. They turned to look at each other. Somehow, she seemed different. There was a strange aura around her.

She said in a clear normal voice, "Thank you for setting me free." She did not whisper, this time, and it was not creepy. Megan listened attentively, as Maggie said, "I will never forget what you've done. You have no idea how much this means to me." She smiled at her. It was such a beautiful smile. Megan had never seen her look so happy. "There's still one more thing I need you to do for me, Megan, before I move on."

Megan nodded at her, unable to speak, for some reason.

All of a sudden, her body felt lighter than air. She floated up from her bed. Maggie floated with her and took her by the hand.

"Come with me," she said. "It's far."

They floated up through the ceiling and past the roof into the nighttime sky. Maggie led her high up into the clouds. They glided through the air swiftly, hand in hand. Megan wondered where they were going. At the same time, she was in no hurry to get there. The experience of flying through the clouds under the starry skies like birds made her feel so carefree. She looked down and could see city lights passing by rapidly.

She looked over at Maggie, who was smiling at her. The aura around her made her body glow, lighting the way for them. It was a beautiful sight. Megan smiled back at her.

They descended over a long highway. Maggie followed its length from one state to another. Megan enjoyed the view, even though she could not recognize any of it in the dark. It was still amazing. Sometimes, they glided over waterways. There were many cities, forests, and open plains, as well.

Finally, they slowed down and moved lower to the ground, until they passed over pretty houses in neat rows. They landed on the ground in front of a beige house. Maggie pointed to the mailbox. It read, "Garrett, C." Megan knew it was Chris' house, but she had no idea where they were.

Maggie explained, "This is my brother's house in Florida. Let him know what happened to me. Remember his address." She pointed to the house address, and then to the nearby street sign. "Write it in your journal, so you won't forget. He needs to know."

Megan could only nod, again.

"I'll take you back home," Maggie said. "Close your eyes." Megan did as she was told and felt a strong pulling sensation in her stomach, which reminded her of being on a rollercoaster. "Okay, you can open them."

Megan opened her eyes and found herself standing in her bedroom. It was still nighttime, but she was alone. She looked around for Maggie. This time, she was able to speak. "Wait! Who's Leanne? Was she a victim?" There was no response. "Maggie?"

She sat down on her bed feeling frustrated. She was unsure if she was still dreaming or if she was awake. It was hard to tell, although everything felt real. She stood up and walked out to the hallway. She peeked into Josh's room. He was asleep. She returned to her room and grabbed the journal from the drawer of her nightstand. She opened it and wrote down Chris' address. She did not know what city, but she had a feeling the address and state would be sufficient. She could give the information to Detective Johnson. It should be enough to help him locate Chris.

After she was done, she climbed back into bed, pulled her blanket over her, and closed her eyes. She tried to fall asleep. Her gut instinct told her to open her eyes, so she did. She nearly screamed. Maggie was lying in front of her.

"It's too late to help Leanne," she said. "She's been gone longer than me. You can wake up now."

Megan opened her eyes. It was morning. She reached for her journal and realized she had not written in it like she thought. It was all part of the dream. However, since she already wrote it in her dream, it was easier for her to remember. She wrote down the address for real, and then described her dream.

She thought about what Maggie said to her regarding Leanne. She was gone long before her, which had to mean she was dead.

Detective Johnson had a long night at work. It was morning and he was still working around the clock with no sleep. While he was tired, there was still much for him to do. Sleep would have to wait. He reviewed the stack of reports he typed during the night in connection with Margaret's missing person's case, evidence vouchers, and a crime report based on the visible injuries and apparent cause of death.

When he thought about it, he was still amazed by everything, which took place the previous evening. Part of him was in denial even now. He could not believe Margaret's body had actually been recovered, after more than thirty years as a cold case file, along with the shovel allegedly used to bury her. Both the body and shovel were exactly where Megan said they would be, which was incredible, considering how she claimed to come by her knowledge.

How the hell was he going to explain these strange facts to the D.A. – *by telling the truth?* He certainly could not lie. There had to be a way around it, which could still result in a conviction.

At least, there was a sufficient amount of DNA to identify the body and eventually prove it is Margaret. There also seems to be DNA on the blanket. He still needed to wait for the results and pray for a match. He would probably need to locate her next of kin to prove it is her. At the same time, he could make a notification to her relative, and finally close the missing person's case.

He frowned. Finding a living relative was going to be a problem. As far as he knew, there was only one known relative, which was her younger brother, Chris. Johnson knew his name and date of birth, but had no idea where he was living, or if he was even alive. A Department of Motor Vehicles search of his name and date of birth resulted in several similar hits from three different states, which was not encouraging. He printed the page. It was going to take time to find the right one. There was a slight chance none of those results were him. If only there was already a way to contact him. Unfortunately, there were no valid phone numbers on file.

To add to Johnson's grief, Nick still had not gotten back to him, regarding those two mysterious missing hair follicles, which had been found in Cameron's vehicle back in 1989. What could have happened to them? Finding them and matching any one of them with the DNA from the body would make life so much easier.

Johnson yawned and rested his head in his hands, while leaning on his desk. He longed for the end of the day, hoping he would finally be able to rest. "No rest for the weary," he told himself.

Just then, his cellphone began ringing. It nearly gave him a heart attack. He checked the caller ID and saw it was Megan. He immediately answered, "Hey, Megan. How did you sleep?" It was his subtle way of asking if she had any revealing nightmares.

"Good morning, Detective. I had a very interesting dream last night. I had to share it with you. I'll skip to the good parts. She showed me where her brother lives. He's in Florida. I have his address for you."

Johnson could not believe his ears. "Are you serious? I'm starting to think you might be psychic. This is the second time you've called me with information I needed desperately. You're a life saver."

She laughed and gave him the address, which was to a house in Stuart. He wrote it down and noticed it matched one of the hits from his search results. He circled it on that page, in case he misplaced the paper where he wrote the address. Next, she told him what she learned about Leanne. He was eager to hear what she had to say.

"Maggie implied she died long before her. She also said we were too late to help her."

"She's dead, huh? Damn," he shook his head sadly. "I was afraid you were going to say that. I hate the idea of Cameron getting away with another murder," he said with disappointment in his voice. "He must think he's so smart. Smug prick. Well, it might be too late to help her, but it doesn't mean I have to stop trying. I'll do what I can to find out more about her. Maybe I can make a few calls. It helps to know I'm looking for a dead person and not a living one. It makes it easier, as long as she has a death certificate and isn't missing, too. Thanks for the info."

"You're welcome," she said. "I'm glad I could help."

"You have been a tremendous help. Believe me." He was concerned about her well-being, so he asked, "How are you holding up, after last night? It was a rough night for all of us. I still haven't slept," he told her. He wanted her to know she was not the only one, who had a hard time dealing with the case.

"I'm very sorry to hear that," she replied. "Fortunately, I'm holding up much better today, compared to how I felt yesterday. I was such a mess. I'm sorry, if I was a nuisance to you or any of your co-workers."

"You were not. No need to apologize," he told her. He noticed he was getting another call. It was Nick. "Hey, I've got to go. Got another call. I'll be in touch, so I can keep you in the loop."

"Okay. Thank you. Bye!"

"Take care." He pressed a button on his phone and took the next call. "Nicky! Talk to me, buddy. Tell me something good." He tried to be hopeful, although he had a feeling it was going to bad news.

"You are not going to believe this, Rob," Nick began. "I found our missing evidence."

"What? No way!" Johnson was delirious with joy. "Where was it?"

"*They* were right in plain sight the entire time," Nick told him. "I have no clue how I kept missing them, but I checked somewhere I've already checked like three times and there they were sitting together. It blew my mind. It's like they appeared out of nowhere because I could swear they were not there the previous times I checked. Suddenly, they wanted to be found."

Johnson wondered if they appeared with help from a certain spirit. Maybe Jack Roe or Margaret Garrett, since she was no longer trapped, as Megan put it. He kept his guesses to himself, although he expressed his delight. "That is fantastic news, my friend! You've just made my day!"

"Yeah, and mine! You owe me lunch and today I'm feeling particularly hungry for some Spanish food," Nick grinned happily with the knowledge he would not be paying for his lunch throughout the next week.

Johnson was okay with the deal he made. He declared, "My man, I would go across the ocean to Spain to get your food, if you asked me. That's how grateful I'm feeling, right now." Lucky for him, there were plenty of Spanish restaurants in the vicinity of the building, where they worked.

"Nah, bro. It's gotta be Puerto Rican, Dominican, or Cuban. I'll settle for nothing less," Nick joked.

"You got it, buddy."

At last, he had what he needed. He would be able to get the DNA tested and see if it matches any of those hair follicles. It would prove the body was in Cameron's car, at some point. Finding Margaret's brother would help him to identify the body by matching their DNA. He had his work cut out for him.

A few days later, Christopher Garrett arrived from Florida at John F. Kennedy International Airport in Queens. Johnson went to pick him up personally. Chris was set up at a nearby hotel in Yonkers, paid for by the Yonkers Police Department. They needed him to stay long enough to participate in a DNA test, and then to identify the body, if the tests were conclusive.

Once Johnson was able to get a DNA sample from Chris, he had everything he needed to complete the testing. Within the next week, he received the results from the tests. Sadly, the recovered body did indeed belong to Margaret, based on the matching DNA from her brother. The blood staining the blanket belonged to her, as did most of the hair within the blanket. In addition, one of the original hair follicles found in Cameron's car, which thankfully reappeared, in the *nick* of time, matched her hair and DNA, placing her in the rear of his vehicle, after her death. Combined with the photos of her in his basement dressed in the attire she wore when she went missing, it was enough to seek a conviction against Cameron.

Oddly, there was another hair found in the blanket, which did not belong to her. It was shorter. Johnson became excited at the possibility it could actually belong to Cameron. It would directly tie him to her death, sealing the deal on an easy conviction. Through a court order, Johnson was able to acquire an immediate DNA sample from Cameron. He put a rush on the tests. He was glad to learn they were a positive match.

No evidence could be recovered from the shovel the diver found in the Hutchinson River, but it was not really needed. It was carbon dated to the 1960s, which could mean it was his shovel.

Johnson drove Chris to the Westchester County Medical Examiner in Valhalla to identify the body, which had recently been transported from Bellevue Hospital, since it was originally recovered in New York City. Identifying the body was merely a formality. Obviously, he was not going to recognize her. It was mainly to gain closure that Chris even agreed to it. Both his parents died before they could get their closure.

The detective was with him at his side when he approached the cold metal table, where the corpse lay under yet another white sheet in an ironic twist. The morgue attendant pulled back the sheet from her face revealing the skeletal remains. Chris quickly looked away, and then left the room.

He was filled with sadness, regret, and anger, but also relief. At long last, the mystery of what happened to his sister was solved. He did not know the details, but he had a general idea, which was more than enough. He did not wish to know any more about that dreadful day, except more about the man responsible.

"Who did this to her?" He asked Johnson.

"His name is Henry Paul Cameron. He was a mechanic on Odell Avenue. He's currently doing time at Sing Sing for doing the same thing to several other women. We'll make sure he answers for what he did to your sister, as well. He's gotten away with it for long enough."

"Sing Sing?" He repeated, sounding interested. He had a passing thought, but kept it to himself.

"Yes," Johnson answered. "It's in Ossining."

"Ah, okay." He asked, "So, it was that serial killer they mentioned in the papers, back then?"

"The Anniversary Killer. Yes, it was him," Johnson confirmed. "I know it's too late and long overdue, but I am deeply sorry for your loss."

"Yeah, thanks," Chris replied. The fury built up within him, although he did well in hiding it in front of the detective. "When can I make the funeral arrangements? I'd like to put her near mom and pop."

"Whenever you're ready. Let's have a talk with the Coroner," which they did.

Arrangements were made for Margaret to be buried with her parents at the nearby Kensico Cemetery within a few days' time. Chris had purchased an extra plot in advance, in case she was ever found. Otherwise, it would have gone to him upon his passing. His sister's body would be brought directly to the cemetery without a church service or wake. Chris did not see a point in it, since most of the people who knew her were dead or old.

After dropping Chris off at the hotel in Yonkers, Johnson returned to his office on South Broadway. He contacted the D.A. and was finally able to get the ball rolling on a conviction. Henry Cameron was re-arrested and charged with the kidnapping, torture, mutilation, rape, and murder of Margaret Elizabeth Cameron.

He had nothing to say on the matter when Johnson went to see him at the prison. He merely displayed a look of disappointment because he got caught lying.

Johnson asked him, "Since I'm here, is there anything else you may want to tell me? Maybe about how Leanne died?" He bluffed, "I know she's dead. You know it, too. Don't you?"

"I don't know what you're talking about," Cameron responded, while looking away.

"Okay, keep playing your games, Cam. Eventually, I'm going to find out more and when I do, maybe I'll come back and see you, again."

Cameron sucked his teeth, "Promises, promises. Whatever, man. Like it even matters to me. I'm in here for *life*. Do you really think another sentence means *anything* to me? Do what you gotta do, Dick."

"I plan to," Johnson promised.

# Chapter 22

## Saying Goodbye

Josh sat on his bed with his Mandalorian action figure. He watched it and wished it would speak on its own, as it had seemingly done so many times over the past month. He knew it was his special friend, Lizzie, who pressed the small button on the chest every time, or the buttons on its shoulders. He loved whenever she did it. It took his mother and Misty a few days before they figured out the toy was not alive. He found it amusing how scared they were of his favorite toy.

Recently, his Mando seemed quite ordinary. He placed it down on the bed.

He missed Lizzie. He thought about the first time he saw her. It was while he was sitting in the very same spot on his bed, where he currently sat. She appeared out of thin air and scared him, although he later learned it was not her intention. She said she was sorry. She was only trying to say hello.

It had always been her, who lifted him up to reach his dresser every time. Lizzie played with him and taught him how to create and build cool things using his LEGOs. She talked his female action figures for him. She read his books to him, whenever he wanted to hear a story. She taught him about the stars and planets, while reading his "*Star Wars*" Golden Books to him. Sometimes, she made up stories to tell him. Other times, she told him funny jokes. She even talked about her life with her younger brother. Lizzie and Josh often ate breakfast and dinner together. Well, he ate. She kept him company. They also watched television together. She was never too busy to be his friend. She always had time for him. She loved him and he loved her.

He thought she would be around forever, but now she was gone. He had not seen her in days. His mother told him she went to Heaven, which was supposed to be a good thing. Still, he missed her terribly. The loss of his best friend brought tears to his big brown eyes. As it turned out, it was his tears, which finally got her attention, again.

"Don't cry, Josh," she said to him, as she appeared beside him, seated on the bed.

"LIZZIE!" He threw his arms around her and embraced her. "I missed you so much!"

"Aw, Josh," she caressed him, while she held him close. "I told you. I will always be with you, no matter where you go."

"You really mean it?"

"I swear it. Forever! If you miss me, don't cry. Just think of me and remember the fun we've had together. If you talk to me, I will hear you. I can't always show myself to you, but I am always listening."

"Really?" He asked with his face still damp from his tears.

She wiped his cheeks dry with her hand and reassured him, "Always. I promise."

He looked at her and smiled. It was then, when he noticed the aura around her and said, "I don't want you to go to Heaven. I want you to stay here with me. You're my best friend. I love you, Lizzie." He hugged her, again.

"I love you, too, Josh, but I have to go to Heaven. It's where I belong. My mother and father are waiting for me. They miss me and I miss them. I want to be with them. You and I will see each other, again, someday, when the time is right, but not until I've seen you grow up and live a wonderful life. I need you to live the life I never could. See the world and all the beauty it has to offer. Make a family of your own. Become a great dad."

"Better than my dad?"

"Much better. You will do a lot of things to make me and your mom proud. I just know it. You're a very special boy, Josh. You have a rare gift. Don't ever lose it."

Curious, he asked, "What gift?"

"This," she answered simply. "You can see and speak to people, who have passed on, like me. Not everyone can do that. Most people would be too scared, but not you." She poked him softly on the tip of his nose. "You're a brave boy. Someday, you'll become a man. Remember to nurture your gift, but be careful.

Not all spirits are good. You will learn to know the difference. I'll help guide and protect you, so you'll never have anything to worry about. Okay?"

He nodded, "Okay."

She said, "I need to leave soon. You might not see me for a very long time, but remember I am still with you. You can talk to me and I will hear you. Never forget I'll always be watching over you and keeping you safe, but what I really want you to do is learn to let go of me. Learn to live your life without me. Make new friends, who are *alive*. Stop being so afraid to talk to people. You can't be shy forever. If you keep it up, you'll live a lonely life. You don't want that. Do you?"

"Uh, uh," he shook his head.

"Good. Soon, you'll begin going to school and it will be like I told you. There will be other children your age, who will become your friends. You'll learn new things together. Sometimes, you'll go on class trips together. It will be awesome. I promise. It's going to be a fun and exciting adventure. You'll see."

He smiled at the prospect and was looking forward to it. However, there was still something concerning him, so he asked, "Will you still be my guardian angel?"

"*Always!* That will never change, Josh. Face it, pal. You're stuck with me for the rest of your life," she told him.

He cheered, "Yay!"

She smiled and they embraced.

While squeezing her tightly, he said to her, "Thank you for being my best friend, Lizzie. I'm never gonna forget you."

"Aw, you better not. You're so sweet," she smiled lovingly at him. A moment later, she stood up from the bed and said, "It's time for me to go. I want you to be a good boy for your mother. Okay? She needs you, so spend more time with her."

"Okay, I will." He waved at her. "Bye, Lizzie!"

"Goodbye, Josh." She waved back at him, before gradually fading away and disappearing.

Josh went into his mother's room. She was reading her journal and going over her notes. He climbed up onto her bed and gave her a big hug. "I love you, Mommy," he said.

"Oh. Hey, baby," he surprised her with his unexpected and affectionate visit. "I love you, too. You came in here just to hug me and tell me you love me?"

"Uh huh," he replied.

"Wow! Thank you, baby."   Megan was truly touched.

"Mommy, can we play a boardgame?"

Playing boardgames was their favorite way to bond. It was exactly what she needed. Spending quality time with her son would certainly cheer her up. She replied with enthusiasm, "Absolutely!"

"Goody!"


On the day of Margaret Garrett's burial at Kensico Cemetery in Valhalla, Detective Johnson gave Chris a ride from the hotel in Yonkers. Johnson also informed Megan of the location, date, and time, knowing she would want to pay her last respects and possibly meet Chris.

On the way to the cemetery, he informed Chris about Megan saying she was instrumental in locating his sister's body. He wanted to put in a good word for her, before Chris saw her in person. He deliberately did not mention anything about ghosts. Chris' mind was elsewhere, so he did not think to ask how Megan helped find his sister.

Chris thought about the last time he saw his sister alive. It was a Saturday afternoon. They met up either for lunch or an early dinner at the Friendly's Restaurant on Tuckahoe Road. It was someplace where they often went with their parents, before the break-up. It remained a special place for him and his sister. He considered going there once, before returning to Florida. Mainly, he was doubtful if he could handle the experience. Being there would bring back way too many memories. The last thing he wanted to do was to have an emotional breakdown in public.

It would break his heart to learn the Friendly's had closed several years ago and was replaced by a diner.

Next, he found himself thinking about the day his sister disappeared. He went over to her building on Walnut Street to meet her. By then, he had been living with their father for a year and a half. His sister promised to go to the movies with him. They had plans to go to Movieland on Central Park Avenue, so they could see *"A Nightmare on Elm Street 4: The Dream Master."* Margaret never came home and he never did see the movie. He couldn't.

Eventually, when the theater closed down in the early 2010s, he was glad. It hurt too much for him to see the building. It always made him think of her. For the most part, he avoided going anywhere near it.

Now, he had a new memory to hate. The last time he looked upon his sister, or rather the first and only time he looked at her rotting corpse on a table in the morgue, was stuck in his mind. He shut his eyes tight, trying to erase the gruesome image. Here he was, on the way to her burial. How could he ever forget this day? He couldn't.

He could not wait to be on a plane heading back to Florida. First, he had one more thing he needed to do, away from the watchful eyes of the police. Later, he thought. He noticed they were almost at the cemetery.

Megan arrived at the cemetery, shortly after them, with Hannah, Josh, Misty, and Leslie. They were all dressed in black. Hannah drove them in her car. There were only a few other people, who Megan believed were probably distant relatives. Some were old, but most were too young. She wondered how many of them actually knew Maggie. It could not be too many. They were most likely at the cemetery for Chris' sake.

She wondered if she would be able to spot him right away, based on the one time she saw him in a dream. As soon as she saw Detective Johnson, she knew the handsome older man with the big brown eyes and thick eyebrows had to be Chris. He was much older than she expected. She had to remind herself she only saw him young in her dream because it was how he looked in 1988. Naturally, he was going to be older in real life.

Megan waved at Johnson. He nodded politely to acknowledge her presence. The burial ceremony was about to begin, so greetings would have to wait. An elderly priest said a few kind words, although it was obvious by how he spoke, he never actually knew the deceased. Megan held Josh's hand to make sure he remained by her side.

When the priest was done with his prayer, the coffin was lowered into a freshly dug grave. It was an expensive bronze plated pine coffin. Chris spared no expense for his sister. There were freshly cut red and white flowers available. Everyone took turns dropping one onto the coffin. Most of the family left, after depositing their flower and giving their condolences to Chris. Afterwards, the priest spoke to him, and then walked away to his car to leave.

Megan waited until they were all gone, before she approached Chris and Detective Johnson. Her entourage followed closely behind her. Johnson introduced them to one another.

After introductions were made, she looked at Chris and said, "I am so very sorry for your loss. You're sister was a special girl. I know she was loved by many people. I have been researching the case, ever since I learned about her. I live in your old apartment at the Hill View."

"Oh, okay," he nodded. "I was wondering how you knew about her. Thanks for coming. And thank you for helping Detective Johnson with the case. He said he couldn't have solved it without your help."

"I was deeply honored to help," she said. "I'm glad she can finally rest in peace. Her spirit must have been at unrest for so long."

Hannah made a face acknowledging that fact. Only Leslie noticed. Megan wanted to tell Chris the truth how she knew about Maggie and him, but she did not want to come off sounding like a psycho stalker. Johnson was grateful she kept that part a secret. It was for the best.

Chris barely remembered Leslie when she told him she lived in the same building. He asked her, "You lived on the first floor?"

"Yes. My father was the super," she explained. "I was a year younger than Maggie."

He shook his head, "Sorry, I guess I don't remember. I left there when I was around fifteen. I never liked it there. My parents were always arguing." He turned to look at the grave and added, "My sister was the only one, who really mattered to me, and then she was gone. I sort of blocked out a lot of those years."

Leslie felt terrible for him. His life must have been hell. She did not know what else to say.

Megan wanted to tell him about her nightmares so badly. She wanted him to know she had a deep personal connection to his sister. In the end, she remained silent.

Josh half hid behind her leg. Chris was a lot older than his mother and the detective, which intimidated him in some way. Had he known who Chris was, he might have said something to him. Instead, he kept looking back at the grave. He was hoping to see Lizzie. He wondered if she was there in spirit, or watching them from Heaven.

He noticed Misty was especially quiet. Could she feel her? No one realized she was fighting with all her strength to remain calm. She felt so many spirits around them, it was making her uneasy. She could not wait to leave.

Initially, Megan wanted to give Chris his sister's diary, but Johnson told her in advance he would need it for the trial because of the one entry Margaret made, where she visited Cameron's garage a year before he abducted her. The way she described his creepy smile when he looked at her implies her death might have been premeditated, which could help the case against him.

On the other hand, she never said his name or the name of his family business, so the diary could get thrown out in court. Not literally, but figuratively.

While Chris took a moment alone to say goodbye to his sister, Johnson pulled Megan and her crew aside to ask how things have been in the apartment. He was surprised to hear things have calmed down significantly. Misty enjoyed the distraction of conversation. She told him she had not felt any spiritual presences in the apartment, since the body was located. Apparently, finding the body and informing Chris of what happened to his sister gave Margaret's spirit what she wanted all along. Peace. Burying her would allow her to finally rest. The only thing left to do was to give her the justice she deserved. Johnson informed them it would come soon enough with Cameron's new trial.

Megan desperately wanted to be there.

After the burial, Megan and her friends returned to Yonkers. Both Misty and Leslie went home, but Hannah stopped by the apartment for a visit. As soon as they entered, they noticed a significant difference in the atmosphere of the apartment. It was so quiet and peaceful. The heaviness in the air had lifted. Megan had never even noticed it before, until today. She finally had an idea of what Misty always felt, which meant Maggie had still been there, until today.

Megan sat at the table and let out a long sigh of relief. "I can't believe it's finally over."

Hannah sat down across from her. "I guess life can finally start going back to normal for you. Huh?"

"Normal? I don't even know what that is anymore," Megan replied. "I haven't lived a normal life in years. This is going to take some getting used to for me. To tell you the truth, I think I'm going to miss having her around. She was a playmate for Josh. I don't know how he's going to take it. He really loved her."

Josh had gone into his room when they got home, so he could not hear them speaking about him.

Hannah suggested, "I think you should try and fill the role she left vacant. Now that you no longer have to be preoccupied with researching and writing in your journal, you can spend more time with your son. It's your time to bond with him. You're pretty much all he has, considering his father is in California."

"I know," Megan nodded. "I want to spend more time with him. I want him to have a good happy life. It's one of the reasons why we came back to Yonkers. Well, that, and to get away from his abusive father."

"Josh is still young. He'll probably forget all about his Lizzie, once he starts school. Before you know it, he'll be playing with other little boys and girls. He just has to get over being so shy around new people he meets."

"Tell me about it. He can't take my leg to school with him," Megan joked.

Hannah asked, "Would you ever consider getting the church to bless the apartment, just in case?"

Megan thought about it and shook her head. "No. Why would I bother now? I didn't do it before when I was going out of my mind. You know I'm not religious like that. Not like I used to be as a girl. It was more my parents. Besides, I think this place doesn't need it. She was never a bad spirit."

Hannah thought about it and commented, "I guess you're right."

Megan suggested, "Hey, would you mind if we play a boardgame with Josh? I could use the distraction."

"Sure. Why not? I think it's a great idea," Hannah replied. "It will be good for Josh, too."

Josh sat on his bed staring at the Mandalorian on his dresser. He closed his eyes and wished as hard as he could for it to say something on it's own. He did not want to believe Lizzie was gone. He waited, but there was only silence. He opened his eyes and pouted.

He laid back on his bed and stared at the ceiling. He pretended he was looking at the sky. Lizzie used to tell him about space, whenever they laid back on the bed. She told him if you went all the way up to the sky through the clouds, you would eventually reach space. It fascinated him. He wondered if Heaven was beyond space. It seemed so far away. How could she watch over him from so far away? It seemed impossible to him.

He heard a loud noise, which startled him. It was followed by his Mandalorian saying, "This is the way."

Josh sat up immediately and looked at his dresser. The Mandalorian had fallen over on his chest. It could have caused the button to be pressed accidentally. Instead, he chose to believe it was her. She made it happen to let him know she was still with him, as she promised. He smiled knowing everything was going to be all right.

A second later, his mother popped her head into his doorway and asked, "Hey, Josh? Do you want to play a boardgame with me and Hannah? We're going to order a pizza pie, too."

He grinned happily and said, "Okay, Mommy. I'm coming." He climbed down from the bed. As he walked out of his room, he stood his Mandalorian up. He had to stand on his tippy toes to reach it, since he no longer had help. He knew someday he would be tall enough. Lizzie told him so.

A few seconds later, Josh joined his mother and Hannah at the kitchen table to play a game of *Monopoly*. Out of respect, they left the usual seat vacant. This time, it was in memory of their special friend.


After a lot of patience, Detective Johnson was able to dig up a death certificate for Leanne Flynn from 1985. According to what was written on it, her nude body was found lying face down on a log in a wooded region of northern New Jersey. The apparent cause of death was strangulation. She had been dead for nearly a week by the time her body was found. It had Cameron's name written all over it. It was his M.O.

Johnson needed to learn more. He contacted several police department agencies from that region, until he found the right one. It was no easy task. Due to how long ago her death occurred, it was hard to find someone willing to do the research and find out what he needed to know. After dealing with laziness and incompetence, he was able to speak to someone helpful. He learned there were no arrests made in connection with Leanne's murder. He was not surprised. She was originally listed as a Jane Doe, when she was found. When she was identified, her family did not care to follow up on the crime because they claimed she was a hopeless case with a drug problem.

It appeared Margaret was right. It was too late to help her.

Johnson knew it had to be Cameron, who murdered her. Her death occurred a year before his first official victim. Maybe she was his girlfriend. It was possible he did not lie about that. Johnson had a feeling when she broke up with him, he did not take it too well. He strangled her and dumped the body in the same exact way he did with most of his other victims. Johnson figured he was able to get away with it once, so why not try it, again?

It was a damn shame there was no way to prove his theory. While Cameron somehow managed to get away with that murder, Johnson swore he would not be so lucky with the case of Margaret Garrett. Not this time. It was high time he paid for his crimes against her. He got away with her murder for far too long.

When "Hank" Cameron's trial began, Megan requested she be there to see him be put away. Johnson arranged for her, Hannah, and Leslie to have front row seats. Chris was also there, after returning from Florida, a second time.

Hank could not believe he had to face a judge in a Westchester County courtroom, once more. He considered getting a haircut for his new trial, but then figured the hell with it. He did not care how he looked. His lawyer insisted he, at least, wear a suit. He reluctantly consented.

After only a couple of weeks, the jury heard both sides of the case, as told by the prosecution and defense. They weighed the evidence against Hank and made their decision. He was found guilty and convicted of the additional crimes of kidnapping, unlawful imprisonment, assault, and murder. As Johnson hoped, Margaret's diary indicated her murder might have been premeditated, even if Hank's lawyer objected to it because Hank's name was never specified. The seeds of intent were planted in the minds of the jury. The bondage photos recovered from the basement of the garage proved Hank had her there against her will during the time when she had been presumed missing. The resentment and frustration was quite visible on Hank's face during the presentation of the photos. The jury observed it. The hair follicles originally recovered as evidence from his previous trial placed Margaret in the rear of his vehicle. His hair sample found neatly wrapped in the blanket with her bloody corpse proved he handled her body. He could no longer deny it.

Hank was only able to get off on the rape charge, since there was no proof to back it up. It did not matter. He was guilty enough to rot in prison for the rest of his life with no possibility of parole.

The prosecution managed to win the case without ever mentioning anything about the paranormal, although they were fully aware of the details. Johnson told them everything and played the recording for them. He showed them the signed affidavits from the girls swearing Margaret's spirit had been haunting Megan's apartment and guiding them to solve her murder. He also showed them the journal.

The D.A. managed to figure out how to use the girls as anonymous witnesses, who he would only call to the stand as surprise witnesses, if things did not go their way. As it turned out, the physical evidence spoke for itself. The jury was satisfied with Johnson acting on anonymous tips to find the metal box and the location of the body. It all worked out in the end.

When the judge sentenced Cameron, Megan and the girls had to hold themselves back from cheering to avoid being found in contempt of court.

However, it did not stop their celebration dinner later on the same evening with Johnson and Misty, after the trial was over. They met up for a nice Italian dinner at Zuppa Restaurant on Main Street in downtown Yonkers. While it might have been a small victory for them, considering Hank was already doing life in prison, it was a significant victory for Margaret, who finally got the justice she deserved.

Johnson knew his old friend, Jack Roe, would have been proud. He himself felt honored to have been invited to celebrate with the lovely ladies, who made it possible for him to close his oldest cold case. He held up a glass of wine and proposed a toast, "To Margaret! May she finally rest in peace, now that justice has been served."

"To Margaret," the girls responded in unison, and then they drank.

Josh was with them, although he did not partake in the wine or toast. He was too busy enjoying his soda and spaghetti. However, his mind was on his Lizzie. He knew she was watching and with them in spirit.

Megan smiled at him adoringly, before taking a long sip from her glass. She felt great satisfaction for her role in helping Maggie. She wondered if her spirit truly was at rest. She really hoped so.

After drinking from her glass, Misty said something, which resonated with what Megan was currently thinking. "My grandmother used to have a cryptic saying, regarding death and the afterlife. Whenever she said it, I always felt scared by her words. I assumed she meant it in a negative way. After everything that's happened, I believe I finally understand what she meant."

Megan asked, "Well? What did she say?"

"Dying is like waking from a dream, or a nightmare. It's an ending and a beginning."

Johnson commented, "Wise words, indeed."

Megan was inclined to agree, based on what she knew.

Sometime during the end of the summer, Megan had an unspoken promise to keep to her son. She dressed him accordingly for adventure. She allowed him to bring his Mandalorian, since he insisted.

He asked, "Where are we going, Mommy?"

"It's a surprise, Josh. Trust me. This is one adventure you and Mando are going to love!" She was so excited. She could not wait to see his reaction when they got there.

They went downstairs and waited outside for their ride to arrive. Minutes later, Hannah pulled up in her car wearing sunglasses. They greeted each other and she drove them toward North Broadway. Upbeat music was playing on the radio to set the mood. The ride only took about fifteen minutes. They reached their destination and turned into the entrance road of Untermyer Park. They parked in the lot and exited the vehicle.

Josh asked with excitement, "Are we here? Is this where we're going for our adventure?"

Megan shook her head, "Not exactly. We're almost there, though. It's just a short walk from here. Come on. Give me your hand." She took his hand, as they crossed the road and stepped onto the path, leading to the walled garden. It was a short walk, which took them past a World Trade Center 9/11 Memorial and the community center.

Soon, they approached the gate leading into the garden. Josh still did not recognize it. He always saw it in his dreams from the inside, as it was when Margaret was a little girl. This time, he would see it in person, as it was today. Sadly, it was not as pretty as it once was so many years earlier, but it was still quite beautiful to look upon.

As soon as Josh saw the long moat leading to the tall twin sets of columns with the two griffins mounted at the top, he screamed with excitement. "MOMMY! THIS IS LIZZIE'S SECRET GARDEN! How did you find it?"

She smirked when she responded, "Honestly, I think she told me most of her secrets, but I sort of came across this one by accident. I had a feeling you were going to love being here." She watched him joyously, as his eyes scanned everything taking in the scenery, as she had done during her first visit months earlier.

Josh was confused at how different certain things appeared, especially the pavilion, which was much older and in worse shape than it had been when he last saw it. In his dreams, everything in the garden looked much better than it actually looked. He was only shown the beauty of the park, not the ugliness that existed. It did not really matter to him. He was just pleased to be standing in Lizzie's secret garden in real life, not in a dream. He could not believe it.

"Wow!" He looked into the moat to see the fish, which he and Lizzie used to feed. Thinking of her made him deliriously happy.

"Josh!" His mother called after him and quickly held him back. "Be careful, baby. Otherwise, you'll fall inside and get soaking wet. Not to mention, the fish might gobble you up! Argh!" She tickled him briefly.

He laughed. "They don't eat people! They're too little," he told her. His voice became high pitched when he said "little," making it sound adorable.

Hannah asked, "Hey, Josh? Do you want to feed the fish?" She showed him a small, plastic, orange can of fish food, which she pulled out of her purse. She picked it up from the pet store, before going to their building to pick them up.

"Yes!" He replied.

"Here," she handed it to him. "But be careful not to drop too much at one time, and don't drop the can," she warned.

"I won't," he assured her.

He gave her his Mandalorian to hold, so he could focus on feeding the fish with both hands. When she grabbed it, she accidentally touched the button on the chest causing it to say, "I want my next job."

Both Hannah and Megan shot each other a sharp look, but then laughed when they realized her finger was touching the button.

Over the next couple of minutes, Megan watched Josh. She loved how pleased he looked, while feeding the fish. She made sure to stay close to him, so he would not fall into the shallow moat. He seemed to know what he was doing. It was great to see he was enjoying himself. She wondered if he was thinking about his Lizzie, as she found herself doing in that moment.

Josh was certainly thinking about Lizzie. With each dash of flakes he dropped into the moat, he could almost feel her presence beside him. She said she would always watch over him. Today, he felt her presence and it brought him comfort to know he would always have his best friend with him.

# Epilogue

## Her Justice and Her Peace

Two months later, at the Sing Sing Correctional Facility…

Hank stepped out to the courtyard for his recreational time. He found a seat on a bench and began mulling over his recent trial. It made him furious how that know-it-all detective was able to figure out he killed Margaret, after so many years. To top it off, he even knew about Leanne! *How?* Would her murder trial be next on the agenda? How did that prick know? More importantly, how in the world did he know where to find the body? Hank was baffled. There were no witnesses and he never told anyone. He was so careful.

The mere thought of it, drove him crazy. The only thing, which made any kind of sense to him, was someone else must have found the body by mistake and contacted the police anonymously. It must have been downhill from then on.

Hank looked up when he spotted a fellow inmate approaching. It was a tall rugged looking guy, who looked to be around the same age as him. He did not look familiar. The inmate asked, "Hey, what's up?"

"Same shit, different person asking," Hank replied sarcastically. "Can I help you, New Jack?"

"The name's Matt. You're that guy from Yonkers. Right? The *Birthday Killer*? I heard about you."

"Well, Matt. It's actually *The Anniversary Killer*. I think you may want to check your hearing, if you heard *Birthday*. While you're at it, take a fucking hike. I don't need a fan club."

Matt chuckled, "A fan club? That's pretty funny. You're a funny guy, *Hank*." His expression changed and he became serious.

Hank grew impatient with him and asked, "How did you know my nickname? You hear that, too?"

"Yeah, I did. By the way, I have something for you." Right then, Matt stabbed Hank in the throat. "This is for Maggie and all those other girls you hurt, you sick piece of shit." He then stabbed Hank repeatedly in the stomach using the same shiv, before jamming it into Hank's crotch and hurriedly walking away. He had been using a handkerchief to hold the make-shift knife, so he would not leave any fingerprints. As he walked away, he did not look back and did not slow down. Within seconds, he disappeared into the prison crowd on the other side of the courtyard.

Hank dropped to the floor clutching his groin with one hand and his throat with the other. There were too many wounds to stop the bleeding by hand. He could not call for help, since his vocal chords had been severed. Instead, he gurgled blood from his mouth. The blood seemed to gush out by the pint. He barely had time to realize what was going on, before it was too late to stop it. He continued to bleed out, fully aware he was about to die.

He expected his life to flash before his eyes, but there was nothing. Just the ground before him and it was rapidly turning red. At first, it was as if no one else seemed to care. Other inmates walked on by and saw him on the ground, but they simply kept walking. Nobody wanted anything to do with him. Soon, his fellow inmates gave him a wide berth to avoid stepping on the sea of his blood.

Finally, a prison guard spotted him lying in a pool of blood and alerted the others. All prisoners were moved back to the other side of the courtyard, while the guard went to check on Hank. By then, his life force was slowly slipping away. In his final thoughts, he wondered who was it that stabbed him. *Who the hell was Matt???*

It's a question that would never be answered for him. Seconds later, Hank lay dead on the ground. At last, true justice had been properly served.

## Several months earlier, after Margaret's burial in Valhalla…

Chris Garrett arrived back at the hotel, after being dropped off by Detective Johnson. His old suspicions had been confirmed. His sister was dead. It was something he always believed. His parents were the ones in denial. His grim opinion eventually caused a rift between him and his mother. After his father died, he tried to reconnect with her, but she held a grudge against him. It was the reason he moved to Florida. He needed a fresh start.

When his mother died earlier in the year, all those ill feelings returned. As did feelings of guilt for not being there during her last days. He also thought about his sister's "disappearance." He always wondered, if she really was a victim of The Anniversary Killer. At last, he knew the truth.

Today, his sister was laid to rest, after so many years of being missing. He felt so angry.

He picked up his cellphone and contacted an old friend. "Hey, Matty. It's me, again. I still haven't heard back from you. I'm in New York. I was hoping you were back in the States, by now. We should meet up. There's something important I need to tell you. It's about my sister. Call me when you get this message."

## Several months later, on the day after the trial…

With the trial finally over, Detective Johnson and Megan agreed it was best for Margaret's diary to go to her brother, Chris. Johnson made copies of the pages for her to keep. He wasted no time and went to the hotel to deliver the diary in person. Chris was extremely grateful. Johnson did not stay long.

Once Chris was alone, he sat down on the bed to read the diary. He scanned through the small pages quickly, before turning back to the first page. He wanted to see how much she had written. There was a lot, which pleased him. It was going to be great reading what his sister wrote during happier times.

However, as soon as he began reading her introduction, he had to stop. Reading his sister's words immediately made him cry.

He reached for his cellphone and made a call to a longtime friend.

"Hey, Matt. The trial is finally over. It ended yesterday. That's partially why I didn't call you back last night. Sorry, bro. My mind is a mess. You'll have to forgive me. I'm literally grieving her all over, again."

"Hey, no worries, Chris. I understand. I've been there," Matt responded, almost coldly. "So, where is he?"

"He should be back at Sing Sing, by now. He won't be going anywhere anytime soon. If you can reach him, he's all yours."

"If? You're a funny guy."

Chris asked, "Are you sure you really want to do this?"

Matt replied, "After what that motherfucker did to your sister, he deserves it. I've been waiting such a long time to do this. I just never knew if he was the one, who actually did it. It seemed too risky to take a chance without being one hundred percent sure. But, hey! If a jury of twelve found him guilty, I'm willing to bet the evidence against him was pretty damned overwhelming. It's good enough for me. My conscience will be clear."

"I'm just saying, it's not too late to change your mind. You don't have to do this for me, or for her. It's too big a sacrifice."

"Don't worry about me, Chris. I know what I'm doing. I'm a professional. It's what I do. This one's on me. I owe it to Maggie. I wasn't around to keep her safe. I'm not the same naïve kid I was, back then."

"You can't blame yourself for what happened to her. You were in the marines, trying to become a better man. She understood. She was okay with it."

"A better man," he chuckled. "There you go, again, making me laugh. That's pretty funny. It doesn't matter anymore. Listen, it's better if we don't say too much over the phone. We've already said enough. Better to be safe, than sorry. Thanks for the information. Have a safe flight back to Florida."

"Yeah, sure. No problem. Thanks," Chris replied. He was concerned for how cold and unfeeling Matt sounded. Then again, maybe it was exactly what was needed. He added, "Hey, you're a much better man than me, Matt. Good luck."

"Trust me, brother. This will be a cake walk for me, compared to other things I've done, since joining the military. I'll do my time standing on my head. It will be worth it. Besides, I feel like I've been preparing for this my whole life."

Chris knew that much was true, although he had no idea what his friend was actually capable of doing. As far as he knew, Matt was willing to end up as an inmate to get the job done. Unlike, Hank Cameron, Matteo Federico was a trained killer. He was even willing to kill, if necessary, just so he could end up at Sing Sing, as an inmate. Since retiring from the marines ten years earlier, he sold his services to certain people, who could afford him. He was good at what he did. He only worked through reliable references and word of mouth, except in this case. This one was personal. It was something he had to do to put his mind at ease. Cameron had to pay.

Chris was grateful. "I really appreciate your sacrifice," he said. "I know my sister would, too. She really loved you a lot. Thank you for your service. I won't forget this, Matt. If you ever get a chance to hit me up, you can always call collect. You got my number."

"No doubt. It's memorized. Like the saying goes, 'No justice, no peace,'" Matt replied, referring to his former high school sweetheart finally getting her justice and her peace.

# About the Author

---

Jason Medina was born and raised in the Bronx, NY. He worked as a police officer in the NYPD for 23 years, before retiring in 2014. He began writing books in 2012, and has continued to publish new books nearly every year, since then. His books mainly focus on the paranormal, such as his locally acclaimed *"Ghosts and Legends of Yonkers."* He currently resides in Yonkers and volunteers regularly for the Yonkers Historical Society. Jason is also a poet, an artist, musician, photographer, and a paranormal investigator.

He can be contacted through his email: *Ginvestigators@aol.com.*

*www.JasonMedinaTribalPublications.com*
*www.YonkersGhostInvestigators.com*

# Other Books by Jason Medina

NO HOPE FOR THE HOPELESS AT KINGS PARK

THE DIARY OF AUDREY MALONE FRAYER

A GHOST IN NEW ORLEANS

GHOSTS AND LEGENDS OF YONKERS

THE MANHATTANVILLE INCIDENT:
AN UNDEAD NOVEL

AFTERMATH OF THE MANHATTANVILLE INCIDENT:
AN UNDEAD NOVEL

KINGS PARK PSYCHIATRIC CENTER:
A JOURNEY THROUGH HISTORY,
VOL. I-III

A NIGHT AT THE SHANLEY HOTEL